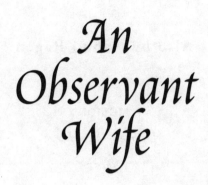

An
Observant
Wife

Also by Naomi Ragen

An Observant Wife

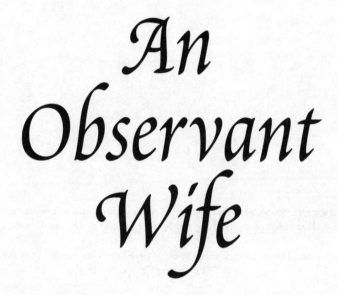

Naomi Ragen

ST. MARTIN'S
PRESS
NEW YORK

First published in the United States by St. Martin's Press, an imprint of St. Martin's Publishing Group

AN OBSERVANT WIFE. Copyright © 2021 by Naomi Ragen. All rights reserved. Printed in the United States of America. For information, address St. Martin's Press, 120 Broadway, New York, NY 10271.

www.stmartins.com

Library of Congress Cataloging-in-Publication Data

Names: Ragen, Naomi, 1949- author.
Title: An observant wife / Naomi Ragen.
Description: First Edition. | New York : St. Martin's Press, 2021.
Identifiers: LCCN 2021016346 | ISBN 9781250260079 (hardcover) |
    ISBN 9781250260086 (ebook)
Subjects: GSAFD: Love stories.
Classification: LCC PS3568.A4118 O27 2021 | DDC 813/.54—dc23
LC record available at https://lccn.loc.gov/2021016346

Our books may be purchased in bulk for promotional, educational, or business use. Please contact your local bookseller or the Macmillan Corporate and Premium Sales Department at 1-800-221-7945, extension 5442, or by email at MacmillanSpecialMarkets@macmillan.com.

First Edition: 2021

10 9 8 7 6 5 4 3 2 1

For Shoshana, Malka, Gladys, and Kathy,
in honor of fifty years of friendship. Thank you.

CONTENTS

Rabbi Hillel used to say: If I am not for myself, who will be for me? But if I am only for myself, what am I?

—*ETHICS OF THE FATHERS 1:14*

An
Observant
Wife

1

✧

DAUGHTER OF
THE GROOM

How strange to watch a woman marry your father, thought Shaindele, a bit stunned, her eyes brimming with the tears she knew would earn her dark looks, if not outright scoldings and exhortations, if certain people in the family noticed. *And who could blame them?* she thought, hurriedly wiping them away. Her initial furious objections to Leah Howard, the bride, her blatant exhibitions of nastiness, indeed outright hatred, for the new woman in her father's life had been so vicious, what else could they think now, seeing her crying at the wedding? But they would be so wrong.

She had not only changed her mind but had been forgiven, and with so much compassion by the woman now sitting quietly in the bridal chair, calm and beautiful, awaiting her bedecking; a forgiveness she believed she had not earned and did not deserve. With her whole teenage heart, she wanted to gladden the bride not simply out of politeness or religious obligation but because she deserved it. And then there was her father. After all he had suffered, would it not be inhuman, almost monstrous, to begrudge him the happiness that now shone from his kind blue eyes, at long last replacing the shock and hopelessness that had taken root there with such vicious tenacity—until now?

But as much as she tried, as much as she *wanted* to, all her good intentions were swept away like dead leaves by the raging current of fear coursing through her.

Her father's unexpected marriage to an outsider, a woman brought up in the tainted secular world, a woman who had eaten pig and shellfish, had unsanctified sexual relations with who-knows-how-many men, and had once *tattooed her flesh*—an abomination specifically proscribed by God Himself!—was like plastering a plague notice across the door to their Boro Park apartment. Who among the matchmakers and their clients would be intrepid enough to push past it and venture inside? No matter that all now agreed that the bride was a pious and worthy penitent who had put her past firmly behind her, adhering to every religious precept—as far as true forgiveness was concerned, among the very pious who made up her world, there was the theory, and then there was the practice.

While in theory the Torah demanded that each Jew imitate a just and compassionate Creator, forgiving each other before each Day of Judgment so that they themselves could hope to earn forgiveness, in practice, the more pious Jews were, the more they adhered to stringency upon stringency, the less likely that was to occur. Ultra-Orthodox Jews, sometimes known as *haredim*—literally "the fearful ones"—referring to their terror of transgression, paradoxically never forgave or forgot even the slightest deviation from social rules etched in the reinforced concrete of community boundaries. And now with her father's marriage to a *baalas teshuva,* he had taken a jackhammer to those boundaries, smashing through them.

While Shaindele hoped that time would eventually dissipate the heavy fog of communal disapproval hanging above their heads as people shifted their idle minds to some other scandal, she had no illusions it might benefit her or her older brothers the way it would her siblings— six-year-old Chasya and two-year-old Mordechai Shalom. Unless her Bubbee's long and distinguished rabbinical lineage could be mustered to mount a successful defense, the matchmakers would be scraping the bottom of the barrel for all three of them, the place where all the ugly, stupid, poor, handicapped singles with bad reputations sank, mingling with the divorced and widowed, as well as the aging never-marrieds.

Her brothers would probably have an easier time, she thought, being well-respected Torah scholars and, most of all, men. Men always had the upper hand, especially when they could bring scholarship to the table. After all, weren't some of the most celebrated heroes of the Talmud former thieves, thugs, and ignoramuses whose brilliance in the study halls compensated for all their former sins?

As for herself, a girl and no scholar, it would be quite another story. She couldn't help her fear. At nearly seventeen, the question of her shidduch was pounding fiercely against the shores of her consciousness like huge breakers on some forsaken island, ravaging her serenity and reshaping the coastline of her thoughts.

But this was not the time to think about that, she berated herself, taking a deep breath as the sound of the flutist's first plaintive notes broke through the chatter, replacing it with the hopeful, almost heartbreaking Jewish wedding song: "And so will be heard in the cities of Judah, and in the streets of Jerusalem, the sound of happiness and the sound of joy, the voice of the bridegroom and the voice of the bride."

She moved down the row of women who stood like phalanxes on either side of the linen-and-flower-bedecked wicker chair in which sat the bride, staring at the little book of psalms in her lap, her lips barely moving in recitation. Only the slight furrows around her eyes revealed the turmoil and sincerity in her heart. When the bride finally raised her head, her eyes looked directly into Shaindele's. For an instant, Shaindele blinked, terrified her thoughts might be leaking out of her eyes. But to her relief, the bride smiled warmly, reaching out to her and grasping her hand with a gentle squeeze of encouragement. Despite all the young girl's efforts, the forbidden tears now overflowed. She smiled through them, hoping that would be enough to dispel any misinterpretation.

But soon the bride's eyes left hers, focusing with joyous intensity on the man moving slowly down the aisle, flanked by his brother, Abraham, and his Talmud study partner, Meir. A light sheen of sweat coated his handsome face beneath the heavy, dignified black hat. His blond beard had been neatly combed, his golden *payos* hidden behind his ears.

His face gave nothing away, thought his daughter anxiously, failing to notice the upturned mouth, the slight overbite as he attempted to quell the rising tide of his hilarity, his eyes like the ocean dancing in the morning sun. Dazzled by her own overwhelming sense of doom, of looking down from a precipice with a mad desire to jump and get it over with, almost relishing the suicidal release that would accompany the long fall, the crash, and oblivion, she was blind to the extent of his utter rapture.

What if right now, a person—respectable and not insane—stepped forward and firmly demanded that the whole thing be called off, the hall cleared, the guests dispersed? *Oh, oh, the horror of it! Oh, oh, the sheer relief of it!* she thought with panic and strange joy. She waited, forgetting to breathe, hoping, dreading. But it was not to be, she understood, as the band picked up the tempo and everyone around her smiled, caught up in wedding happiness. They all seemed so . . . *so pleased, so normal.* She exhaled in resignation.

The weight of a soft, heavy hand suddenly fell upon her like an admonition, draping her shoulder. Shocked and filled with guilt, she looked up. Bubbee. Her rotund and elderly body was clothed in the utmost of sumptuous yet subdued and modest Boro Park finery. Shaindele felt herself clasped in sure hands like a wailing infant put to the breast. *"Ich farshtey,"* her grandmother breathed into her ear, so low Shaindele wondered if she'd imagined it. *I understand.* The girl exhaled, her body suddenly limp as her heart slowed with relief and a strange acceptance. She squeezed her bubbee's hand gratefully.

All around the wedding hall, male friends, relatives, and acquaintances frolicked and danced as was the custom, steadily encroaching upon the women's space, forcing them to move aside. The women, crushed together, refused to give way completely, intent on catching every nuance, their faces expectant and amused, but also slightly puzzled. Grandmother and granddaughter wondered if the bride had noticed, praying she had not.

They needn't have worried. Leah Howard had no eyes for anyone save the man who was slowly, steadily bringing himself to her. She watched, mesmerized, as his face grew brighter with each step, the years sloughing off and the shine of renewal and youth washing over him.

When Yaakov finally came within arm's length, he stopped, trembling, as he looked down upon her face. *This young woman, this stranger,* he thought, marveling once again at her willingness to give herself to him, to become part of his pitiful life, in full knowledge of all his shortcomings and tragic mistakes. *This lovely woman who knew him completely, yet* still could love him so wholeheartedly. *How is that possible?* he wondered. It was a miracle. A gift from God. He drank in her glowing face, her sweet eyes filled with hope and happiness. *My dear God, thank you! Please, please, never let anything happen in our life together to wipe that look off her face.*

And then, despite himself, those thoughts were silently pushed out by others that encroached, unbidden, desperately unwanted. He fought against them. *No!* he exhorted himself, his smile contorting with the effort. He mustn't think about that time, the very first time he had pulled a bright, white veil over the face of another lovely, smiling young woman who had, in the end, disfigured by despair, become almost unrecognizable. He had not been able to make her happy. He had not been able to save her, the wife of his youth. Zissele. Poor Zissele. *Oh no! Not now, please,* he begged for the countless time, for absolution, for forgiveness and ultimately for release. *Please,* he begged some implacable force in the universe that controlled all that was meant to give human beings joy and meaning. *Please, let me . . .*

The bride, blinded by love and happiness, saw none of this. Thankfully, the almost-opaque veil was soon gently lifted over her head and pulled down over her eyes, sparing her the astonished looks and pinched mouths of many who followed her progress down the aisle toward the marriage canopy.

And who could blame them? On one side, she was supported by a woman in a shocking red dress wearing red patent leather heels so high and so thin each step was not to be taken for granted; while on the other, by the highly respected widow of a great Torah scholar, *mother of her groom's first wife,* the epitome of religious dignity and modesty. It was this very lack of symmetry that provided the counterbalance which made it impossible for onlookers to make up their minds if they were witnessing a travesty or a blessing. Yes, the girl's mother was a definite *prutza.* But what could one say to the vision of Rebbitzen Fruma Esther Sonnenbaum tenderly holding the bride's arm, not only giving the match her blessing but physically leading the bride to the saintly man who had fathered her grandchildren?

Shaindele watched it all from the sidelines with her little sister and brother. The children were jumping up and down with excitement and joy. Shaindele hoped some drops from their overflowing cups of happiness might anoint her, too. Just at that moment, as if her thoughts had been read, the bride turned and smiled at her directly, beckoning her to climb up and join them under the chuppah along with her older brothers, who were holding the canopy poles aloft. Grabbing Chasya's and Mordechai Shalom's little hands, she nodded, leading them briskly down the aisle and up the steps toward the couple about to be wed.

The little ones, put off by the strangeness of the veil and the white dress, approached the bride shyly. But Leah bent down to them, whispering endearments, and they stretched out their little arms around her, clinging hopefully, until Shaindele quickly led them away toward the back. Perhaps some of their joy *had* rubbed off on her, Shaindele thought, finding herself smiling through her tears in the shadows as she contemplated the newly expanded circle of her family. That was until she caught sight of Leah's mother: the spiky, dyed blond hair, loosely covered by the gold-spangled headscarf more appropriate to a Middle Eastern belly dancer or a gypsy, dangling there for all to see like the red handkerchief taunting the snorting bulls of disgrace and ostracism, goading both to aim for her, Shaindele, right between the eyes.

2

❦

THE WEDDING DANCE

As prescribed by Jewish law and tradition, soon after their wedding vows, Yaakov and Leah were ushered into the seclusion, or *yichud*, room, where for the very first time in their entire relationship they found themselves completely alone behind locked doors, a state forbidden to them as an unmarried couple.

Yaakov stood there for a moment, frozen, the sweat pouring down his forehead. Leah looked at him and laughed. Reaching up, she removed his heavy black Borsalino. Then, taking a napkin off the tray of food thoughtfully provided them to break their wedding-day fast, she gently dabbed his forehead, his brows, and the sides of his cheeks.

"Can this really be happening?" he asked her in wonder, catching her hand and bringing it to his lips for a kiss.

She put the napkin down, nodding, her hands slipping around his shoulders as she pressed her soft, dry cheek against his, rubbing off some of the moisture.

He put his hands on her shoulders, his fingers tingling with joy as he held her, filled with a happiness he had never expected to feel again *and had never felt before,* he finally admitted to himself. Not that he hadn't loved the pretty young girl who had been his first wife. But they had both been so very young and inexperienced. As a yeshiva student, he had been carefully trained by his teachers and his rabbis on how to repress all his sexual feelings, sublimating them into a love of learning, good deeds, and loving the Most High.

But now, with years of marriage behind him, having experienced sexual love and arousal and consummation, he was no longer that young virgin. He pulled this beautiful, soft woman gently into his arms, as close as he possibly could, his lips finding hers for the first kiss they had ever shared. Time seemed to stop as this wild new experience enveloped him body and soul. He pulled her closer, not wanting to let go, wanting to feel the newness of her lips, how they touched his with equal passion, her body leaning into him without shyness or reluctance. He felt ecstatic.

Someone knocked on the door.

With a start, they pulled apart, shocked, then suddenly shy. They laughed awkwardly, their eyes bright with happiness.

"Tell them the bathroom's down the hall," she whispered to him, smiling.

He grinned. "Yes?" he called out.

"Catering. We brought you cold drinks."

"But we already have cold drinks . . ." Then he understood. It was Meir and his other friends, keeping up the jollity. He turned to her, shaking his head with an apologetic shrug. "They want us to come out so they can start the dancing."

"Soon," she whispered in his ear, her breath tickling and flirtatious, so very different from the one woman he had ever known. In that breath, in those words, he found the promise of a new life, a real life of intimacy and passion as yet unexplored, he realized. He was not old, not anymore. The old man he had seen in the mirror over the last two years since losing his wife had disappeared. Instead, here was this vigorous, expectant person; this *young* man heading out into uncharted wilderness, daring, almost giddy with the opportunity to slice another piece of life for himself, prepared from a different recipe. It was a gift, a replenishment, the dry wadis of his heart suddenly streaming with spring water, moist and blooming again. Hopeful, but also frightening. This was going to be very different from the first time around, he realized, finding that thought overwhelming in so many ways. There was the excitement and longing for new sensations, yet simultaneously the fear of the unknown, and the utter terror of falling short, of disappointing her.

For the first time, he allowed himself to acknowledge that this woman he had married, although younger in years, was far more experienced in passion. She had had several partners, he only the one. What if he didn't . . . couldn't . . . measure up? What if she was annoyed—disgusted, even— with his naivety? A cold shiver ran up his spine.

"Let them wait, Yaakov," she answered gaily, uncovering the tray and setting out two plates for them on the small, decorated table.

He sat across from her, allowing her to fill his plate with food, which he dutifully chewed and swallowed, but of which—even if his life had depended upon on it—he would not have been able to recall even a single dish.

"But why aren't *you* eating?" he questioned, suddenly noticing.

She smiled at him, shrugging. "How can I? I am so full, filled to the brim."

He put down his fork, reaching across the table. "Leah, my Leah," he whispered softly, almost to himself. "My reward and my gift. Please be patient with me if I make mistakes, if I . . ."

She stood up. Going around the table, she sank slowly into his lap, her arms around his shoulders, her head resting on his neck.

"Your beard tickles," she told him, laughing.

"Does it?" he murmured into her soft neck, wishing he could skip the dancing, the well-wishers, the entire demanding world outside the door; wishing himself already in his own home, in his own bed, all the old, sad ghosts banished, all the tragedy and loss scrubbed away, leaving it glowing with vitality and renewal. But it was not to be, he realized reluctantly, the banging of the wedding guests growing too insistent to be ignored.

"I guess we have no choice, my Yaakov," she said, sliding her feet to the ground and allowing her arms to fall to her sides. She grabbed a piece of fruit, cupping her hand carefully around it so the sweet juice would not stain the white satin of her borrowed wedding gown, which needed to be returned in good condition to the free loan fund to clothe the next thrifty ultra-Orthodox bride.

"If only there were a back door where we could escape," he said, surprising her.

"Would we do it?"

"How I would love to!"

"We couldn't!" she laughed.

"No, probably not." He took a ripe, red strawberry, biting into it and letting it stain his lips.

She watched him, almost tasting the juice. Then she went to the door and unlocked it, opening it wide and letting the world course in, the women taking charge of her and leading her away as the men surrounded Yaakov, taking him along in a flood to the men's side of the impenetrable *mechitza.*

Oh, the dancing! Oh, the circles of men, the circles of women, each on their own side of the high partition! How people swirled and dipped, holding hands and singing as they surrounded the bride and the groom, each in their own separate kingdom, until someone brought chairs and shockingly stormed the *mechitza,* hoisting up a terrified Leah and a reluctant Yaakov and carrying them away to sway in the air as they clutched the sides of their chairs with one hand and the end of a long rope with the other, their only public physical contact their entire wedding.

Once the festivities had moved over to the men's section, Fruma Esther allowed herself to be led to a chair and plied with cold glasses of water. Someone thoughtfully brought her a large, cloth napkin, and she wiped her sweating face. She had been dancing with the others, of course; a wedding guest could not very well refuse to get up and perform the mitzvah of gladdening the bride, no matter her feet felt like lead and she could hardly keep her head up, blurry with fatigue from all the days of planning and preparation, most of which had fallen on her. She didn't mind. She'd even enjoyed it. A simcha, after so much tragedy. Funerals, after all, also took planning and food preparation; they were also exhausting.

Besides, who if not her? She looked around for the bride's mother, hoping she was hiding herself in an appropriate corner with her red dress and her turbaned boyfriend. She shuddered, wondering what people were saying. Then she shrugged, setting her mouth grimly. *Let them think whatever they want, but if they open their mouths, mine will also not stay closed.* She knew exactly which principals' ears to bend when children applied to the most prestigious schools, exactly which matchmakers should be dropped dismaying hints about *yichus* and unseemly behavior, exactly which *rosh yeshiva* to approach concerning hopeful applicants. And all of *them*—she told herself with steely conviction as her eyes swept around the room—knew it, too. Not that she was a vengeful person or a gossip, God forbid, both traits being absolutely forbidden by the Torah. But like a security guard at a bank, who mostly just smiled at you as you entered, it was important that everyone knew you also had a loaded gun dangling from a holster in case of emergency.

Rebbitzen Fruma Esther Sonnenbaum, although unconnected in blood to either the bride or the groom, nevertheless considered herself the patron of these festivities. After all, had she not arranged the hall, addressed and mailed the invitations, including personal notes to the most prestigious of the rabbinical guests to make sure they didn't imagine their absence would go unnoticed (or forgiven)? As she sat in her chair wiping away the beads of moisture from her forehead and holding court among the many guests who came by to pay her homage as the formidable widow of the late, revered Harav HaGaon Yitzchak Chaim, she watched approvingly as the young married women and girls twirled around the hall, bright and glowing in their fashionable, modest finery, their lavishly styled wigs almost indistinguishable from real hair.

But soon her eyes misted. If only it were one of her grandchildren getting married instead! But to witness her former son-in-law, her Yaakov, paired with another woman was almost more than she could bear. She should be here, her pretty Zissele, dancing with the others. Such a tragedy!

When she looked back upon her long life, it was as if so much of it had never happened. Like pages in a book left out in the rain, most of it was blurry and unreadable, except for a few scattered sentences describing deaths and births and memorably awful sicknesses she had nursed herself and others through. Why was that? she wondered. Was it because there was only so much room in her mind and the bad was stronger than the good, and today always crowded out yesterday? Or was it because she didn't want to remember?

She found that idea frightening. For what is a life, especially the life of a family, if not memories? It had been a good life, she exhorted herself. A life filled with blessings. After all, what is a handful of funerals and sick days compared to thousands of ordinary good days of waking and sleeping and kissing the young, and caring for them as you watched them grow up strong, healthy, God-fearing, and good? Every moment, one must recognize with gratitude the overwhelming goodness one had been granted in life.

That was the way it should be, she mourned, even as she knew it was not. The death of Zissele at such a young age by her own hand had canceled out so much of the light and blessing of her life, casting a shadow over the past and the future that obscured what she wanted to believe in and hope for. She would never recover from it, the way you could hope to heal from the inevitable death of a person racked with disease or simply old age.

Was it my fault? She shrugged, the question like a carpenter's sharp tool used over and over to deepen already chiseled grooves, each time threatening to destroy the good wood that was the center of her being. It was dangerous to think that way, she scolded herself. As God was compassionate to repentant sinners, so must she be like Him, and find a way to forgive herself, for she was truly, abjectly, profoundly sorry for her part in her life's tragedy; for every tiny moment, so vividly remembered, where she had gone wrong: the second she had held the phone in her hand and began to dial the hospital, then put it down. The moment she had let her mouth utter the words, "Give her more time!" to her son-in-law, convincing him that it was possible for Zissele to heal on her own, with their help. Even the moment when she had turned her head and pretended not to see when Zissele had slumped to the floor, wetting herself.

It's enough, enough, she pleaded with the relentless foe lodged in her soul, unconvinced and unappeased. Like the prosecuting angel that appeared before the Throne of Glory every Yom Kippur, clutching his laundry list of your sins that could not be pried loose no matter your tears or atonement, she held this enemy close to her heart, almost welcoming his wounding thrusts against her. One day, she thought, when her battered soul had had enough, she would finally be released to join her Yitzchak Chaim, her dearest. And then the prosecuting angel would have both of them to face as well as the good Lord Himself, Who—kind and forgiving and compassionate as always—would, she had no doubt, be standing there by their sides.

"Don't let it slip!" Yaakov admonished his friend and *chavrusa* Meir, whose pudgy body in the warm wool suit was melting from fatigue as he held one of the ends of the chairs aloft.

"I'm going to let you fall?" Meir laughed. "Me?"

Yaakov smiled down at him to show he had not meant it seriously. How could you admonish Meir? After all, it if hadn't been for him picking up the phone and arranging that first date with Leah when all the official shadchonim of Boro Park had categorically refused to get involved, there wouldn't be a wedding!

Meir smiled in return, willing his weakening arms to stiffen under the unfamiliar assault of physical exertion. After all, as a Talmud scholar, he did nothing more strenuous all day than turn the pages of his holy books. In many ways, he thought, he had already gone beyond his strength in playing matchmaker at his friend's request. There had been consequences, whispered in his ear by angry members of his congregation and fellow students in the kollel, who questioned not only the suitability of the match but opening the door in general to the slightest whiffs from the depraved secular world.

Meir, the most naive and innocent of men, was downright shocked at some of the uglier and more sinister hints of his friends at the kind of life a girl like Leah might have experienced before she saw the light.

"What she's done and what she knows . . . ," they whispered to him, shaking their heads sorrowfully. "How do you bring such a woman to our saintly, innocent Yaakov?"

What could he say? He didn't know anything about the depraved secular world or what young women did there. Instead, he had sweated and gone red and answered with all his heart: "As our sages tell us in Talmud *Yoma,* 'Even willful misdeeds are accounted to the penitent as merits,' and in *Bava Metzi'a:* 'Once a man repents, stop reminding him of his past deeds.'"

Chastised, but unconvinced, they had slunk away.

But now, sweating beneath the burdens he had taken upon himself, he wondered. Being from such different worlds, could they make a successful life together? He studied the face of his dear friend looking down at him, then followed his happy gaze to the bride's excited and ecstatic smile. It should only continue this way, he prayed, unable to forget the more urgent warnings of his critics to "think what example such a match sets for the community." As it is written: *A man in a boat who bores a hole under his own seat cannot say to his fellow passengers when they protest: What do you care? It is under my own seat.*

Eventually, long after the remnants of roast chicken, brisket, and potatoes had congealed on their plates and been removed, but before the sugary chocolate cake and petit fours had been served, wedding guests got up to leave. The first to go were the elderly rabbis, who took their leave of the bridegroom as their wives said goodbye to Fruma Esther, and only then to the bride they did not know. Leah responded by gratefully taking their proffered hands into her own with real warmth, accepting on faith that their kind wishes for a happy life had been sincerely expressed.

Once the honored rabbis had gone, the lesser luminaries—teachers, community leaders, young scholars—followed, signaling across the *mechitza* to their wives, who reluctantly left the lively discussions at their friendly tables, ending the rare night out when they were served a fine meal in such delightful company, to accompany their husbands back to a house full of laundry and demanding youngsters. These women, mostly only a little older than the bride herself, fixed smiles on their faces as they studied the sweetness of the bride's smile, the joy in her eyes, fighting valiantly against their galloping cynicism to envision a bright future for this clueless girl who had no idea what she had just gotten herself into.

They could not help but imagine with horror being in her place at such an age, forced to undergo all they had experienced without the twin buffers of youth and naivety that had cushioned their own crash into the harsh realities of married life. "Now she is in love. But the tension of making ends meet, the endless housework in that drab little apartment, caring for stepchildren, and then hopefully her own pregnancies and births . . ." Even the most solid foundation of real love grew soft and muddy under the steady, daily downpour of troubles. The more empathetic could not control themselves, leaning in and kissing her cheek, a kiss full of hope and pity. "You must come to us for Shabbos," they whispered. "Any time at all, you must call me, if you need anything," they added with real feeling born equally of true, womanly solidarity coupled with an avid curiosity to follow the progress of this strange story to its conclusion.

The last to go were the people Yaakov and Leah actually knew.

"I'm so happy for you, my dear friend," Shoshana Glaser said, wrapping her arms around Leah, who hugged her back with love. Newly engaged to the love of her life after years of hiding her scandalous affair, she looked more like a *Vogue* model than a pediatrician, Leah thought in wonder, always surprised at her best friend's slim loveliness, the warm sheen of her glowing olive skin and straight, dark waterfall of hair.

"Is everything all right with you, with John?" Leah asked softly, looking around anxiously for the tall, handsome pediatric surgeon who she knew was not only in the midst of converting to Judaism but was also finalizing the divorce from his first wife.

"He's fine. Sends his love. He was on call tonight."

"And your parents?" Leah whispered, knowing how hard the revelation of this relationship had hit her friend's elderly, ultra-Orthodox parents, who had so hoped their only daughter would marry a distinguished Talmud scholar with parents from the old country.

Shoshana shrugged, not meeting her eyes. "No heart attacks or strokes, thank God! I know they'll never really get over it, but at least now they'll get to dance at my wedding. I'm sure they're also relieved to know the real reason why all those shidduch dates never worked out."

"Oh, those shidduch dates!" Leah groaned, remembering the ladies' room in the Marriott Marquis on Broadway where they'd met, hiding out from blind dates—hers an on-the-spectrum misfit, and Shoshana's a balding fiftysomething who had lied about his age.

Shoshana laughed, hugging her. "No more shidduch dates! Imagine!"

"There she is, *delira* and *excira,* the bride!" It was Dvorah, the Irish convert roommate who had first introduced her to religious life. "The good Lord works in mysterious ways." She shook her head, smiling and shifting the weight of her toddler above her burgeoning belly. "Can't wait to see you in maternity clothes, all fat and happy! A regular Boro Park matriarch!"

"Give her time." Shoshana shook her head, taking the little girl's pudgy hand in her own. "Your little girl is delicious. No wonder you can't wait to have another."

"I've already got children, remember?" Leah protested. "Five wonderful, perfect people I adore." She looked over to where the two little ones were turning circles in the middle of the dance floor, sticky with sweets, their new shoes dulled by splashes of Coca-Cola and pink ice cream, their festive clothing stained with chocolate and who knew what else. They both needed baths.

"And three of them teenagers," Shoshana murmured meaningfully.

"I love them all," Leah insisted.

"Where are you spending the night?"

"At home. The children are staying the night with their grandmother and uncle." *Home,* she thought a little frightened. Going home. A new home in an ultra-Orthodox Jewish neighborhood in Brooklyn. Her final, forever home. Such a different life from what she'd planned or could even have imagined growing up in San Jose, California.

"Whose idea was *that*?" Shoshana asked with raised brows.

"Mine. I *love* my new life, and I can't wait to start."

"I'll call you," the two young women said, blowing kisses as they moved off to allow the long queue of well-wishers to advance. There was Rabbi Weintraub's wife and Rebbitzen Basha, who had mentored her in her new life. And finally, there was her mother and her partner, Ravi.

"So you survived, Mom?"

"Well, if I would have known there was going to be so much wild dancing, I would have worn more comfortable shoes! My feet are killing me!" she groaned, lifting her feet out of the five-inch heels and resting them on the floor. "That's okay, right? I'm not scandalizing you around your new religious friends, am I?"

"No, Mom. And who cares anyway?" She leaned forward to hug her mother's stiff, resistant shoulders, massaging them. "When are you going back to Boca Raton?"

"We have a 6:00 a.m. flight tomorrow."

"It was so wonderful of you and Ravi to come," she said, nodding at the tall, dark man by her mother's side, the only man on this side of the *mechitza*. He was back to wearing his traditional Sikh turban, Leah noted, wondering how her mother was dealing with it. She'd sworn to leave him if that ever happened. Her poor mom! First her daughter, now her boyfriend! She kept running away from religion, and it somehow kept finding her.

"So what now, honey?"

"What do you mean, Mom?"

"What is life going to be like for a married woman in the ultra-Orthodox world?"

"I suppose I'm about to find out." She laughed.

Her mother took her head. "I really hope this works out, Lola—"

Leah flinched at the sound of her given name.

"Sorry, sorry. I sometimes just forget. Leah."

"It's okay, Mom."

"But I want you to know, whatever happens, you can always come home. We will always be there for you. You are my baby girl." She drew her close and kissed her.

Leah rested stiffly against her mother's shoulder for a moment, annoyed and disappointed at this implication of impending failure. *She's never going to get it,* she thought, straightening up and fingering the flimsy red scarf with gold spangles resting lightly over her mother's spiky platinum-tipped hair, a knee jerk to the Orthodox demand that married women cover their hair. She sighed. You only had one mother. Their relationship, imperfect as ever, would go on the rest of their lives.

"Mom, I am really, really, really happy."

Cheryl nodded, tears making her eyes sparkle.

And then finally, when the hall was almost empty and the *mechitza* removed, the family stood together. Shaindele held a sleeping Mordechai Shalom in her arms, while Fruma Esther held Chasya's hand. Her two teenage stepsons stood shyly behind their father.

"We will all meet tomorrow at the *sheva brachot,*" Fruma Esther told her.

"But the children," Leah protested as Chasya finally succeeded in squirming out of her grandmother's firm grip, running to Leah, and burying her sticky face and hands in the silky folds of the long white gown. Leah lifted her, burrowing her nose into the child's soft neck. The wedding dress would just have to go to the dry cleaners. "You smell like bubble gum ice cream."

Chasya laughed, shaking her head. "Strawberry. I want to come home with you and Tateh."

"Tomorrow, Icy," Leah murmured, reluctant to let her go.

"But why?" the child protested.

"Don't bother your mameh," Fruma Esther admonished her.

The little girl turned around to look at her, astonished. "My mameh?"

Leah looked down at her, her face radiant. "Yes, I'm your mameh now, my lovely girl." Now and forever and forever.

The child laughed and jumped up and down, suddenly full of energy. "But can I still call you *Mommy*?"

"Yes, my darling." Leah smiled, a sweet bud of happiness opening inside her.

"Come, we have presents for you at Bubbee's house. Say good night to your parents," Fruma Esther said firmly, her eyes blinded by tears.

Leah kneeled next to the child, taking her little body in her arms, breathing in the childish warmth that mingled joyously with the honeyed drips and spills of the celebration. "Good night, my sweet little Icy," she murmured into her hair, which badly needed a shampoo, kissing her stained cheek. She got up and looked at the little boy cradled in an exhausted sleep of oblivion in his older sister's arms, gently smoothing his tousled blond curls out of his eyes. She put an affectionate arm around Shaindele, kissing her flushed cheek. "Thank you so much! We'll come to pick them up tomorrow before you have to leave for school."

"I can take the day off," the girl offered, a little too eagerly, Leah thought. She studied her a moment, troubled. Shaindele was very committed to her schoolwork. "No, you have exams soon."

The girl shrugged, a bit sullenly.

But then Yaakov was moving past her, hugging his children and talking to Fruma Esther, saying his final good nights and making it clear it was time for all of them to leave.

And then, it was just the two of them.

"Come," he whispered thrillingly.

3

❦

A VIRGIN
WEDDING NIGHT

Lugging their wedding presents, Yaakov and Leah stepped over the threshold of the apartment. Its worn, familiar furniture, vigorously polished, winked dully from the shadows as the overhead fixture with its yellowish bulb came to life. On the walls of the old Boro Park apartment, newly plastered and painted a too-bright white in honor of its new occupant, hung the laminated jigsaw puzzles his first wife had patiently assembled with their children during long Sabbath afternoons, lovingly rehung by his daughter and his first wife's mother. The family portraits, including the photographs of Zissele, also remained where they were. He saw Leah glance around, her eyes stopping to stare at them.

"Maybe I should have . . . ," he began uncertainly. *What is the etiquette in such matters?* he thought, lost. But she moved close to him, putting two fingers over his mouth.

"I love these photos. They're the first time I laid eyes on you. And the jigsaw puzzles. Zissele will always be here in this house, because her children are here."

"Do you mind? Does it hurt you?"

"What?"

"Does it hurt you that you have to share them with her? Take care of another woman's children?"

She could have given him a quick, reassuring answer, she thought. Instead, she tried to tell the truth. "The older ones, the boys and Shaindele, will never be mine. I wouldn't even want that. I just want to be there for them if they need me. But Icy and Cheeky"—she shook her head with a smile as she used her nicknames for the little ones, given when she was only a babysitter doing a good deed for a desperate and unhappy widower—"I don't think of them as someone else's. I fell in love with them long before I ever met you."

"Thank you."

"For what?" She smiled.

"For loving them and . . ." He stopped, taking off his big, black festive hat and laying it carefully on the dining room table. "For loving me," he whispered.

How is this going to work? she wondered, her body yearning for his but held back by invisible wires. *How do you get into bed with a man when your entire relationship has been absolutely nonphysical, even the slightest touch forbidden? How do you release the lock on passions chained and jailed by religious law? And how am I supposed to know what is acceptable among religious people once we are in bed? No one ever talked about that!* Her counseling by the bride teacher, a *frum* woman with a huge scarf over her blond rebbitzen's wig, had done little more than elaborate the final points of the laws governing abstinence and separation during her menstrual period. As for the rest, the woman had summed it up thus: "I'm sure I don't need to tell you the things I tell young virgin brides."

She'd gone home devastated at the insult. But perhaps the woman had been right. She wasn't, after all, a virgin, not technically. But the men she had known, the life she had lived as an American woman in the new millennium, bore no resemblance to the life she had now embarked upon among the ultra-Orthodox Jews of Boro Park. In that sense, she was like any other virgin bride going into the unknown, unsure of what she was allowed to do, to feel; unsure of what her new husband would permit himself to do in bed. What kind of behavior would he expect from her? Could she be herself, adventurous and unrestrained? Or would that offend his piety, his modesty? Would it, she thought with a heavy, frightened heart,

disgust him, a man who had only ever known one woman—a timorous, eighteen-year-old virgin who had no doubt worn an ankle-length, long-sleeved nightgown to bed and shrunk from his touch?

Yaakov stood motionless, studying her. *What happens now?* he thought, a bit terrified. *What should I do? What is she used to men doing?*

As a man who had been brought up with the idea that passion between a man and a woman was a dangerous thing that must always be contained and fought against outside the very clear parameters of marriage, he was used to closing down his feelings and burying them. There was no such thing as a private life in the haredi world. The society had an opinion and a rule about everything. Some liked to put a positive spin on this, lauding the interference of the community that butts in, succors, directs, lauds, excoriates, and teaches every one of its members concerning every situation they might possibly encounter in life, demanding they always choose the accepted norm. Sex was no exception. What, after all, was private about marital relations? It, no less than every other part of their lives, required complete submission to the unwavering strictures of their community no less than to the actual God-given rules outlined in the Torah, Talmud, and book of Jewish law. Without that, their little enclave—huddling together like emperor penguins against the fury of soul-chilling blasts from the dangerous, immoral, and alien modern world—would be weakened. Thus, no member could be allowed to defect and chart a new path in any area, not only for the good of the community but also for their own sake, lest they be lost to the howling furies of an inimical culture waiting to pick them off and destroy them one by one if they ever dared venture out on their own.

He had never questioned this. He and his first wife had been innocent teenagers when they married. They had navigated the space between them like astronauts taking their first steps on the surface of the moon, unsure of the very ground beneath their feet. And for a long time, their relationship in bed had been as fragile as crystal they risked shattering with every hesitant touch.

Zissele had come with a list of explicit instructions given to him by his rabbinical groom advisor a few days before their wedding night, as well as a detailed anatomical chart he was exhorted to memorize. He remembered some of the rules:

The room must be in total darkness. Even the windows must be blocked by a cloth. Both of them had to wash their hands three times both before and after "doing the mitzvah." Appropriate prayers must be recited: the prayer that one might fulfill one's obligation "to be fruitful and multiply," and the prayer which asked the Almighty to infuse one with courage and strength so that the body "not contain any weakness or any limpness or any confusion of thought that may negate me, so I may fulfill my desire with my wife, and may my desire be available to me at any time I wish without hesitation or any limpness of the member forever and ever. Amen."

He was exhorted to go to the bathroom, and when coming out, to gently rap the bride on her knees seven times to get her attention "so that her mind not wander from the holiness of fulfilling the mitzvah." Both of them had to remove all their clothes in total darkness, leaving on just a nightgown for her and some robe for him. He was even told precisely how many times before and during he was required to hug and kiss his bride! And the more resistant she was, the more times he had to hug and kiss! The act itself was described in detail, as if explaining it to a child or a blind man or a complete idiot.

He knew that Zissele had also received instructions. She had been taught to examine this place in her body a week before, and familiarize herself with it so that "if the groom should call out to her in a loud voice to guide his member" she would be able to do so. And if he found himself in the right place, he was warned that the "opening was small and narrow and that he would have to enter with great force."

He had found all this material horrifying. Even the promptings of his groom advisor, who had exhorted him on the vital importance of fulfilling the physical act on the wedding night, had not gotten him through it. Every step of the way had been a struggle—to keep his mind pure, his actions in check as his new bride lay beneath him motionless.

He had not followed any of the instructions, finding them instinctively wrong. Neither had Zissele. She was all confusion and fear of not fulfilling her religious duties. In the end, instead of rapping her knees or forcibly hugging and kissing her, he had simply sat on the edge of the bed, his hands folded between his knees, filled with pity for her and for himself. Sex never happened that first night. Instead, they had separated

in fear and confusion, the failure devastating to them both. Nevertheless, looking back, this had been far better than forcing himself to do things he despised and forcing her to do something she wasn't ready for.

Eventually, of course, like every other devout couple, with time and patience and without knee-tapping and forced embraces, they had figured it out. But for both of them, their wedding night had remained forever a shameful secret, a failure, when it could have been a fond recollection filled with teasing, secret laughter, and joy, he thought. And even as the years passed and the walls between them had crumbled, children blessing their union, still, rules and obligations, duty and piety had intruded upon their intimacy like phantom eyes in the darkness for the rest of their marriage.

He didn't want that with Leah. He wanted—so much—to make her happy, and to be happy himself; to firmly close the door of their bedroom, locking out the niggling voices in his head of rabbis and teachers and pious texts. He wanted, once and for all, to banish the doubts, the self-hatred, the awful memories; to be free.

Where to begin?

She took a hesitant step toward him.

"Yaakov, shut off the light."

His heart did a somersault. Of course, the light. He moved quickly.

But the room was still bathed in pale shadows from the streetlamps of Brooklyn that washed through the newly polished windowpanes in their splintered wooden frames. He inhaled, wondering if she'd also demand they close the blind, or cover the windows with thick cloths, as they'd been instructed. To his relief, she didn't.

He stood there foolishly, he thought, not knowing what to do next. How he wished he could say something funny or witty or romantic! How he longed to behave in a worldly, confident way that would impress her! How he longed, in short, to be someone else. But he was stuck with himself, he thought dismally, looking at this young woman he had fallen in love with so deeply, afraid of making some fatal error that would reveal to her what a profound mistake she had made to connect her life to the shambles that was his own.

They waited in silence, paralyzed by uncertainty. And then, for some reason he himself didn't understand, he moved toward her, taking her hand in his and entwining his long fingers with hers. "Leah," he whispered, kissing her fingertips. "My beautiful bride."

She leaned into him, kissing the space where the stiff white collar of his shirt met his neck. He felt a thrill that mesmerized him. Wordlessly, he led her to the bedroom.

To his surprise and discomfort, the brand-new twin beds had been pushed together and covered with a colorful, king-size comforter.

"Do you like it, the comforter? My mother bought it for us as a present," she told him shyly. "All we had were twins."

Her mother. *Of course,* he thought. No religious person would make up the beds of a married couple this way. The very suggestion that their bed was a king and not twins that could be pushed apart during the many days when they would be forbidden to even touch, or pass each other a plate, let alone share a bed, would be considered by Boro Park standards shockingly inappropriate.

"It's wonderful," he answered with a strange enthusiasm she found amusing. It was true. He loved it; loved the illusion it created of a space that would always unite them, brushing over the reality.

"Should I use the bathroom to get undressed?" she asked uncertainly.

Disappointment filled his heart. He had so looked forward to something banishing the old ghosts. "Of course."

He waited patiently. To his surprise, she soon returned, still fully dressed.

"I can't manage these buttons."

He smiled, pulling her close. His fingers fumbled in the darkness, missing the tiny lace hoops.

"Wait." She switched on the small night lamp, turning her back to him. "Can you see them now?"

He nodded, the flicker of light forbidden and thrilling. Slowly, carefully, he pushed the little, slippery pearl buttons through the tiny hoops, his fingers tingling with desire. And when he had unfastened them all, she held the dress against her chest modestly.

"The lamp, Yaakov?"

"Please, Leah," he begged her suddenly.

She turned to him, startled. Then, looking into his pleading eyes, she deliberately withdrew her arms from her sleeves, stepping out of the dress and her half-slip, laying both carefully over a chair. Slowly, one by one, she pulled out the little pearl pins that had held back her hair, letting her reddish-gold curls cascade down her back.

He reached out tentatively, running his fingers through her curls, something he had been longing to do from the moment they met. Lifting her hair in a bunch off her back, he was shocked at the smooth, pearly whiteness of her skin, the way it glowed with youth.

She didn't mind being in her bra and panties, but him being still fully clothed made her feel shamefully exposed. She reached over, moving his black suit jacket off his shoulder.

A light seemed to go on in his head. He smiled a little mournfully. "How stupid! Of course," he murmured, stepping back to undress.

She crawled beneath the covers, pulling them modestly beneath her chin as she slipped out of the rest of her clothes. She thought about the chaste white cotton nightgown bought in a Boro Park lingerie store still packed in her small suitcase. *Let it stay there,* she thought, a shiver of happy anticipation going through her at the feel of the cool, crisp sheets against her naked body.

She watched him undress. His body surprised her with its beauty, the broad shoulders, the firm jut of his collarbone, the tapering waist. There was not an ounce of fat on him, no paunch at all. Still, the naked male body topped by the pious, rabbinical beard . . . The contrast was almost too much. *But that's who he is,* she understood. That was the package deal, the man, his beliefs, his lifestyle. She opened her arms, ready to embrace all of him.

The gesture, the fullness of her acceptance, made him want to cry as he hurried to join her, slipping inside her arms. He, too, against all the rules, wore nothing.

"Do you want to shut off the light now?" she murmured.

Years of Talmud study made it impossible for him to escape the words whirling around in his head like bats escaping from a cave, slamming against his skull: *Shulchan Aruch,* 240–11: *It is prohibited to have marital relations by day unless the house is dark.* But it wasn't day, it was night! And even if it wasn't, according to some authorities a Torah scholar who covers himself is also permitted to have marital relations by day! It was also written that since a scholar is modest in his ways, he won't look (at his wife in the light). But this was only in the case of a great need or if his evil inclination overcame him.

His chest contracted almost angrily. Another old ghost.

"No, let's leave it on," he said defiantly. "Besides, the Rambam says a man and woman can do anything they want in their marriage bed."

"Let's not bring rabbis into our bedroom tonight, my Yaakov, even the magnificent Maimonides."

His heart secretly filled with joy, but also misgivings. "But if *you're* uncomfortable. If *you* want to turn it off . . . Do you?" he asked simply, ready to be disappointed by her reply.

"Uh, well, not really . . . If you're sure it's all right . . ."

In answer, he laughed, pulling her toward him, crushing her body to his with tenderness and gratitude. "Please, Leah, can we leave the past, everything we've experienced, outside this door? Can we leave all the rules about piety and modesty in the kitchen and living room? When we come here, can we just be ourselves?"

A great weight lifted from her heart. She couldn't believe he was saying everything she had wanted to say but was afraid to because it might make him doubt the sincerity of her transition from a girl who picked up men in bars and saw forbidden movies to a devout Boro Park wife and mother, a member in good standing in their community, the woman she thought he wanted her to be. It was as if someone had turned a key, opening the padlocks on both their hearts and bodies.

What happened next was thrilling, astonishing, tender, exciting, and surprising to them both, leaving them exhausted, battered by wave after wave of emotion so deep and real it was almost destructive, changing them both in fundamental ways that only much later would they fully comprehend.

Blessed are You, Eternal God, Source of Life, who has kept us in life, sustained us, and enabled us to reach this joyous moment.

They were one now, Leah thought, truly. Pray God that would never change.

4

⚛

SHAINDELE'S
NEW BEGINNING

What a difference a year had made, Shaindele thought, settling into the familiar, rickety wooden chair with its long, scuffed writing arm, junked from some New York public school that had long since modernized to plastic. In that the furniture mirrored the building, an old public school whose Irish and Italian second-generation tenants had long since disappeared, replaced by Hasidic Jews who had bought the abandoned building, outfitting it with scraps and leftovers and their own version of an education, which would have scandalized their American-born predecessors.

She was seventeen, going on eighteen. Long gone was the dread of running into the likes of Freidel Halpern, the principal's perfect daughter, who had graduated months before, taking her perfect French braid, her snobbery, and her ugly insinuations with her. Gone, too, was Gnendel, her sidekick and echo, who had left without graduating to marry the son of one of the area's butchers. With glee, Shaindele imagined her in a stained white apron standing behind the counter.

Although one was forbidden to hold grudges, she would never forgive those two who had orchestrated and led the vicious bullying she had suffered in wake of her mother's death: the little hints about how early death was a punishment for sins and the high-handed disdain over her father's relationship with a *baalas teshuva*. How they had made her suffer! She wondered if the recent wedding was going to put an end to it or, as she most dreaded, become the jumping-off point for yet another round?

But so far, the girls had been kind about her father's new wife.

"Such a beautiful wedding, *kaynahora*," little Esther Shulman had whispered sincerely. "May your family know only joy from now on."

"It must be a blessing to have a mother to take care of your little brother and sister and the house. Now you won't have to work so hard," Raizel Liba added sweetly, while chubby Adina Sara had stood by, nodding in agreement, dispensing a big, warm hug.

But it was not the approval of the B- and C-listers she craved—daughters of pharmacists and shopkeepers—but those of the elite group who had once been her peers, daughters of rabbis and kollel-heads. Freidel's father was principal of the school, while Gnendel's headed his own kollel (no doubt the reason she'd found anyone at all to marry her, with her face! And no doubt they'd held the wedding three weeks after the engagement so as not to give the groom an opportunity to change his mind).

When her mother had lived and her father had been a full-time scholar, her place among them had been assured. She'd been a princess, community royalty, her lineage linked from both sides to distinguished rabbis and scholars going back a hundred years.

But her mother's sudden death had put an end to all that. For not only had the shocking details surrounding it fueled the rumor mill, but it had also triggered the economic necessity for her father to leave the kollel and take up full-time employment—a disgrace in their scholarly community. Perhaps worst of all was her father's shocking determination to make a redheaded *baalas teshuva* his wife.

Now, instead of concrete, she stood on beach sand, she thought, her status shifting with every new wave of community gossip. In every word, every glance, every gesture toward her by others, she searched feverishly for sly suggestions of disdain, conjuring insults and slights out of thin air. And even when she failed to find them, it did little to assuage her anxiety or dissipate the clouds of disparagement she imagined hanging over her head. The only thing that had so far kept her from collapsing altogether were her grandparents. Living and dead, they were still all indisputable community luminaries.

It might still be all right, she comforted herself, still buoyed by the wedding in which her grandmother's power and influence had been displayed in all its glory, bringing together the top echelon of the community's Torah scholars to lend an aura of respectability to what would otherwise have been a disgraceful debacle that would have muddied the family's name and ruined her chances of finding a good husband. As it was, despite the mother of the bride dressed like a harem dancing girl toting along her gentile boyfriend in his Aladdin headdress, no one had dared to boycott or even breathe a bad word. That is, at least not to their faces. To do so would have been to openly challenge the stamp of approval given the occasion by the community's éminences grises of Torah scholarship and piety. And no one would, she thought, unless something happened that set the pot to boiling once more. Shaindele found herself obsessing over what that something could be.

There were so many things.

First, Leah could make a mistake—an innocent mistake—that would set the whole neighborhood wagging their tongues. She could, for example, wear socks and athletic shoes. After all, she had friends who went Rollerblading, and even skiing down the streets in Boro Park! Or she could buy the wrong clothes for Chasya, something red, or forget to dress her in long tights when the weather got warm. But that was the least of it.

What if down the line her father and Leah argued and the neighbors heard? She remembered that terrible time between her parents before her mother . . . Oh, how awful that had been! What if it happened again? What if her father realized how different Leah was? What if Leah realized what it was to live such a strict, difficult life? What if they fell out of love, separated? The whole burden of caring for her family would once again fall upon her shoulders.

It was all horribly plausible. More than once, she had pondered the strangeness of a young, secular woman choosing to live among them despite all their niggling rules and annoying restrictions. Why would you take that on yourself if you didn't have to? Surely, it must have been fun to be secular, to go to movies and plays, and go ice-skating in Rockefeller Center in the winter, and swimming at Coney Island in the summer, all things forbidden to haredi women by virtue of the endless strictures concerning modest dress and deportment? Until Leah entered their lives, she had seldom, if ever, given such possibilities a moment's thought.

From birth, she had lived in a walled city on a planet in which all the paths had been clearly delineated, the rules made crystal clear. And behind those battlements, she had been happy with those childish amusements that had been permitted her, never feeling any sense of deprivation. But the encounter with Leah, coupled as it was with the loss of her mother, had made it shockingly clear that those walls were not in fact made of bricks and mortar. If you pushed against them, they gave way immediately, opening up a road toward a million unexplored possibilities.

Looking beyond them to see where her stepmother had come from, trying to imagine the life she had lived, had begun as an exercise in contempt to strengthen her opposition to a match of which, she told herself, no one approved; an attempt to strengthen her solidarity with those respectable and wise people around her who had so clearly communicated their disgust and rejection.

"*Baalas teshuva* with the wild red hair," Freidel had called Leah, egging Shaindele on to do things that almost destroyed her relationship with her father simply to placate what she now realized were an ignorant and hateful girl's ugly prejudices. Why, she'd even been ready to run away from home and get married, convinced that Leah would destroy her family's reputation, reducing her own value in the marriage market to little more than zero!

Had she really been that silly, she wondered, that self-absorbed and vengeful she'd been prepared to destroy the happiness of her family simply to assuage some worthless acquaintance's sense of propriety? She shook her head in self-amazement, thinking of the home she had come from that morning. The smell of coffee and orange juice had filled the clean, orderly kitchen, and folded laundry sat in baskets waiting to be put away. Chasya and Mordechai Shalom, both beautifully dressed, their little faces scrubbed, their hair combed, sat chattering amiably over a table of freshly made omelets and toast. Most of all, she recalled her father's newly serene eyes as he'd sat back watching, a gentle smile on his lips.

It was his last week in kollel. What a relief it probably was to him to know that when he started work full-time in the city, his home and his children would be in competent, loving hands, not those of some silly, resentful teenager who couldn't cope, she thought with surprising candor, both surprised and pleased at how much she had grown to finally admit such a thing. She looked down gratefully at the blouse she wore, newly laundered and ironed by her stepmother, and the brown lunch bag filled with nonfattening, nutritious treats Leah carefully prepared for her each day.

Right after the wedding, she had found it hard to become accustomed to such luxuries. "I'm not a child! I can take care of my own clothes and make my own lunches, Leah," she'd protested. But Leah had only laughed.

"There is plenty I expect you to do, Shaindele. Don't worry that I'm going to spoil you! Now off you go, you'll be late."

"But don't you want me to drop off the children?"

"I'll take them in the car," Leah said. "It'll be quicker."

The car—the gleaming blue Honda Civic, purchased secondhand with Leah's income and the wedding gifts—now parked on the street right outside their apartment building, ready to take them on Sunday picnics and to museums and zoos. If anything delineated the border between their old lives and this new one, it was the car, and her father's suddenly youthful face as he kissed everyone goodbye in the morning.

As Shaindele walked to class with carefree ease, she couldn't help but remember the old days when all of it had been her responsibility: cooking, cleaning, laundry, childcare; the feeling of panic and self-hatred as dirty dishes and pots left over from the Sabbath piled up on the counters and hampers stinking of a week's worth of soiled children's clothes fouled the air. The disorder, the unhappy, crying children, her schoolwork, the missed days of classes . . . She must never go back to that again, never!

She sat down behind her desk, closing her eyes for a moment before steadying her shaking hands to grip a pen and notebook as she waited for the lesson to begin. She wasn't the same person as the young girl who had come to school the year before, she realized, her heart broken from the loss of her mother, her head a mass of confusion, struggling with an anger and resentment that often boiled over, threatening to tear her fragile young heart apart.

But with the healing had come some scars. In witnessing the pitiless end that had come to her mother, part of her youth had been robbed from her, part of her innocence. She would never again be able to look out at the world through the eyes of a child. She had seen a part of the world she had never been meant to see, and which now could never be unseen.

She wanted so much to live a good life. She wanted to be happy, with that unique yearning felt by the young who are full of health and dreams and energy. Even with all the pain she had experienced, the optimism that is part of having lived so few years was strong inside her; the idea that it is possible to change things, to make them different, better; the idea that it is perfectly feasible to overcome the past and forget it. The proof of that was in her father's eyes. He was walking a new path, and so could she.

She could go forward in a way unique to her alone. And it could be light-filled, with a luminescence that would shine brighter and brighter with each step, the way her father's eyes shone now with something new, something surprising and unexpected, that had happened to him. She did not yet know where to find that path, only that it was out there, waiting.

Leah, the young woman she had fought against for so long, was now part of her life, taking on herself so many of the burdens people had thoughtlessly piled on her, mistaking her youth for competence, resilience, and strength, when just the opposite was true. She'd been inexperienced, rigid, and weak. But that was the past. She felt confident that at the very least all her tragedies and missteps had taught her something about the world and particularly about herself. She felt sure it was possible to grow and get better.

She didn't know what the future would hold, but her young heart yearned that it be a better life than a short and troubled one filled with pain like that of her poor mother. Her heart still ached for her mother, but now, finally, she felt the possibility of healing was not so far off. Only then, she told herself, could her heart truly open to all life's possibilities.

How strange that this young woman she had feared, despised, rejected, and battled against had become the catalyst for that opening! As if she were a flower and Leah rain.

Whatever ugly things people said about *baale teshuva*, there was something comforting—inspiring, even—about a woman raised in the great, free outside world leaving it all behind to join them in their narrow lives. Far from weakening her faith, it had strengthened her belief and her understanding, making her feel that she needn't doubt the path she had been raised to follow, because even others, who had followed a wider road, had voluntarily chosen to find their way there.

By the time school ended, the short daylight hours of winter had already faded as she headed home through the smoky glow of streetlamps that filtered through the thinning autumn leaves. All around, she saw people moving, hurrying—bewigged mothers pushing baby carriages, young Talmud students carrying heavy books, children balancing on bicycles.

There was something beautiful, she thought, in just putting one foot in front of the other, propelling yourself forward through the onrushing flux of time; something rewarding in motion itself. The life force inside her rose to the surface of her consciousness in a way it had never done before. She was aware of herself being alive, being human. And this seemed to her the opposite of where she had come from the year before, when her heart had been filled with death, with stasis and mourning.

She could feel the world yearning for her. She wanted so much to embrace it, to become part of it. But could she? Did she have the ability, the will, to push her life force, frozen by the agony of loss, into vitality again, into the future? What could she do? How could she make this happen? She felt paralyzed, afraid of missing her chance. And yet, because she was young, so hopeful, too.

She wondered if everyone felt like this at some time in their lives. But no one she knew talked of such things. *I'm lonely,* she realized, wishing once more she could talk to her mother. But she would have to do this alone now, this reaching, this growing. And the thought of that terrified her.

5

❧

JOY

Something was sweeping over her, Leah thought as she strapped Mordechai Shalom securely into his car seat and helped Chasya close her seat belt. The rhythm of her life, so long dictated by her own ideas and needs, was no longer under her control. She was surprised at just how radical the change had been from her previous life once she moved into the Lehman household.

She had not expected that. After all, she had been taking care of the house and the children for months before the actual wedding. But coming in during the day was not the same as living with them, she realized. Lifting the baby out of his bed as he awoke first thing in the morning, his body soft and still heavy with sleep as he curled up in her arms, caressing her cheek with his own; Chasya jumping into her lap as she sat drinking her morning coffee, the lingering smell of her evening bath and shampoo rising like incense from her warm scalp.

The very sound of their voices whether in unhappiness, hilarity, or sweet entreaty—even their silence behind closed bedroom doors—made demands on her attention, her heart, her mind, evoking a vigilant watchfulness and a degree of obligation she had never before experienced. Most of all, the magical, transformative word *Mommy,* addressed to her in laughter or bawling misery, tugged at her heart, burdening it and filling it with joy in ways she could not have foreseen or even imagined.

Their own mother had been *Mameh.* If Mordechai Shalom remembered her at all, he showed no sign of it. But Chasya did. Once when Leah had found her sitting by the window looking out into the street, her little face somber and forlorn, she'd made the colossal error of asking her what was wrong. The little girl's response had been devastating.

"She didn't come to the wedding," Chasya answered without looking up.

"Who, sweetie?"

"Mameh."

Leah stood staring down at her, dumbfounded.

"I haven't seen her in such a long time," the child continued, shaking her head. "Maybe she forgot where we live? If I see her, I'm going to go get her."

The lump in Leah's throat made it impossible for her to speak. So she gathered the little girl into her arms and sat with her silently, stroking her hair, accepting and sharing her matchless grief. The idea of making up stories about heaven and angels and paradise and how one day she would see her mother again seemed wrong somehow. As much as Leah wanted to believe in such things, she knew that telling that to Chasya was simply a heartless detour around the inescapable heartbreak of her present reality. It was almost obscene.

"If I do a lot of mitzvoth and *daven,* will HaShem send her back?"

Leah swallowed hard, remembering her own magical thinking when her fiancé Josh had shockingly slipped and fallen to his death: the hope that it was all a mistake, that it wasn't as bad as it seemed; that a doctor would come and give him a magic little pill that would cure him. He'd open his wide, brown eyes and smile his unique lopsided smile, his eyes filled with familiar, self-deprecating humor. "Wow," he'd say. "That's something I won't try again!" And they'd pick up their backpacks and continue their pre-wedding hike through beautiful Zion National Park.

She held the child closer, shaking her head. "You are the best little girl in the world, Icy, and HaShem loves you just the way you are. But that's not the way the world works, sweetheart. When someone dies, they don't ever come back to this world, no matter how much we pray and how much we miss them."

The child seemed to accept that as if she'd known it all along. "Mommy, I have a secret," she whispered, snuggling closer.

"Do you want to tell me what it is?" Leah whispered, rocking her.

Chasya nodded solemnly, pressing her small soft lips so close to Leah's ear that her breathing moved the tiny hairs inside. "Every day, I'm getting smaller. Smaller and smaller. Maybe one day, I'll get so small, you won't be able to see me. I'll just disappear, like my mameh."

Leah pulled her gently away, turning her by the shoulders so that she could look deeply into her eyes. "Chasya, look at me. Every day, you are getting bigger and bigger, and smarter and smarter, and more and more beautiful. Every day, you make me and your tateh so happy. Even if you hide, we'll always be able to find you. Do you believe me?"

The child thought about it for a few moments, then nodded.

"And now I have a secret to tell you."

Chasya looked up expectantly.

"It's okay to feel sad, to miss your mameh. But it's also okay to be happy. That's what your mameh would have wanted for you. For all of you. To have fun! And you and I and your tateh and Cheeky and Shaindele and your big brothers are going to be a very happy family. We are going to be the kind of family your mameh would have wanted us to be. We are going to have a lot of fun together, every single day!"

Ever since that conversation, that had become her mantra, Leah thought. To have fun; to bring joy to the home she had moved into and to the motherless children under her care. She had never understood before how simple a mandate that was.

In the past, she'd always thought joy came after huge successes or immense expenses. But now she found it was at the end of a sugar cone or a lollipop, in front of the monkey cages in the zoo. It was sometimes just as simple as putting on music and dancing around the living room as the children whooped and danced around her.

She got into the habit of playing music for them right after their baths as they waited for their tateh to come home for dinner. First she used

Yaakov's ancient boom box, putting in outdated cassette tapes of young yeshiva boys singing liturgical songs. But one day, she simply connected her iPhone to the speakers on her computer, putting on her favorite playlist. The first song was Foo Fighters' "Everlong": *If everything could ever feel this real forever, if anything could ever be this good again.* And then the music just kept blasting out: oldies like the Beach Boys' "Wouldn't It Be Nice," the Supremes' "You Can't Hurry Love," Justin Timberlake's "Can't Stop the Feeling," Avicii's "Wake Me Up," Lady Gaga's "Poker Face," Katy Perry's "Hot N Cold."

At first, the kids seemed a little uncertain at how to react to the unfamiliar music, but they got into it quickly, she saw, wildly throwing themselves into stamping and shouting and twirling around the living room. Chasya, sweating, peeled off her pajama top, laughing. The baby soon followed suit, left with nothing but his diaper. Her own hair covering had long ago been flung to the floor, her tight, frizzy red curls spilling down her back, flying in all directions. She hardly noticed. Twirling around the room in some kind of trance, the music bringing back so many memories of the life she'd left behind, she almost didn't hear the banging on the door until it did the impossible, becoming even louder than the music.

Only then did Leah think of the neighbors and the curtainless windows whose shades she had not bothered to pull down.

———

Fruma Esther Sonnenbaum didn't listen to gossip. As every person harboring an unquenchable desire for a large and respectable portion in the World to Come knew, gossip was a surefire way to erase your merits and get yourself permanently banned from heaven. After all, were there not thirty-one commandments and four curses in the Torah specifically aimed at the sin of malicious talebearing? As it is written: *You shall not go up and down as a slanderer among your people.* Gossip, as she and every other God-fearing Jew well knew, was the leading cause of baseless hatred, the reason our temple was destroyed, why our people were exiled from their land, and why God did not listen to our prayers. Indeed, as the sages declared, gossip, slander, and talebearing were worse than murder, immorality, and idolatry, the three mortal sins one was ordered to give up one's life rather than commit. A gossiper, they said, denies the existence of God, and the Almighty "cannot live in the same world" with such a person. Even the "dust" of evil talk was toxic. So you couldn't get away with saying things like: "Oh, what I could tell you about her if I wasn't a pious person." Sorry, no. As Solomon, the wisest of all Israel's kings said, "One who guards his mouth and tongue, guards his soul from tribulations."

Nevertheless, as the rebbitzen was also well aware, in Boro Park, among the pious, not listening to gossip was almost impossible. In fact, it was one of the tools of the community to keep itself pure, guarding against the insidious dangers coming from those troublemakers and misfits in their midst who threatened to unravel the fabric of their lives, the well-being of their children. For how could you function as an enclave of holiness if you did not guard against interlopers filled with evil intentions, who must be expelled by collective ostracism? And how would you know who to expel and ostracize if no one told you?

So when her phone began to ring off the hook with stories about her former son-in-law's new wife, she was faced with a dilemma of no small proportions. Was it permissible, she pondered, to hear what her friends and neighbors wanted to tell her? The nosy strangers, the mere acquaintances who had the temerity to call her or stop her in the street were not the problem; she dispatched them with a withering look and an on-high quotation about the evils of gossip. What, there was a shortage of quotes? But the others—people she had known all her life, people she respected, who like herself had on their bookshelves well-worn copies of Rabbi Yisrael Meir Kagan's seminal book on *loshon hara* called *Chafetz Chaim,* meaning "desire life," after the verse: *Who is the man who desires life? He who guards his tongue from evil and his lips from falsehood;* people who had Talmud scholars for husbands and sat next to her in the synagogue on Yom Kippur quaking with fear that their prayers for a good year might not be accepted—if people like *this* were willing to risk their eternal souls by selflessly bringing a matter they considered of vital importance to her attention, how could she refuse to listen?

What made it more difficult was the suddenness and volume of these tales after months of quiet in which she had congratulated herself on removing her opposition to the strange match as well as single-handedly facilitating the wedding through the shameless use of her considerable prestige as the widow of the great rav, cowing all opposition. Moreover, she had personally taken it upon herself to convince the loudest and most vociferous opponent to the match, her granddaughter Shaindele (who had even gone so far as to run away from home) that her father deserved to go ahead with his life, even if it meant accepting his less-than-stellar choice in a new wife. Selflessly, she had made it happen, which wasn't to say that she didn't occasionally indulge in secret fantasies about how different things might have been had Yaakov settled on one of the Flatbush widows or Monsey divorcées for whom the matchmakers had so vigorously campaigned.

Most of the time, though, she grudgingly admitted to herself that he had chosen well, for himself at least. Gone was the listless, defeated widower with rounded shoulders who had allowed tragedy and loss to drain the sparkle from his eyes and the hope in his heart. He was—she thought a bit resentfully—as happy as she had ever seen him, including during his marriage to her Zissele. In fact, he seemed like a different person altogether. Realism had replaced idealism, and instead of floating through the air on Talmudical exegeses, he wore sturdy walking shoes that were planted firmly on the ground. He'd finished his accounting course, passed the CPA exam, and had just accepted a job offer. Soon his years in kollel would be behind him, along with all the dreams of his youth of becoming a great and revered rav.

It was tragic. But who was she to criticize? Earning enough to provide for his family was a necessity, although a heartbreaking one. Such promise! He had been a shining star in the yeshiva world, or so she had always told herself. Otherwise, she would never have considered the match for Zissele. It was what her daughter had wanted also. This she believed with all her heart.

But tragedy tested a man, and challenged him. There was always a tension in their world between the spiritual and the material, a conflict between sacrificing all for the sake of learning the Torah and working to provide a better life materially for one's family. While their world theoretically lauded scholars and looked down on wage earners, the wealthy among religious Jews were viewed with respect bordering on craven approbation, and young Talmud scholars vied with each other in seeking out the well-to-do daughters of wealthy businessmen, ignoring the poor offspring of fellow Talmud scholars. Still, a scholar who left the study house to work full-time was a rarity, and not a welcome one. It was a situation that invited hostility and criticism among religious Jews (which she would have preferred to believe came out of conviction rather than envy), which would fall not only on Yaakov but on herself and her grandchildren as well.

She had hoped that with Leah's computer business doing so well, that the girl might suggest—of her own accord of course—that Yaakov surrender the burden of *parnosa* to her completely. But this, she saw, was not to be. Yaakov had made it clear that he felt he owed it to his new wife to do his share. It was, he insisted, a matter of self-respect as much as necessity.

But since when did a Talmud scholar believe earning a living instead of allowing his wife to support him took away from his self-respect? This was a secular idea, from the immoral secular world whose notions of what made an admirable husband and wife bore absolutely no resemblance to those of their own world, where admiration could only be earned in the study halls of the yeshivot and *kollelim* and where a woman of valor was the woman who works and runs a business (in addition to housework, childbirth, and child-rearing), freeing her husband to learn without such petty distractions.

But his new wife, she sighed, was not from their world, and Yaakov, she supposed, was desperate to please her. This was the way of the world, she told herself, secretly mourning the distinguished young Talmud scholar who had sat in her living room as he courted her daughter, his face beaming with joyous possibilities as he talked of his love of learning, his plans to become a great scholar and found his own yeshiva.

The children, too, had undergone a transformation since the wedding, but in their case, a blessed one, she thought, her features suddenly brightening. Shaindele had stopped stuffing herself with Swiss chocolates and rugelach to feed some hunger she hadn't been able to assuage, her once chubby body slimming down. She was a pretty seventeen-year-old who had blossomed. She had even grown taller by an inch or two. The stodgy Bais Yaakov uniform—the blue, long-sleeved blouse buttoned to the neck and calf-length, pleated navy skirt—looked almost chic on her newly taut body. But most of all, her face had changed. Gone were the ugly grimaces of resentment and sullen rebellion. If she was not exactly the bubbly teenager she had been before her mother's death, she was at least once again the diligent, promising student. Otherwise, Fruma Esther would have heard about it; she checked in with the girl's principal and teachers weekly.

As for the little ones—it was like night and day! Instead of soiled, wrinkled clothes, they were dressed like little dolls, their faces scrubbed pink, their little bodies filling out with good, regular home-cooked meals. Most of all, they seemed happy. Gone were Chasya's constant stomachaches that had had them rushing to the emergency room. And little Mordechai Shalom had a full-time mother again he could depend upon, instead of herself, an aging Bubbee who had doctors' appointments she couldn't skip, bad feet that hurt her when she took him for walks, and arms too frail to even lift him up for a good hug.

Fruma Esther, be happy! she admonished herself. *Who more than you knows how close the family had come to the brink of despair, disgrace, and financial ruin!* Maybe Leah couldn't support Yaakov as a full-time learner, but the money from her thriving internet business was at least helping to pay off the endless loans from the interest-free loan funds, taken out in desperation to make up for the loss of Zissele's teacher's salary after she died. The loans, financed by the tithe money from generous members of the community, were not like getting money from a faceless bank. It was from someone's pocket, usually someone who knew you, and whom you knew well. Defaulting on such a loan was not a private, personal matter but a widely known disgrace with immediate consequences to a family's communal standing.

Yet, despite it all, she admitted to herself that even her happiness over these good things was tinged with a strange resentment as she watched the consequences of her daughter's tragic death slowly fade from the consciousness of her family and the community. They were going on with their lives in happiness. It was so unfair! While her love for her grandchildren and her sincere desire for their well-being sweetened the bitterness in her soul, the current rumors gave her a perverse satisfaction. No one could take her Zissele's place.

Still, she did not look forward to the possibility of hearing something scandalous about her grandchildren's new stepmother. Having prominently championed the match, the opprobrium would fall heavily on her as well. With a great intake of breath that made her enormous breasts heave and tremble, she buttoned her coat. True or false, the stories making the rounds must be quashed immediately and decisively, especially if they were accurate. Her own and her grandchildren's well-being depended upon it.

As for the Torah's many prohibitions about listening to gossip, well, permissible or forbidden, she could not very well turn a deaf ear to what was being said about her family. It was, she reasoned, like taking an ambulance on the Sabbath: a desecration of one of God's commandments in order to preserve a life that in the future would faithfully observe many other commandments. Still, for a woman as devout as Fruma Esther, who believed herself to possess an absolute, iron-clad grip on right and wrong, it was no trifling matter. Her present moral confusion was rare, even a bit frightening. And thus, she felt she had no choice but to risk the dust of slander by talking the matter over with her dearest friend, Basha Blaustein.

Wife of the deeply respected *posek* Rav Aryeh, Basha had been in school with Fruma Esther from kindergarten through graduation from Bais Yaakov Seminary. Both coming from established and respected Boro Park families with long lists of distinguished rabbinical forebears, they were top merchandise in all the matchmakers' bride pools that summer and months before. Both had been offered and had accepted Grade A candidates— long-bearded young scholars with reputations for brilliance in Talmud study who, the matchmakers assured their parents, were worth every penny of the colossal financial settlement they needed to provide for years of continued study. Within two weeks of each other, and several weeks shy of their eighteenth birthdays, both had gotten engaged.

Their friendship had become even stronger through the years as they helped each other survive the difficulties of financially supporting their husbands through kollel and giving birth to many children. There was no one Fruma Esther admired and respected more.

She took out the cell phone her family had insisted on buying and teaching her to use following her scandalous, solo journey to a New York hospital for an eye operation that had left her stranded and in need of a secular hospital volunteer to get home. Now the phone helped everyone to keep track of her comings and goings. Even her daughters in Israel had taken to calling her a few times a week on it just to check there were no new surprises. Despite the rabbis' harsh condemnation of cell phones, almost everyone in Boro Park had one now, connected—of course!—to the kosher internet that pre-blocked all unacceptable websites.

"Basha, I need to speak to you. You have maybe a minute?"

"Such a question! Talk."

"No, I'll come over. You're home this morning?"

"I'm baking for Shabbos."

Although the Sabbath was four days away, this did not surprise Fruma Esther. After all, Basha had ten children—all married except for one—numerous grandchildren and great-grandchildren as well as a husband active in the effort to encourage secular Jews to become more religious. As a result, Basha's table regularly seated thirty or more family and guests for the traditional Friday night dinner and Saturday afternoon lunch. To do it properly, you needed almost a week with all the food buying and preparation.

They sat companionably on the worn sofa in the sparsely furnished living room, dwarfed by massive wooden bookcases filled with holy volumes.

"The phone doesn't stop ringing, Basha."

The other woman sighed. "It's about Leah and the music, right?"

"Music?"

Basha studied her friend's genuinely puzzled face. "So you didn't hear even what it's all about?"

"I don't listen to *loshon hara*."

Basha shook her head. "You have no choice."

"Why?"

"Because if you don't know what's going on, how can you help her?"

"She needs help?" Her voice quivered.

Basha nodded.

"But *loshon hara* . . . it's forbidden, Basha."

"It's permitted when your *kavanah* is not to disgrace or belittle someone but to warn others about their faults. In that case, it's not a sin. It's a mitzvah."

"Before you tell me what's going on, tell me this, Basha: Is it true?"

Basha pulled down her headscarf, tucking in a few gray hairs, as if to shore up her piety against accusations from a bad conscience. "It might have some seeds of truth. After all, I heard it from so many people, and not just the usual yentas."

Fruma Esther braced herself. "What are they saying?"

"That she is bringing secular music into the house, and they are . . . dancing wildly."

Fruma Esther swallowed hard. "What exactly does that mean?"

"What part?"

"Every part! *Vus is dus* 'secular' and 'they' and 'wildly'?"

"I don't know the details. The neighbors complained the music was loud and noisy, and the children, Chasya and Mordechai Shalom, and even Leah, were jumping up and down."

"So they were playing a game, having fun?"

"It's more than that. The children were naked, and she had no head covering."

Fruma Esther inhaled a sharp, involuntary gulp of breath. "The doors were open?"

"No, of course not. But the windows had the shades up."

"They are on the second floor! Who could look in?"

"People in the apartments across the way."

"How can they see anything? They're across the street."

"The neighbors came up to complain about the music, and when Leah finally opened the door, they saw the children."

"She opened the door without her hair covering?"

Basha shook her head. "Not exactly. They said it was 'loose' and her bangs hung down over her eyes, and a few red curls were hanging down her back."

"So the noise upset them. This is not a crime. They make loud Purim parties and no one complains."

"It wasn't just the noise. It was the music."

There was, as far as Fruma Esther knew, no prohibition against listening to secular music, as long as it wasn't religiously based like church music or Hare Krishna chants, and as long as the lyrics didn't have any lascivious or foul language. Lustful songs, *shira agavim,* were another category. Anything that aroused the sexual desire was banned completely, especially when children were around.

"No halacha prevents us from listening to music, Basha."

This, of course, was true, and both women knew it. But they also knew the problem went far deeper.

"Of course, investigate. That is only fair, but . . ." Basha hesitated. She loved Leah, whom she and her husband had mentored all through her difficult search to return to her roots. She had even championed her all through her fraught courtship with Yaakov, encouraging Fruma Esther to relent. But she couldn't help but be disturbed by these rumors, which fit in perfectly with all the conventional wisdom about not welcoming even sincere *baale teshuva* into the community for fear they would backslide, polluting the holy streets of their tight-knit communities with the remnants of their past, secular lives. For a woman deeply involved in bringing secular Jews into the fold who had spent years fighting against such prejudices, such rumors were drops of poison into the water she drank.

"Even if it isn't exactly what they're saying, still, you need to remind her that everything a religious Jew does or says or sees or hears has an effect on the pure *neshama* God gave them. Especially on the children, who are so innocent. Tell her that sometimes we can't allow ourselves even those things that are permitted because it might taint our purity. Talk to her, Fruma Esther. Explain it to her."

Fruma Esther got unsteadily to her feet, the sweet crumbs from the rugelach turning bitter in her mouth as she envisioned what was to come.

6

YAAKOV LEAVES KOLLEL

Amid the usual cacophony of voices involved in lively debate, Yaakov's footsteps fell softly on the floors of the kollel as he entered for the last time. As he made his way across the large hall, he saw (or thought he saw; it was no longer possible to separate his imaginative fears and shame from reality) familiar faces looking back at him, their warm smiles hiding pity and contempt. And then, of course, there were those who did not look up at all, immersed (or pretending to be) in their sacred Talmudical studies, the same studies he was now preparing to abandon for the mundane, petty existence of a *balabus*. And each time he felt he was being ignored, the slight was as sharp as a stiletto scraping the vulnerable underbelly of his despair.

He looked fondly at the peeling walls with their sagging bookcases, the chipped wooden chairs and tables, rubbed to a fine patina by the hands and bodies of his fellow students over decades. This had been his home for so many years. He had progressed from *cheder* to yeshiva to *mesivta* to the *bais midrash*, landing finally in kollel. While many of his fellow students had dropped out along the way either from disappointment in their progress or financial constraints, he had had the good fortune to be burdened by neither. For over twenty years, he had been part of the elite of this community, learning full-time, and was well on his way—or so he had always told himself—to becoming a respected *rosh yeshiva*. It was in this conviction that he had heretofore invested the entire value and meaning of his life, believing wholeheartedly that only this had earned him the respect of all those who knew him: his children, parents, former in-laws, neighbors, the parents of his children's friends, as well as the butcher and the grocer, who waited patiently each month to settle his bill. It defined him to the world. It defined him to himself.

How could it be otherwise? From his earliest almost toddling steps into *cheder,* where the kindly rebbe had smeared honey over Hebrew letters and allowed him to lick it off, impressing him with the sweetness of learning the holy alphabet in which God's word was written, it had been drummed into him that learning was the highest form of living and serving God. Doing anything else was a mistake, a failure, a sad burden. At the very least, it was settling for second-best. Not the smallest factor in this feeling was the way all the women in his world looked up to Torah scholars and how they looked down upon everyone else.

And so it was that he had gone step by step down that path, almost without being conscious of making a choice. It was what everyone else in the community was doing; what all his friends were doing.

And now, suddenly, it was over.

Despite the fact that this, too, had been his own choice, he found that devastating. It was the heartbreaking relinquishment of his lifelong dreams.

His eyes smarted as he weaved through the crowded rows, avoiding the eyes of others. The sensation of coldness, of being shut out, was not new. It had begun simultaneously with his secular night studies. He couldn't help but notice that his voiced opinions, insights, questions— once regarded as extraordinary, the epitome of intellectual vigor—were suddenly less interesting to those around him. Whereas before, people were eager to engage with him, they now seemed to sigh and look restlessly over his head as if he had not spoken at all. Or so it seemed to him.

"How are you, my friend?"

A familiar voice broke through this painful reverie, and a kind arm draped itself across his shoulders. He looked up, startled, finding welcome in the upturned lips of his *chavrusa,* Meir, as well as an unaccustomed sadness in his friend's usually cheerful, large brown eyes. Wordlessly, the two men embraced.

The years studying with Meir had been the best years of his life, he thought. The pure intellectual challenge of interpreting the holy texts, squeezing out the nectar of God's truth, God's will, had been his highest calling, challenging all his mental faculties and the deepest instincts of his heart. It had been a privilege to share these precious hours with a partner whose dedication matched his own.

"Have you found . . . Are you going to . . . ?" Yaakov began, finding it hard to discuss his replacement.

Meir nodded. "Someone new. The rav suggested. But it won't be easy to start over."

Yaakov nodded gratefully at this kindness. "Maybe we could still find time on Shabbos, or in the evenings, after work?"

Meir hesitated. "We are moving next week. A bigger apartment, but a longer walk." Yaakov understood. Neither he nor Meir were the most athletic of men, and learning together on the Sabbath when it was forbidden to drive or use public transportation would entail a long trek through Brooklyn streets.

"Maybe during the week, then? I could drive over?"

Meir smiled. "What a question!"

Yaakov exhaled. Once a week, then. It would be something to look forward to. And then there would be the early mornings on the subway on his way to work, and the late afternoons on the way back, and perhaps an hour or two in the late evenings, before bed and after the children had been put to sleep. He *must* find the time to continue his lifelong passion for learning the Torah. He couldn't imagine life without it.

"And maybe then you could summarize what you were doing all week?"

Meir nodded kindly. "But as it is written: *It is not the study that is essential, but rather the actions,*" he said in Hebrew, quoting from *Ethics of the Fathers*. "We learn in order to live a good life. And that's what you are doing."

"Rabbi Akiva would not agree with you."

He knew he didn't have to elaborate. The famous debate from the Babylonian Talmud between Rabbi Akiva and Rabbi Tarfon, in which the two sages argued over the primacy of study versus action, was well known to every yeshiva boy. Rabbi Akiva had championed study above all.

"Yes, Rabbi Akiva won the debate. But only because he argued that study leads to action, and is therefore greater. Rav Huna said this clearly in *Avoda Zarah* 17b: *He who occupies himself only with studying is as if he has no God.*"

"I will miss this so much." Yaakov's voice caught.

Meir squeezed his shoulder consolingly. "It is not forever, my friend. A time will come when your children are grown, and you will have more time to devote to the things you love."

Yaakov thought of the years ahead: the older children's weddings; raising Chasya and baby Mordechai Shalom to adulthood and then their marriages. Perhaps more babies with his young wife . . . He would be an old man by then, his mind grown dull and inefficient. As the sage Rabbi Eliezer ben Jacob wrote: *He who studies the Torah in his youth, is like writing on clean paper, while he who studies in his old age is like writing on used paper.* It tore at his heart.

"I hope you get your own yeshiva one day soon, Meir. You deserve it."

"You have always been the greater scholar, Yaakov. It isn't fair. Twenty years of your life!"

Yaakov shrugged. It might not be fair, but it was God's will. Who was he to question it? "God has blessed me in other ways, my friend."

"You're happy in your new life?"

Yaakov brightened. "I feel as if I have been given a second chance."

"Did you ever speak to Leah about your learning?"

"Of course! She wanted me to continue. She told me she could manage to support us for now, that I should continue if that is what I really wanted."

Meir could not hide his surprise. All along, he thought Yaakov's working had been one of the conditions of their marriage; that Leah, coming from the secular world, must have insisted upon it. "So then, why?"

"Why? Because this is my chance to be a better husband than I was the first time, Meir. Maybe if Zissele had had less to do, if she hadn't had to work along with giving birth and taking care of the house and so many children all by herself, maybe . . ."

Meir lowered his arm and stepped back, shaking his head slowly. "Yaakov, you know that wasn't the reason. Zissel had a sickness."

"Yes, but maybe she wouldn't have gotten sick if she hadn't worked so hard all those years. I was blind to it. I am not going to do that to Leah. Never." He shook his head vociferously.

"All the women in our world work hard. They wouldn't want it any other way!" Unspoken between them was the assumption that a woman's portion in the World to Come depended upon her husband's victories in the study hall. When a woman supported the family financially, leaving the man free to learn, she did it not only for him but for herself. They were partners, sharing in the reward.

"So we were taught. So we believed," Yaakov answered, his jaw suddenly clenching, his lips white.

Meir was shocked. "And now, my friend, you no longer believe?"

"Since I lost my Zissele, so many things no longer make sense to me. And so many of the things I trusted blindly, so many of the things I was taught, the community itself has stopped believing and observing, if they ever did."

Meir, gentle, trusting Meir, was shocked. "Really?"

"Yes, Meir. Are we not taught to welcome the stranger? And yet, how was my Leah treated when she decided to live among us as a God-fearing woman? The matchmakers treated her like dirt. They matched her with the mentally ill, the physically disabled. They even gave her phone number to an African convert who had abandoned a wife and six children back home!" Yaakov put up his hand to halt Meir's attempts to comment. "I know what you are going to say. The sins of a few. But it isn't a few. Remember how I had to beg you to play matchmaker because not a single matchmaker in Boro Park was willing to get involved when I wanted to go out with Leah, simply because she was a *baalas teshuva*?"

"I remember." He shifted uncomfortably. His brief foray into the murky realm of go-between to facilitate romantic liaisons was something he had still not gotten over.

"Everyone was against her, despite all the things written in the Torah about welcoming the stranger. So now I don't care what anyone else thinks, Meir. I will do exactly what I know is right according to the Torah I learned all those years."

Both of them knew this wasn't true. Yaakov—perhaps even more than Meir—cared deeply, passionately, about the exalted and honorable place he had earned over so many years among his peers and neighbors. "What will the neighbors think?" had been drummed into him—into all of them—from earliest childhood, like a mantra. It was inescapable.

"And what about the rav, his opinion?"

"Of course I care about the rav! But he is not an ordinary person."

"Maybe you should talk it over with him, then, one last time?"

Yaakov shook his head. "No, I've made up my mind. I'm going to work. If it was just to help pay the rent and buy food and clothes, maybe I would hold on a little longer. But it isn't. It's all those loans I took out. Why should my Leah work so hard to pay off *my* debts?"

"Debts you made to keep a roof over your children's heads, food in the refrigerator, when you lost your income from Zissele's teacher's salary! What else could you do?"

"Exactly. So now I also have no choice, Meir. I have to work to pay it all back."

"Will it take a long time?"

"It will take what it will take. I know my obligations. Is it not written in my wife's marriage contract that I must provide for her?"

They both knew that clause in the Jewish marriage contract was practically fictitious, piously ignored even (especially?) by the same rabbis who were fanatical in every other regard concerning strict observance of even the most minor of religious duties or customs. But it wasn't right. Bitter words rose to Yaakov's throat, but he forced them back. He looked at his innocent, happy, fortunate friend Meir, who was learning full-time, his wife, Bruriah, and her parents supporting him and their children. He was happy for him, and devastated at how their ways had finally—and irrevocably—parted.

Yaakov took a deep breath, then sighed. "We have the whole day, Meir. My last day. Let's not waste any time, my friend. Let's learn."

As the day drew to a close, there was one last thing he had to do. He went to Rav Alter's office and knocked on the door. The assistant let him in. The office, as usual, was packed with petitioners: housewives anxious to save a meat pot and its contents from being discarded because a drop of milk had leaked upon it in the refrigerator; busybodies wanting to enlist the rav's endorsement for various causes—worthy and less so; poor people needing charitable donations; yeshiva boys in moral turmoil; parents inquiring about certain shidduch prospects . . . It was endless.

"It is my last day in kollel," he told the assistant. "I wanted to say goodbye."

"Your last day, Yaakov? Come," he said firmly, leading him past the others directly into the rav's inner sanctum. "And may HaShem bless you, Yaakov."

Yaakov looked at the mahogany bookcases that reached from floor to ceiling on every wall, crammed with heavy books. Volumes of the *Jerusalem Talmud,* the *Babylonian Talmud,* the *Code of Jewish Law,* and hundreds of commentaries and exegeses stared back accusingly. His legs trembled with sudden weakness. The room, so familiar to him from the countless times he had found his way there seeking comfort, inspiration, or just a simple human connection, seemed almost hostile now.

But there was the rav. He exhaled. He never really understood what it was about this elderly man that mesmerized him so completely. Perhaps it was simply the knowledge that each word he uttered came from huge treasuries of wisdom garnered not only from decades of intense study but also countless interactions with people from every background who streamed unceasingly through these doors seeking answers that touched on every aspect of human existence.

He remembered the time so many years before when he'd sat across from the cluttered wooden desk as a young bridegroom barely out of his teens, entering kollel for the first time. How he had poured out his grandiose dreams of achievement, as if diligence alone could uncover the wellspring of every sacred mystery of life, allowing him to find the answers that had eluded so many great scholars before him for centuries, men who like pearl divers had held their breath, diving into the bottomless wisdom of God's sacred words, hoping to come back to the surface without drowning, bearing the rare jewels that would illuminate mysteries of life for all mankind. The rav's face, he remembered, had been warm, betraying no skepticism or amusement at these naive outpourings. How difficult it must have been for him to hide a smile as he listened! And how kind.

He remembered those days after the birth of his children, when the rav had been with him, rejoiced with him. And then there had been the time when death had come, and he'd sat on a low stool during shiva, his shirt ripped in mourning like the heart beneath it, his eyes wild with incomprehension and despair. The rav had sat beside him, saying almost nothing, and his presence had brought an infusion of strength and faith.

And then there was the time that the rav had forced him to come to him, and he had entered this office a broken man. How the rav had urged him to find new life, new love! And how he had resisted that advice! But now here he was once again, instead of opening a chapter, closing it. Of all the people he knew, only Rav Alter, this man of Torah, could possibly comfort him and give him hope for the future.

But it was a different rav he faced now, he realized, one in the midst of his own heartbreaking tragedy as his elderly wife lay in agony from the merciless disease that did not differentiate between saints and sinners, the very old and the very young. The cold lips of the Angel of Death were already brushing her forehead as the rav helplessly watched, his prayers unanswered.

He'd aged, shockingly, Yaakov saw, startled. Always impeccable, now ill-fitting black pants fell around his ankles in folds, and the fringes of his tzitzis hung outside his white shirt and dark jacket reaching sloppily almost to his knees. His long salt-and-pepper beard, normally meticulously groomed, was untrimmed and almost completely white. The velvet skullcap worn beneath his huge, respectable black hat sat askew on his suddenly fragile skull, exposing the vulnerable pink scalp beneath. His tall, distinguished frame seemed to have shrunk, the shoulders bent in suffering as they made an effort to straighten every now and then as if buckling beneath a familiar weight that had gradually—without his even being aware—grown too heavy to bear.

Yaakov cleared his throat.

The rav looked up, a surprised smile brightening a face that seemed already deeply etched in mourning.

"I don't want to bother you, Rav. You are so busy. Your office is full."

"Yes, always full," he murmured distractedly. "But come sit down a little, Yaakov. How are you?"

"Baruch HaShem," he answered mechanically.

"Of course. Baruch HaShem. But tell me anyway." The old man's eyes sparkled almost mischievously for a moment.

"It is so hard to leave, Rav. I feel my heart is breaking."

The rav seemed surprised.

Could he have forgotten that this was to be his last day? But before Yaakov could belabor this hurtful suspicion, the rav came around from behind his desk, taking both of Yaakov's hands in his own.

"A beginning and an end. That is every day of our lives. That is what we have in common as human beings, Yaakov, every day of our lives. And to every ending, there is a new beginning."

"I dreamed of a different life."

"Yes, it is so hard to dream and live and not to find what we want. So much has been given to us, but somehow not what we want. There is always something missing, always something we could have had, should have had. We do not understand why God denies us these things; why He is deaf to our prayers." The rav glanced out the window, his eyes suddenly unseeing. "We cannot understand, but that doesn't mean our just and loving God doesn't have His reasons. If we have faith, every experience we undergo in life, good or bad, will bring us closer to Him."

"Sometimes, it doesn't feel like that. Sometimes, it just feels like a punishment. It is so painful."

"Yes, very painful," the rav repeated, unseeing. "Like a burning, taking away all our impurities with it."

Was that true? Yaakov wondered. Did suffering refine, or did it simply destroy? He didn't know. But what he did know was that his life had undergone horrors that had ended in transformation, and in the end, he had found great joy. What he did know was that the future was unknown. What would it be like to wake up in the morning and take the subway to an office where not the words of Torah were spoken but only numbers? How much money was earned? How much was spent? At what profit? All of his days were already bartered and sold to this slavery. Out of this, he would have to do the impossible, squeeze out time for the glory of studying the word of God.

There would be compensations. When he came home, his children—well-dressed and well-fed—would be there to greet him, and his wife—his lovely wife, who gave meaning to his life, his beautiful Leah, who had helped him rise above his despair—would also be there waiting.

What would he have done without her? What would he have *been able* to do without her? It could have all happened in exactly the same way and he could be alone, or greeted by some widow into a living room with a white linen upholstered couch no one was allowed to sit on, and fancy armchairs covered in plastic that would have stuck to the back of his thighs. Or some bitter divorcée, her face filled with annoyance and hatred, watching his every move, waiting to catch him out, to say, "Ah, you men, you are all the same!"

Instead, he would come home to a happy place, a kind woman who loved him, children jumping into his arms, smiling, his children, his motherless children, with a mother now, to care for them and love them . . .

"Are you all right, Yaakov? Sometimes I think maybe I pushed you too hard to remarry."

He smiled into the rav's anxious face. "Finding a new wife was the best thing that could have happened to me, Rav. You were so right. I was broken, and she helped me to heal. She's a gift from God."

The rav seemed glad to hear this, but surprised. "Yes, when we are young . . ."

There seemed to be a question at the end of that statement, something unsure, incomplete.

"I don't think age matters, Rav. Wasn't it you who told me that this is what God asks of us, to live in partnership, men and women, not to be alone, that this is God's will?"

The rav gave a self-deprecating smile. "Yes, I remember something of that nature. I remember telling it to you. And was it true?"

"Yes, Rav. It was true."

The two men, the older man who had fulfilled every dream that Yaakov had ever had, and the young man about to plunge into a life he had never planned for, never expected, and really never wanted, embraced, each feeling their courage and ability to face the future somehow strengthened.

"Don't be a stranger."

"Never, Rav. And I wish a *refuah shlama* to the rebbitzen."

The rav nodded, his eyes once again seeking the unknown.

7

LEAH'S SHAME

One look at Fruma Esther's face told Leah everything she had to know.

"Come in, please, Bubbee Fruma. I can explain."

The old woman crossed the threshold cautiously, looking around as if she expected some evidence of an infestation—mice, rats, roaches—that would turn the familiar terrain of her deceased daughter's home into a suddenly foreign and slightly disgusting place. But there were only the baskets of laundered clothes, the newly vacuumed old carpet, the well-dusted photographs, and beyond them the made-up beds. Order reigned. And except for the industrious sounds of the hardworking dishwasher and washing machine, the silence was broken only by the whirr of Leah's computer sitting in the center of the dining room table, surrounded by piles of folders.

"The children?"

"All in school and day care. It's ten o'clock, Rebbitzen," Leah answered patiently, wondering what was implied by the question.

"Baruch HaShem," the old woman replied automatically, sighing.

"Baruch HaShem," Leah echoed nervously. Was the sigh a sign of relief? And if so, what was she expecting when she showed up midmorning?

"It's good we can talk, Leah-le," Rebbitzen Fruma Esther murmured. "You know what it's about."

"Yes, the music."

"Sick? Who's sick?"

Leah looked at her, confused. "The music," she said again, louder.

Fruma Esther touched her ears, embarrassed. Maybe the hearing aid batteries were low? Not *sick*. Mu-sic.

It had been three days since the neighbors knocked on her door. In that time, Leah Howard Lehman had had time to consider the matter. Her initial reaction had undergone a gradual shift from horror, embarrassment, and an acute desire to apologize profusely to that of a considered defiance: this was the privacy of her own home, after all! This was her music, lively and joyous, which she had been sharing with the sad orphans that had become her stepchildren, giving them some joy. They were doing nothing wrong, and it was certainly no one's business, except her own and probably Yaakov's. Her only sense of discomfort came from the fact that she had not shared what had happened with him.

There were several very good reasons for that, she told herself. First, he was so busy with the transition out of kollel and into his new job. She knew just how much this weighed on him. Why should she add to his cares by sharing this petty confrontation with the neighbors? Besides, she told herself, hadn't she settled the matter? Hadn't it all blown over? At least, she had not heard anything further since she'd gone back to playing the yeshiva boy choir tapes. Finally, and most truthfully, she hadn't broached the subject because she was ashamed of herself for having given into her longing to revisit a little bit of her old life.

What was so terrible about that? Not everything in the secular world, in the first thirty-four years of her life, had been bad. In fact, she had enjoyed so much of it: the concerts in Carnegie Hall, the ballet and opera at Lincoln Center, the Sunday strolls through MoMA and the Metropolitan Museum of Art. And yes—if you were asking—her old playlists.

She remembered the girls in the women's religious study program in Israel who'd ripped out their nose and belly button rings, lasered off their tattoos, and draped their bodies in the drabbest, most middle-aged, calf-length skirts and button-down cotton shirts available to mankind. How they'd vied with each other to adopt ever-more radical stringencies, as if a sincere belief in God and adherence to His actual commandments wasn't good enough! They wouldn't wear a jean skirt even if it went down to their ankles. They wouldn't wear the color red, or a white blouse that might allow a hint of what lay beneath. They ate nothing that did not come straight off the shelves of tiny haredi grocery stores, even if supermarket shelves were groaning with products that were perfectly kosher, bearing the stamp of approval from the Orthodox Union. They even boycotted milk chocolate from Israel because the cows might have been milked by non-Sabbath observers! Who thought this stuff up? There was a whole playbook of piety-signaling signs that they hoarded and displayed with zealous delight to impress each other and their rabbinical mentors. She had always found this kind of behavior a bit sickening—childish, even—with a large, disgusting dollop of self-hate. She had always refused to participate, earning herself more than one pious lecture and dirty look.

But the time she had spent in Boro Park had altered this firm stance, she realized. There were some things to which you had no choice but to submit, like the length of your wig (not too long or too short!) or the height of your heels. Stilettos were considered whore-like, and flats too stylish. Even before she married Yaakov, especially in the throes of trying to convince skeptical and hostile matchmakers of her sincerity and worthiness to join the community, she had taken care to present the outward appearance of conformity to the dress codes around her. When in Rome . . . right? she'd told herself.

But as time went on, she'd found herself being forced more and more to conform to new (and often, in her eyes, irrational) demands that always took it a little bit further than the time before, until she felt almost crushed beneath their weight, and the self she had been close to disappearing altogether.

The latest was water. Water! Some rabbis were forbidding using tap water to wash dishes, or brush your teeth, or wash vegetables because they claimed there were bugs in Brooklyn water, particularly in Boro Park and Flatbush, which broke the biblical prohibition against "eating any crawling thing." They demanded that you filter all the water you used.

She'd tried. Then one day, when the children were fighting and the phone was ringing and she was trying to prepare soup for dinner, she gritted her teeth and filled the soup pot directly from the faucet. While she still diligently checked over lettuce leaves and cauliflower, holding them up to the light; still poured rice and lentils out onto the table then carefully checked them grain by grain as she swept them into a container, her days of boycotting the Brooklyn municipal water pipes were over.

Strangely, she hardly felt any guilt. The only thing that bothered her was how she hadn't had the courage to talk it over with Yaakov first. But the water supply and the Foo Fighters music were the least of it. There were other things, far more serious and gargantuan, that she was keeping from the man she loved. How had that happened? And how much longer could she keep it up? Perhaps, she admitted to herself, dancing to her old playlist had been her stubborn way of fighting back against so many things she was being forced to do that she couldn't bring herself to talk about or share.

"What happened that the whole neighborhood is talking?" Fruma Esther demanded, settling herself heavily into the sinking cushions of the worn sofa as she gave up the effort to divide her dwindling strength between this confrontation and the considerable effort needed to keep herself standing upright.

"Is it?" Leah swallowed. "No one has said anything to me."

"It's spreading around the neighborhood like a disease, a virus. My phone doesn't stop ringing."

"And what are they telling you?"

"Loud, *prutza* music coming from my saintly Yaakov's apartment. The children like wild animals jumping up and down, naked. And you . . ."

Leah's heart contracted. "What about me?"

"Without your hair covering, behaving just like them . . . like the two-year-old."

An ache stabbed her heart, yet she refused to give in. "My hair was covered. The children got hot, so they took off their shirts. Look, all I did was try to bring some joy to your poor grandchildren. They are suffering, Bubbee Fruma."

All the exasperation suddenly left the old woman's face. "What did you say . . . suffering? Since when?"

Leah moved her chair closer, describing the conversation with Chasya. Fruma Esther leaned forward, listening intently, her face pinched.

"She said that . . . my little Chasya? That she looks out of the window, waiting for her mameh to come home?"

Leah nodded, unhappy to bring this elderly woman such news even in self-defense.

They sat in silence for a few moments. "So you wanted to make some fun for them, to make the house *freilich,* that's all, right?"

"That's all, Bubbee Fruma."

"And they were playing, and the music was on?"

Leah nodded.

"But why secular music? You couldn't find an Avraham Fried tape? Yaakov Shwekey?" Her eyes lit up. "Or Lipa Schmeltzer? He's very *freilich,* they tell me." She never listened to music, except at weddings and bar mitzvahs when she had no choice. A person had time for such things? And anyway, her hearing . . .

"I got a little tired of playing the yeshiva boy choir tapes. And you know what? Maybe I also needed some cheering up! It's sometimes not so easy for me either, Bubbee Fruma."

The elderly woman straightened her back, her hands suddenly gripping each other. "Something is wrong between you and Yaakov?"

"No, of course not. But it's not easy," she repeated. "I have all this work to do"—she waved toward the computer—"and there is no money left over for a cleaning girl. And I need to shop and cook and take the children to school and pick them up . . . and sometimes, the children need me at the same time my computer needs me. I'm trying my best."

So this was a different story altogether. She had come to chastise and warn but found herself aching to comfort and protect.

"I will talk to them, Leah-le, find out which one of the yentas is spreading these lies. God watch over us, they should be so ashamed, so ashamed!" She shook her head. "Just wait," she fumed. "Wait until I get my hands on them. *Keiner zet nisht zein eigenem hoiker. People who see dirt everywhere except on their own faces!* The sin of gossip is worse even than the music of *shkotzim.*" She stood up unsteadily. Leah jumped up to offer her an arm. She took it gratefully.

"Don't feel bad. It's a big mitzvah, Leah-le, what you are doing for Yaakov, for the children. To make them a clean home, a kosher home. To bring them happiness. There can't be a bigger mitzvah in the world, my child. I wish I could help you more." She shook her head helplessly. "There was a time in my life, not so long ago, when I was a real *balabusta*. You wouldn't believe! Shabbos dinners for twenty-four. Cholent pots as big as potato sacks! And the challahs I'd bake! Twenty challahs for every Shabbos, hand kneaded with the finest flour and oil. And now . . ." She shrugged. "What am I good for? I can't even lift little Mordechai Shalom anymore; he's too heavy for me. The *Aibishter* should only bless his *shaine kepelah*. My eyesight is not good." She didn't continue her litany of woes, somehow ashamed of admitting how swiftly the floodwaters of age were rising over her head.

The latest disaster was her hearing.

While she had worn a hearing aid for years, somehow it wasn't working as well anymore. When people spoke to her, she sometimes had to pretend, half the time guessing when she answered. And sometimes she got it terribly wrong. She could tell as people smiled at each other at her answer in a mocking way and repeated the question. She had to go back to the ear doctor. But she was putting it off. What if . . . what if nothing could be done anymore, and she'd be deaf as well as half-blind? Oh, it was no fun to grow old! Thank God Yaakov had found a young woman to care for her grandchildren. To love them. She tightened her lips. Let anyone say a word against her Leah-le. Just let them.

"And Shaindele, her friends, the girls from her school, they also heard the rumors? They are teasing her again like before?"

Leah felt her cheeks grow warm. She hadn't even considered that! How awful if it was true! "She hasn't said anything. At least not to me." Their relationship was so much better now, but still tentative—as it was between any adult and teenager—the ups and downs rapid and unpredictable. What if she ran to Yaakov with the gossip like before? That's all she needed!

———

At least it isn't as bad as last year, Shaindele thought. Those horrible days! The whispering behind hands, the giggles, the side glances, the silences when she entered the classroom that filled her heart with apprehension and dread. This time, only a few of the girls had even mentioned it, *dafka* the nice ones. A few of her friends had come to her privately, asking straight out about the rumors flying around. They'd been honest and respectful.

And even though this was exactly the kind of disaster she'd been dreading ever since her father walked down the aisle, now that it had actually happened, she found herself strangely indifferent. So much had happened to her over the last two years!

She'd experienced unfathomable grief, searing hatred, jealousy, bitterness, and finally a painful push into adulthood and maturity. There were things she understood now that even a few months before she had not. For example, the fact that human beings were imperfect and not all tragedies could be prevented or even correctly assigned to an individual perpetrator for absolute blame. She understood, too, that many of her schoolmates and others around her, untempered by the kind of tragedy that had shaped her young life, were simply silly children whose opinions on most subjects didn't matter. Their simplistic view of life—to which she had always subscribed—dividing people into saints and sinners, "good" families deserving of the best *shidduchim* and "unworthy" families whose background, finances, and history relegated them to Grade B or even Grade C shidduch prospects, was simply ridiculous.

Wasn't her own family the perfect example that disproved that rule? As far as *yichus* was concerned, no one could deny their distinguished pedigree as descendants of European Ashkenazi Torah scholars who had settled in Brooklyn and become the much-lauded and much-loved members of Boro Park's elite. But on the other hand, there was the difficult and undeniable matter of Zissele Lehman, her mother, who had died by her own hand, an unforgivable sin that the family had managed somehow to shroud in secrecy, even arranging for burial on sacred ground forbidden to suicides. Her father's defection from the study house, and his choice of an unacceptable partner, had also somehow been smoothed over.

But there was a tipping point, she thought. If this latest rumor gained momentum, it was going to be bad, even very bad. Even Bubbee, the resident family expert in quashing such scandals, was going to be hard-pressed to do anything about it. This was true because people so loved to have their suspicions confirmed, to feel that common wisdom and gossip were ultimately vindicated and that the snobbery against outsiders from those born into well-connected religious families, far from being an ugly display of the bad character and causeless hatred strictly forbidden by the Torah, was nothing of the kind. Oh no! If the community had been against the match between Yaakov Lehman and Leah Howard, it had only been for the purest of motives, they told themselves, because the community was wise and learned in the ways of putting up walls to protect the precious society they had created out of the ashes of their European ancestors, the burned-down yeshivas of Poland and Lithuania.

We came to America bereft of everything and rebuilt and prospered, they told themselves. And this rebuilding and this prosperity must be protected at all costs from the invasion of destructive hordes, which included murderously hostile, ignorant, and hateful gentiles of all colors and races, as well as Jewish outsiders who came banging on the door wanting to abandon their meaningless secular lives and partake of the light and joy of the community that had been rebuilt with such ceaseless toil after the Holocaust.

But one couldn't open the door too widely. No, indeed. One moldy potato tossed into a pile of perfect produce was enough to spread the rot, to spoil years of painstaking educational efforts to nurture the next generation of Torah scholars and faithful, God-fearing Jews. Vigilance was necessary. Which is why Yaakov Lehman should never have married Leah Howard, the community decided. The music and the naked dancing were to be expected. It was inevitable, whether or not it had actually happened.

Shaindele understood all this intuitively, revealing to her just how far she had traveled in her beliefs from her childhood and from the community in which she had grown up. Only a few months ago, such a rumor would have started her down a spiral of humiliation and devastation ending in a bitter confrontation with her father and Leah. But now, she had no intention of mentioning it at all. Why should she give the perpetrators the satisfaction of causing heartache and tension between her parents?

Honestly, she felt sorry for Leah. A rumor like this once started never really went away. It was as sticky as superglue, adhering forever to those it shamed. Whatever the truth, Leah honestly didn't deserve what was coming her way. But she was mature enough to understand that she,

Shaindele, was helpless to do anything about it. It was not for nothing the sages compared repairing the damage caused by *loshon hara* to gathering feathers from a pillow shaken out in the wind. Go talk to everyone who had heard or was spreading this rumor! Go find them! And even if they could be tracked down somehow, what could you say to convince them that what they had heard, what they so wanted to believe, was monstrously wrong?

"It's their sin," her friend Shulamis comforted, her kind blue eyes narrowed, and her pretty, soft mouth pinched. She was a new friend, recently transferred from the women's seminary in Gateshead, England, as her father took up a prominent rabbinical post in a prestigious Torah institution known for its emphasis on perfecting one's character traits, or *middos*. Unlike the other girls, she was meticulously careful never to speak or listen to a word of *loshon hara*. The other girls, however, had kept their distance, unsure of how this would affect their own reputations.

Walking back into her classroom after recess, Shaindele stared straight ahead. To her surprise, instead of mortification and helplessness, she felt a sudden surge of strength. Let them talk then, the useless cows! God heard all, saw all. He would decide who deserved to be punished. As it is written in the Yom Kippur prayers: He alone "brings down low and raises on high."

She had embarked on a new path in life, she told herself, one that would shock everyone she knew—especially her family. But she didn't care. Why should she? Had concern for the family reputation prevented anyone in her family from doing precisely what they wanted, and the consequences for everyone—herself most particularly—be damned? So who cared that this rumor about Leah would shorten yet another leg on the already shaky stool that was her shidduch chances, putting them in danger of complete collapse? Who wanted to get married anyway? What she wanted, she realized, was something else.

Living in a house with newlyweds had brought other ideas to the forefront of her mind. Day after day, she was witness to the interaction between her father and her stepmother: the way they stood beside each other doing the dishes, their shoulders almost touching, exchanging warm, secret smiles. The little, unexpected bursts of laughter. The way her father sang *Eishes Chayil* to Leah on a Friday night, his blue eyes deepening in color, his forehead glistening with a newfound youth. The way Leah touched him, so casually and delicately, her hand seeking a shoulder, a finger, his back. How they were together had awakened something within her, something new: a curiosity, a longing, to know more of that great mystery that existed between men and women.

Until now, she had found no outlet for her desires, except to buy a ticket and take a seat on the staid, socially acceptable shidduch merry-go-round. But that wasn't what she wanted. First, she felt much too young. And second, it wasn't a husband she was looking for. What did she need a husband for? All she wanted was to simply explore how it would feel to be with a young man who would look at her the way her father looked at Leah. What was wrong with that?

Up until now, it had been hopeless. But all by herself, she had finally found a solution, which albeit completely socially unacceptable, was one that felt right to her. And even though at the moment it was more like a fantasy than reality, still its promise lay close to her heart. She realized, of course, that if it were ever exposed, there would be hell to pay. But that only made it more thrilling, increasing her excitement and her desire.

"You should ask your parents about what's being said," Shulamis suggested, interrupting her thoughts. "Maybe even talk to the rav? He'd put an end to it."

But Shaindele had stopped listening, her mind a few blocks away. She blushed. Let her father and stepmother and Bubbee deal with this. It had nothing to do with her. She had a life of her own, she thought with sudden joy.

8

⚭

THE BOY FROM THE
PIZZA PARLOR

It was one of the few places where young men and young women mingled in Boro Park: Moishy's Kosher Pizza and Dairy on Fourteenth Avenue. Children and teenagers stopped by on their way home from school or ran over an hour after Shabbos ended, magically already starving despite having stuffed themselves all day. But you didn't have to be hungry to order a slice from Moishy's. Even when you had no appetite at all and had no intention of going in, the smell wafting out into the street of baking dough, melting cheese, and tomato sauce fragrant with basil and oregano drew you in like sea sirens.

In September, right after school started but before the High Holidays, Shaindele noticed a new boy behind the counter. She realized he was a little older than the last one as she studied his handsome dark eyes and the attractive hollows emphasizing his high cheekbones. She watched, almost mesmerized, as he insouciantly flicked his thick, dark bangs coolly out of his eyes at regular intervals while opening and closing the heavy oven doors to check on the dough's progress.

"I've never seen him here before," she whispered to Shulamis, who took a quick look and then piously averted her eyes.

"Don't you know who that is?" interjected a girl who was one year behind in school but a very well-informed and talented yenta and professional buttinsky. "It's Duvid Halpern, the principal's son. They say he got in trouble in yeshiva, and his rebbe kicked him out."

"That's not what I heard," another girl jumped right in. She was two years younger than Shaindele and loved attention. Everyone turned to her.

"Really, I don't think we ought to be—" Shulamis began but was immediately hushed by the others.

"What did you hear?" Shaindele encouraged the girl, dying to know.

"I heard he dropped out of Yeshiva Gedolah in Lakewood. That he wants to go to Yeshiva University, to be a doctor or a dentist."

"College!" Shulamis whispered, scandalized.

All the girls were staring now, but he ignored them. He was shockingly clean-shaven, and his bare arms were tan beneath the rolled-up sleeves of his white, button-down yeshiva boy shirt. The skin of his neck—barely visible beneath the carelessly undone collar button—was the color of a delicious latte.

One of the handsome Halpern boys, Shaindele thought, wondering where one got a tan in September in Boro Park. It must be left over from the summer, which meant he'd been lying around on the forbidden beaches in Coney Island or out in the Rockaways, violating a long, long list of well-known and clearly stated rabbinical prohibitions that included indulging in mixed swimming (males and females sharing the same ocean) or ogling almost-naked women. Was she shocked, appalled? Or pleased? She honestly didn't know.

Without even realizing it, her mind slowly began to undress him. Off went the black jacket and tie he wasn't even wearing—uniform of every other yeshiva boy she had ever seen—and then the white shirt, the tzitzis, and the undershirt. Before she could even consider stopping herself, there he was, practically naked except for a bathing suit, sitting for all the world like some *shegetz* on forbidden sands.

She blushed deeply.

To their disappointment, someone else came to take their order, a short, heavy Israeli in his late forties, Moishy himself.

Secretly, she followed the young man's every move as he put on an apron and moved inside the alcove behind the pizza ovens in the narrow space that fronted the floury counters with their bins of yellow and white cheese and big, red vats of sauce until she could barely make him out. A sense of irrational loss welled up in her heart. Subtly changing places behind the counter, she got a much better view.

Her heart beating furiously, she watched as his graceful hands turned white with flour, conscious of their strength and competence as he kneaded the dough, then pommeled and flattened it mercilessly with a lethal-looking rolling pin. But there was delicacy, too, in the long fingers as they stretched the dough thin without tearing it. And just as she thought he had finished, he lifted the whole disc on his palms, tossing it thrillingly in the air, then catching it deftly just as it seemed it might fall.

"Maybe stop showing off already?" Moishy shouted at him.

A sudden, irrational hatred welled up inside her, filling her eyes with tears as they narrowed in hostility toward Moishy. How dare he speak that way! She looked anxiously at the young man to see if he'd been wounded, but his face was turned away from her. It was then she noticed it: his feet. Even though he was standing in the same place, his feet were moving endlessly with a sure, jazzy rhythm—right foot forward, left foot back and behind, then right foot over and back, responding to music only he could hear.

She lifted her eyebrows. *Where does a yeshiva boy learn how to dance? Where can I learn how to dance?* Her whole body tingled, thrilled.

From then on, she could not pass Moishy's without slowing down, her heart pounding faster even blocks away at the very thought that he might be there, that she might catch a glimpse of the long, dark bangs, the tiny triangle of tanned flesh beneath the open collar. Of course, she did not even dream of speaking to him, the very idea making her quiver with helplessness. What would she say to him, the principal's son, the brother of her nemesis, the insufferable Freidel?

But Duvie-leh (as she thought of him—in her heart of hearts, they were on the most familiar of terms) was nothing like his snobbish family, she told herself, determined not to allow the scantness of the information on which such a conclusion was necessarily based to interfere in any way with her daydreams. No, Duvie-leh was a sensitive soul, too sensitive for the brutal yeshiva world that demanded total dedication, total commitment.

Had he been, perhaps, less attractive—say, five foot three, with a mousy-colored short beard and glasses—perhaps Shaindele Lehman would have reached the same conclusion that most right-thinking citizens of Boro Park had already arrived at about Duvie: that he was a yeshiva bum who had neither respect for his parents nor fear of God. There was no other explanation for a boy who should be diligently poring over the Talmud in Lakewood choosing instead to pour tomato sauce over pizza dough while imitating Michael Jackson dance moves in Moishy's on Fourteenth Avenue.

While at the time she did not consciously realize this, her defiance of this common Boro Park wisdom signaled a wide-ranging and dramatic turning point for Shaindele Lehman, a silent rejection of everything that had been drummed into her since childhood. While this had yet to find any tangible expression, it was an upheaval in the making that would soon upend her life in ways she could not have imagined.

———

"Vus machstu, Yankele?"

Through the earsplitting screech of the dirty old F train to Brooklyn, Yaakov heard the diminutive of his name that no one who knew him ever used. He was *Reb* or *Rav Yaakov* to those who were his friends and acquaintances. Standing in the unbearably crowded train, he lifted his heavy, exhausted head to search for the speaker. What he saw was a vaguely familiar face he couldn't quite place. Someone he knew from shul? A neighbor, perhaps?

"Feivel, from the chair *gmach*." The man chuckled, noticing his confusion.

The man from across the street who had loaned them chairs for the shiva. Yaakov's face reddened. So now they were the best of friends? Yankele? He felt his temper rise, forcing him to summon all that remained of his self-control after a soul-shriveling first week at a job he had never wanted.

"Shalom, Reb Feivel," he answered wearily.

Someone in front of them vacated a seat, exiting the train. Yaakov eyed it longingly, but before he could make a move, Feivel swiftly settled himself into it, smiling up without apology.

Yaakov shifted from foot to foot, giving him a weak smile in return.

"My wife tells me your family are lovers of music," he began with a snicker.

Yaakov looked at his smirking face, only half hearing him. "What?"

"That you love music!" the man shouted above the din of the train.

Yaakov stared at him, bewildered.

His eyebrows shot up. "Nu, you don't know? You haven't heard?"

"Heard what?"

He shook his head. "The whole neighborhood is talking, Yankele."

Now there could be no mistake. The use of the unfamiliar nickname was meant as an insult. Yaakov stiffened.

"May God bless you, my friend, but I'm not sure what you are trying to say."

"Your wife, your children, dancing practically naked to goyish music. The whole street heard them and saw them. You need to find out what happens at home when you are not there, my friend."

Yaakov felt his head spin. For a sickening moment, he actually thought he might faint. But the thought of giving this disgusting person an opportunity to offer him a helping hand suddenly gave him strength.

"In our home, we listen to music, not *loshon hara*. And you'd do better to learn a few dance steps instead of using your feet to run around bearing tales. As it is written: *Thou shall not go up and down as a talebearer among thy people.*"

The man's mouth dropped open, but before he could think of a worthy response, Yaakov wound his way shakily through the crowded train, opening the door between cars and walking through until he had distanced himself as far as he was able.

To his relief, there was an empty seat. He collapsed into it gratefully, pressing his hands to his forehead to stop the spinning and wipe away the newly formed beads of sweat as he struggled to decipher what had just happened. Had his transformation from Torah scholar to accountant stripped him instantaneously of any dignity so that a virtual stranger felt comfortable accosting him in public with this vile story? And what could it possibly mean? If there had been some troubles with busybody neighbors, surely Leah would have mentioned it, no?

He trusted her completely: trusted her heart, her deep religious feeling, her commitment to him and to their children and to the life they were building together. The last thing he considered was that the man's words might actually have some basis in fact.

As his stop neared, he felt himself growing lighter, envisioning Leah's smiling face, his children bright-eyed and bubbly jumping into his arms, and the tasty, hot dinner awaiting him on the table. By the time he got home, he had almost forgotten the stranger from across the street.

Just seeing her brought comfort to his heart, he thought, wishing he could reach out to her as usual as soon as the children stopped climbing all over him, and that she could respond by kissing his cheek, something Zissele had never done in front of the children, something he loved. But she was in her impure days, and no physical contact was permitted between them.

"How was your day, my love?"

The children tugged at his pants, wanting to be picked up again.

"Let your tateh breathe, Chasya, Mordechai Shalom!"

"I want to show him my new dance!" Chasya insisted.

At that word, Yaakov saw Leah's face suddenly cloud with sadness and something else. Guilt? A tremor of cold fear gripped him. He fell into a chair.

"Leah-le, please tell me what is going on here."

"What have you heard?" Her voice was higher pitched than usual, defensive, he noted fearfully.

"Some neighbor I don't even know, from across the street, was *draying my kup* with some story on the subway—"

"Not now!" she whispered fiercely, with a significant glance over at the children. "Have your dinner. Then I'll give them both a bath and put them to bed. We need to talk. No, no, don't look like that! It's nothing, I promise you, *bli neder.*"

He believed her. Why shouldn't he?

They had always been honest with each other, almost brutally so, holding nothing back. And it had been in that brightly lit space of truth, devoid of shade, that their love had been able to blossom, overcoming so many obstacles: the shame over past mistakes and tragedies that had for so long been hidden from others and even from themselves.

Oh, the joy of being loved for who you are, despite all your failures, mistakes, and deficiencies! The joy of being comforted, admired, and accepted! This defined the bond between them.

Besides, to hide what you are ashamed of from the person you love is such a Sisyphean task. In the end, you wind up so exhausted, it is almost a relief not to have to love or be loved anymore, not to care enough to hide.

They had never allowed that to happen. Right from the start, she had admitted to him being an unwitting part of a fraud that sold worthless medical tests that had endangered the well-being of countless people all over the world. He had expressed his sense of responsibility for giving into the entreaties of his young wife—in the throes of severe postnatal depression—not to be committed to a mental hospital because of the shame involved, resulting in her suicide. All this was known between them. And it had only brought them closer. There were no festering lies, only forgiveness and compassion. That was the basis of their relationship.

Leah placed a skillfully prepared meal down on the table in front of him, careful not to hand him the plate (another intimacy forbidden during her impure days). It smelled divine, he thought: thyme and lemon chicken breast, wild rice, and sweet potatoes. There was even a dessert, Yaakov noticed, an apple oatmeal muffin. It had all been made from scratch from fresh ingredients. He rejoiced with every bite. How did she manage it all? Such a wife, such a treasure! When he finished, he carried his dishes and utensils into the kitchen, adding soap to the sponge and washing them off before placing them in the drainer. Then he walked into the children's bedrooms.

They were both wrapped in towels, warm and fragrant from their baths. He helped Leah get their little struggling limbs into the pants and sleeves of their clean pajamas, all the while pretending to have lost an elephant in their room, which he insisted on searching for in their armpits and belly buttons, while they screamed in high hilarity. "Oh, you probably put it in the closet so you can play with it in the middle of the night. Is that what happened?" He tickled them.

"No, Tateh!" Chasya screamed. "It's not an elephant. It's a monkey! And it's up there, hanging from the ceiling, waiting for you to leave!" She screamed, overjoyed, while little Mordechai Shalom repeated, "Monkey, monkey!" until Leah finally told Yaakov his "help" was no longer needed, and she'd meet him in the living room.

The reminder of the serious talk ahead wiped the smile off his face as he kissed his children good night. He sat down on the living room sofa, taking out a volume of the Talmud as he waited for Leah to join him. But he couldn't concentrate, waiting impatiently for the moment they would face each other in the quiet room to renew their bond of trust and put this obvious misunderstanding behind them. He could not imagine any other outcome. He loved her, his children, this home, and for all its difficulties, his life.

He listened to the voices of the little ones as they said their bedtime prayers. And just then, the front door opened. It was Shaindele.

It was almost eight and already dark outside. He tried to remember where she could have been until this hour but could think of nothing.

"How was it, Tateh? The new job?" she asked him breathlessly, in a move he sensed was a deliberate attempt to forestall any interrogation.

"It was all right. New beginnings are always hard, child."

She nodded. "I know it will go well with you, Tateh. May God bless you."

"Thank you. You ate?" he asked her.

She hesitated. "I . . . I got a pizza. On my way home from studying with Shulamis."

"A new friend?"

Shaindele nodded. "From Gateshead. We are good friends."

"A fine institution, Gateshead. Best seminary in the world for Jewish girls. What is she doing in Boro Park?"

"Her father got a job as a *rosh yeshiva*."

"Really? How wonderful for him." His heart ached. "You go over there to study a lot? Did you tell Leah you'd be late?"

"I . . . I think so, but sometimes we just stay after school without planning it."

"Ah, finally, asleep." Leah sighed, walking into the living room. "Oh, Shaindele. I was wondering when you'd be getting home. Why so late?"

"She says she was studying with her friend from Gateshead, Shulamis."

"So much work for seniors, right? I remember my last year of high school. It was a killer."

Shaindele's whole body seemed to exhale a sigh of relief.

"But the next time, you should let me know. I was beginning to worry," Leah said.

"I'm sorry. I'll try to remember."

"Sit down, eat something," Leah said generously, overcoming her disappointment over their lost privacy. It would just have to be put off.

"She ate already. A pizza," Yaakov said mildly but pointedly. "Your stepmother and I need a little privacy, Shaindele."

Shaindele looked from one to the other, surprised. Her father had never before even used that word! "I'm going to my room."

"Thank you," Leah called after her.

Shaindele closed the door behind her, leaning her back against it and exhaling like a mountain climber who has just navigated a treacherous rock wall. Such luck! They were busy with each other. Otherwise, she might have been facing questions that were difficult, if not impossible, to answer. Questions she hadn't even asked herself.

What am I doing? she thought, looking into her eyes in the mirror that hung over her desk. Her cheeks were flushed, even more so than usual, the high color deepening into a blush of red. Her pupils were dilated, and her lips seemed soft and vulnerable. After two weeks of sitting by the counter, Duvie Halpern had finally noticed her. He smiled! He didn't do that often. She should know. She only saw that smile twice in the two weeks she'd become a daily visitor to Moishy's: once when his boss had dropped a few boxes of pizzas ready for delivery, splattering tomato sauce and hot cheese everywhere, and another when a friend from his yeshiva days had told him his former rebbe had broken his arm on the way to shul.

While the other smiles had had something mean in them, the smile he had given to her was perfect, she told herself, all flashing white teeth and warm brown eyes. It made her tingle all over.

"I guess you must really like our pizza," he'd said jokingly.

She'd sat there stupidly, tongue-tied.

Moishy had given Duvie a dirty look. "Don't talk. Work."

But just before he'd reluctantly turned away, Duvie had whispered, "Or maybe there is another reason?" And then he winked.

She'd looked down at her trembling hands, gripping the counter. When her pizza arrived, she'd fled.

Now what will I do? She could *never* go back now that he'd noticed her coming so often! But when she did (how could she pretend otherwise even to herself, even in the privacy of her own bedroom?), the next time, she'd have to think of something to say to him, something clever, so he wouldn't think she was just some silly Bais Yaakov girl who fainted if a boy ever looked at her.

She couldn't even imagine such a conversation. She had absolutely no experience in talking to boys. The only young men she knew were family members, like her brothers, who although the same age as Duvie, were totally different: devout, studious young men who would never talk to girls, and—of this she was positive—didn't even know how to wink!

What did a young woman say to a young man? What could you talk about? Torah, of course, the way the family did around the Shabbos table, picking apart all the little inconsistencies in the text of the Torah portion of the week and putting them back together with learned rabbinical commentaries. For example, what did Pharaoh's magicians mean when they called the plague of lice "the finger of God"? And how do we know that Moses was a preemie? But somehow she didn't think that such things would interest Duvie Halpern, yeshiva dropout.

Don't plan anything, she decided. She would just go and sit and wait. Whatever happened between them would be God's will, of this she was certain. You could never know what plan was in the Ruler of the Universe's mind. If He wanted something to develop, it would. And if He didn't, it wouldn't. So what was the point of planning and scheming?

But somehow this wasn't as satisfying as imagining all the possibilities in which she could become the catalyst in this process, bringing it to a boil. She lay down restlessly on her bed, letting her tense, young body relax while her mind chased around in circles. What was happening to her? Even when she'd run away from home before the wedding, telling herself she should get married before her father's wedding ruined her shidduch possibilities; even when she'd sat next to a strange man on the train to Baltimore, these kinds of thoughts had never gone through her mind. The opposite! All she'd felt was revulsion and fear. In fact, the journey had convinced her she *never* wanted to get into bed with a man.

But with Duvie . . . her fingers played with the buttons of her blue shirt, digging beneath to find the taut, tender flesh of her abdomen. What would it be like to be touched, to touch someone so different from herself, such a strange, foreign body? A man's? The very idea brought a riot of feeling to her heart, an ache to her stomach, and a tingling lower down. What was that, that tingling, that ache? What did it mean? And what was she going to do about Duvie Halpern?

9

A DIFFICULT CONVERSATION

"Finally, quiet," Leah whispered as she joined Yaakov on the sofa.

He looked up at her. Kissing his Talmud, he got up to place it carefully upright next to the other massive volumes weighing down the bookcase that dominated the room.

He turned to her. "Maybe we should sit by the table?" he suggested delicately.

She nodded, her jaw tightening. She'd been about to suggest they retire to their bedroom to talk. But if even sitting near each other on the sofa was too intimate during her "impure" days . . .

"Let me first go check if Shaindele's door is closed."

He shifted uncomfortably. "Is there something you don't think she should hear?"

She felt sweat blossom beneath the head covering that was squeezing her forehead and temples, crushing her ears. "I don't want her to hear any of it, Yaakov. This is just between us."

She disappeared for a moment, then returned. "It's all right. Her door is closed. We'll speak quietly."

They took their places, facing each other across the large dining room table.

"So what is going on, Leah-le?"

"I . . ." Where to begin? The conversation with Chasya about her dead mother? Her own sudden desire to dance to the music of her youth? Or perhaps the neighbors banging down the door?

Seeing her hesitation, his face took on a new concern. He didn't care what had happened, whatever it was! But this reluctance to speak to him, to open her heart, to be honest, was terrifyingly new, with echoes of past tragedies he just wanted to forget. "You know you can tell me anything, Leah-le. Don't you know that?"

Did she? Could she? She couldn't even sit next to him on the sofa because she'd had her period eleven days ago! What did she really know about this man or his world?

He had grown up so differently from her in this strange, closed-off place she hadn't even known existed for most of her life; this little enclave, like some Krishna cult, whose members were born into it and had it in their DNA. How could she ever hope to understand, let alone to fit in and become one of them?

Yet she loved a great deal about her new life, especially this man, her husband. She loved him so much, so much! A love based on real respect, compassion, and shared values. What if she opened her heart to him and he stopped looking at her the same way? What if she disappointed him? Worse, what if he suddenly came to the realization that the many opponents of the match between them had been right all along?

"I . . . I've . . . done something wrong, a mistake, Yaakov."

He wanted to no end to reach out to her, to caress her and comfort her, but it was forbidden. In frustration, he clenched his hands into fists and thrust them deep inside his pockets. "Please, just tell me. What could be so bad you're afraid to just tell me?"

In a rush, she suddenly told him everything, from the encounter with little Chasya sitting by the window searching for her mother, to the moment she'd reached for her music, to the nasty faces of the neighbors standing by the door. She didn't leave out the children's state of undress, or her own dishevelment. She even gave him an account of his mother-in-law's recent visit.

What she failed to mention, however, was the most important thing of all, that elephant in the room that, unlike the imaginary creature he conjured to tease the children, really did exist—something so big, so important, she simply did not have the courage to raise it.

He exhaled, actually relieved. While his heart ached for his little girl's grief, what business was it of the neighbors to butt into how Leah played with the children in their own home? He shook his head, annoyed. Another yenta parade. More troublemakers. What else was new?

"You did nothing wrong, Leah-le. Nothing at all."

She was a bit astonished to hear this. "Yaakov, I've brought disgrace down on this family, your family!"

"My neighbors and 'friends' don't need your help. They bring it down on this community all by themselves with their wicked talebearing."

But that was not all. She took a deep breath. "They've stopped sending their children for playdates. Chasya sits alone, playing with her dolls. They won't let their children into our house anymore."

His heart contracted. He could bear the idiot from across the street with his slimy smile and innuendoes slithering up to him on the subway. But his children! He felt rage bubbling up from his stomach, choking him. With great effort, he cleared his throat. "I'll talk to them. Bubbee Fruma will talk to them. Don't worry!"

"I'm so sorry, Yaakov. It's all my fault! I'm still so new to all this."

"Nothing to apologize for. But, Leah-le . . ." He hesitated. "How long has this been going on?"

She looked up at him uneasily. It was not in her nature to lie, and she had never lied to Yaakov. She tightened her lips, her heart contracting. "It started two weeks ago."

"*Two weeks?*" He jumped up, pacing the floor. Two whole weeks. "Why didn't you say something?"

"I didn't want to worry you! You have so much on your mind, leaving kollel, the new job . . . I thought it would all blow over, that it was just some little thing with the neighbors. I didn't understand."

Two weeks. Day after day. Night after night. And her looking at him across the kitchen table every morning and turning to face him in bed every night. And the children playing alone, all by themselves like outcasts. And nothing. Not a word. He felt the fury explode in his brain, at his neighbors, at the community, and, yes, at her. He was devastated. He wanted to smash something. But more than that, he was gripped by a cold fear. In this state, he was afraid to say or do anything.

The minutes ticked by as he composed himself. And in that interval, Leah saw her new life dissolving, all she had achieved becoming flotsam, wreckage floating out on the edge of complete devastation.

He sat down again. "You've never been afraid to tell me anything before. So what is happening now, my love?" he asked as gently as he could.

Hope flashed through her. But still, she did not have the courage to tell him the whole truth, finding it hard to face it herself. So she took the easy, convenient way out. "I don't know, Yaakov. I think . . . I think I'm just tired."

He was immediately sympathetic. Of course! How had he not realized that? The house, the children, the business. And no money for a cleaning girl or babysitters! But that was going to end. He was going to be bringing in a salary, a paycheck that would make her life easier. He suddenly forgot the dreariness of his day, his longing for his old life. If he could make her life easier, it was all worth it!

"We will find someone to help out."

"But the expense . . ."

"I will bring home my first paycheck soon. That is the first thing we will spend it on. Help for you, my dear Leah-le."

She studied his handsome, kind face, flushed now with the effort to be understanding, to reach out to her, to make things better. Her whole body tingled for his touch, wanting to kiss him, hug him. But the enforced physical separation could not be breached. This was the halacha. She wanted to cry with frustration.

And so they patched things up. But it was not over, she knew. It was just beginning. One day, she would be forced to tell him everything.

———

"Shoshana, it's me. Are you busy?"

"Leah, how are you? It's been so long."

Since her marriage, Wednesday nights at the skating rink had been put aside along with her Rollerblades. There was simply no time.

"How are the wedding plans going?"

"It's . . . complicated."

Oh no! Leah thought. Like her, her friend Dr. Shoshana Glaser had crossed a minefield to achieve her engagement to the man she loved, a fellow medical doctor, newly divorced and undergoing the conversion process to Judaism. "I thought you were all set!"

"Nothing is ever easy, is it?" She sighed. "But let's not talk about that. How are you doing?"

"Could we meet for coffee? Do you have time?"

"For you, Leah, I'll make time. Evenings are best for me."

How could she get away in the evening? That was the most hectic part of her day! Someone would have to put dinner out for the kids, then put them to bed. Yaakov would find the house empty. No, evenings were impossible. "Do you have a morning free?"

"You know I love you, but I can't do mornings. I have rounds and then the clinic. Can't you get a babysitter one night?"

She had never left the children with a babysitter. Maybe she could ask Fruma Esther? She didn't think the old woman would mind, so little was asked of her these days since she had taken over all the cooking and childcare. But then she remembered what Fruma Esther had said about not being able to lift Mordechai Shalom. What if she tried and broke something! Was it even responsible to leave the children with her? Yet it was urgent she speak to Shoshana, her best friend in the haredi world and a fellow rebel; the only person she knew who would understand and wouldn't judge.

"I don't know."

"Why don't you just ask your husband to watch them for an hour one evening?" There was a bit of exasperation in Shoshana's voice.

Of course. She could put them to bed first. He wouldn't have that much to do; he'd be happy to do it. But then she remembered: he was starting his learning program with Meir in the evening. But surely not every night! He would have one night free. She needed to find out which.

"Of course. I'll call you back. Which night are you free?"

"Let me see."

Leah heard the rustling sound of flipping pages.

"I have a meeting with my parents' gerontologist Monday, and John and I are looking at halls on Tuesday. Thursday, I have to go out of town for the weekend. Hey, what about Rollerblading on Wednesday, like old times? I still go every week. I couldn't survive without it."

"I hope I haven't forgotten how." Leah laughed ruefully. Look how complicated their lives had become! She felt like crying in frustration. But she didn't want to talk about this while Rollerblading around a rink with dozens of strangers. "Please, Shoshana. I need to talk to you."

Something in the timbre of her voice must have conveyed the urgency to her friend.

"Okay. No Rollerblading."

"Thank you so much! Let me see if Yaakov is free. It will be so wonderful to see you."

He didn't like to take personal calls at work unless it was an emergency, he'd explained to her, because it was like cheating his employer, siphoning off time he was being paid to work. In such matters, he was absolutely scrupulous, which only made her respect and love him more. After all, if a man wouldn't cheat his employer out of two minutes' time, what were the chances he would cheat on his wife? Or lie to her?

"Yaakov?"

"Something happened?"

"No, everything is fine. I'm sorry to call you at work. I just . . . I need to know what evening this week you are going to Meir."

"Why is this so important it couldn't wait for the evening?"

There was a pause as she took in the uncharacteristic harshness in his tone.

"I'm sorry, but it can't wait," she answered unapologetically. "I am arranging to meet my friend Shoshana, and she is very busy."

Unlike me, he thought with a touch of bitterness. But this was his wife, his Leah-le, he quickly reminded himself before his frustration could seep into his answer. He exhaled. "I arranged to see him on Wednesday."

"Oh," she sighed. "Well, never mind, then."

"No, wait, what—?"

"Never mind. I'm sorry I bothered you."

"We'll talk this evening. Goodbye, Leah-le."

She sat with the cell phone in her hand, tears falling softly down her cheeks. *I'm trapped,* she thought with a sense of near panic. *Trapped.*

And then it came to her. Shaindele.

She had been so careful not to take the girl's time for granted. She never asked her to babysit or pick the children up from school. But this one time, perhaps she wouldn't mind. Lately, though, the girl had taken to coming home later and later each evening. Remembering her own teen years, she didn't like to interrogate her. After all, she wasn't a normal American teenager. She was a Bais Yaakov girl, held to the strictest possible standards of behavior. Besides, she'd heard Yaakov asking her about it, and he seemed to find her answers satisfactory. Something about studying for exams, was it? A strangely typical teenage cover story, she thought skeptically. But if, in the unlikely scenario Shaindele *was* lying and was actually off living it up somewhere, why would she want to be the one to blow the whistle? More power to her! Soon enough, she'd be living a staid, middle-aged life as a teacher, having a child every year, and working like a dog.

She was shocked at herself. *Where are these negative thoughts coming from?* She was suddenly frightened. She really *must* talk to Shoshana, and she needed to do it now, she told herself urgently, before things got so bad there would be no turning back.

———

To her surprise, Shaindele was strangely evasive. But she didn't say no, just maybe.

"I have to have a definite answer, Shaindele. I can't make an appointment to meet my friend with a 'maybe.'"

She was sullen when she looked up. "I don't know what's happening on Wednesday."

Leah was aghast. "What do you mean?"

"I mean, I could be busy."

"Well, maybe you could rearrange your time so you *won't* be busy? Just change it to another night?"

"I'm not sure," she repeated stubbornly.

"Well, I *am* sure!" she exploded, despite all her efforts and good intentions. "I don't ask you to do *anything*! I wash and iron your clothes, wash the dishes, make you dinners, and even pack your lunches! What am I asking from you that makes it so hard for you to say yes? One hour on a Wednesday night? We are a family, and I need your help!"

"You could find a babysitter," Shaindele insisted, bringing Leah's frustration to the boiling point.

"You know, I think the time has come for you to tell me exactly what you are doing every night until so late," Leah said, her voice uncharacteristically steely. That got the girl's attention, all right, Leah saw.

"I . . . I already told Tateh."

"I know what you told your tateh. But maybe I'll just call this Shulamis Glickstein's mom and ask her about it."

"No, don't do that!" Shaindele shouted.

"Lower your voice, young lady."

"You can't tell me what to do. You're not my mother."

"And you can't tell *me* what to do. What's Shulamis's phone number?"

"None of your business!"

"Okay, never mind. I'll look it up on the computer. Glickstein." *There were probably two million Glicksteins in Boro Park,* Leah thought, *but the threat should be enough.* It was.

"All right already! I'll do it. I'll babysit for you on Wednesday night," she said ungraciously.

"Thank you, Shaindele," Leah answered with a corresponding lack of grace, shutting the door to her room with a little bang.

The children heard the raised voices and heard the door slam. They had never seen Leah angry. Mordechai Shalom began to cry, and Chasya sat on the floor with her back to the wall, holding her stomach.

What have I done? Leah thought, terrified.

She lifted Mordechai Shalom into her arms and hugged him, then crouched down next to Chasya. "Shall we put on some music and dance?"

The tears immediately disappeared, and the child jumped up and put her soft little arms around Leah's neck.

"Not Pirchei," she demanded, referring to the yeshiva boy choir.

"Okay, not Pirchei. But we'll have to play it softly, and you can't jump up and down. Mrs. Weitz downstairs doesn't like the noise. And we have to pull down all the shades so nobody can see us."

"Why can't they see us?" Chasya asked.

A question! "Well, because when you have so much fun, people get jealous and then they want to join in and have fun, too. But I don't want Mrs. Weitz to dance with us, do you?"

Chasya shook her head, beginning to giggle, astonished at the idea of the harried, heavy woman with her huge, pendulous breasts hopping up and down the way she did when she danced.

"So we'll be very, very quiet and dance like this," Leah said, putting Mordechai Shalom down, then pulling down all the shades. She began tiptoeing softly in circles around the living room, humming her favorite sixties songs, waving her hands wildly, and shaking her head up and back like vintage Janis Joplin. The children laughed hysterically, following behind her, imitating her, not bothering to wait for her to put on music.

Their laughter, she thought, *is better than any music, any antidepressant. I must never compromise or endanger it for any reason that is in my power to prevent. Please, God, make this my prayer. Help me to keep my word.*

10

❧

THE ELEPHANT
IN THE ROOM

She got to the coffee shop early, taking a seat by the window so that she might at least see her friend's little red car pass by—there was no way she'd find a parking space nearby. It was an Italian convertible, an extravagant engagement present from John. "Who needs a diamond ring when all I do all day is sterilize my hands and put on rubber gloves?" Shoshana laughed.

He'd given her a ring anyway, a circle of marquise diamonds with a sapphire center stone, the "color of your eyes, my love."

Leah looked at her own simple wedding band, which by custom must be of plain, unengraved, solid gold. Yaakov wanted to buy her an engagement ring. He was going to sell Zissele's jewelry to pay for it, but she'd stopped him. "Put it away for Shaindele. She should have something from her mother."

She really didn't care, she kept telling herself. She'd known the life she was choosing when she fell in love with a haredi widower with five children.

She remembered her days as a hi-tech product manager and sales representative earning bonuses so obscene that she'd been able to afford anything: a Manhattan apartment she'd shared with Andrew, who made even more than she did; designer purses; season tickets to the Met and ballet. Often she'd pass by Tiffany's and Bulgari on Fifth Avenue on her way to work, stopping to stare at the bling in the windows. She loved bling as much as any woman, she told herself. Just not enough to barter body and soul for it.

There she was, her dear friend, as slim and beautiful as ever! As usual rushing, just a little late.

"Shoshana!" She rose, throwing her arms around her friend.

"Sorry I'm late."

Leah waved her explanations away. "Do not apologize. I'm the one who is stealing your precious Rollerblading time. It was very good of you. I would never have asked unless it . . ." Her voice trailed off.

Shoshana looked at her searchingly as she shrugged off her coat. "Spill."

Leah swallowed. Could she? Would she? She thought of Chasya holding her stomach and Mordechai Shalom's tears. She had prayed, and now she had to do the work. *Hishtadlus,* it was called. You prayed, but then it was incumbent upon you to make every effort humanly possible to solve your own problems. Only then would God intervene to help.

"Shoshana, I'm struggling. I don't know how much longer I can go on."

Her friend reached across the table, taking Leah's hand in both her own. She was shocked. "But I thought you were so happy! That you and Yaakov . . . the children . . . that it was everything you ever dreamed of. What's happened?"

"Nothing . . . everything. I am happier than I have ever been in my life and more in love with the man I married than I ever dreamed possible. He is the best person . . . the most loving partner, father . . ." She choked, the tears rolling down her cheeks shamelessly, the floodgates opening. She tried to stop, taking the tissue hurriedly offered by her friend and blowing her nose as she wiped her eyes on her sleeves.

"Yes, you look ecstatic," Shoshana drawled, which just started Leah off again. "Okay, okay. Sorry. We'll be serious now." She waited for a few moments until Leah was able to compose herself, the appearance of a waitress with notepad in hand speeding up the process.

"I'll have a latte with soy milk and a butter croissant," Shoshana told the girl, who was trying not to stare as Leah dabbed her eyes and straightened her *tichel.* "What do you want, Leah?"

But she couldn't speak.

"She'll have an almond croissant and a cup of green tea. Jasmine, if you have it." Shoshana turned her attention back to Leah. "Is that okay?"

Leah nodded.

The girl disappeared.

"I'm sorry. I . . . I just have no one to talk to about these things."

"What things?"

Leah took a deep breath. "*Taharas hamishpacha.*"

Shoshana leaned back. *Family purity,* the umbrella term for everything relating to sex. Of course. What else? The one thing you could never bring up with your sex partner! So ridiculous. But she tried to be kind. "I'm a little surprised, Leah. I expected you to have problems, but I thought it would be all the housework and childcare being dumped on you, in addition to developing your business and paying the bills—"

"Yaakov started working full-time!" She felt compelled to interrupt, to defend him.

"You know I love Yaakov. He's one of the good guys," Shoshana placated. "But sex? Really?" She raised her eyebrows in amusement.

"What, because I wasn't a virgin?"

"Well, sort of. And even though this *is* Yaakov's second marriage, I expected you to be the experienced one in this relationship."

She shook her head miserably. "It's not the sex. That's been wonderful."

"Glad to hear it!" She blushed, then smiled. "Then . . . ?"

She lowered her voice to a whisper, looking around. "It's the lack of sex! It's the whole thing. The counting seven clean days after your period, the vaginal inspections, and the mikvah—that bewigged matron examining my naked body, picking off stray hairs—I could really live without that, believe me . . . but it isn't even that. The worst thing, the very worst thing is . . ." She paused, swallowing a sob caught in her throat. "It's that we aren't able to touch each other, even hand each other a plate of food, or sit on the couch together, and our beds are pushed apart for almost *two weeks every month.* It's driving me insane! I don't know how much more of this I will be able to stand." Again, the tears rolled down her cheeks.

"Wow!" Shoshana handed her another tissue. Then she sat silently, rearranging the packets of sugar.

The waitress arrived, placing their orders in front of them. The croissants smelled heavenly, as did the coffee and tea. They waited silently until the girl unpacked her tray and left. Shoshana leaned forward, sipping her drink, then crumbling the pastry before slipping only a tiny fraction into her mouth.

"Honestly, I don't know what to say. Remember, you're talking to a girl who's never been married. And while I admit John and I haven't exactly been saints, there is so much I still don't know. Have you talked this over with Yaakov? Does he know how you feel?"

"How can I?" Leah burst out, gripping the table. "He'll hate me. He'll be so disappointed. It will just confirm for him everything people told him before he married me: that my religious commitment wouldn't last, that I'd change my mind and want to go back to my secular life as soon as I figured out how hard this would be."

"But, Leah, why now? I don't remember you complaining about your wedding night. I'm sure it wasn't what you were used to, but the two of you seemed to manage that all right."

"Because we could talk about it. Because Maimonides says a man and a woman can do anything they want during the times they are permitted to be together. So everything else is custom, stringency, not halacha. *Taharas hamishpacha,* that's halacha. No way around it. How can I ask Yaakov to sin?"

"You know, I think you are misjudging the situation. A lot of what goes on in the haredi world—including *taharas hamishpacha*—aren't biblical laws carved in stone on Mount Sinai. They are customs or rabbinical add-ons, strictures created simply to keep a fence around the actual biblical laws. Like not touching a pen on Shabbos when the actual prohibition is not to write."

Leah leaned back. "So does that mean we can . . . that there is room to navigate?"

Shoshana shrugged. "You are the two people in this relationship. It is going to be what you both decide it's going to be."

"But how can I ask him not to follow the laws? It's his life. He is so scrupulous. Such a tzaddik."

"That's fine when it comes to personal mitzvoth. He can be as uncompromising as he wants when it comes to what he puts in his mouth to eat and the length and sincerity of his prayers. But you are talking about mitzvoth that concern the two of you. You have to decide this together."

"I didn't know there was anything to decide."

"I'll give you an example. Do you cover your hair when you are home with the children?"

"Of course!"

"Well, that is not the halacha. Jewish law says a married woman needs to cover her hair only when she goes outside the house."

"But everyone in Boro Park covers their hair inside!"

"First of all, you don't know that. All you know is that when someone comes to the door, their hair is covered. But what goes on inside when they are alone, you can't know."

"That's true."

"But even if every woman in Boro Park covers her hair twenty-four seven, that still doesn't make it the halacha, and you still only have to cover your hair when you go outside."

"I didn't know that."

"I'm not surprised. Most *baale teshuva* blur the lines between law and custom and practice. But if you are finding certain things absolutely disgusting and it's ruining your *shalom bayis,* you need to talk it over with your husband."

"Or a rabbi."

"Oh, right. Sure thing. Bring a rabbi into your bedroom!" Shoshana rolled her eyes. "But you should be prepared. Yaakov will probably want to do just that."

"No, he won't. We actually discussed that on our wedding night."

"What?"

"That we should keep rabbis out of our bedroom, that what went on there should just be between us. Like leaving on a light."

"You see? He sounds absolutely reasonable. There is no reason to be afraid of talking to him about this. Discuss with him what you can and can't do. Compromise."

Leah stared at her, dumbfounded, finally realizing the truth. For the first time since completely altering her life and becoming an Orthodox Jew, she felt unwilling and unable to compromise anymore. Not on this.

"I will keep going to the mikvah. It's not so bad. I even sometimes enjoy it—all that pampering, the long baths, the lovely soaps and creams afterward. And the mikvah I go to is so clean and pretty, and the attendants are friendly and not intrusive. They treat the whole thing so modestly. But all the rest of it . . . Why should having my period, which is such a natural thing for a woman, make me feel like an outcast, like I'm unclean, untouchable? It's disgusting. I hate it."

"Oh, finally, the good girl has reached her limit. Congratulations!"

"I don't understand why you're not shocked and disappointed."

"Don't you think women like me who are born into haredi families and grow up in that world have the same feelings about certain things? Especially some of the more stringent rabbinical decrees that were dreamed up in the Middle Ages? The lives of modern women are so removed from all that."

"So what is the solution, Shoshana?"

"I'm not going there, even for you, my friend. As they say, consult your local Orthodox rabbi. But in your case, I'd say talk it over with your husband. He's spent twenty years learning Talmud in kollel. If anyone can tell you what the true halachic limits are, he can."

"But what if he takes a very hard line and won't budge?"

"How much do you love him?"

"How wide is the ocean? How many stars are in the sky?"

Shoshana shrugged.

"But that's irrelevant. It's not a question of love. It's a question of life. My life. It's degrading! I can't do this to myself! I became religious to live a higher, purer life. This feels like the opposite, like I'm turning into some woman in a mud hut, put in purdah because I'm menstruating. It's primitive, and it's ugly. I'm not doing that, Shoshana. Not because I don't love God, or love my husband, or the Torah. But because I can't do it and still be who *I* am. And if after knowing how I feel, Yaakov still insists on it, I don't know how I'm going to feel about him and our life together."

For the first time, Shoshana looked shocked.

"You understand? That's the reason I'm terrified to talk to him about it, why I keep putting it off."

"But not talking about it isn't a solution either, my friend."

"I know that! The other day, I was playing with the children, and we were dancing around the apartment, and I reached for one of my old playlists of rock songs. I put it on really loud and danced wildly with the kids. I didn't even think about pulling down the shades or what the neighbors would think, not until they came banging down my door! For the first time since I became religious, I reached for my old life. You understand? I'm so scared."

Shoshana leaned forward, taking both Leah's hands in hers and holding them. "I wish I had some words of wisdom for you, my friend. But I don't. I understand you only too well. But I can't tell you what to do. Yaakov is very *frum,* and he is uncompromising when it comes to halacha. I really don't know what will happen if you are honest with him. But this much I do know: if you're not, if you don't sit down and talk to him, tell him the truth about how you feel, your marriage is over."

———

Leah returned home that night feeling drained, almost shaking with despair. But determined, too. Yes, Shoshana was right. She must talk to Yaakov. Nothing could be as bad as this avoidance, which amounted to a life built on lies. Their life together had to be based on truth. She told this to herself over and over again, trying to convince herself to crack open the Pandora's box and let loose those very monsters that could gobble up her new life and spit it out.

Yaakov was still out learning with Meir, she saw. The rest of the house was silent. She knocked on Shaindele's door.

"Come in," the girl called, not bothering to get up.

"Hi. Everything all right?"

Shaindele swept her open palm in an arc as if to say, *Voilà, see for yourself!*

"Did they give you a hard time, Shaindele?"

"Well, they asked for you, and Chasya was a little weepy, wanting to know when you'd be home. But she was okay after dinner and a bath."

"Thanks so much for your help. I'm really sorry I had to bother you."

Shaindele got off her bed and walked toward her. "No, *I'm* sorry. I don't know why I gave you such a hard time. You can ask me to babysit. I don't help you as much as I should."

Leah was touched and relieved, glad that the bad old days when she and her oldest stepdaughter were adversaries weren't coming back for a sequel. Under all that bravado and occasional nastiness, she was really a sweet kid. Just a typical teenager.

"So are you going to tell me the truth about what you're doing out so late every night?"

Shaindele blushed, shaking her head.

"Okay, I'm not going to pressure you. I'm not a warden, and this isn't a jail, and you are old enough, and smart enough, to think about your choices. But if you want my help or advice, I'm happy to talk to you anytime, Shaindele. All right? I was also once a teenage girl."

Shaindele nodded gratefully. They wished each other good night.

Actually, Leah was relieved to be spared an outpouring of teen angst at the moment, facing as she was her own difficult, life-changing choices. It almost made her feel sick. She poured herself a cup of tea, nursing it in the darkened kitchen, rehearsing what she was going to say when Yaakov walked in. But then she thought, *Tomorrow is my mikvah night! Why would I want there to be bad blood between us after two whole weeks of separation?* No, she would put it off, at least until after she did her ablutions, when she could at least hold his hands as she spoke to him. It made so much more sense, right?

When Yaakov returned, they spoke to each other softly about their day, the usual small talk, falling asleep in their separate beds. The following day, she woke up with a smile, just thinking of the night ahead. She whistled as she dressed the children, who laughed and tried to pucker their lips and whistle, too, with little success but much laughter. And after she'd dropped them both off at school and day care, she hurriedly took care of her computer clients, creating a new email list for one, posting a few ads for others, then working on an online campaign for a local dress store.

She took care of the housework, the children, as efficiently as she could, all the while her mind and heart open to the night ahead. Yaakov came home early to help her, taking over dinnertime and bath time so she could leave early for the mikvah.

And when she returned, the house was quiet, the children already asleep, and Shaindele behind her closed bedroom door.

In their bedroom, she saw he had lit some candles and moved the beds together.

"I brought you a present," he murmured after taking her into his arms and kissing her—lingering kisses filled with longing, amplified by the many unbearable days of separation they had endured.

She opened the small package, her eyes bright with pleasure.

"It's a CD, *Dance Neginah.*" He smiled. "Jewish music for dancing at weddings. I'm sure the kids will love it."

Such a thoughtful gift, she thought, her eyes sparkling with tears. He'd forgiven her; forgiven her ignorance and all the trouble she'd caused him with the neighbors. He'd forgiven her for holding back, keeping secrets for two weeks. He wasn't angry. *He is a saint,* she thought. *And I am worthless to have doubted him and our life together. I must be stronger, for his sake. He deserves it. He went against the world for my sake, and for his sake, I can sacrifice a little.* Why would she want to do anything to hurt such a wonderful man? She had signed up for this. She'd known exactly what she was getting into. She would just try harder.

At that moment, it all seemed so possible. Curled up in his arms, the horrible separateness dissolved, becoming blurred and indistinct, almost as if it had never been. It was simply in the past, she told herself. Besides, every other woman in the haredi world seemed to manage with it just fine. She didn't think about Zissele, the first wife, the one who had not managed at all.

She wouldn't think about this now. What was the point? They had two weeks together! Two whole weeks. She would wait. Maybe it wouldn't bother her so much the next time. Maybe she'd get used to it, like she'd gotten used to putting away her cell phone on Friday night until sundown on Shabbos. The way she'd gotten used to wearing long skirts, and shirts with long sleeves, and stockings even in summer. The way she'd gotten used to how her hair covering pressed in on her scalp and temples, giving her a headache. It was possible, wasn't it? There was no point in upsetting him now, no point at all, when it was possible that for his sake she might get used to it. She would think about it some other time. She would wait and see, she told herself, pressing her cheek into his bare shoulder and breathing him in.

11

⚭

AN ELDERLY ROMANCE

Close to Chanukah, the holiday of light, the darkness finally overtook Rav Alter. His beloved wife of almost fifty years passed away quietly in her sleep. Rabbi Alter was at her bedside, and when she took her last ragged breath, he sobbingly ripped the collar of his suit jacket, the traditional sign of mourning.

The funeral was held immediately, as is the custom, and word of mouth spread the time and place. It seemed that everyone in Boro Park knew within the hour. Like one big family, the inhabitants of the crowded apartment houses and little brownstones put aside their normal activities and made the pilgrimage to fulfill the mitzvah of comforting the bereaved.

For Fruma Esther, it was more than an obligation. She had known Malka Alter almost all her life, having grown up in nearby streets and gone to the same Bais Yaakov.

Another funeral, she thought as with a heavy heart she walked down to the funeral home on Sixteenth Avenue. She couldn't believe how many people were there! *Only the death of a Hasidic rebbe draws more,* she thought proudly.

Little Malka Ruth Alter. She shook her head. As frail as a bird with her skinny legs and long, scarecrow arms. And that was before her illness, God should watch over us. But from that scrawny body, she had brought forth six healthy children, four of them sons. A true miracle. It had never been easy for her; she was never robust. But she had done her duty toward her husband and her family, may her memory be forever blessed! Fruma Esther pressed her lips together tightly as if she could say more about the burdens that had been put on this good woman, some of them enormous and unnecessary.

As the rebbitzen of a community that encompassed one of the most respected *yeshiva gadolas* and kollelim in the neighborhood—known all over the haredi world for its depth of commitment to learning and to strict observance—as well as the synagogue attached to them, she had overseen an empire that required endless participation and dedication. Dozens were hosted for meals every Shabbos, and double that for the holidays. Of course, she had help. But to oversee all the buying and storing and cooking was also no small thing.

And this was her reward: packed crowds waiting to recite psalms and prayers that would accompany her soul on its journey to the highest levels of the World to Come, where a chorus of heavenly angels would sing her name to welcome her soul's arrival.

At least, that is what Fruma Esther so wanted to believe even when all the evidence of her eyes showed her nothing of the kind. There was only the plain pine box covered with a velvet, gold-braided cover wheeled in on a metal gurney by bearded men. And there it sat at the front of the room, as the women and men, separated by an impenetrable *mechitza,* crowded each other to catch a glimpse of the strange and pitiful sight that was all that remained of this fine woman's existence in this world, the same as for any ordinary, even evil, person whose soul had left their body.

It was an unfathomable thing, Fruma Esther thought. Unfathomable. You could never understand how the sacred life that had flowed so strongly through a person suddenly stopped, leaving behind this useless carcass that one could do nothing but hide away in the earth as quickly as possible.

The service started with the chanting of psalms, chosen because they began with a letter of the deceased's name. This was followed by the first of many eulogies. Sons and grandsons rose up to give learned discourses on the week's Torah portion, doing their best to relate it to some sterling quality of the deceased. The more ambitious calculated the numerical value of the letters in her name and found parallels with other things of the same numerical value.

Unlike a man's funeral, where one could go on and on about all the public offices and communal activities of the deceased, when a woman died, the relatives had to be content with talks praising her "modesty, hard work, and love of Torah." Of course they would mention how wonderful her cooking was and how generous her hospitality to strangers and the poor. But central to women's eulogies was the statement that "she never said a bad word about anyone, and always judged people favorably." Silence was a virtue for women, as well as not rocking the boat.

Sometimes this irked Fruma Esther. Several very close friends had lived difficult lives with unreasonable husbands who had put them into early graves. To hear their self-imposed silences praised seemed wrong. *What will they say about me,* Fruma Esther wondered, *those faceless crowds huddled beneath their wigs in the women's section, those men in long beards and black hats on the other side of the mechitza? What will my daughters and sons and in-laws say? My dear grandchildren?*

It was usually the grandchildren, or great-grandchildren if you were so blessed, that gave the best eulogies, their young faces naked with raw grief as they wept, recalling the honest pleasures of their bubbee's Shabbos seven-layer cakes and Yom Tov brisket with prunes and apricots. The children were more removed, restraining their grief, or perhaps more conflicted. A mother was not a grandmother. You had other responsibilities that sometimes necessitated measures that were often severe and unpleasant in order to keep your children from straying off the right path. They would only forgive you when they used the same methods on their own children. *Forgive, but not forget,* she thought.

She looked around at the other women, realizing with a shock that she was one of the oldest. Yes, this was the way it was. You got married, and everyone around you seemed to be getting married. Every other week, there was another chuppah you were invited to—years of cakes with white frosting and vigorous Hasidic dancing. And soon it was the circumcision ceremonies you were attending, the crowded synagogue halls, the mohel and sandak in white—the former to do the slicing and the latter to hold the baby still while reaping the honors of being enthroned in the Chair of Eliahu the Prophet. Before you knew it, it was the bar mitzvahs you went to, boys in their first Borsalinos and custom-made dark suits that could do nothing to hide the fact that the guest of honor was still a little boy playing dress-up. Then suddenly all the little boys and their sisters were getting married. Suddenly, the cycle started over again, this time with the grandchildren. But the invitations were fewer. Sometimes they invited their grandparents' friends, and sometimes they didn't. If you got an invitation, you went gladly, sending your wig to the beauty parlor, buying another silver kiddush cup engraved with the young couple's names as a gift, and forcing your arthritic legs to get up and dance a hora.

And after that it was a simple hop, skip, and jump (actually, more of a long downward slide, she thought) to this, the rectangular box on the metal gurney.

It was an hour before Rav Alter finally got up, the last of the eulogists. They were all used to hearing him speak. He did so every week in the short break between the end of the Torah reading and the beginning of the Musaf prayers. He was a good speaker, not taxing his audience with too many complicated *pilpulim* or burdening them with heavy doses of *mussar*. His eulogy was short, and to the point, his face open and lively with a natural warmth.

But this was not the familiar face they had known. He looked ravaged, she thought, finding it hard to catch her breath. Like a completely different person! Without the shine of joy that usually moistened his face like an expensive cream, his face sagged in all directions. The deep lines of aging that smoothed out when his cheeks were raised in a smile, making them hardly noticeable, now dug deep canals into his forehead and around his eyes. His complexion was frighteningly white, and his head seemed too heavy for his frail neck to hold it erect so that his hat seemed to fall forward, as if even its slight weight, added to all his new burdens, could no longer be borne.

Worst of all, when he began to speak, he was almost unintelligible. Someone hurried to adjust the microphone, placing it nearer his lips. To her relief, she could now understand him. "We know that when the soul departs the body, it lingers. We know that you are here with us, Malka, that you can hear all that is being said about you. I ask you, my dear wife, to forgive me for every trespass against you; every unkind or angry word; for every time you were silent and I did not reach out to ask you what was troubling you; for every time my work kept me away from home so that all the burdens of caring for the family and household fell on you. My dear wife, you gave me everything I have. You supported my learning. All my Torah is yours. You taught me so much: how to be a mensch, how to love. You taught me to care when I asked someone, 'How are you?,' to listen to the answer. You taught me that the people who don't ask, who don't speak, who are sitting alone on the sidelines, they are the people we need to sit down next to, not the ones who crowd around us. And all day, every day, you worried about your people: the widows you brought charity to, the orphans you arranged to get into yeshiva, the young girls of marriageable age from poor families that needed new clothes, the tired parents caring for sick children. You do not need an angel to accompany you on your way to heaven. Your good deeds will crowd around you as you ascend, each one a winged angel. Ah, my dear wife, my life. What will I do without you?" He wept helplessly until his sons and a few of his students hurried to help him down from the podium.

Fruma Esther felt tears come to her eyes. She had not expected this. She had expected, along with everyone else, a learned discourse based on Talmudic sources and obscure midrashim, not the raw outpourings of a wounded heart; not something so real, so intimate and sincere, naked to the world, unshrouded behind philosophical and biblical imagery and allegory.

Ah, my dear wife . . . what will I do without you?

She felt her heart expand and go out to him in his grief. Perhaps this was the true sign of greatness, she thought. The ability and modesty that allows one to be human and without pretense. Only a rav of his caliber, known for his scholarship and magnificent oratory, someone held in such respect, could publicly risk such a thing.

———

The funeral was followed by shiva, seven days in which all those at the funeral and many more besides would show up at the house to pay their respects and offer words of comfort.

Rav Alter found all the bustle wearisome. But he had no choice but to submit, sitting on a low stool and receiving the well-worn phrases in which religious Jews express their sorrow: "May God comfort you among the mourners of Zion and Jerusalem," they murmured, shaking his frail old hand or putting an arm around his bent shoulders.

Women came, too, bringing meals and snacks for the mourners and their visitors, keeping the living room table groaning under numerous plates of cakes and cookies, drinks, and sweets. Fruma Esther was among them.

She went out of her way to make *p'tcha,* the strange calf's foot jelly that none of the young, *frum* brides knew how to make anymore and which she knew Rav Alter loved. She also whipped up a huge batch of chocolate rugelach—prepared according to Rebbitzen Alter's own famous recipe— which she covered with a festive blue napkin.

Of course, there was a *mechitza* in the house that separated the men from the women, and thus she was not allowed to serve her dishes directly to the rav. But she asked one of his daughters.

"He loves this," she informed the married woman in her forties wearing a towering headdress of vertiginous height that according to the laws of gravity threatened to send her toppling backward. It was the new style. Fruma Esther shook her head, examining the turban's many elaborate folds and tucks and wondering how the whole thing could be induced to stay in place without nailing it to the skull.

"God bless you, Rebbitzen," the rabbi's daughter thanked her.

But Fruma Esther wasn't satisfied. "Tell your father it's from me, Fruma Esther Sonnenbaum. I was dear friends with your mother, and these are made according to the same recipes."

She sat among the other women relatives, neighbors, and friends in the roped-off and curtained section of the dining room, her eyes peeled for the moment her food was delivered. To her annoyance, the daughter took her time. But then, finally, she saw a white plate with a colorful blue napkin make its way from the kitchen to the little table before the rav. She watched as the rav's daughter peeled off the napkin.

Did the rav's face light up? Or was that her imagination? No, he was definitely picking up a rugelach, she saw, watching anxiously as he placed it in his mouth and took a bite. She saw him close his eyes for a moment, then open them. To her joy, he took two more quick bites, polishing it off rapidly. She waited only long enough to watch as he picked up another one. As for the *p'tcha,* they were no doubt saving it for dinner. She understood. You needed privacy to attack the quivering, Jell-O-like delicacy that was *p'tcha.*

It was a wonderful good deed to bring a little comfort to the bereaved, particularly during the first seven days of mourning, when death and loss were still painfully razor sharp, she told herself with quiet satisfaction as she got up to take her leave.

She remembered those days, those terrible days and worse nights, when her dear Yitzchak Chaim had left this world, making her a lonely widow who often cursed the misery of still being alive. It helped that at that time, all her daughters still lived nearby. With time, of course, they and their husbands had moved away, all except her Zissele. And when Zissele's children were born, one after the other, she was kept busy cooking and babysitting, educating and scolding. All that helped. To be busy, to have your *kup drayed*—day in day out—helped. But then tragedy had again overwhelmed her life.

Zissele, my little Zissele.

She would never recover from that, she understood. That perpetual sorrow was lodged in her heart forever, softening it to the sorrows of others, making it compliant and responsive. She never went to a shiva house now without becoming part of the mourning, whereas before, she had kept it all at arm's length, happy to put in her time, chalk up her mitzvah, then escape back to her own life.

As she moved toward the rav to say the ritualized words of comfort and farewell, her heart ached with loss, not only because the deceased had been a friend but because death tested even the strongest of faiths. The darkness that came with death cast a deep shadow over the life-affirming rituals of even the most devout. From the moment you opened your eyes in the morning to the moment you fell asleep, your heart was ripped asunder anew. Was not the first prayer of the day, *Modeh Ani,* thanking God for restoring your soul, a reminder that the precious soul of your beloved would never again be restored to their body except during the Resurrection of the Dead? While she sincerely believed that would happen, as did every pious Jew (according to Maimonides, it was one of the fundamental articles of faith), she also knew that, like the coming of the Messiah, it could take a while.

Throughout the day, every time one whispered a blessing over food or drink, over thunder and lightning, one was reminded of one's connection to the dear Lord of the Universe, and that it was He who had taken the living to "sleep with their fathers." You accepted this, of course you did! What choice did you have, after all? But each acceptance of the proper order of things in the universe was also a reminder and a reinforcement of your human powerlessness and utter vulnerability, your inability to stem the ravaging tides of time and chance that swept in suddenly to drag those you loved out to the endless sea from which none have as yet returned.

The only real comfort, she considered, watching the rav's ravaged face, was to surround yourself with life: your children and grandchildren, your friends and neighbors. But that, too, she pondered, was never enough. The Talmudical saying that "a man only dies to his wife" was equally true of the death of a wife to her husband. The loss of a longtime partner was the cruelest loss of all.

She would do what she could, she thought, to make it easier for him to bear. At least, she could bring him the foods he loved. Now that Leah was cooking for her grandchildren, she had time on her hands. She thought of all the delicacies she hadn't prepared in so long: stuffed cabbage, *falsche* fish, *gribbenes,* latkes, tzimmes, knaidlach . . . But maybe not. *Gribbenes* had been banished by the know-it-all young doctors along with schmaltz, she mourned, even though plenty of *Yidden* had been brought up on such things and died peacefully in their nineties. She herself hadn't touched such foods in decades. Never mind, she would prepare traditional foods the new way, with olive oil, she told herself, her nose wrinkling in distaste at the very thought.

Just then, Suri Kimmeldorfer, the matchmaker, walked up next to her, nodding hello.

"May we meet only at simchas," she said primly.

The two had only recently reconciled, Fruma Esther holding her fully responsible for the debacle of Yaakov's recent remarriage. It was her fault that instead of a proper, Boro Park bride, he had wound up with a *baalas teshuva.* And even though she had decided to make the best of it, it still rankled.

Suri, for her part, had been doubly outraged over all her wasted time and effort in pushing *frum,* blameless divorcées from excellent families as well as rich, Flatbush widows in Yaakov's direction to no avail. And if that wasn't enough, she'd forfeited a hefty fee by refusing Yaakov's request to play matchmaker with Leah, something she had only done out of loyalty to Fruma Esther! Injury added to insult! But if you were a matchmaker in Boro Park, you didn't have the luxury of holding on to grudges—no matter how justified—against respectable and influential members of the community who not only could sabotage your work with others but withhold their own kin from entering your bride-and-groom pools.

"Such a tragedy!" Suri shook her short, wig-covered head, sending the stiff plastic-looking bangs swinging. "The rav will be lost without his wife." Her eyes glittered.

Yes, another client for you, Suri, Fruma Esther thought, but said nothing, simply letting out a long sigh.

"How are you feeling, Rebbitzen?" Suri asked anxiously.

"Me? The same as everyone else in this room, Suri." *Except you.*

"And how is the young couple?" Suri probed, finally getting to the real reason she had zeroed in on Fruma Esther the moment she entered the room. Who knew? Divorces were not unheard of anymore these days. Especially when scholars like Yaakov Lehman got entangled in frivolous matches with wild, redheaded *baalos teshuva.* She had already heard rumors . . . She would be more than happy to give it another shot.

Fruma Esther, however, had her own agenda.

"They are very happy together, Suri. But I think the community could be a little more welcoming to Leah. She doesn't have many friends, and sometimes her neighbors are not keeping the mitzvah of loving the stranger, bringing sin upon the whole community."

"*HaShem Yishmor!*" Suri murmured, clicking her tongue nervously as she wondered where this was going.

"Really pious people among us need to help her," Fruma Esther told her pointedly.

That got Suri's attention. "Of course! But how?"

"You know, Suri, you have great influence in our community. You are one of our leaders," Fruma Esther told the astonished matchmaker.

"Well . . . I . . ."

"No, no. Don't be modest, Suri. You and I both know what people will do to make sure their children get a good shidduch. You investigate every match, talk to the bride's kindergarten teachers, the groom's rabbis, the storekeepers who deal with the parents to make sure they pay their monthly bills . . ."

Suri squirmed. "People depend on me to find out the truth before getting mixed up with some family that is trying to hide all its problems. Better you know what's happening before the *chasuna* than after!" she cried.

"Of course, this is not, *chas v'shalom,* a criticism. You have to look into every match. Which is why you have a chance to let people know that their reputations could suffer if they are known not to be God-fearing."

"What do you mean?"

"I am talking about how they welcome a *baalas teshuva* to the community, and especially if they take it so far they are willing to hurt poor orphans who lost their mother so recently."

"People are hurting your grandchildren? People in Boro Park? Our people? What does this mean, Fruma Esther?"

"Some people won't let their children come to Yaakov's house to play with the children anymore."

All her red flags went up. "But they must have a reason."

"What reason could they have?" Fruma Esther demanded, pulling herself up to her full height and adjusting her head covering. "I want you to know I intend to get to the bottom of it, Suri Kimmeldorfer. I want you to know I'm going to knock on the doors of all the neighbors to find out who's behind this wicked thing, and then I'm going to talk to every rabbi and every rebbitzen, every admor and every rosh yeshiva in the neighborhood and their wives and daughters."

Suri Kimmeldorfer listened in amazement. This was a real tzimmes Fruma Esther was cooking up. It could ruin reputations, pitch neighbor against neighbor. The more turmoil there was in the neighborhood, the more her bride-and-groom pool shrank: this one not talking to that one, this rebbe not approving of that rav's *talmidim* or the daughters of certain families . . . A frisson of terror like an electric shock coursed along her varicose veins. "But Fruma Esther, isn't it better to bring peace and love to our community than stir up conflict?"

"Ah, so it is, so it is. I see that you understand me perfectly, Suri."

"You think so?" The confused matchmaker stared at her.

"Yes, we must bring peace to the community. You can help by telling all the families you are working with that all the rabbis in the community are now very involved in *kiruv,* in bringing newcomers into the fold, and that no one will marry into a family that treats newcomers shamefully."

"I haven't heard of that."

"Well, believe me, the rabbis are all going to be making speeches about it this coming Shabbos. Trust me. Just imagine how impressed your clients will be when they hear it first from you!"

This was true. Her reputation for being a welcome guest among the most important rabbinical families in the community would soar! "I'll mention it to them," she promised. But what she could really say was that Fruma Esther was on the warpath against those who were turning their backs on her former son-in-law and his family and that they should be cautious not to be one of them if they knew what was good for them. And for her.

12

DUVIE

She stood waiting for him in the shadows of the elevated platform of the subway train out of Boro Park. Above, the F train rumbled ominously as it came and went, the time intervals uneven and unpredictable. After weeks of meeting Duvie in various deserted parks, it was the first time that Shaindele had agreed to actually go into Manhattan with him. This was a thrilling decision that pitted her caution against her growing desires and expanding curiosity.

She thought back to the first time she had ever left Boro Park on her own. It had been more or less a disaster, a secret escape to Baltimore via Grand Central Station, in turn both terrifying and impressive as she tried out the consequences of adult decision-making without parental or rabbinical supervision. It had ended in an ignominious return home by Greyhound bus; her aunt and uncle, whom she had fully expected to supply both sheltering arms and a sympathetic ear did neither, instead traitorously informing her father and handing her a bus ticket and a brown paper bag containing a challah sandwich and high-calorie snacks. But the trip had still proven a milestone, giving her the first taste of what it would be like to meet men who were neither relatives nor friends of the family. Mostly, these random encounters had been unsatisfactory, leaving her disheartened, even a bit disgusted. The irony was not completely lost on her that in running away to find a husband, she'd ended up deciding never to get married at all.

Duvie Halpern had changed all that.

At first, it was just banter and random smiles, as impersonal as the wedges of cardboard on which he served up his soggy pizza triangles. After a number of disappointing forays to Moishy's when he wasn't there at all, Shaindele made a chart of what she observed was his work schedule. Sometimes he only worked evenings, starting at seven or eight, thus forcing her to find places to linger after school until he arrived. This was better, really, because if he came in really late, she could go home and then go out again, unaccompanied by Shulamis or some of the other girls. Even early on, she realized she didn't want anyone looking over her shoulder where Duvie was involved. She never bothered explaining to herself why. And the plan had worked. Without the prying eyes of her Bais Yaakov friends, she was able to relax. Her tongue untwisted, and her lips lost their thin, tight stretch. She was able to smile at him.

"Do you want extra cheese, mushrooms, tuna?" he asked solicitously. Of course, that is what he asked everyone who ordered a pizza, but she could tell just by looking at him, he found *her* special. Unlike the others, it wasn't really a question, just an excuse to linger and spend time with her, she told herself. And after he brought the pizza, he would wait a little while and then come back. "How was it?" he would ask her. "Good?"

She had always just nodded woodenly, until one day she finally got up her courage and said, "A little overdone, to tell you the truth. Look at all this black on the bottom."

He seemed taken aback, but amused, expressions of mock horror and chagrin flickering over his handsome face. Then he broke into a smile, leaning over the counter toward her and whispering in her ear, "It's the worst pizza in Brooklyn. In New York State. In the universe." With lightning speed, he turned his back, disappearing behind the ovens before the eagle eye of Moishy caught him out.

The next time, he was even bolder. "Your face is as pink as a rose," he'd murmured instead of talking to her about toppings. And she'd blushed furiously, walking out into the night with her limp pizza dripping oil. The entire week, she'd locked his words deep in her heart like a secret treasure, taking them out periodically to wonder over them.

After that, she began taking different clothes with her to school so she could change out of her Bais Yaakov uniform before going to Moishy's, using the public bathrooms in one of the coffee shops. But that didn't work out very well; the clothes, wrinkled badly from being stuffed in beside her notebooks and heavy texts, were not very attractive. She'd kept her winter coat zipped up. So the next time, she wore the clothes *underneath* her dowdy school uniform, grateful for the unusually cold weather and her under-heated classrooms. She chose a pretty, flowered Sabbath blouse and a slim, dark skirt that showed off her petite, slender figure, changing in the school bathroom and only unzipping her coat when she got to Moishy's.

The effort had proved worthwhile. Not that he had actually said anything, but she could see how his eyes left her face and traveled up and down her body. Then he gave her that smile, that special Duvie smile she knew was meant only for her. It was thrilling.

The very next time, she found a note slipped between the cardboard and the pizza so discreetly that at first she didn't notice it until she practically took a bite out of it. Delicately, she removed it, slipping it swiftly into her coat pocket without daring to even glance in Duvie's direction. She fingered it for two blocks until stopping to unfold and read it.

Curious? Meet me after work, 8:30, Dome playground, 16th Avenue, between 37th and 38th, on Thursday.

What was that supposed to mean, *curious*? Did it mean *he* was curious about her, that he wanted to get to know her? Or was it a challenge, questioning if *she* was curious about him? Or was it about something else entirely? And if yes, what else?

She stood there a long time, confused, the paper crumpling in her hand as she squeezed her fingers into a fist. *Am I? Curious?* she asked herself, feeling something heavy—almost oppressive—mingling with her excitement and joy.

Of course she went to meet him, despite her anxiety about being caught. The playground would be deserted at that time of night, she convinced herself, and dark enough so that people looking out their windows in the neighboring apartment buildings wouldn't be able to make them out.

Shivering, she opened the gate and walked inside, taking a seat on a bench near the jungle gyms behind a large tree.

What am I doing? She shuddered, her eyes searching the streets, panicked she would be discovered by the eagle eye of someone she knew. The consequences would be devastating. Her reputation—or what was left of it, all things considered—would be ruined. But most people she knew were home eating dinner, or learning the Torah, or listening to a *shiur,* not wandering the streets of Boro Park or sitting in deserted, ill-lit parks. Right?

He was twenty minutes late. She had almost given up when she saw him coming toward her in the distance, his dark hair glistening in the yellow light of Boro Park streetlamps.

He nodded to her, a bit impersonally she thought, chagrined. Then he sat down next to her, his legs wide, and his elbows resting on the back of the bench.

"So what yeshiva are you in? Who is your rebbe?" she asked him innocently, smoothing down her skirt.

He leaned back and laughed, digging into his pocket and pulling out a pack of cigarettes. He lit one and took a deep breath, exhaling smoke rings at the night sky.

"Listen, honey . . . ," he began.

"Shaindel," she corrected him.

"Okay, Shaindel. Just so we get this straight, this is not a shidduch date, okay?"

"Who said I want a shidduch?" she replied, hurt. "I just turned seventeen."

"Is that so?" He moved in closer, offering her the pack.

Why not? she thought, reaching inside and for the first time in her life touching a cigarette. Everyone else was allowed to break the rules, right? Her mother could kill herself, her father could drop out of kollel and marry a girl who once relished pig and shellfish, her stepmother, Leah, could dance around the house naked to forbidden music (or so the latest embellishments to the vicious rumors going around suggested, spread by oh-so-*frum* people. Not that she believed a word of it. Seriously, Leah? They had no idea. But Leah must have done *something*.). *So I can also break a few rules,* she thought, defiantly taking one out and holding it awkwardly between her fingers.

He laughed. "Here, let me show you." His fingers felt electric as they touched hers to reclaim the cigarette. Placing one end against the glowing end of his own, he blew patiently until it caught fire. Then he placed it between his lips and blew some more. "Here," he said, handing it back to her.

She felt more than strange putting something in her mouth that had been in his. But fearful of evoking still more mockery, she inhaled. A horrible choking feeling immediately filled her lungs. She couldn't breathe! She coughed furiously, panic-stricken. Was this some kind of evil trick? Angrily, she spit it out.

He patted her gently on the back, grinning and unsympathetic. "Don't worry about it, Shaindel. It happens to everyone the first time. Now, try again, but don't breathe it in so deeply this time. Just a little bit, into your mouth."

"You think I'm really stupid, don't you? I'm not touching that thing again!"

Ignoring her, he retrieved it from the ground and dangled it in front of her. "Don't be a baby," he taunted, inhaling it and exhaling smoke rings.

She watched him doubtfully. But he seemed fine. Her childishly smooth fingers shaking, she took it back. This time, she inhaled with caution. The mildly acrid sensation of having bitten into something spicy and overcooked enveloped her mouth and throat, but the lethal sense of drowning was gone.

"See?"

"See what?"

"You won't die if you break the rules."

"Why did you want me to meet you here?"

He closed his eyes and looked up at the sky. "I don't know. You keep coming around. I guess I wanted to figure out why."

Why, she thought. The question she had been afraid to ask herself. She didn't have an answer, not one she could give *him* anyway. So she changed the subject.

"You know your father is the principal of my school. Freidel was two years ahead of me."

"Yes, my dear sister Freidel. She's getting engaged, you know. Some future *gadol hador,*" he said mockingly, grinding his cigarette under his foot.

"She was horrible to me."

He looked up, grinning. "Freidel's a bitch. And her husband is a yeshiva moron. She got what she deserved."

"I won't be invited to the wedding."

"Don't worry about it. Neither will I."

"Really?" She was shocked. "Why not?"

"Because 'what's not nice we don't show.' And I'm not nice."

"What did you do?"

"I dropped out of Lakewood."

"Oh. My father just dropped out of kollel. He was there for twenty years."

He leaned forward, suddenly interested. "How come?"

"My mother died. We need the money, so he's working full-time now. He has a new wife. A *baalas teshuva* from California."

"I think I heard about that . . . A redhead? Right?"

"I guess everybody heard."

"Lucky him. How did he get away with that?"

"He wouldn't take no for an answer."

"And how is it now, for him, for you?"

She hesitated. "Better than it was. I had everything dumped on me. My little brother and sister. The housework. The cooking. I hated it. And I don't think I did a very good job. Freidel used to gang up on me with her friends, make me feel ashamed of . . . of . . . losing my mother, that my father had a *baalas teshuva* girlfriend . . ."

"Yeah, I bet. She's so good at that. A real *tzadakis.*"

"What did she do to you?"

"Nothing special. She just made sure I knew she sided with the rest of the family, and that I was damned to hell for ruining her shidduch chances."

"Did you?"

"If only! But no. She's marrying exactly the kind of idiot my parents wanted her to."

"What's wrong with him?"

"Nothing—if you want to be tied to some guy who is not planning on doing anything the rest of his life."

"Why nothing? He's learning."

"He's sitting on his backside, making phone calls and drinking coffee. And after the wedding, he'll be busy working hard to get my sister pregnant. In the meantime, she and my father and his father will be sending him money every month to pay the mortgage on an apartment they bought for him until they get him some cushy job as a teacher or mashgiach. That will take a while. He's got to put in the time."

"Maybe he loves learning. Maybe he'll be a great teacher or mashgiach."

"Right. And I'm going to be a chef at a four-star restaurant. Give me a break. It's all a big joke, don't you know that?"

"What's a big joke?"

"That all the *frummies* who decide to sit and learn are going to be great scholars. They are just too lazy to get a degree and earn a living. They're taking the easy way out."

She knew that wasn't true. Her father had sacrificed so much to sit and learn. It was his passion, not an easy way out. But she decided not to contradict him. "Is that the reason you dropped out?"

"Well, I didn't, actually."

"What do you mean?"

"It was more like I was politely told that I should find another 'more suitable' place for myself. In other words, I got kicked out."

She absorbed this. Only real bums got kicked out of yeshiva. It must have been something awful. She didn't pursue it. It was much too much information already.

He didn't seem to mind or even notice her silence. "So what about you, Shaindel? Do you have a boyfriend?"

She shook her head. "And I don't want one."

He laughed. "So why do you keep coming to visit me at Moishy's?"

She shrugged. "I like the pizza."

He slanted his head, studying her. "Soooo. What is it you like about me, little Shaindele?"

"Who says I like anything?"

"You change out of your Bais Yaakov clothes when you come in. I'm not stupid."

She blushed. "What do *you* like about *me?*"

He turned his head toward her, resting his elbows on his knees. "Well, you're not fat. And you seem a little more interesting than the rest of the girls around here, who would have gone screaming to their parents and gotten me fired for sending a note."

So he liked her because she had agreed to do something no respectable girl in the neighborhood would have done! She was hurt. But he had also noticed how she was dressed, that she had been trying to please him. And he as much as admitted that he found her attractive ("You're not fat"). But in the turmoil of her mixed emotions, she found it hard to separate that out from the rest. It was just one more thing in this whole experience that confused and excited her.

Altogether, it wasn't exactly what she'd imagined young men said to young women they admired and were falling in love with. But, hey, hadn't he asked her to meet him here, alone? Weren't they sitting here side by side in the dark? And perhaps, most of all, wasn't he the elusive, handsome, older brother of her nemesis, Freidel, one of the boys she'd always fantasized about? It was almost as if in enticing him to single her out, she was getting back a little of her own against her tormentor. *The enemy of my enemy is my friend, right?*

She liked talking to him. It was so easy, she thought. She didn't have to pretend, or be on guard, because he didn't seem to have the same view of things as the rest of the people she knew in Boro Park.

He didn't touch her, not that first time.

13

※

LEAH TALKS TO HASHEM

"Dear God," Leah prayed, sitting in the living room after dropping the kids off at school and day care. "I just thought I'd catch up with You. It's been a while. I'm sorry. I think about You all the time. I'm so grateful for everything You've done for me. Thank You for my husband, for Yaakov. I was so lonely, and in such despair that I'd ever find a man who would love me and be faithful to me. He is everything I could have wanted, HaShem. They say that after the creation of the world, You have time on Your hands, so You use it making *shidduchim*. You did a great job for me. Thank You. Thank You so much.

"And thank You for the children. Please, keep watching over all of them, keeping them safe and healthy. Keep the little ones, Chasya and Mordechai Shalom, away from sharp objects and hot stoves and the more frightening illnesses kids pick up from the other kids they play with. Please keep helping me to find ways to make them happy.

"I worry a little about Chasya. She is so sensitive and so deep. I know there is a well of sorrow in that little girl. Help me to show her how much I love her and how precious she is to me and to her father and whole family. Don't let those vicious little snobs in the neighborhood hurt her in any way. And thank You for sending Fruma Esther on the warpath against them. It has helped a lot. Okay, not everyone is on board—there are still a few holdouts—but Chasya has some friends to play with now who come over, Baruch HaShem.

"Now I need to talk to You about myself. Dear HaShem, my dear, dear Friend." She sighed. "I'm in trouble. And I'm a little embarrassed to even share it with You after all You've done for me. It feels . . . ungrateful. Which I'm not. At least I don't think I am. But some days, I am finding it impossible to imagine going on this way.

"I'll start with the easy things. This neighborhood. It's so dark, so gray. There are no mountains, hardly any trees, and only tiny little patches of grass behind chains and fences. I miss California, the beautiful views, the sunsets, the forests and mountains. I'm starved for them. I can't stand being in the city . . . these dusty streets." She took a deep breath. Facing yourself wasn't easy.

"And . . . the truth is . . . the fact is . . . I'm lonely."

Even as her lips formed these soundless words, she felt shocked.

It was true. But how could that be? She had a loving husband, sweet little children who called her *Mommy!* And she loved them all sincerely, with her entire heart. And they loved her.

"You see, Yaakov isn't around very often. He works hard all day, and when he does come home, he's committed to dedicating some of his time to learning. Don't get me wrong, I don't resent that . . . at least I know I shouldn't. How can I? He loves learning so much, and I knew who he was when I married him. Actually, most of the time, I'm sincerely proud of him, and I'm sure You are, too; he's earning all of us Your blessings.

"Yes, I love the life You've given me, and I'm grateful but . . . but . . . You see . . . I'm home alone all day with the kids and when they leave in the morning, just with my computer. Business is going well, thank You so much! But I go a little stir-crazy. And . . . and . . ." This was hard, so hard! But she could tell Him, because of course He knew all about it anyway. "I don't have any friends in this neighborhood."

She had expected in time to become a part of the social life of those around her. She'd been realistic; it would not happen overnight. But she'd expected that after a year among them, they would have thawed somewhat; that she would invite and be invited in return for Sabbath meals. That she would be asked to join the other women in participating in local *chesed* efforts—collecting donations for poor local brides and grooms, baking cakes for newlywed *sheva bracha* dinners, bringing meals to new mothers . . . But somehow none of that had happened. The neighbors, who had all been friends with Yaakov's first wife, had very politely begged off her dinner invitations with one excuse or another and had failed to invite her in return. And no one had come knocking on her door to ask her to join in their little local projects. In fact, except for a polite greeting when coming across each other, they pretty much ignored her. And now, with the whole music fiasco, their children had followed suit. If not for Fruma Esther going door to door and basically twisting their arms, Chasya would still be playing all by herself.

While the intervention had alleviated the problem of the children, it had not endeared her to her neighbors. They still kept their distance. At this point, she didn't really care anymore. *Who needs people like that as friends?* she told herself angrily. Which was fine except that it meant she didn't have any friends.

Of course, there was always Shoshana. But as sympathetic as her best friend in the neighborhood was, she was unable to do much. She was in her last year of residency, and her working hours were off the charts. In addition, she was planning her wedding, a complicated and lavish affair that had to include all the religious strictures necessary to keep her parents and their friends happy, as well as all the American wedding aesthetics taken for granted by the groom's upper-class Bostonian family. In other words, mission impossible. Shoshana was struggling with it. While they spoke on the phone several times a week and had managed to sneak in time for coffee, Shoshana clearly wasn't going to be much of a companion.

"I know I should try to help myself, HaShem. I could go back to our skating group on Mondays. But that's the night Yaakov meets with Meir! I explained this to him, and he really tried to change to another night, but it's the only night Meir can do it . . . so I said okay." She sighed. She hated the way this was sounding. Saint Leah, the martyr.

"I guess I could get a babysitter, but the thing is, even though we are both working so hard, a lot of the money is going to pay off loans, and what's left is eaten up by taxes and rent."

Ironically, even though they were both employed, they were worse off than their neighbors, most of whom were being subsidized by some kind of government program, many of them fraudulently. She knew for a fact that many couples got married in a religious ceremony but didn't register their marriages with the government so they could apply for rent and food subsidies as unwed mothers. With the government paying their mortgages, some even purchased second homes that they rented out. Honestly, she couldn't get her head around this kind of dishonesty among so-called God-fearing people. Religious law demanded that Jews strictly keep the secular laws in every country they lived if such laws didn't contradict the Torah. These kind of unethical shenanigans were strictly forbidden: *Chuka d'medina Chuka.* The law of the land was also the law under halacha.

But there was the law, and then there was how people actually lived. The more she lived in Boro Park, the more she understood how wide the gap was between the two. It was very disappointing. And as a result, honest, hardworking people like themselves were often not better off financially than those who were learning full-time.

Of course, Yaakov's salary would increase as he added experience to his résumé, and her business was growing month by month according to the hours she was able to devote to it. And truthfully, she'd learned to care less about material things. It helped that she'd grown up with an unwed mother, and fairly poor. You could get your clothes in Goodwill, take the kids to all kinds of free museums and parks, buy generic food in bulk. People in Boro Park were the hands-down champions of living on the cheap, making her mother look like a rank amateur! And she'd learned from them.

"No, being poor isn't the end of the world, HaShem, and I guess this is more or less what I expected when I married a debt-laden, widowed Torah scholar. But the loneliness! The number of hours I'm here in this apartment on my own, or just with the children! Well, HaShem, it surprises me. I thought there would be more *us*."

She hesitated. Could she do it? Talk to the Holy One Blessed Be He, Master of the Universe, like one of her girlfriends? Repeat all those things she'd discussed with Shoshana? Was she really going to entreat Him to help her overcome her revulsion to one of His commandments? She swallowed hard. How could she tempt making the God she loved, Who had given her so much happiness, angry? How could she bear to disappoint Him? Worse, would He find it sacrilegious, offensive? These were, after all, His laws. Or so she had been led to believe. He must have a reason. What could she say? And then the words came to her.

"I know, HaShem, You can read my thoughts and see into my heart. So You already know I'm finding it agonizing to be separated from my husband for two weeks every month. It's not . . . well . . . the actual"— was she really going to use the word *sex* in a prayer?—"intercourse part; *that* I suppose I could learn to live with. But the idea that my husband can't touch me, sit on the same couch, hand me a plate . . . It makes me feel like I'm tainted. It makes me feel crazy. You made me a woman. All the things that happen to me are Your will. How could any of it be impure or unclean? Please help me to understand. Give me the courage to talk to Yaakov, to tell him the truth, and give Yaakov the wisdom to hear me and understand and help me through this, because—I'll be honest with You—I just don't know how much longer I can go on like this. You see, it's just that, and please forgive me for pointing this out because I know You can do anything, but it's just that . . . I thought I'd be pregnant by now! *But how is that ever going to happen if Yaakov and I are separated two weeks every month?*"

She felt hot tears sting her eyes. *How could I have spoken to God like that?* she thought, shocked. But it was no use holding back. This desperate urge for a child had taken her completely unawares. It was an unquenchable fire that burned away her hopes. She'd even gone so far as to ask advice from Rabbi Weintraub, the principal of the girls' program for the newly observant to which she had first applied when deciding to live a religious life in Boro Park.

He was sympathetic, but felt she was rushing things. "It's only been a little while," he reminded her. "HaShem hears your prayers, but He works in His own good time."

Others, women like Rebbitzen Basha, had showered her with what she imagined they saw as encouraging miracle tales, stories of barren women who started volunteering at orphanages and were soon pregnant with twins. Others suggested special prayers, amulets, certain diets, visits to the graves of famous rabbis . . .

The problem was, of course, that all of those spouting these well-worn suggestions already had children, not to mention grandchildren and even great-grandchildren! They would have been shocked if she'd allowed them a glimpse into her absolute fury at hearing these clichés. What could they know about her despair? About how her hopes—charred in the dark flame of monthly failure that flared up like clockwork, blackening her vision of the future, her self-image, her most cherished hopes and dreams—were wearing thin, almost disappearing? Sometimes she looked in the mirror and found someone else, a washed-out older woman whose lips, with their downturned corners, already hinted at bitterness.

But it was not only herself she was failing, she knew. Yaakov, too, expected to have more children. He was still young. By not getting pregnant immediately, she felt—in the unreasonable and impatient way women often feel about pregnancy—that her body, which had always served her so well, and which she had always nurtured and cherished—was dealing her an unspeakable betrayal. It did not help that she lived in a place brimming with pregnant women pushing baby carriages with toddlers trailing after them. In the fecundity of Boro Park, she felt like an outcast, cursed and punished for some unforgivable sin.

Having herself checked out medically had only made it worse, for they had found nothing physically wrong, which meant that they could do nothing to help her. When she tried to talk to Yaakov about it, as sympathetic as he was, he seemed a bit impatient. "Have faith, my Leah-le. Wait." Easy to say if you already had five children!

Wait. It was what everyone counseled her.

Why was it that she could not? Why was it she was so anxious? Was it because the minute you got pregnant, all the laws of separation magically vanished for nine glorious months? Or because Yaakov had already proven his fertility with another woman, and thus the only possible place fault could be laid was at her own feet? Or was it the sad reality that these children whom she loved so much would never truly be hers, that—in the end—she was no more than a glorified babysitter?

She rejected this shattering idea furiously. She loved all of her step-children like a mother, she told herself, including Shaindele and even the two older boys she saw so infrequently. As for the two little ones, Chasya and Mordechai Shalom, her Icy and Cheeky, she knew how precious she was to them and they to her. Perhaps because of that, she mourned with excessive zeal all the time she had missed out on in their lives.

How lovely it would have been to have known Chasya when she was a week old, a month old! To watch her give her first smile, grow her first tooth, take her first step. She had been denied all that and couldn't help but envy the woman who had gotten to spend every second with them, the woman Chasya still searched for. She wanted that for herself, to be part of a child's life from the very moment they were born.

How terrible it would be to never hold a child in your womb and hear its heart beat against yours, an experience that had no substitute in the life of a woman. The happier it made her to be a beloved wife and mother, the more she longed to deepen and expand that matchless experience with a child of her own, someone who would join them together forever.

Give yourself time. But time was exactly what she didn't have! Thirty-five going on thirty-six! But so what? Women were having babies well into their forties, even fifties these days, she tried to comfort herself. And sometimes you even read in the newspapers about a sixty-year-old becoming a mother! Yeah, right. That was all she needed—to look like her baby's grandmother; to have children when she had no strength left to raise them.

She didn't want to have a second family, to have a baby in the house when Shaindele had already made Yaakov a grandfather, and Chasya was fifteen and Mordechai Shalom was having his bar mitzvah. She wanted to raise them as brothers and sisters; for them to play together and to be part of each other's lives. And that could only happen if she had a baby soon, she thought.

But what about the economic situation? Having a baby wasn't practical, she reasoned with herself. After all, it was going to take years for Yaakov to earn significantly more money, and she was going to have to cut back when she gave birth and had a little one to care for.

All that was true, but unconvincing. So what? Nothing she had ever done had been practical! And yet all of those impractical things had brought her so much joy: becoming a religious Jew when it was so easy to be a secular one with no restrictions, no don'ts—don't eat this, don't eat that, don't watch television or go to movies. No nosy neighbors. No scanning the labels of food for exactly the right rabbinical endorsements. No dress code. No horrible wigs.

But anything worth having, she thought, was also worth the trouble of dealing with all the problems that came with it. The easy way had not brought her joy. All those orchestra tickets to the ballet at Lincoln Center and concerts at Carnegie Hall; all those movie tickets and cable subscriptions and Hermès bags had never brought her anywhere near the kind of happiness she had experienced in Boro Park with Yaakov and his children. It was the real life she had wanted and dreamed of, full of so many good and important things.

It was worth the effort.

She remembered the biblical passages in which the barren matriarch Rachel passionately declared to her husband, another Yaakov: "Bring me children, or I will die!" And his testy answer: "Am I God Who can open your womb?" And then there was Elkanah, the husband of Hannah in the book of Samuel, also a second wife, who writhed in agony for her childlessness under the pitiless taunting of her husband's fecund other wife, Peninnah. "Am I not better to you than ten sons?" the clueless Elkanah tells Hannah, missing the point completely.

And yet both men, like her own husband, were good men who had loved their barren wives above all. A man's helplessness and inadequacy in the face of a barren woman's suffering was a theme in the Torah, whose sacred writings were filled with endless compassion for such unhappiness. In both cases, the women, despairing of their husbands' understanding, had opted to open their hearts to God, Who had answered their prayers and opened their wombs.

"Please, dear God, help me!"

She sat there, her mind poring over all she knew about the divine, her imagination soaring like someone in a hot air balloon, up and up until she felt her consciousness expand so that she was in the clouds, above the highest mountaintops. And still her mind and soul rose, entering the blackness of outer space where stars were flung like diamonds across the firmament, sparkling with light from distant planets billions of light-years away.

It was unfathomable, the idea of God, the one, indivisible, supreme Creator who had designed and built the entire universe and every creature in it. How could you speak to such a Creator? How could your mind encompass Him? How could your tiny, human heart, beating for such a short time, ever contain more than a minute fraction of the gratitude you owed Him for all you'd been privileged to experience in your short, earthly sojourn?

This wondrous creation! she thought, overwhelmed by love. *Who can know the astonishing, ineffable complexity of it? The beauty of it? Each thing that grew, each creature that lived, a whole universe of such magnificent and awesome diversity that the mind could never wholly grasp even one thing in its totality of being, let alone the combined marvel of it all. How is it possible to open my heart to Him, Who is the repository of all this power, all this creativity, all this goodness? How can I tell Him my petty woes and troubles?*

She felt ashamed. But she, too, had been formed by His hand. She, too, was His creation.

"My tiny heart aches for You, dear Lord. Help me. Look into my heart and give me what I need, if not what I long for. Dear God, HaShem, My Father. Help me."

All afternoon as she went back to her work for her clients, she felt a sense of renewed hope, as if her soul had made a connection, touched God. It was exhilarating and exhausting. She was looking forward to getting the children home and into bed so she could make an early night of it. But when she went to pick up Mordechai Shalom, he wasn't waiting for her outside with the other children. "He's sick," his teacher said. "He's inside, lying down."

He was burning up with fever, she saw as she touched him, her heart contracting in fear. "What's wrong, Cheeky?" she murmured, taking his hot little body in her arms. He flung his small arms around her neck, his little face with its still-big baby cheeks flushed a deep crimson. He pointed to his ears and tugged at them, weeping.

"Don't worry. It's just a virus. It's going around," the teacher comforted.

Leah nodded, concerned but not overly so. Children caught things. They got sick. It would not be the first time she'd nursed him through something. She picked him up, cradling him in her arms, clueless to the anguish that lay ahead.

By the time Yaakov came home, the toddler's fever had risen from 101 to 103, and was still rising. While he had spent the first few hours crying in pain and tugging at his ears, he was now apathetic, almost drugged.

"What does the doctor say?" Yaakov asked anxiously, rocking him.

"He said it's a virus, and I should give him baby aspirin. Which I did. He said if it gets worse, to call him."

Together, they fed Chasya and put her to sleep in a roll-out cot in Shaindele's room in the vain hope of trying to isolate her from catching it. She wasn't happy about it.

"I want to be with Cheeky," she wept.

"I know, sweetie, but he's sick. He'll be better soon, and then you'll go back to your own bed."

"I want to go now, please, Mommy, Tateh!"

Yaakov transferred the baby to Leah's arms and picked her up. "What if I tell you a story before you go to sleep? Would you like that?"

"What kind of story?" she asked suspiciously.

Despite their worry, Leah and Yaakov exchanged a secret glance above her head, amused and proud. She was so smart!

"Well, what kind do you want, Icy?"

"With a princess, and a golden fish, and two angels," she demanded, her eyes beginning to close as she rested her cheek on her father's strong shoulder. Yaakov and Leah smiled at each other as he bore her away.

"What if it has three angels and a golden lion?" he whispered. She raised her head and smiled at him.

It was no more than an hour later when the baby's condition suddenly changed.

"*Yaakov!*"

The child was jerking his arms and legs, and his eyes had rolled back into his head. At his mouth, a white foam was forming. He seemed to go limp and have difficulty breathing.

"Oh, *HaShem Yishmor!*" he whispered, horrified, as he lifted the child from the bed. "I'll call the doctor!"

"No, we'll take him to the emergency room!"

"If you come, who will watch Chasya?"

"Call Shaindele to come home. She's with her friend, right around the corner. In the meantime, we can ask a neighbor to watch her," she said hurriedly, taking the baby from his arms and handing him the phone. "He's burning up!"

"Hello, is this the Glickstein home? My daughter is studying with Shulamis, Shaindele Lehman. What? She's not? Can I talk to Shulamis, please? Hello, this is Shaindele's father, I need to . . . What do you mean? You have no idea? But I thought . . . she said . . . All right, all right. Thank you."

His face was ashen. "Shulamis says they had a falling-out and haven't been seeing each other for weeks. She has no idea where Shaindele is."

"Oh, Yaakov . . ."

His jaw flexed. "I can't deal with this now! I'll ask the neighbor to come and then call Fruma Esther."

The baby was crying now and exhausted, but fully awake and breathing normally. Whatever it was, it seemed to have passed.

Mrs. Weitz came bustling in. "What's wrong with the baby?"

They told her. "My Heshie used to get this all the time. It's from the fever. You need to bring it down. Put him in a cold bath. Put in ice."

"Until we get him to the hospital, it could happen again," Yaakov said, considering.

"I'll call the doctor's emergency number and see what he says." Leah dialed.

"Let me help you," Mrs. Weitz offered kindly, going into the bathroom and filling up the bathtub with tepid water.

"The doctor says to put him on his side and let him rest. Then to try to bring his temperature down immediately. Even if it goes down, he says we should still bring him to the emergency room and have a doctor look at him. But if he has another convulsion and it lasts more than three minutes, we need to call an ambulance."

"*HaShem Yishmor*," Yaakov murmured, white with fear.

They undressed the little boy and put him on his side. Then they lifted him into the tub. At first, he didn't move, but then he started to splash around sleepily. He even smiled. A stone rolled off their hearts.

"I still think we should take him to see a doctor, Yaakov."

He nodded, taking out his phone and calling Fruma Esther.

"She's coming over. She'll be here in fifteen minutes."

"Go, go. Poor baby! Not to worry. I'll watch Chasya." Mrs. Weitz shooed them out the door.

"Thank you so much, Mrs. Weitz," Leah said, close to tears at this kindness.

You can never know the whole of a person's heart, she thought, ashamed now that she had never liked this big, bustling woman with her ugly, short, dark wig covered with an equally ugly hat, whose loud voice echoed through the hallways all day long as she tried to rein in a house full of unruly children.

"Do you want me to try calling some of Shaindele's other friends?" Leah asked, picking up the unfinished conversation that was on both their minds as she buckled her seat belt and started the car.

He didn't speak for a moment, holding Mordechai Shalom close to him. Then he just shrugged painfully, shaking his head as if he couldn't find the words.

"Yaakov, I'm sure it's fine. She's a good girl. She's changed so much."

But he just shook his head.

14

WHERE IS SHAINDELE?

"Where are we going?" Shaindele asked Duvie, who just shrugged with a lopsided grin as he swiped his metro card at the turnstile.

"I suppose you never use the subway?" he said from the other side. "Here, take my card."

"I use the subway," she responded, a little insulted, taking the card and swiping herself through. "In fact, last year, I even ran away from home. Got all the way to Baltimore from Grand Central, just so you know."

He peered at her a little more closely. "*Gevaldik,*" he murmured appreciatively, laughing. "I want to hear all about it."

From the decrepit outside platform, the bulky, graffiti-scarred buildings of the surrounding neighborhoods looked like the decaying carcasses of some hulking prehistoric beasts, she thought, shuddering. It was all so ugly when viewed from this unfamiliar height and angle. The wind blew cold and wet against them until she felt utterly chilled. She glanced at him to see if he felt the same. But he was studying the subway map, ignoring her, completely oblivious to what she might be feeling. She seriously considered going home and leaving him there. But then, finally, she glimpsed the approaching lights of the Manhattan-bound F train.

They sat next to each other in the crowded car, barely speaking.

"So are you interested?" she finally asked him.

He looked at her blankly.

"About my running away?"

A light went on in his head. "Oh, that. Sure. Why not?"

"Well, you don't seem very interested."

"Look, Shaindele. I'm as interested in you as you are in me."

She swallowed. "What do you mean?"

"How come you never ask me a single thing about myself? About what happened in yeshiva? What I want to do?"

She was taken aback.

Honestly, almost nothing about him interested her, she realized, except for the physical attraction between them.

It was pretty obvious Duvie wasn't what anyone would consider a "good shidduch." He was clearly the black sheep in his family of Torah luminaries, rabbis, and principals; a yeshiva dropout going nowhere fast. She didn't want to hear about it or to give him a platform to air all his whiny bad excuses. She was still her father's daughter. Hearing the details would just make her even more ashamed of herself than she already was for being attracted to him and meeting him behind her father's back.

She kept showing up because she had never experienced lust before. It fascinated her. After the ordeal of meeting strange men on her brief escape to Baltimore, she'd been terrified that she might never want to be a wife and mother. These new feelings, even toward someone as unacceptable as Duvie, were a huge relief. As it is written: *Were it not for lust, man would not marry, bring up children and do business.*

"So tell me. What *are* you up to, Duvie Halpern?"

"Wish I knew!" he laughed uproariously, slapping his thigh.

She looked around the car anxiously, embarrassed. She sniffed the air to see if she could detect the scent of alcohol. That would have been nothing new for Duvie. Often he had shown up at their meetings smelling like the inside of an Irish bar. Not that she had ever been inside such a place! But long ago, she had passed by outside just as someone was swinging open the doors and been engulfed by that pungent, slightly sweet-and-sour smell. She didn't smell it now. But he kept laughing. Soon, the whole train would be looking at them, she thought, mortified.

"Shh! What's wrong with you?"

"Nothing. What's wrong with you?" He took a few deep breaths, putting his hand in his pocket and pulling out his cigarettes.

"You can't smoke in here," a man across the aisle called out to him.

"What's it your business?" he answered belligerently as if he, too, were six foot two with the girth of a heavyweight champion like the man now looking darkly across at them, as if he were about to spring up from his seat. Duvie sullenly put the pack back into his pocket.

"Let's go," he told her, suddenly grabbing her hand and pulling her roughly through the aisle to the next car.

"You're hurting me!"

"Sorry," he mumbled, letting go and motioning her to two empty seats.

Reluctantly, she joined him.

"Why aren't you interested in me?" he asked again, sliding his arm around her shoulders.

"Don't!"

He removed it peevishly. "Such a *tzadakis* all of a sudden."

She blushed, looking at him sullenly.

"So okay, I'm sorry. But, *taka,* are you or aren't you interested, huh?"

"What's with all the questions, Duvie?" She was getting more and more annoyed until she suddenly noticed his hands were trembling. "What's wrong with you tonight?"

"Nothing . . . Well . . . I had this . . . thing . . . with my parents. They are kicking me out of the house if I don't go back to yeshiva."

She caught her breath. "*HaShem Yishmor!* So what will you do?"

He clasped his hands together between his knees and stared at the floor. "How do I know?"

"So go back to yeshiva. What would be so bad?"

He lifted his head and stared at her pretty, childish face, flushed pink from anger and the cold. "I'm *never* going back to yeshiva. I'd rather live on the streets." He sat up, his eyes suddenly bright. "Listen, I've got this plan. I started playing poker on the internet. First I did it for fun, just a few dollars. But I was really, really good at it. Every time I played, I made money! So I'm going to get a stake together and start playing for real. And when I have enough, I'm going to buy a ticket to Vegas and play there for real. You know, they have, *taka*, these poker tournaments and you can, *taka*, like win a million dollars! Yeah, a million dollars." His eyes shone.

"Isn't that . . . like . . . *assur*?"

"What's that supposed to mean?"

"You're not allowed to gamble."

He grinned at her. "And isn't it, like, *assur* for a nice Bais Yaakov girl to meet boys in dark parks and take the subway into the city at night?" he mocked. "Where do your parents think *you* are?"

She blushed a deep crimson. "What's that your business?"

He leaned back, spreading his arm casually behind her, almost touching her shoulders. This time, she let him. "So let's make a deal. No *mussar*, okay? Let's just have some fun tonight?"

"Where are we going?" she asked again, leaning back. It was a relief to be with someone as bad as Duvie, who you knew was in no position to judge anything you did. No matter how bad you were, he was always worse. All her wrongdoings seemed so mild compared to his.

"You'll see," he said mysteriously.

They got off at Broadway-Lafayette. The neighborhood didn't look too promising to her.

"What's so great about this?" she asked him, wondering why they hadn't gone to Forty-second Street and Broadway. She'd had her heart set on seeing all the bright lights, the theaters and movie houses, places she'd only ever heard about.

"Stop complaining already, or I'll leave you here!"

This was new, this nastiness. She wasn't sure how a boy you liked was supposed to treat you, but this didn't sound right. She looked around at the dark, unfamiliar streets. She didn't even have a subway card to go home and had no idea where to buy one. Reluctantly, she followed him.

It was a long walk. The houses seemed exactly like the ones in Boro Park, cramped old brownstones with no yards or driveways.

"What a dump!"

"Yeah, a five-million-dollar dump!" he hooted. "You see over there, that's Bedford and Grove Street!"

"So?"

"So that's where the *Friends* apartment is!"

"What friends?"

"The television show! With Jennifer Aniston and Courteney Cox and Matt LeBlanc . . ."

"From where do you have a television?"

"You can watch it on the internet. On your phone, even. It's very famous. I've watched the whole series, start to finish, about six times. Wait . . . you don't have internet?"

"Why would you think I do?"

That question, of all the things she'd asked him that night, was the single time he actually looked puzzled. "I don't know, I just thought, if you were meeting me in the park, you were like me. Fed up with people telling you how to live, what you can and can't do. I thought you wanted to be free, too."

"I do want to be free!" she answered him stubbornly. "I'm just not sure yet of what!"

"Well, you'd better find out soon, little Shaindele. Because if someone sees you out with me, very soon you're also going to be kicked out of Bais Yaakov and probably your family. So you'd better have a plan B."

"B?"

"Yeah. It means another plan when your original one doesn't work out. What was your original plan?"

"I want to be a teacher in Bais Yaakov. Like my mother, God watch over her."

"Such a rebel!" he mocked, grinning, taking out a cigarette and lighting it. He offered her one, but she refused.

"What do you like about them?"

"About what?"

"Cigarettes. I just don't get it."

He took a deep drag, considering as he blew out smoke in rings under the powdery yellow halo of a streetlamp. "I don't know. I guess the way it makes me look. Tough."

Now she laughed, relaxing. "You don't look tough, Duvie."

He glanced at her, annoyed. "So what, then?"

"You look like a boy trying really hard to pretend he's a man."

"And you look about twelve. I mean, except for the boobs." He stared at her pointedly.

"What makes you think you can speak to me this way, Duvie?" She was close to tears.

"Okay. I'm sorry. I ask *mechilah*. Let's just have some fun, all right?" He put his arm around her shoulder and squeezed. She slipped decisively out of his embrace.

He shrugged, taking another deep drag on his cigarette and moving ahead. "Do what you want, little Shaindele."

Grudgingly, she followed him to the brightly lit but somewhat seedy commercial area. There was a Black man with pink hair and tights, and groups of teenage tourists all weaving their way through ordinary working people entering McDonald's and Ace Hardware. Her feet were cold and tired when Duvie finally said, "We're here."

It was a bar with a shiny black storefront and a marquee in the shape of a grand piano. It jutted out fantastically, covering their heads.

"Best jazz club in the world!" he exulted, throwing open the doors.

"Jazz?" Shaindele repeated, following close behind him.

"Such a Boro Park girl." He shook his head sadly. "Wow, look who's playing tonight! Jimmy Cobb! He's an old-timer. Played with Davis and Coltrane!" he rejoiced, uncharacteristically super-excited.

She was glad of that, although she couldn't understand what in all this had achieved such an instantaneous transformation. She looked around, searching for answers in the people sitting at tables and all along the bar, packed together as tightly as women crowding up to the *mechitza* to get a glimpse of the men dancing during Simchas Torah. Waitresses weaved around them, balancing trays of alcoholic drinks, hamburgers, and fries.

Up front, a blue-lit stage held a large piano, drums, and a double bass. The musicians didn't look anything like what she'd imagined. Instead of tuxedos and evening gowns (this she'd once seen in a wall poster advertising a concert at the Brooklyn Academy of Music), they wore sleeveless undershirts, their arms covered in tattoos, or black jackets and baseball caps, their eyes surprisingly shaded with sunglasses in the gloom. One even had a long beard. All he needed was a black velvet skullcap and a black *bekesha,* she thought, and this could be Fourteenth Avenue . . .

They squeezed into the bar, mostly to get out of the way.

"What do you want to drink?" a bartender asked.

"Not sure," Duvie answered, taking out his thin wallet and flipping through it.

"There's a twenty-dollar cover charge for the show if you don't order," the bartender informed him. "So maybe you'd like some food?"

"Well, in that case, sure. How about a hamburger and fries, and a large tap beer."

Shaindele gasped, but he just grinned at her.

"And for your girlfriend?"

"Oh, she's good," Duvie said. The bartender glanced sympathetically in her direction, rolling his eyes.

"I'll have a Diet Coke with rum," Shaindele suddenly spoke up. "And can you put that into a paper cup?"

The bartender winked at her.

"I hope you have some cash on you, Shaindele."

"I have," she answered him defiantly. "I didn't know you eat *treife*."

"There's a lot you don't know about me." He shrugged.

I bet, she thought. *And even more I don't want to know.*

She watched as the plate of food was set in front of Duvie, almost holding her breath as he took a large bite out of the still-red meat encased in the whitest and softest of buns only gentiles ate. In Boro Park, the equivalent would have been challah rolls, smaller versions of the braided egg bread that graced the Shabbos table. Something about the roll's spongy whiteness stained with the hamburger's bloody residue nauseated her.

"Here, take one," Duvie said, offering her a fry dipped in ketchup.

She shook her head, fastidiously removing the paper from her straw and sticking it into the paper cup.

"What, even the glass here isn't kosher enough for you to use?" he scoffed.

"We said no *mussar* tonight, right? So leave me alone!"

Before he could answer, someone got up to the microphone. She could hardly understand anything he was saying, although Duvie and everyone else seemed ecstatic, laughing and applauding. And then this person put down the microphone and sat down by the piano and began to play. As soon as he did, someone else began to play the drums, and someone else plucked on the long strings of the double bass.

It was a funny kind of music, she thought, without a real beginning, middle, or end. It just seemed to ramble on from place to place without giving you a clue what was coming next and why. It wasn't that she didn't like it, she just didn't understand it, the way you understood wedding music that had a beat you could dance to and came with words everyone knew by heart. And even though the people around her were nodding and snapping their fingers, it didn't seem to have any particular rhythm.

"Isn't this fantastic?" Duvie said, his eyes shining.

"What kind of song is that? What are the words?" she asked him.

"It's not . . . a song. It's . . ." He stopped, exasperated. "They are just making it up as they go along. Somebody starts and the others kind of feel the vibe and pick it up and add their own. It's like they're each doing their own thing, but also making something together."

She listened to him, surprised. It was probably the most intriguing and intelligent thing she'd ever heard him say. He wasn't stupid, she acknowledged, sipping her drink, trying to hear what he heard. Then someone new came onstage and started blowing a kind of horn. *A trumpet, like in the Bais Hamigdash?*

A strange feeling came over her, spreading through her chest and stomach along with the alcohol in her drink. The notes were sad, but sexy, too, and a bit dark, she thought, suddenly understanding the lighting. If you could hear the color blue, it would sound like this. When they stopped playing for a moment and everyone hooted and applauded, she found herself clapping as well, genuinely looking forward to when they would begin again. The next set seemed happier, almost jolly, but equally unscripted and wandering. She wondered how the musicians knew how to do that—to put their feelings into the music—and if they all really felt the same way at the same time, or if they just adapted themselves to get along and support each other? She wondered if they took turns taking the lead, or if everything they did surprised each of them as well?

To her surprise, she forgot about Duvie, about him sitting there eating his bloody, *treife* piece of meat in a roll so white it no doubt had been made with milk, which was forbidden to eat with meat, still another transgression. The music, which she had found so unsettling, suddenly seemed to flow through her, exciting her with its spontaneity.

What would it be like to live the way those men played, each day a new flow, in directions you couldn't predict but just try to follow? To experiment every day? To be open to the lead of others, to the strangeness, to the newness?

It was the very opposite of everything she had ever been taught—that there was only one path, well traveled by every good Jew who had ever existed, and to step off it was to step into the uncharted wilderness leading to sin, ugliness, and death.

Then she suddenly thought of her poor mother, locked in the bathroom, bruised and broken, wandering in the darkness. She had never strayed, never taken a spontaneous step into foreign, untested terrain. How, then, had she wound up there?

A startling thought suddenly ripped through Shaindele Lehman's seventeen-year-old heart—her mother, faithfully putting one foot in front of the other, doggedly keeping to the path of righteousness, the path of her forefathers, and still it had led her there! How could that have happened? Her poor, devout mother! She felt tears of sorrow fall quietly down her cheeks. She turned to Duvie, reaching out for him. But he was turned away from her, oblivious. His bangs were plastered to his sweating forehead like a little boy's, his fingers moist and discolored by a sticky brown-and-red stain that also stained the white cuffs of his yeshiva boy shirt.

Stupid idiot, she thought, disgusted, wiping her eyes. She felt nothing for him, she realized. He was just another stranger who didn't even know she was weeping in the darkness touched by blue light. He didn't know that terrible things happened to Jews who went off the right path, the ancient path of their forefathers, or that the same things could also happen to those who never strayed, those who loved God and the Torah. He would make up his life as he went along, each day a random note in blue-tinged darkness.

———

It was well after midnight when she finally got home. She placed the key in the lock and almost held her breath as she turned it as silently as possible. But as she looked down, she realized that light was pouring through the space underneath the door.

They were all there, waiting for her: her father, her stepmother, Bubbee.

She turned to face them wearily, taking off her coat and hanging it in the closet.

"Shaindele," her father began, his jaw clenched in fury.

"Please, Tateh. Can we talk tomorrow? I'm so tired."

She had left Duvie sitting at the bar without saying goodbye, finding her way back to the subway. A kind Black woman had swiped her through the turnstile and even refused to accept payment. "We've all been there, honey," she said.

She remembered the Black woman in Grand Central on her way to Baltimore who had showed her the way to her platform, the first Black person she had ever spoken to, and how she had been terrified to even walk near her and had never even thanked her. She wouldn't let that happen again. "Thank you so much!" she'd told the woman, who'd smiled and waved.

She'd dozed off on the train but had luckily been shaken awake by a sudden movement of the rattling old car just before her stop. Otherwise, she would be wandering on the tracks in Coney Island.

"We'll talk about this now!" Yaakov said firmly.

"Shaindele, we were so worried. We called your friend Shulamis," Leah said softly.

"Shulamis? You called Shulamis? Why?"

"Because your brother was very sick, and we needed to go to the emergency room!" Yaakov slammed a hand against his fist.

"We wanted you to come home and babysit," Leah continued patiently.

"Mordechai Shalom? What's wrong with him? Is he all right? What happened?"

"He's sleeping. He had a very high fever and started to shake," Fruma Esther chimed in. "And you, where were you? *Yenne-velt!* Who knows what could have happened to you, a young girl out alone at this time of the night?" She shook her head, heaving a huge sigh that made her breasts rise and fall like dough. "HaShem be blessed for watching over you! So foolish! Why do you worry your parents like that? Again! After Baltimore! Your family was on *shpilkes*! I'm very disappointed in you, *maideleh*. Explain yourself."

What could she say? She was actually too tired to make up a story.

"I went to Greenwich Village with Duvie Halpern. We listened to jazz."

"Duvie Halpern? Rabbi Halpern's—your principal's—boy?" Yaakov asked, hoping for some reprieve from the awfulness of this story.

She nodded. "The one that works at Moishy's Pizza."

"Rabbi Halpern has a son who works in a pizza store? Aren't all his sons in Lakewood?"

"No, Tateh. Not Duvie. He got thrown out."

Yaakov collapsed into the sofa.

Fruma Esther sat down heavily beside him. She was astonished at what direction this conversation was taking. That a granddaughter of hers, her flesh and blood, child of her saintly Zissele, should go off at night to meet strange boys. What a nightmare! Forget about dancing around with the *kinderlach* to a little music! If the yentas got hold of *this* story, there would be nothing she could do! She fanned herself.

"Can I get you some water, Bubbee?" Leah asked her anxiously.

She waved her away, but Yaakov brought her a glass anyway.

As she sat there stupefied, taking small sips, her mind suddenly recharged and refocused. Duvie Halpern! One of the handsome Halpern boys, grandsons of the admor, sons of Reb Shlomo Halpern, principal in Bais Yaakov. Not a bad shidduch. If her family was going down, it wasn't going alone. But why did anyone have to go down at all? After all, they were both single, both from good families.

"How could you do such a thing, Shaindele? How?" Yaakov beseeched, beside himself.

Fruma Esther made a dismissive motion with her hand. "Let's not get too excited, Yaakov."

"What?" He stared at the old woman, shocked. "You? How can you say that? She's been lying to us for weeks! Meeting with a boy on her own! Is this how your saintly mother and I raised you, Shaindele?"

The girl hung her head wordlessly. A livid color, like that of wine, rose in her pale cheeks at the onslaught.

Leah got up and put her arm around Shaindele's shoulder. "Are you all right? Nothing happened to you?"

Shaindele looked at her, surprise and gratitude welling up inside her, along with her suddenly misting eyes. "I was scared by myself on the subway."

"He let you go by yourself!" Yaakov exploded, jumping up and smashing his hand against the wall, rattling the laminated jigsaw puzzles in their frames.

"No. I just left without telling him."

"What were you doing with him there in the first place, Shaindele?" Yaakov shouted.

Leah put a calming hand on his shoulder, shaking her head almost imperceptibly. "You'll wake the baby. Look, it's been a really hard night for all of us. We're exhausted. Maybe we really should all talk about this tomorrow?"

To Yaakov's surprise, Fruma Esther agreed. "Yes. This problem isn't running anywhere. *Morgen iz oich a tog.*" *Tomorrow is also a day.*

Outnumbered, Yaakov gave in. Honestly, he was stunned, heartbroken, and defeated. How had he failed his little girl that she had behaved in such a way? How? And what was the right path to take now?

They bid good night to Fruma Esther, and Yaakov insisted on driving her home.

Leah listened sleepily as he returned, coming into the dark bedroom, changing into his nightclothes, then sliding in beside her.

She reached out for him, touching his shoulder gently. "Yaakov, don't take it to heart. She's just a teenage girl. They all get crazy ideas in their heads. At least she didn't try to excuse herself or lie. Shaindele is a good girl, but she's young, confused. She has a crush on some teenage boy, went off on a date with him. It's no big deal. All of us did things like that when we were young, no?" she whispered.

He turned his back to her, stiffening. For the first time since falling in love and marrying her, Yaakov realized how much he didn't know about this woman he had defied everyone to marry. What kind of things had she done as a young girl? And what kind of a mother could she be to his innocent young children?

Leah watched his back. In her heart, she felt the first fluttering of fear.

15

CONSEQUENCES

Shaindele would come home directly after school. This would be strictly monitored. If she wanted to go somewhere else, either Leah or Yaakov would have to check it out thoroughly in advance. She would write her school assignments in a special book, and this would be checked each night to see if they had been done. She would not be allowed to go out by herself to the store without either a parent or one of her siblings. Her time would be calculated to the minute. The list went on and on and on . . .

"Is all that really necessary, Yaakov?" Leah questioned. "After all, she seems really sorry. And nothing actually happened."

His reply was stiff and formal, she thought, making it clear to her that this was not up for discussion. When he left for work, it was with none of the usual kindness and affection that accompanied his goodbyes. It was almost as if he considered this *her* fault! But what had she to do with the actions of a seventeen-year-old girl she had known barely two years? It was very unfair!

Still, whatever she might have felt, she passed over these decrees to Shaindele in her most draconian manner. To her surprise, the girl took it all meekly, almost relievedly. It was as if she'd been expecting the slash of a guillotine and had only gotten a paper cut.

Leah couldn't understand it. She tried to think back to her own teen-age years. Why, if her mother had tried to impose *any* of these restrictions on her, it would have been the French Revolution, complete with barri-cades and cannons! There would have been full-blown mayhem! As much as she had tried, as long as she had lived in this world, she just didn't un-derstand this girl, or the family dynamic, or this community. She found this not only sad but frightening. It made her feel as if she were living in a fog, judged by secret rules in a secret book that someone, somewhere, pos-sessed but refused to let anyone—at least her—read.

A few days later, there was no sound from Shaindele's room long after she should have been up and dressed for school.

Leah knocked on her door.

"Can I come in?"

When there was no reply, Leah opened the door. The girl was still in bed, the covers over her head. Leah sat down on the edge, reaching out to smooth back Shaindele's hair, feeling her forehead. She seemed warm, but not feverish.

"How are you feeling?" she asked sympathetically.

Shaindele turned over, her eyes wet with tears. "I'm so ashamed."

Leah caressed her forehead. "Why don't you take the day off from school? I'm going to drop Chasya off. Can you watch the baby for me? And when I get back, we'll talk."

When she returned, Shaindele was sitting on the living room couch, Mordechai Shalom ensconced in her lap. To Leah's relief, they were both smiling.

"He isn't coughing, and he doesn't feel like he has a fever anymore, Leah. Here, you touch him."

"Is that right, Cheeky? Are we all better now, my sweet little boy?" she cooed, taking the child into her arms. A huge smile lit up his little face as he nuzzled into her neck. "What are we going to do with our Cheeky?"

"Pops," he demanded, giggling.

"Oh, you want a reward for scaring me to death the other day? Well, we'll just have to see about that, young man," she told him, tickling his round little stomach as she hoisted him onto her hip and walked into the kitchen. Her lips grazed his forehead in a gentle kiss. He really was all right. No fever. Thank You, God! She exhaled, retrieving a big box of mango pops from the depths of the freezer. She sat him in her lap, peeling off the paper, then handing it to him. Then she looked over at Shaindele sitting alone in the living room.

"Come and take one, too, Shaindele," she called out to her.

The girl got up and joined them in the kitchen. She said no to the pop, but sat down at the table across from them.

"Maybe a hot drink instead? I'm making myself some fresh coffee."

"Tea? Chamomile?"

"Sure."

"Thank you, Leah," she said gratefully.

Leah strapped Mordechai Shalom into his high chair, filling his sippy cup with chocolate milk and setting a bowl of dry Cheerios in front of him on which the mango pop dripped its sticky orange residue. He found the combination gourmet, gobbling it down ecstatically with his spare hand. His appetite was definitely back, she saw, and she breathed out another prayer of grateful thanks. She filled two mugs with hot water, handing one to Shaindele with a spoon and a tea bag and placing some coffee and sugar in the other for herself.

"Sugar?"

"Yes, please."

Leah handed her the bowl of sugar cubes, and she absentmindedly added four as Leah watched, amused.

"So you want to tell me what's been going on with you, Shaindele?"

"You know."

Leah shook her head. "Not really. I mean, I heard what you told your family. But you haven't said a word about why. Why did you do it, Shaindele?"

The girl stirred in the massive sugar infusion, studying the inside of her cup for a few moments as if coming to a decision. Then she looked up into Leah's concerned face. "I met a boy, and for the first time, I liked him," she blurted out. "I didn't even know that was possible."

Leah smiled. "Yeah, I know what you mean."

"Do you?" Shaindele whispered, surprised, the smile disarming her. It was so unexpected, so nonjudgmental.

"Of course! It happens to every girl at some point. It's normal—like waking up one day to find all your beloved dolls have suddenly turned to plastic."

"It happened to you, too?"

"Shaindele, it's what *all* young girls go through. You have a certain point in your life when you figure out that boys exist and that they're fun to be with and you care about what they think about you and—I don't know—something will just pull you toward them—the way they look or . . ." She smiled. "I remember this one boy—I was about your age, maybe a little younger—and I was just fascinated by the way he held a pencil! I know it sounds crazy, but that's the truth! There was something about his fingers. They were so long and manly and just had this way of twirling the thing around so confidently, or holding it so delicately to the paper, as if he were caressing it."

Shaindele's sad face suddenly broke into a smile. "You're right. It's meshuga."

Leah smiled back, sipping her coffee. "So what was there about Duvie?"

Shaindele hesitated. "I don't know, *eppis*. Maybe that his hair fell all the time into his eyes and he didn't even brush it away. He just left it there, as if it didn't matter."

"Right. The hair in the eyes, and then he just swings his whole head and the hair moves up a little and falls back again. So sexy."

Shaindele blushed. That word, in any conjugation or form, was never spoken aloud among the people she knew, and—if you were a good Bais Yaakov girl—you were supposed to pretend it never entered your mind. She quickly changed the subject. "Tateh is so mad on me."

Leah nodded. "But I think he was worried most of all. The idea of you being on the subway by yourself, walking home in the dark."

"I was also scared! But no, Leah, Tateh is right to be mad on me. Leah, you don't understand. You're not from here. This thing . . . what I did . . . it's a *shandah,* unforgivable. If anybody finds out, I'll get thrown out of school, and I will *never* get a shidduch—except some convert or *baal teshuva* nobody else wants." She stopped, biting her lip. "Oy, I didn't mean—"

Leah reached out and took her hand. "It doesn't matter. I know what you meant. Are *you* worried about it?"

Shaindele looked defiantly into her teacup. "So what?" she said softly as if to herself. "Who cares? I mean, after what happened to my mameh, do I really *want* to get married? Do I really *want* to have children? She did everything right, everything people expected from her. So how come all those terrible things happened to her anyway? I mean, how could a kind God let it happen, if there even is a God."

Leah felt her mouth suddenly go dry. "Of course there is a God, Shaindele!" she said hoarsely, helplessly, shocked.

Shaindele shook her head. "I don't understand you, Leah. You came from outside. You had everything. Nobody bothered you or told you what to do. You didn't need a shadchan. You could just meet a boy and it was nobody's business. Why did you give all that up? Why do you even *want* to be one of us?"

Leah felt a deep chasm open in her heart. It wasn't an innocent question. It was a challenge to all she had so painfully and arduously acquired over the past few years, demanding that she relive every fork in the road, every footfall. It was gut-wrenching and a bit mortifying to have to do so under the scrutinizing gaze of this young, troubled girl who had never liked her and always viewed her beliefs and practice with suspicion. It was like being cross-examined by a particularly cynical and unfriendly detective. But it was also, she realized, absolutely crucial to her stepdaughter's well-being at this delicate point in her life to give her some real answers. She was at a dangerous crossroads, and these were vital questions that she couldn't ask her father, or her grandmother, or her teachers without arousing hostility, calumny, and misgivings.

"Once, when I was very small, my mother took me to the zoo. I remember being in the snake house. There was this gorgeous snake with different colors and markings, as if some artist had painted its skin. I couldn't stop staring at it. And I thought, *I love the artist who made that beautiful creature.* So I guess you could say I started believing in God right then and there. I became religious because I love the world, Shaindele— every animal, every tree, every flower. The sea. The sky. Mountains. It is all too complex, too fantastic, to be just some random accident. There *has* to be a Creator. And I love that Creator."

"The goyim also love the Creator. But why did you choose to love

HaShem, our HaShem? The One we say took us out of Egypt, gave us the Land of Israel, gave us the Torah and all the laws. Why do you love *Him*?"

Leah felt the dread familiar to every *baalas teshuva* when confronted with such basic questions. How to distill into a few words, a few sentences, the epic journey they have been through without sounding ridiculous? But it was usually a secular interlocutor with an axe to grind who posed such challenges, not someone who had been a religious Jew from birth. What to say to this troubled girl that would not sound like some cliché from a proselytizing website? She agonized.

"I never felt at home in the family and place into which I was born. I always felt something was missing. Everything I did, even the fun I had, it all seemed artificial and a bit hollow, like a child pretending to be a mother or a soldier or an actress. I never felt grounded, at home, in my own skin, until I came here and fell in love with your tateh."

"But all the laws, all the rules!"

Leah nodded. "It's hard, I'll admit it. And I don't always understand the reasons for so many things. But in the end, it has truly brought me closer to my Creator. I feel I know Him better now. Every struggle I have in keeping His laws—even the ones I can't understand—brings me closer to Him and Him to me." She hesitated. That was really not the whole story, not even the most important part of it.

"Look, Shaindele. I love HaShem, our HaShem, the God of Abraham, Isaac, and Jacob, because He gave us the Torah, all the laws we live by. What is the Torah really asking of us? To be kind to one another. To be just. Not to harm anyone or cause them pain or loss or embarrassment. The Ten Commandments that were written by God on two tablets of stone, what do they say? Don't steal. Don't lie in court as a witness. Honor your parents. Don't murder. Don't commit adultery or even secretly covet anything in your heart that belongs to someone else. And if you don't worship idols, and have only one God, who you love and fear, and respect, never throwing His name around, then you'll keep the other things He's asking of you as well."

"Like Shabbos."

"Yes. Like the Sabbath."

"It sounds so goyish when you say it like that."

"Well, the Commandments are part of all Western religions. It's something we Jews gave the world to make it a better place, a kinder, more just place. This is our God. He belongs to us, and we to Him."

"Okay, I understand. But what does that have to do with not meeting a boy and going to a jazz club in Greenwich Village? What does it have to do with not dancing in your own house to music?"

Now I'm in hot water, Leah thought. *I shouldn't have said anything to the girl; I should have told her to ask her local Orthodox rabbi, or her bubbee or her father!*

"I'm not smart enough to answer those kinds of questions yet, Shaindele. I don't understand the connection either." *And I don't know if I ever will.* "I'm also learning, day by day. But I really do believe that this community, in its own way, has created these rules to keep people close to God and to encourage them to keep the Torah."

Even as she said it, Leah wondered if that was as true as it once was. Or if she even believed it at all anymore. Or were the social rules piled on top of God's rules just a misguided attempt by very limited and small-minded people to keep control of the little society they'd created and wanted to rule with an iron fist? And did it expand hearts and minds, or simply harden and close them? She felt her face flush.

"Sometimes," Shaindele began wistfully, oblivious to the struggle going on inside the woman across from her, "I wonder what it would have been like to have been born into another family, from another religion, maybe even another country. Is that terrible?"

"No, of course not. All of us wonder that."

What are they teaching her in Bais Yaakov? All those religious lessons, over all those years, and still they had not instilled in her even the most fundamental loyalty and appreciation for the basic tenets of her faith! And were the rigorous and never-ending attempts to seal off members of the community from the outside world simply the recognition of the abject failure of the educational and spiritual training given to their children, leaving them so weak that they'd crumble with the first whiff of a challenge from outside the community's high walls? *But no,* she thought. *It's more than that.*

"Shaindele, you have lived such a sheltered life. You go out into the world and listen to some music, and it all seems so much fun, and so innocent and enjoyable. The world outside of Boro Park *does* have many good and interesting things, but it is also full of real horrors."

"What do you mean?" Her eyes were wide.

"Well, some of these places are dangerous. The secular world isn't a place that respects women. There is so much pornography everywhere."

"What's that?"

Oh boy. Just shut your mouth, Leah. "Ugly movies about young women who are attacked and molested. It encourages normal men not to respect women, to behave badly toward those who are vulnerable or in the wrong place at the wrong time. Your father, your teachers, they want to protect you from those risks. They don't want you to learn about such terrible things or to be in any danger."

"Were you ever attacked, Leah?"

"No, because I knew how to protect myself. But I hated living in such an unsafe place. I wanted to build my real home among people who respected women. Many—most—of the men I knew were like your Duvie. Sure they wanted to be with me, but only to get whatever pleasure they could without giving me any real commitment in return to be together, to build a family. I felt used. So I came here and met your tateh, who loves me and respects me. And that is what you should want for yourself, child."

"Then why did Mameh kill herself?" she blurted out. "Did she hate being a mother and wife so much? And how do I know the same thing won't happen to me?"

"Come here." Leah reached out for her, taking her into her arms. The girl moved closer, laying her head on Leah's shoulder, wiping hot tears from her eyes.

"I'm so afraid there is something wrong with me, Leah, something sick inside me like there was in Mameh. What if it comes out when I start having babies? What if I do the same thing to my children she did to us?"

So that was it, the bedrock of this young girl's most terrible fears, the source of her rebellion and rootlessness. Leah hugged her. Her bones felt like those of some fallen bird, so young, so fragile! How had she not understood how young Shaindele really was? How had she had no inkling of what she must be going through?

The idea that she now had the responsibility of helping this truly troubled girl was horrifying. *What do I know? What can I say?* But there was no choice. "Shaindele, you can't think like that! No one knows what tomorrow will bring us. There are accidents, and people die or get crippled in all kinds of strange and sudden ways we never even imagine. Does that mean we should never leave the house? There are children whose parents abused them. Does that mean that they won't have any choice in life and will wind up abusing their own children? The most precious thing every human being has in this life is the freedom to choose how to live. But we can't use that gift if we are cowards, afraid to get out of bed in the morning. I always say, 'Choose wisely, then do it! Whatever is going to happen is going to happen. But at least, I'll choose my life, and not be paralyzed with fear.' Does that make sense?"

"I don't know."

Leah sighed. "There was this story I once read called *The Beast in the Jungle* by Henry James. It was about this person who was always afraid something terrible was going to happen to him, that some beast would pounce on him at any moment. So he never did anything in his life. And then, when he got old, he realized that none of the things he feared had ever happened. What had ruined his life was the fear itself, which kept him from living; the fear was the beast in the jungle."

"I am trying! That's why I spent time with Duvie. He wasn't even nice to me most of the time, to tell you the truth."

"What do you mean?"

"He made fun of me. Called me a baby. All he wanted was to touch me."

Oh no. Leah took a deep breath. "Did you let him? Did you want to?"

Shaindele looked across at her defiantly. "Sometimes."

Oy vey. "What, exactly—"

"I don't want to talk about it! But I never let him do anything I didn't want. And in the end, I decided I didn't like him, after all, and I walked away. Isn't that enough?"

"But you do know, right, about the birds and the bees?" *Even that I can't be sure of with this kid and the kind of education she's gotten in this place,* Leah thought, furious.

"Oh, the things they teach you in bride school, right?"

Leah's heart skipped a beat. "Right."

"I wouldn't do that. What for? That's between me and my husband, if I ever have one. If I wanted to do that, I'd go to the shadchan and find someone to marry."

Leah felt the breath come back inside her lungs. "But he, Duvie, wanted to?"

She nodded. "He was always pushing me to try things. But I didn't do what he wanted if I didn't think I'd like it."

"But some things you liked, you tried?"

She nodded.

"Okay, it's good that you kept control, because that is your right as a woman. What you say goes when it comes to your body."

"Even when I'm married?"

"Of course!"

"That's not what I heard."

"What did you hear?"

"That on your wedding night you have to do exactly what he wants. Otherwise, you're a 'rebellious wife,' and he can divorce you."

"Now you listen to me, Shaindele Lehman. You never, ever have to let anyone use your body in a way you don't like. Period."

The girl looked relieved. "Are you going to tell Tateh?"

Leah considered that. What part of this was she referring to? Her fears? Her guilt? Her sexual experimentation? Telling him everything would be honest, but foolish, she realized. If he was upset now, this additional information would just ignite all burners and take this problem zooming to another stratosphere. And she loved him too much to do that to him.

"Shaindele, I honestly don't think that I need to tell him everything you told me, at least not right now. But I should tell him some things. He loves you, and I'm sure he'd want to help you."

The girl looked down, exhaling long and hard. "Don't tell him I don't believe in God. Don't tell him I let Duvie do things to me."

Leah nodded. She'd been thinking along exactly the same lines. "Okay. But that doesn't mean we can forget about all this: your fears about getting married, about what happened with Duvie, even about your faith in God. These are very important things, and I think you need to talk to someone, a professional."

"Like Mameh did? A psychiatrist?"

"I don't know exactly. But someone a lot smarter than I am, someone who can help you get over your fears and can give you some good advice. Would you be willing to do that?"

Shaindele nodded gratefully, feeling a weight roll off her shoulders. "But this person, it would be private what I tell them?"

"Completely private. It would just be between the two of you."

"That would be good," the girl nodded eagerly.

Goodwill and relief flooded them both as they held on to each other affectionately, neither dreaming about the far-reaching and unimaginable consequences of this decision.

16

IT IS NOT GOOD
TO BE ALONE

"I tell you, Basha, when you get to a certain age, you want to feel some *nachas;* you want to feel that you've built something, something that will last after you're long gone. But then you see things, in the *ayniklach,* your hope for the future, that make you afraid, that make you ashamed, like you didn't do your job for the *Aibishter.*"

Under normal circumstances, Fruma Esther Sonnenbaum would never have shared such thoughts with any living being. But now, after what had happened with Shaindele—something she could not share with anyone, even her best friend—her heart drowning in sorrow, so heavy she felt she could no longer carry it, she had no choice but to open the floodgates before she was dragged under, breathless from the weight of it.

She was sitting on a park bench beside her friend as they tried to angle their faces toward the weak rays of an unseen sun. Despite being early spring, just a few days before the merry Purim holiday, snow was still on the ground, blackened by dog excrement, polluted city air, cigarette butts, and various pieces of trash. The sight of it further depressed her.

"This is not like you, Fruma Esther." Basha shook her head.

"You should only know what's like me these days, Basha. But I don't know what to do. My sins overwhelm me," she murmured sadly.

"Sins? What sins, Fruma Esther?" the other woman scoffed, a small ironic smile twisting her kind face into one of surprise and skepticism. "If your sins are sitting so heavy on you, what should the rest of us say? You are the most pious person I know."

Fruma Esther—longing to abandon herself completely to the joyous comfort of complete self-recrimination and disgust, feelings that demand nothing but shame, which she could supply in abundance—was flattered. "I have always tried, Basha. My whole life. With my whole heart."

"Not a question even." Her friend shook her head, scandalized. "We have all looked up to you, Fruma Esther. Believe me. You gave strength to so many. Just to see how you handled your *nesyonos* gave everyone *chizuk*. How you behaved when you lost your beloved Yitzhak Chaim, may his soul rest in peace! Like a queen, your head up, taking care of your family, comforting all the mourners, feeding all the yeshiva boys who came to recite the kaddish by you . . . What? How many were there? Twenty? Thirty?"

"Seventy, one Shabbos alone! Oy, did I cook!" She sighed. "My dear husband . . . Cherish your Aryeh, Basha. Every moment you are together. To be a widow is to be half-alive. The loneliness . . ."

"I don't know why you never thought to remarry. You were young when you lost him."

"Young?" she scoffed. "I was sixty-three, already a grandmother many times over."

"Until a hundred and twenty!" Basha blessed her friend. "If you had only listened to the matchmakers then. There was Rav Eichenstein, who lost his Peninnah just a few months later."

"I was still in mourning! It was out of the question."

"And then there was that Admor of Chemnitz, whose wife was in that car accident, *nebbech*."

"A hit-and-run, God should wreak a terrible revenge on the *rosha* who left her there! But what would I have done among the Hasidim?" She chuckled, finding the very image of walking side by side with some man in a big fur *shtreimel* and a long, black *bekesha* so fantastic as to be irresistibly amusing even in her present mood.

"It's not unheard of. Remember when Rebbitzen Erlich went off to B'nai Brak to marry the head of the Mezhbizh?"

"Her children were shocked."

Basha nodded. "It was a surprise. To everyone. But so what? I heard from my cousin Malka who saw her at a *tisch* just last month that she's very happy. Wears a big turban instead of a wig. The Mezhbizh don't wear wigs."

The two women looked at each other and couldn't help laughing. "Imagine! A turban! Well, if it was too late for me then, it's certainly too late for me now." Fruma Esther shrugged.

"No, you are wrong, my friend. As it is written: *It is not good for a man to be alone.* Or a woman. I happen to know for a fact that there is a very pious widower who is also lost without his dear wife."

"Who are you talking about, Basha?"

"I have to tell you? You don't know? A certain person who loves your *p'tcha!*"

Fruma Esther Sonnenbaum felt her face grow hot. "It was a kindness. I knew his wife's recipes. And during shiva, it's a mitzvah to bring food to the house of the mourners. It wasn't personal."

"Didn't you say his daughter has been calling you to thank you? That you promised her you'd bring more?" Basha probed.

Fruma Esther squared her shoulders a little defensively. "It's a *chesed.* The young girls, they don't know how to cook. Not like we cooked for our husbands. Everything is takeout." She paused. "I have been there a few times since the shiva."

"I knew it! You talked?"

"Of course. What, I'll run into the kitchen like I'm delivering from China Glatt? Of course I sat. We talked. His daughter was also there. And the grandchildren."

"So he said something?"

Fruma Esther leaned back against the hard bench. How wonderful it had been to share her loneliness with someone her own age who under-stood the heartbreak of losing a partner of so many years! "We talked about our wedding days, and how it seemed like only yesterday . . ." Tears came to her eyes. Basha quickly offered her a tissue.

"The Torah doesn't say what's not true. It's not good to be alone, Fruma Esther."

"I'm not alone! I have also my daughters, my sons."

"Busy with their own lives, or thousands of miles away in Israel!"

"So they don't call? Every day, almost. You can even see them on the little phone."

"Really?"

She nodded. "My *ayniklach* showed me how. They are my life now."

"They have their own lives, Fruma Esther. And their own parents to take care of them."

"They need as many pairs of hands as they can get to bring them up right, Basha. Believe me."

"I'm not saying not."

"So what are you saying to me?"

"I'm saying that you're lonely, and he's lonely."

"It's not even three months! She's still warm in the grave!"

"Loneliness is suffering, Fruma Esther. And three months of suffering can be like a hundred years."

There was nothing to say. It was true.

"Let's not even talk about such a thing." Fruma Esther sighed.

"Think about it."

How strange, Fruma Esther thought later that evening as she lay down in her solitary bed in her empty room, that something that was never even in your head for a second can suddenly take over your whole mind. It was like a bad virus, she thought, the idea of a shidduch with Rav Alter, spreading and infecting her every waking moment.

As she tossed and turned, she tried to shift her thoughts to Shaindele. Now *that* was something to keep you up all night! *Maybe if I had had a husband, a pious scholar at my side all those years, I could have done better, been wiser. Maybe Zissele would still be here, and Shaindele would still be that frum, dutiful little girl.* For sure there would have been no redheaded *baalas teshuva* dancing around the apartment to the music of *shkotzim*, scandalizing the whole neighborhood. Why had it never once crossed her mind to find another man after her dear Yitzchak Chaim left this world for his reward? Despite all the exhortations in the holy books that we are meant to have partners, the thought had never even crossed her mind. It seemed ridiculous to even imagine another chance at love, at companionship.

But as it is written, when a person sees troubles brewing, let him examine his own acts. Could it be that all this was God's way of showing her that her self-imposed loneliness was not His will? And if so, was this now His plan for her?

Alone in her bed in the little apartment that had grown increasingly solitary with every passing year as one by one the children and grandchildren grew up and moved away, she thought about it. But it was ridiculous. Seventy-five. How does a person that age even stand beneath a chuppah? *Everyone will laugh on me,* she thought. But it wouldn't have to be like the wedding of a young person, she suddenly thought. It could just be a rabbi, a few friends, a few of the children from both sides. No catered hall and groaning, heavy-laden buffet tables; no prancing musicians, no hysterical dancing circles of sweating guests. Just a simple gold ring, the recitation of "You are hereby consecrated unto me by the laws of Moses and Israel." Just a heel smashing a napkin-wrapped glass. Just a simple supper afterward, she yawned, already seeing the table set with challah and gefilte fish. Maybe even *p'tcha.*

It wouldn't be like her first marriage, she thought. It's so different when you're young. The blood races, the stomach knots. You are excited, terrified, too, of the unknown, the forbidden territory of sexual love opening up like iron gates long locked by custom and tradition and law, suddenly, thrillingly, flinging open wide to let you pass through with God's blessing. It would be nothing like that. Just two lonely human beings finding refuge and comfort with each other, leaving enough room between them for all their memories. *He'll bring his Malka Ruth, and I'll bring my Yitzchak Chaim,* she thought. *All four of us would be in such a marriage.* But so what? The table was big enough to hold them. And as they sat across from each other, she could put down a bowl of good soup in front of him and then in front of herself, and a potful would last a week, instead of a month in the freezer like now, with no one to eat her cooking but herself. Who can cook for one? It was depressing and impossible.

Yes, she thought, changing sides again. It could be a good thing. But how to go about it?

She couldn't even imagine. Why, the very idea of approaching the subject with a matchmaker made goose bumps rise on her arms beneath the ankle-length, long-sleeved flannel nightgown and on the scalp beneath the *tichel* that covered her hair even in sleep.

He would have to initiate, not, God forbid, her! It would have to be his idea.

She began to think of ways in which Rav Alter might be helped along to come up with this idea all on his own.

17

⚜

YAAKOV STRUGGLES

His heart was aflame with the kind of passion he had seldom known in his life. *It is all going to hell,* he thought as he tried to concentrate on the numbers and ledgers and computer spreadsheets that took up his desk.

Why is this happening to me? he thought helplessly. *That a daughter of mine could do such a thing . . . go alone into the city at night with a young man who she had been secretly meeting for who knows how long?* A terrible, debilitating thought struck him. Had Leah known about it and kept it from him? And worse. Had she encouraged it?

She was, after all was said and done, and as much as he believed in her and loved her and trusted her, a *baalas teshuva.* She had grown up in a different world, the debased world that he and his whole community invested everything in keeping at bay like a dangerous plague, sheltering the purity of their children from its toxic influence. And here, he had invited a person who had been sick with it into his home! *Had* been sick and sought help and recovered, he chastised himself, ashamed. He hung his head. But while Leah's encounter with the disease of secular life might have given her antibodies and immunity, perhaps it had also seriously clouded her judgment. Just look at her reaction to Shaindele's deceit! As if it were some little, minor problem all teenagers go through, like a bad grade on a test or a pair of stockings in the wrong shade! Imagine! And perhaps in *her* world—that is to say what was *once* her world, he chided himself—it was. But not in his. In his world, it was a complete catastrophe. How didn't she understand that if it got out, his daughter would be ruined: expelled, prevented from graduating with her class, and forever barred from fulfilling her dream of becoming a teacher like her mameh? More, that she would be blackballed by the matchmakers!

Even worse, perhaps, her brothers—those blameless, pious, studious young men far away with their aunt and uncle in Baltimore, innocent of any connection to their sister's waywardness—might also find themselves cut off. If the word spread, no matchmaker in good conscience would be able to offer them the daughters of men willing and able to support them through years of kollel study, men who asked only that their future sons-in-law be serious scholars from impeccable families.

He pinched his forehead, closing his eyes. How had it all come to this? And what was he going to do about it?

It wasn't Leah, he finally understood as he pondered this problem with the sincere honesty and self-reflection that had guided his whole life. It was him, this new life, he thought, looking around at the office with its six-foot-high cubicles and friendly, bareheaded coworkers, a place where strange women wore sweaters and skirts that made him blush.

At first, he had been vigilant in keeping his distance, aware of the dangers inherent in their very proximity. But after a few months, when he got to know them, he realized that they were kind, considerate, and intelligent. He even had to admit that some of them had much better manners than the people in his own community, who were often impatient, pushy, and less than totally ethical. (He thought of Leah's constant battles with her clients to get them to pay their bills.) His ideas about goyim—formed in the insular world of his upbringing—were shamefully stupid, he realized, born of ignorance and prejudice. After months in Manhattan among such people, the yeshiva world, which had once been his entire universe, seemed small and provincial in comparison to the sophisticated, massive life that went on daily in the city. The idea that only in the life of the yeshiva was there meaning and value, everything outside being worthless, seemed as unbelievable now as it had once been the gospel truth.

As this realization stole over him, his steady resistance to the friendly overtures of his work colleagues to join them for lunch or out for drinks began to weaken. He wondered if he was being unfriendly for no reason, especially since it could affect his chances for promotion and raises. And so he'd gone out with them one evening when his boss insisted.

It was a neighborhood restaurant with a long bar. They'd all ordered from the menu, but he'd had no choice but to choose something unmixed for fear of unkosher additives. He'd asked for vodka, which he knew was kosher. "Do you want a twist of lime with that?" the bartender inquired.

"A twist? You mean a piece of fresh fruit, fresh lime?" he ascertained to make sure it posed no halachic problems with kashrut. Assured by the answer, he agreed.

Outside of a sip of wine on Friday nights, four cups during the Passover seder, a tiny plastic cup of scotch after prayers on Shabbos morning, and various drinks on Purim, Yaakov Lehman was a stranger to alcohol. Now he faced a large glass of colorless but potent liquid that he had no choice but to consume to prevent offending those around him. He sipped it carefully. It was actually . . . quite . . . good, he thought, gulping it down.

"Another?"

"Why not?" he laughed, suddenly extremely calm and strangely delighted with himself and everyone else.

After that, the conversations with his coworkers seemed unforced. He gave his opinion on the coming mayoral elections and listened good-naturedly to a detailed analysis of the chances of the New York Jets to make the playoffs, of which he understood nothing.

"So how do you like our little company so far?" one of the secretaries asked him, taking a barstool next to his and staring at him with unfeigned curiosity and admiration as she took in his handsome face and the black velvet skullcap that covered his head.

"Fine, fine. All is good," he said, staring into his drink, mortified by her proximity.

"I don't know how you numbers guys do it all day. I'd go bonkers keeping track of all that." She sighed, wiggling just a little to get comfortable, which brought her stool even closer to his.

"Well," he said, getting up with measured speed. "I have a wife and children waiting at home for me."

She shook her head and laughed. "Okay, whatever."

After that, he begged off such occasions except when he absolutely couldn't get out of it, like company celebrations, birthday parties, or going-away parties. This same woman—her name was Joelle—always seemed to find him.

Maybe that was it, he thought. God was punishing him for talking to Joelle, for trying to be part of this company socially. The more he thought about it, the more upset and confused he became.

I was once a kollel man, a yungerman. *But who am I now?*

He had no time to think about it. His employer was paying him to work, not daydream or worry. It was a sin not to give a full, honest day's labor, he scolded himself. With the self-discipline that comes with decades of training in fulfilling the will of God with meticulous, wholehearted obedience, Yaakov forced himself back to his work.

As he stood swaying from the subway pole in the crowded F train on his way home that evening, his weary mind searched for answers, for encouragement, but it was simply blank, a used canvas muddied by failed attempts to create something skillful, something beautiful. He just wanted to go inside the small, rented apartment that was his home and be served a hot dinner by the woman he loved, surrounded by his children, with no questions asked, no tasks required of him as the moral head of his household. He did not want to fight with his beloved young wife, his Leah. He did not want to show an angry, bitter face to his beloved Shaindele, to fill the room with outpourings of indignation and disappointment. He just wanted to be left alone.

But when he got off the subway and crept down the stairs, to his surprise, his feet took him in another direction altogether. It was only when he stood before the door of Rav Alter's home that he understood where he had been led and why.

The door opened slowly. It was the rav's married daughter.

"I'm so sorry. My name is Yaakov Lehman. I must speak with the rav."

"Does he know you?"

"Ah, yes, for many years. I used to learn with him."

She sighed, but opened the door wider. "Sit down, I'll tell him you're here."

"Oh, I don't want to bother—"

"Please, sit. He'd be upset with me if I let you go without asking him first."

He sat down nervously, his fingers drumming on his bent knees, feeling ashamed at this imposition and yet helpless to do anything about it.

"He says to come into his study."

He followed her. As many years as he had known Rav Alter, he had never been to his home except once during shiva. There was an unwritten rule that it was off limits to all those beseeching his counsel and time, the last bastion of peace for the old man, his sanctuary. The study was empty.

"He says to sit; he'll come in a minute."

He sat down, every passing second like a slap in the face for his shamelessness in intruding on the old scholar's private time. But before he could flee in shame, the door opened, and Rav Alter entered.

"My dear Yaakov." The rav smiled.

Yaakov remembered their last meeting, and the shiva call after the rav's wife passed away. But for some reason, even after all he'd gone through, the rav looked better now. All the tension had disappeared, and a transformative serenity bathed all his features. He actually seemed younger, steadier. It was almost a miracle, and one that gave Yaakov hope.

"I'm so sorry to come here without calling. I just had to talk to you."

"You need to call me? Yaakov, Yaakov." He shook his head in mock remonstrance. "Does a son need an appointment to see his father?"

Yaakov blushed, the hard lump of agony in his throat, and in his heart, dissolving. "I wouldn't have come, but I'm so lost!"

The rav put his arm around Yaakov, leading him to a sofa. "Tell me."

"All those years I spent learning. Were they a mistake?"

Rav Alter seemed surprised. "Do you think they were?"

"I don't know. Look where I am now. Like everybody else, in an office, using my brains and skills to earn a living, to make money. When I was in yeshiva, we were taught that: 'God would provide for our every need.'"

The old man shook his head. "Those were wonderful years, your years in yeshiva, in kollel. We convince our young men to give up everything, to learn. To become like the caretakers of the Holy Temple, the tribe of Levi, who were supported by the rest of the tribes to do their holy work. But each man also has his private destiny. Didn't Yaakov our forefather work from sunup to sundown tending the flocks of Laban, a dishonest employer who changed his salary dozens of times? God could have given him gold and jewels, but instead He let him succeed at supporting himself through honest work. Moses, too, worked hard tending the sheep of his father-in-law. This was the task that fell to him, his destiny. Only when God intervened and changed his destiny did he do something else. Was Moses the shepherd less worthy than Moses the prophet? Both tasks were given to him by the same God, and he served his Creator in both."

Yaakov was still not convinced. "But is it right for *me* to abandon the role I always thought was mine?" he cried, his heart aching.

"You know, the great Rav Avigdor Miller once said, 'To be in kollel when it's possible to be in kollel is a beautiful ideal. But when it's not possible, it becomes a sin.'"

Yaakov looked up, startled.

"You are struggling, Yaakov, I can see that. As do we all. Every creature who lives must struggle. Did you ever watch an ant?"

Yaakov thought back to the miserable day he had decided to go to Lakewood and become a beggar. Forlorn, he had realized that he couldn't even eat the lunch that had been packed for him because there was no water to ritually wash his hands. Instead, he had crumbled the bread and cast it on the sidewalk, watching a colony of ants bear it away with single-minded strength and courage. That was the pivotal moment he shamefully realized that he had no other choice but to leave the kollel and go out to work.

"But my life has so many challenges—my marriage, working, bringing up my children—I don't know if I can do it all. I feel so lost outside the yeshiva. So incompetent."

Rabbi Alter placed a fatherly arm around Yaakov's broad shoulders. "You must have faith that this is the situation into which a loving God has placed you. He would not have given you these challenges if He did not believe you could overcome them. Believe in God, Yaakov. Believe in yourself. As it is written: *The righteous man shall live by his faith.* It is just ego that prompts you to want the glory of being the next Rabbi Akiva. Instead, let your goal in life become being a better Yaakov Lehman—a better husband, a better father, a better accountant."

Something in those simple words struck him. Yes, that was the real answer. Yaakov nodded. "But I also want to keep learning. I have to."

"Of course! The Torah you learn will remind you that every small, ordinary thing you do is also for His sake." He took Yaakov's hand and pressed it. "Know Him in all your ways."

Yaakov looked into the old man's eyes. *No, it wasn't a mistake, all those years I spent learning,* he thought, remembering those glorious moments in time when he felt he had succeeded in looking at his life and the world through the eyes of God. *I would not be Yaakov Lehman without that investment of time and effort but someone else, someone lesser, in my own eyes.*

"Thank you so much, Rav. I can't tell you how you've helped me. May HaShem bless you and your family. Please forgive me for stealing from your private time. It won't happen again."

"Yaakov, my dear son, if you need me, come to me. It is always a joy to see you."

They embraced, then parted.

If only he could speak to the rav every day, he thought as he hurried home through the dark streets; get such encouragement every day as in his yeshiva days, when all he needed to do was go up one flight and stand outside his door!

But what he had done tonight couldn't happen very often, however generous the rav had been to make him feel otherwise. He suddenly felt as bereft as a child whose mother had dropped him off at a strange new boarding school. He would have to learn to manage on his own.

As he walked home through the dark streets toward the family and home he loved, he prayed that his years of learning had given him the wisdom to bring with him through his front door the kind of answers that would bless them all. The alternative was unthinkable.

18

$$\approx$$

A FAMILY IN TURMOIL

"Yaakov," Leah said, opening the door with an uncertain half smile on her face. She was happy to see him; she couldn't help that, but also filled with a certain dread of what was going to happen now. So much had been left unsaid after the bombshell of Shaindele's revelations. Aside from the harsh restrictions now in place, they had failed to be honest with each other about how they were going to get through this together, as man and wife, parents, lovers.

"My Leah-le," he said with something of the old affection of their courting days.

A huge wave of relief coursed through her. Her eyes brightened as she brought her hand to his shoulder, lightly touching his coat. "You are so late. I was worried."

Of course! How had he forgotten to call her? "I'm so sorry, Leah. I went to talk to Rav Alter," he said, coming into the living room and clasping her hand until he reluctantly released himself to take off his coat and hang it in the closet.

There was so much she wanted to say to him, but soon the children were streaming out of their bedrooms.

"Tateh! Tateh!" they shouted, running to him. His face lit up with joy as he gathered his little boy and girl fondly in his arms. From the corner of his eye, he saw that Shaindele, too, had come to greet him, hanging back in the hallway, her shoulder pressed against the wall, her arms crossed protectively.

He put down Chasya and with his newly freed arm beckoned to his daughter. She, too, was his little girl. "Come," he said.

She approached him with the caution of a small creature facing the unknown.

He kissed her forehead warmly. "My Shaindele," he whispered.

That hard nugget inside her she had been nurturing, polishing to a dark gleam, suddenly shattered like a ball of ice, melting away. She raised tear-filled eyes to his face. "I'm so sorry, Tateh. For everything. I'll do better, *bli neder*. I'll make you proud of me."

"I am always proud of you, even when I'm not so happy about the things you decide to do." He smiled at her.

Leah stood back, watching, amazed. It was almost a miracle, she thought. She had expected a confrontation, stubbornness, recriminations. And while her experience with him had never included shouting matches in anger or deliberate cruelty, she had seen him capable of detachment and coldness, which for her was just as devastating. Honestly, she had been preparing herself for rejection. It was inevitable that he would blame her for his daughter's waywardness, given her own upbringing. Why should he be any different than the rest of Boro Park?

Yet here he was together with them again! A father, a husband, not a judge, jury, and executioner. Her own eyes reflected the relief in Shaindele's as the girl's young body went limp against her father's, allowing him to support her, Leah noticed with enormous relief. Rejection from her father at this moment, when she was so confused and rebellious, would have been akin to lighting fireworks during a gas leak.

"Why don't we all sit down and have dinner?" she suggested with a smile, looking around the table. And then, privately, to him alone, "Afterward, when the little ones go to sleep, we need to talk."

He nodded, fear in his heart, dreading it, but grateful to have her honesty and her wisdom. Another woman might have taken advantage of his obvious attempt at placation and let it slide, instead of seeing it for what it was: a desperate and perhaps a bit cowardly attempt to salvage something useful and whole from a disastrous wreck.

Mordechai Shalom was beginning to yawn.

"Better lay him down," she told Yaakov, who bore him into his bedroom and tucked him in with a kiss.

But Chasya wasn't going anywhere, Leah realized. The child's eyes were bright, and a nervous vivacity informed all her movements.

"I learned how to say a new *bracha*," Chasya announced, climbing up into her father's lap as he sat down at the dining room table, settling in comfortably even though she'd already had her dinner hours ago. Leah, who was attached to the child body and soul, understood that her sharp, sensitive little mind had absorbed all the disharmony in the house with growing agitation. *Let her sit in her father's arms,* she thought wisely.

"I thought you knew them all already!" Yaakov teased her. "So what new thing did you find to make a blessing over?"

"A tree. With flowers on it!" she exclaimed triumphantly. "You say, 'Blessed are You, God, our God, King of the universe, Who left nothing lacking in His world, and created within it good creatures and good trees with which He gives pleasure to people,'" she recited in Hebrew, her tongue tripping a little over the unfamiliar words.

Yaakov looked over her head, exchanging a small smile of quiet pride with Leah. He bent his head forward, lowering it so that his eyes were level with the child's. "And what did you see that made you want to say this *bracha*, Chasya?"

"An almond tree. It was all white, like a bride!"

Yaakov laughed, kissing the top of her little head.

My Yaakov, Leah thought, feeling the moisture gather in her eyes.

"Such a thing there is in Boro Park?" he asked.

Leah smiled, shaking her head. "I know, right? But there's a private house next to her school with a garden in the back that she can see from her classroom window. Chasya has apparently been checking out this tree every day. Yesterday, it finally blossomed. She was so excited, she started jumping up and down. Until her teacher figured out what was going on . . ." She shook her head with mock horror. "But when Chasya pointed out the tree, the teacher decided to use it for educational purposes."

Her mind drifted back to California, to Santa Clara, where she had gone to university. It would be filled with budding trees this time of year. And lawns would be like carpets, the scent of mown grass perfuming the air. Chasya would love it there.

Yaakov noticed her preoccupation. He was attuned to her now with a kind of hypersensitivity to compensate, he realized, for those secret, shameful thoughts he had harbored against her. What was she really thinking about? And how had it come to pass that he didn't know and was afraid to ask her?

Leah suddenly noticed him staring at her. She got up abruptly. "I'll go get the soup."

As she served the meal, she thought, *I should be thrilled and grateful that he has come home with such a different attitude!* And part of her was. But another place in her heart that was more obstinate and harder to reach held back. Today he had obviously gotten some *mussar* from Rav Alter. But what of tomorrow? How would they navigate raising these children when there was such an enormous gap between them of background and culture?

Someone making a video of this meal from a drone hovering above their heads, she thought, would have seen a relaxed, normal family, sharing delicious food, asking each other about their day, laughing at the little girl who sat ensconced in her father's arms making jokes and preening in the adoration of her family. They would not have noticed either the tenseness in the eyes of the eldest daughter, or how she merely pushed the food around in her plate, eating almost nothing; nor the overly solicitous way the young wife and mother made sure to keep all the serving platters filled and the water pitcher replenished; nor even the strongest hint of all that something was amiss from the husband and father, who hardly stopped talking and joking and smiling, but with a smile that stayed captured at his lips, never rising to his eyes.

After the dishes were cleared away and Chasya had been reluctantly tucked into bed and Shaindele had wished them both good night, they sat back down at the newly scrubbed dining room table across from each other. The sofa—the only other place they could sit together aside from their bed—seemed too intimate a space somehow for the kind of conversation they needed to have, an exchange that despite all their good intentions would inevitably pitch them against each other harshly. It was the first time she had felt so alienated from him during the precious time they were allowed to be together. *What a waste!* she thought, heartsick.

"Yaakov, I spoke to Shaindele about what happened."

He lifted his head alertly. "And what did she tell you?"

She sighed. How to say this to him without breaking his heart? "I think we both haven't realized how much her mother's death has damaged her."

"Damaged?" His heart lurched at the word, which intuitively he knew was the correct one. It terrified him.

"Yes. She is having all kinds of doubts."

"About what?"

"Well, about herself mostly. She wonders if what her mother suffered from, that disease, is inside her, too, and if she gets married and has children, if the same thing will happen to her."

"*HaShem Yishmor!*" What was there to say? Of course, it should have been obvious. But then everything should have been obvious. His young wife's depressions after each birth and their escalating nature. Why, any educated person would have known it for what it was immediately! But he along with his community were too *ignorant,* too *backward,* and too *primitive,* he thought bitterly, getting a dark satisfaction in choosing the harshest words possible, not only to recognize it but to find her the help she needed in time.

"But what does this have to do with the boy? The lying? The trips to the city?"

She exhaled, lacing her fingers through his. "I don't know, really. I can only tell you what she told me. She said she was afraid that she would never want to be together with a man and that she was encouraged when she found she liked this boy and wanted to be with him."

"But what of all the rules of modesty we taught her? What she knows from living in a religious community all her life? What about the dangers? She knows better than anyone what will happen to her and her brothers if this gets out. Better than anyone!" he repeated with savage satisfaction. "Wasn't she the one who was most upset about us getting married? And just because she thought it would hurt her shidduch chances? Hysterical enough to run away and plan to get engaged before it happened, when she was barely sixteen?"

"Please, lower your voice."

Yaakov leaned back, removing his hand and using it to cover his eyes. All his good intentions!

"Yaakov, she was absolutely clear about understanding that what she did could have terrible consequences for herself and for the family. She was not confused about that at all. But you are talking about a young, troubled girl. Someone who lost her mother and blamed herself." Should she tell him the rest, about her loss of faith? About how far it had gone with Duvie? *How can I? How can I not? It's his daughter, after all. He has the right to know. He has to understand.* She inhaled sharply.

"There is something else."

He looked up at her, frightened now. "There's more?"

She nodded, taking both his hands in hers. "She is questioning everything she's ever learned or been taught right now. Even"—she hesitated— "her faith."

He flung himself off his chair and paced the room frantically. "Even that," he muttered to himself. He looked at Leah. "And what did you tell her?"

She didn't like his tone of voice. Was that an accusation, a reprimand?

She equivocated, somehow losing confidence in the things she had told the girl about the origin of her own faith, which at the time she had felt to be beautiful and heartfelt. But what if it wasn't? What if it was wrong? What if it upset him? "I don't remember every word I said. But I know I told her I wasn't qualified to answer her questions. That she should talk to you or to a rav."

Was that even true? But it must be! It's what she should have said.

He nodded, relieved, taking his place again across from her. "And what else?"

"She asked me why I'd left the secular world where I could do anything I wanted, to come to Boro Park."

"And what did you say?"

"I told her that it was better here. I told her about all the dangerous things out there and how you were just trying to protect her. But honestly, Yaakov, your daughter needs real help. A person with psychological training who can listen to her and understand how to help her overcome her real fears before she destroys her life."

The cold clutch of the icy hand of terror laid hold of him now. Her mother's daughter, he thought, horrified. He couldn't make the same mistake twice.

"You are right. She needs a psychologist. But if you say she has problems also with her faith, then it must be a *frum* one, someone who understands our beliefs, our way of life."

"There has to be someone that the rabbis recommend, no? You can ask around. This would be better than punishing her, which won't help, believe me."

He was heartbroken at the recognition that it was not within his power to reach his own child with the burning certainty of his own deep faith, as well as frightened of the consequences of sending a young girl off to some stranger who would hear her most intimate thoughts, who would come to know her better than he, her own father. But when a person is sick, he needs a doctor, he told himself. If he had learned anything in this life, he had learned that.

19

THE RABBI-PSYCHOLOGIST

But before Yaakov could even make any inquiries, something happened that tied his hands. Or perhaps made things easier and clearer? He could not decide. He received a phone call from Shaindele's school. Rabbi Shlomo Halpern's secretary informed him that he and his wife and his daughter were to meet with the rabbi in his office the next day.

"But I work. I can't take a day off just like that," Yaakov protested to the woman, his heart sinking at what this could mean.

"Well, this is up to you. I'll tell him," she said without a hint of understanding or compromise. "But in that case, you should tell your daughter not to come in to school."

He felt faint. But then a sudden anger shot through him like righteous wrath. "Well, *in that case,* please tell the rabbi that we'll come only if his son Duvie is also there. Either that, or we'll come to talk to him when I get home from work. And," he added pointedly, "Shaindele comes home from school." He hung up. It didn't take long for the phone to ring again.

"Seven o'clock," the woman said.

"Seven thirty," he answered firmly, then hung up.

"What should I wear?" Leah asked him, almost trembling.

"Why, Leah-le, you always look beautiful and modest. Wear whatever you always wear, my love."

Comforted, but not convinced, she put on her longest sleeves and highest neck, the blouse she called her "*frum* fantasy." It was an itchy material, and the collar, so high, grazed her ears with annoying frequency. The cuffs, made of some ruffled pattern, were useless anywhere except the synagogue, where all you had to do was hold a prayer book; even just washing out a cup, they'd be soaked and ruined. The skirt was equally useless. Midcalf and A-line, its dark blue linen wrinkled the moment you sat down or bent over. But it was the right length and suitably boring. The hair was the easiest problem to solve. A wide turban allowed her to heap her abundant curls to the top of her head, tying them down with so many hairpins that a wisp had as much chance of escaping as the Boston Bomber. No makeup, she decided. Nothing.

Yaakov looked her over and smiled. "You look like a nun." He chuckled.

"I just want it to be all right. For Shaindele."

He inhaled. "We don't have to impress *him*. He has a lot of explaining to do, and he knows it, my love. *He* is the one who should be ashamed of himself. To raise such a son!"

She listened to him with surprise. After all, a call from the principal's office had been their worst nightmare in all this, no? Yet Yaakov seemed not only calm but indignant and more than ready to do battle. Shaindele appeared in her school uniform, her face closed but calm and without a trace of the fear and dread Leah had expected. It was actually impressive, the two of them, Leah thought, surprised.

"Ready?" Yaakov asked his daughter gently.

In response, she shrugged.

Leah reached out, caressing her shoulder. "We are going to be there with you the whole time. No one will dare to hurt or insult you. Whatever you've done, you didn't do it all by yourself."

Yaakov, hearing her, winced but did not contradict her. Even if he had wanted to, it was too late, as the teenage daughter of their upstairs neighbor, hired to babysit, walked in, ending their privacy.

He reached out to his daughter. "Come, child."

The school was deserted, the classrooms silent, the halls dark. It was, Shaindele thought, like walking into a nightmare. Everything the same, but subtly, eerily sinister. Like your bedroom as a child when there is no moon and the lights go out.

Was she about to be thrown out of school? And did it matter? She wasn't sure. But then, what would her life look like? The dream of being a teacher would be flushed away like an appetizing meal that had undergone a process of digestion, leaving it putrid waste. This bothered her more than the idea that the shadchonim wouldn't want to find her a husband. Who needed a husband? Only you didn't want your family to suffer because of you, of what you'd done. You didn't want your good and pious tateh looked at sideways, whispered about; or your kind if clueless stepmother maligned and turned into the butt of jokes or malicious lies and gossip. And why should your blameless, naive older brothers ensconced in their comfortable little haredi lives, the lives they'd been brought up in and were eager to continue, be thrown off course by roadblocks they'd done nothing to erect? Let them punish her all they wanted, she thought bravely. Just let them leave her family alone.

But would anything be up to her at this point? Or was it all a lost battle and they'd been summoned simply to negotiate the terms of their surrender?

They ascended the stairs where a sliver of light banded beneath a single door. They didn't knock, walking immediately inside. The secretary was gone, her desk a pile of loose papers in disarray. The door to the principal's office stood open. Yaakov walked through, beckoning to his wife and daughter to follow.

Rabbi Halpern didn't get up, waving off-handedly toward the hard chairs that were arranged in a semicircle at a safe distance from the large desk behind which he was barricaded.

Yaakov ignored him, standing tall, but nodded to Leah and Shaindele to be seated.

"Rav Halpern," he said, offering the man his hand, "*Shalom aleichem.*"

Reluctantly, the other man half rose, taking it. "*Aleichem shalom,* Rav Lehman," he responded without enthusiasm, averting his eyes from the women with a thin pretense of piety that did little to mask the obvious hostility and arrogance transparent in the twisted puckering of his thick lips beneath the heavy dark mustache and even heavier beard.

Shaindele glanced at him, shot through with the shocking realization of how much he looked like his son. He had Duvie's large, arrogant, widely spaced eyes. Even his face, gone slack and jowly through overindulgence and weakness, still held a hint of his son's handsome high cheekbones. *This is how Duvie will look in twenty-five years, with or without a beard and tzitzis and a yarmulke. He'll be a weak man who loves his pleasures, and he will never have his fill of them,* she thought with surprising insight. Staying religious wouldn't make him a better man, just one with different vices. Anything spiritual in such men would always be just a light first coat slapped on a ruined, distempered wall full of cracks waiting to show themselves.

Then he caught her eye for a moment, and a look passed between them that sent a chill up her spine. Was it an appraisal? Was it a sensual, older man looking at a young girl, imagining her body beneath her clothes? Was that even possible? She shivered, lowering her eyes quickly and staring at the floor.

Leah reached over and squeezed her limp white hand, surprised that despite Shaindele's outer show of complete indifference, it was trembling. Shaindele didn't let go.

"We all know why we are here," Rabbi Halpern began.

"Not really," Yaakov countered. Why should he give an inch?

Rabbi Halpern cleared his throat. This obviously wasn't going as he had expected. "Your daughter's behavior. Let me be frank, if she were anyone else but Fruma Esther's granddaughter, she would have been thrown out of our school long ago."

"And why is that, Rav Halpern?" Yaakov said mildly, raising his brows.

"Don't pretend you don't know what's been going on!"

"I think your family is more to blame for that than my innocent young daughter!"

Rabbi Halpern leaned back. "*HaShem Yishmor. My* family?"

"Yes, your son. Your Duvie. Don't *you* pretend we don't know everything."

Rabbi Halpern sighed heavily with a show of saintly patience, as if greatly put upon without justification. "Yes. With my son. My Duvie. But if not him, it would have been someone else."

Yaakov slammed a fist into his open palm. "That is *mamash* a *farsh-tunkene* chutzpah! You sit behind that desk, you think you're so important you're *potur*? Your son took that job in the pizza place to meet girls, girls from *your* school. My innocent young daughter is not the only girl he started up with. You think you're the only one with informants?"

Like chalk from a blackboard, the arrogant certainty was suddenly erased from Rabbi Halpern's face, Leah saw with a mixture of satisfaction and fright. She could not believe Yaakov was behaving like this! It was thrilling.

"You knew he was a danger to the community, yet you sheltered him instead of sending him away."

Rabbi Halpern visibly shrank. "A father does not give up on a son so easily. We had hopes—"

"You should have been more concerned for the girls in your care than your son! But *gornisht*! Aren't you the principal? Don't you have responsibilities?"

"We aren't here to talk about Duvie!"

"And why not?" Leah interjected firmly. "*K'vod harav,* that is exactly what we are here to talk about."

"And your child, your Shaindele? She bears no responsibility? She has been meeting with Duvie for months."

"Months?" Yaakov lost his certainty.

"Ask her!" He nodded disgustedly toward Shaindele, who for the first time looked up.

"It's true," she admitted, shaking.

"So what now?" Leah said, wanting it to end for all their sakes.

"Tell me why I shouldn't throw your daughter out of our school before she infects the *hashkofa* of the rest of her classmates."

"If you tell me one good reason I shouldn't go to the *rabbonim* and the entire community and tell them how you protected your son and endangered our girls when for months you obviously *knew all about it.*"

The two pious, bearded men looked across at each other like well-matched, battered prize fighters in the tenth round.

"Let me . . . I have a suggestion," Leah interjected. "We are all pious people here who love HaShem, are we not? As it is written: *Be compassionate because He is compassionate.* Where is Duvie now?"

Rabbi Halpern shrugged. "He's gone. We think he went out west."

"Las Vegas," Shaindele mumbled.

"What?" Rabbi Halpern asked, all ears.

"She doesn't know," Yaakov said firmly. "In any case, you say he isn't around anymore?"

"Let him go to *Gehinnom*. I was done with him anyway. He's a jerk," Shaindele continued under her breath.

Yaakov shook his head at her fiercely, and she went silent again. "What is your idea, Leah?"

"Rav Halpern, you know the Lehman family has undergone a terrible tragedy. I'm sure you can imagine, *k'vod harav,* how very hard it was for Shaindele to lose her mother at such a young age and to have so many responsibilities fall on her young shoulders! It has left her traumatized. Even before this meeting, her father and I spoke about getting her psychological help."

Rabbi Halpern sat back in his chair. He nodded. "This is a good idea. But on one condition—that you use the psychologist approved by *our rabbonim,* the only one we send our girls to."

"So you agree she can finish her year and graduate?" Leah pressed, not taking any chances.

"If you arrange for Shaindele to have counseling, we will consider this whole matter closed—that is, if she keeps up with her counseling and we get good reports, and of course if she keeps up her grades," he added almost as an afterthought.

"And Duvie isn't coming back to Boro Park?"

Rabbi Halpern nodded stiffly. "He is dead to me now."

"Surely—" Leah began, shocked, but one look from Yaakov silenced her. This was none of their business.

"And who exactly is this psychologist?"

"Rav Yoel Grub."

"I will look into it," Yaakov said.

"He's the only one we'll accept," Halpern repeated.

"I said, I'll look into it."

———

According to everyone Yaakov spoke to, Yoel Grub was a tzaddik. "He helped my child. She was broken, and he made her whole again," said one of the people he turned to. "He has been treating young people for twenty-five years. All the *rabbonim* send young people to him." "He is a close friend of the Bobelger Rebbe." Of his professional qualifications, the same people were a bit less certain. "A degree in psychology. From Brooklyn College," they offered. "I heard rabbinical counseling training from Yeshiva University," someone else said.

But it was useless. When Yaakov called to make an appointment for Shaindele, he couldn't even get through. "Leave a message, and God willing, I will get back to you," the recording said. "This is normal," his advisors assured Yaakov. "He is up to the roof in clients. He is the best. It could take months."

Yaakov didn't have months. So he called Rav Alter, who agreed to intervene.

"Yoel Grub, you say? And he is a psychiatrist?"

"Psychologist. They say he is very close to the Bobelger Rebbe. Please, Rav Alter, it's my Shaindele. She needs help, after all she's been through."

"Yes, yes. Of course. Don't worry."

Rav Alter, who had never heard this name, was troubled. He picked up the phone wishing to speak to his old friend, the Bobelger Rebbe himself, but was surprised to find himself stonewalled, only getting as far as the nephew. "Hundreds of our girls have gone to him over the years," the nephew told him enthusiastically. "He specializes in these kinds of problems, especially the ones who start to have doubts. God be blessed. He helps them and their parents. I can recommend him without a single hesitation. Don't worry. I'll ask the rebbe to call him to make room for the girl immediately."

Through this exalted connection, the phone soon rang, and an appointment was arranged for Shaindele. And because Yoel Grub was a respected member of their own community, whose character and piety had been vouched for by numerous acquaintances as well as many *rabbonim*, Yaakov was spared the anxiety of this damaging the family's reputation in any way. Such a man knew how to be discreet.

For the first time in months, Yaakov felt he was truly leading his family down a safe and comfortable road. He was grateful and hopeful. Shaindele, too, felt the world was becoming a safer, saner place. She was actually looking forward to it.

No one had a clue.

20

❧

SOME ENCHANTED
EVENING

After much consideration and the weighing of many options, Fruma Esther decided on rugelach.

"I'll make them pareve, so he can eat them with coffee and as a dessert after meat." Having resolved that dilemma, she went on to the next serious hurdle: chocolate, nuts, or cinnamon? Chocolate, while the hands-down favorite in certain circles, was not so good for people with indigestion, which she assumed Rav Alter must have. After all, didn't most elderly Jews? Cinnamon, the healthier option, was popular, too, but bland as far as she was concerned. After deep reflection, she came up with the following compromise: cinnamon with nuts, with just a trace of chocolate. It was pure genius.

She took out her baking pans, bowls, sifter, and rolling pin. She didn't own measuring cups and wouldn't have known what to do with them since all her recipes had come from watching her mother and grandmother and aunts cook, and they measured by seeing how much fit into their hands. As for liquid, you just had to have a feeling for it, she'd been told, and she had certainly developed one.

There were two camps about pareve rugelach: the ones that added yeast and the ones that insisted on cookie dough. She thought yeast made them doughy and little more attractive than soggy bread. A crisp, sweet cookie dough, on the other hand, was irresistible. As for rugelach dough made with cream cheese, she would have been shocked and scandalized. "What is the point of a rugelach that you cannot eat on Shabbos after a heavy meat meal?" she would have scoffed, resisting the very notion.

Still, her mother's recipe had undergone some variations over the years, the most shocking of which was the addition of a secret ingredient that she guarded zealously even from her friends and relatives. She did not feel guilty or give into pressure as—rugelach in hand—they approached her at a kiddush, Shabbos meals, or festive holiday occasions, swooning over her rugelach and begging, demanding, and finally pleading to know how she got them so . . . so . . . indescribably scrumptious. Light, crispy, they melted in your mouth like butter, even though they were nondairy! She smiled to herself. *Why should I tell them? Let them remember what I was worth. Let them know I knew some things they didn't. Let them miss me when I'm gone.*

She sifted the flour carefully, checking for bugs. Only when she was satisfied the flour was perfectly clean did she add it to her food processor. She had tried her mother's way with two knives—such a pain in the neck! This way was perfection. Next she added the cold margarine cut into cubes. The machine took two minutes to turn it into a perfect mixture of pastry dough beginnings. Now was the time for the secret ingredient. Taking it out of her refrigerator carefully, she was cautious not to shake it and have it overflow once she opened it. It was only a small bottle, and losing a large amount would leave her short. Knowing this, she nevertheless never went for a larger size. She was aware some people actually drank and enjoyed it, and it was always prominently displayed on buffet tables along with Coca-Cola and 7 Up. But after trying it once, she had almost gagged and would have as soon drunk it willingly as dishwashing liquid. Anything left over from the bottle when she finished making the rugelach dough would be poured directly down the sink. Adding some sugar, she buzzed the whole thing a few more minutes, then wrapped the light, fluffy dough in parchment paper and placed it in the refrigerator. When she was done, she threw away whatever remained of the secret ingredient—a little bottle of Sprite.

Now all she had to do was wait. It would take a few hours before she could roll out the dough and sprinkle it with the cinnamon and nuts and cocoa, rolling it up into the delicious crescents that would surely be something Rav Alter would soon realize he couldn't live without.

Like a general back at headquarters, she calmly and expertly considered every aspect of her upcoming campaign. Long ago, she had dismissed the idea of going to a shadchan. At her age, why involve some middle-aged yenta in her private life? So she could have a good laugh and tell all her neighbors and friends? Ridiculous. Besides, why give Rav Alter the idea he had a choice?

Instead, she worked on what she considered a far more problematic issue: *yichud*. So far, Rav Alter's daughter had always been there and hadn't thought it odd that she'd been coming by a few times a week to drop off food. Why would she? Many women were doing the same, of all ages and marital statuses. But having the daughter in the way had become an impediment, she realized. Like the pillar of fire in the desert that protected the fleeing Hebrew slaves from their pursuing Egyptian slave masters, the young woman hovered protectively between the do-gooders and her father, never letting anyone get near enough for a private word. But the daughter had her own family to care for. Someone had dropped the golden nugget of information into Fruma Esther's lap that today, the daughter would be home nursing a sick husband. *Nebbech*.

How this information got to her was as circuitous as it was reliable and unique. She had spies everywhere: the woman who prepared food for the kollel students where the son-in-law learned. The grocery lady where he picked up supplies for the family on his way home. Even the dry cleaners who saw to it his black suits were immaculate and his white prayer shawl as white as snow. Reports had come in from all over. So today was her opportunity.

Her usual time to come was the morning, just as Rav Alter was coming home from his morning prayers. But everyone was in such a rush that time of day, especially Rav Alter, who hurried through breakfast to get back to yeshiva where a horde of yentas and needy yeshiva *schlimazels* awaited him, lined up outside his office door to bother him over the trivial details of their lives because they couldn't fend for themselves for two seconds! So coming in the morning was a waste of time. What she needed was to find a time when he was alone and in no rush. How else to get his attention and show him she wasn't like the others?

Then the thought struck her with such simplicity that she couldn't imagine that she'd missed it. Early evening, right after he came back from evening prayers, but before he started his evening *shiur*. Even if his daughter stole a few minutes to look in on him, she'd be long gone by then, at home taking care of her own troubles.

As she took out the chilled dough from the refrigerator, dividing it into four round pieces, each one of which she divided into numerous triangles that she then rolled into crescents, the idea went dreamily through her head. Yes, he would be grateful for a little company from a woman his own age, a woman who had experienced loss, a pious woman who knew what it was to live by the side of a revered scholar and *posek* whose doorbell never stopped ringing. A woman who knew how to fill a man's home with good cooking smells and cleanliness and order; who knew how to talk to such a man without making him feel burdened, weighed down with responsibilities to come up with solutions to problems that only God Himself could solve; a woman who knew when to put in a comforting word and when to keep her lips sealed.

She had a vision, right there in her kitchen. It was a modest one, nothing like the prophets who saw dry bones rising and being covered with sinews and flesh and becoming a great army; nothing like chariots with four-headed horses. It was a vision of lamplight and an old armchair in which an elderly, bearded man sat with his holy books while in the corner, on a flowered sofa, she herself sat with her long plastic knitting needles twining fine wool around her arthritic fingers, content to be once more a wife, part of a couple, useful, the long loneliness banished, and the blackness of the street—which held within it hints of the terrifying descent into the permanent darkness to come—was held at bay by the reflections of light from within the room, creating a bastion, a shining fortress, that would comfort her frightened and aching heart.

She rolled out the dough—which was perfect—then pinched generous amounts of the sweet, cinnamon-chocolate filling with its chopped walnuts, sprinkling it evenly over the smooth surface. Finally, she rolled each piece into a little crescent, which she dabbed with egg yolk, then sprinkled with more nuts. Placing her little treasures carefully in the oven, she set her timer, waiting for the glorious moment when her entire apartment would be filled with the heavenly scent like incense on the altar in the Holy of Holies. As she opened the oven door, she breathed it in. To fill Rav Alter's sad home with such a smell! She straightened her back. Now all she had to do was wait for them to be cool enough to handle.

21

❦

FIRST MEETING

The office of Yoel Grub was in a run-down office building housing a dental clinic, a chiropractor, the headquarters of some *schnoring* organization, and what seemed to be a factory producing orthopedic shoe inserts. Leah could hear the machines whirring from the moment she opened the front door to the building.

"Rabbi Yoel Grub, rabbinical counselor, fourth floor, number fifteen," Leah read out loud from the building directory on the distempered wall.

Rabbinical counselor? Leah raised her brows. The word *psychologist* was nowhere to be found. But given the stigma of such things in Boro Park, she thought she understood.

"Okay, let's go."

But Shaindele didn't immediately follow her to the elevator.

"What's wrong?"

"I don't know. Maybe this is not a good idea."

Leah was stumped. "But, honey, I thought we agreed that this way you can finish school, go to seminary, start teaching. Isn't that what you want?"

"*Avadeh.* But this place . . ." She rolled her eyes.

Leah couldn't disagree. In fact, she was getting the same feeling. It just didn't look very professional. "But it's not the place that's important, honey, it's the person. Maybe this is all he can afford. Fancy offices come with fancy prices, and most of the girls he treats are from our kind of families." Not that this was going to be free, mind you. She shuddered to think how the family was going to manage the hundreds of dollars this was going to cost. But as Yaakov said, nothing was more important than the welfare of the children. Besides, the alternative was going to destroy any chance this young girl had of moving forward in life. It was unthinkable.

Shaindele nodded, unconvinced. She pressed the button on the elevator in the dingy lobby. But Leah hesitated. "They said to use the service elevator," Leah told her, reading the signs that indicated it was in the back of the building.

"Why?"

Leah shrugged. It seemed odd to her, too.

They opened the heavy, old elevator door and entered. Thick, musty carpets lined the inside, giving off the acrid smell of a long-abandoned factory. They walked out into a dark and deserted hallway that stank of dust and despair. Most of the doors were boarded up, they saw, the entrance obviously being from the other side. Shaindele walked ahead quickly.

"Here."

A small hand-lettered sign with the number fifteen—the number they'd been given when they'd made the appointment—was the only indication they'd arrived at their destination. While Leah hadn't thought anything about it at the time, now she wondered. Why was there no normal professional office sign indicating *Dr. Yoel Grub* or *Rabbi Dr. Yoel Grub*? It just looked so disreputable, like some secretive criminal enterprise selling stolen goods or hash. A chill went through her.

"I'll come in with you and wait."

"No! I mean, thank you, Leah, but I don't want. I'm not a baby."

"I know. Of course. But maybe just this first time?"

Although Yaakov had thoroughly checked out Yoel Grub's references, Leah still wanted to look him over.

But Shaindele was adamant. "I can take care of myself." Then she softened. "But thank you, Leah. For everything."

"You know the way home?"

"Of course!"

Reluctantly, she hugged the girl's stiff body, coiled in resistance. Like dropping off a small, helpless child at a day care center for the first time, Leah looked on helplessly, her heart sinking with an inexplicable heaviness and guilt as she waved goodbye.

Shaindele waved back, watching as Leah opened the elevator door and disappeared. When she was gone, Shaindele stood there uncertainly for a few moments. Then she rang the bell.

"Come in," a deep voice said. Something about its timbre frightened her. It sounded demanding, even on something this neutral, she thought, her hand hesitating as it clutched the doorknob. She inhaled then shrugged, gathering her courage. After all, what choice did she really have?

There was no waiting room, she saw as she opened the door, surprised. Just a strange orange couch so wide it could have been a bed. At the far end of the room was another door. *That must be where the main elevator left you,* she realized. So why had they been told to come in the back way? Inside, up against the wall, was a desk without a single piece of paper on it. And instead of the massive bookcases she'd imagined, there was only one small shelf with different-colored business binders. There wasn't a single psychology book or a single diploma or certificate. Instead, there were a few pictures of nature: a waterfall, a clump of trees in the forest, and, strangely, a picture of the beach with a few women in immodest bathing suits, the kind no Boro Park matron would ever wear.

She felt her face grow hot.

He stood up and walked toward her. "Already a red face? Why?"

He was short and overweight with a graying beard and salt-and-pepper hair, dressed in the uniform of the Hasidim: black suit, white shirt, pants wide at the cuffs over white socks and laced-up black shoes. On his head was a large black velvet skullcap.

Somehow, she found this reassuring: his outfit, his age, his girth, his grayness, his stubby fingers. He was indistinguishable from the kind of men she passed by on Boro Park streets every two minutes. Only the beach scene grated. It was absolutely incongruous with who he was presenting himself to be. She looked at it again in case she'd missed something.

"Ah, the beach," he smiled, not unpleasantly. "Yes, surprising. But what is the matter with having a scene to look upon in the privacy of our homes and offices that reminds us how beautiful the world is, and how many things there are to give us pleasure? Even if our faith prevents us . . . ," he added quickly as her eyebrows rose.

She didn't disagree. Yet it jarred. After all, wasn't he supposed to be "reforming" her? Wasn't that his expertise? She'd expected long sermons and admonishments. How was that going to work under the gaze of women in bikinis? She tried to tell herself she should feel relieved, that he couldn't be all that stringent if this was hanging over his desk. But for some reason, she wasn't, feeling instead only a strange sense of vague alarm.

"Come, make yourself at home. We'll begin."

She looked around. There weren't any chairs except for the one he was sitting in. Just the couch. She hesitated, taking it in.

"What, you're not comfortable? You want a hard chair like mine?" he joked. "Come, I'll switch with you." He laughed, getting up.

She suddenly felt foolish. Smiling shyly, she sat down carefully on the edge of the couch. But there was no back support that way, she realized. She'd have to lean all the way back, almost lying down, and put her feet up.

"I see, you're thinking, it's not respectful to lie down. But in this office, between the two of us, there are no rules. Except this—you have to be absolutely honest about your feelings. *Farshteyst?*"

She nodded. "Well, to be honest, I'm not comfortable lying down here. I'd rather sit up, in a normal chair, but not your chair."

He looked down at his desk, gripping a pencil between his thumb forefinger and tapping it impatiently on his desk. "And why is that— Shaindele, is it? Do I have your name right?"

"Well, actually. It's Shaindel. Why what?"

"Why aren't you comfortable lying down, relaxing, putting up your feet in my office?"

She knew why. It felt too intimate, too vulnerable. But she didn't know how to say this without insulting him. "I just like to sit," she said.

He raised his hands. "All right, all right. Wait, I'll bring you a chair."

He flung open the door at the far end. She glimpsed people sitting in chairs and doors leading to other offices. She exhaled, reassured by the knowledge that other people were nearby, just outside the door. But when he returned with the chair, he locked the door firmly behind him, then bolted it.

A chill went up her spine. She looked around. Now both doors were closed, and there were no windows. That meant that he was now in violation of the religious prohibition of *yichud*, she thought, alarmed. And instead of putting the chair on the other side of his desk, which is what she'd expected, he dragged his own chair around, placing the two chairs next to each other so close they were almost touching. Her heart did a somersault.

"I think the couch, after all," she said, sitting down quickly and moving to the far end of it, near the wall. She sat there, her short legs out before her in a childlike pose she found undignified, close to ridiculous. She pulled her skirt down as far as it would go, suddenly glad it was mid-calf.

All the while, she was conscious of him watching her every move, a small, unnerving smile on his thin lips.

"So tell me, Shaindel, why are you here?"

"You don't know?"

"*Avadeh.* But I want you should tell me why *you* think you're here."

"Because I disappointed my parents. I didn't tell them the truth."

"You lied?"

"Not really, I just didn't tell them what was going on with me."

"And what was 'going on with you,' *maideleh*?"

She hesitated. This was really hard, and honestly, she didn't feel comfortable talking about her sex life with a Hasid who had a couch in his office and pictures of women in bathing suits on his wall, not to mention a man who was ignoring the laws of *yichud*. But again, what choice did she have?

"I met a boy, and we started going out."

"A shidduch?"

"No," she answered, knowing perfectly well Halpern had told him all about it. If it had been a shidduch, she wouldn't be here. "We met on our own."

"And how did that happen? Explain it to me."

She told him about the pizza parlor, about the boy behind the counter, the notes, the clandestine, thrilling meetings in the evenings. She even told him about Greenwich Village and the jazz club. To her surprise, he didn't seemed shocked or even disapproving. She found herself relaxing.

"So you started to think about sex, no? What did you do with this boy you met in the pizza parlor?"

"Nothing."

He looked skeptical. "I'm not here to judge you, Shaindel. But if you don't tell me the truth, I have better things to do, and I'm sure you do, too. You're a senior this year in Bais Yaakov?"

She nodded sullenly.

"That's a lot of work, being a senior. You are working hard?"

She nodded, slightly relieved that the conversation had taken this turn.

"Do you like school?"

"Very much. My mameh—"

"The one who died?"

She nodded. He really did know everything. "My mameh was a teacher. I also want. I want to go to seminary when I graduate."

"So, my dear Shaindele—you don't mind, do you? If I call you that?"

She did, actually. Although perhaps kindly meant, it felt diminishing, swatting away any semblance of emerging adulthood, reducing her to a silly child who was to be pampered with diminutives of her anyway silly name. Shaindel—beautiful. Shaindele—pretty little thing. In the end, it was a galling liberty, a pretense of closeness to which he, a stranger, was not entitled.

"If you want, *k'vod harav*," she said formally, her lips stretched tight.

"All right, all right, Shaindel it is." He laughed. "But on one condition: stop with the '*k'vod harav*' stuff, will you? I'm not here as your rav—there are plenty of those in this town—but your advisor, and I hope"—he caught her eye and held it for a moment—"a friend."

She felt herself grow warm, a blush creeping up her neck.

"In fact, maybe you'd like to sit here, on my knees. All my patients are like my family, like my daughters. Maybe you'd feel more comfortable, more able to open up to me?"

Instinctively, she pressed her back against the wall as far as it would go, shaking her head vigorously.

He raised his hands and laughed as if she were being exasperatingly, childishly ridiculous and unreasonable, foiling his sincere, professional efforts to help her. "I'm offering, but if you don't want . . ." He shrugged. "So tell me, Shaindel, what does a girl who wants to be a teacher like her late, saintly mameh, a serious girl who wants to go to seminary, do at night with a boy she met at a pizza parlor?"

Her face broke out in a fierce red bloom. She took a deep breath. "What do girls and boys do?" she answered defiantly.

To her surprise, instead of being offended, he laughed and pulled his chair closer. He reached out his hand, briefly touching her skirt just above her knee. (Was that even possible? she thought with alarm. Or was it simply an accident? An unintentional, awkward miscalculation? Or perhaps she had just imagined it altogether?)

"I want to know every detail—what you did with him and why. I want to know if you enjoyed it or if you are sorry. I want to know what you were imagining doing with him but didn't. I want to know everything."

She shot up. "I'm not comfortable with this, *k'vod harav*."

He reached out and touched her hip. Now, there could be no mistake! He was calm, unmoved. "Sit down!"

She obeyed.

"Well, you'd better *get* comfortable with it, little Shaindele, and fast. Because otherwise, I'm going to be forced to tell your principal—who is a very close friend of mine—and your parents, who are paying so much money—that you are refusing to cooperate, and I can't do anything to help you. And what do you think is going to happen to you then, little Shaindele? Huh?"

She looked him over, feeling the tingle of shock and fear. Yes, her world had always been full of bearded men laying down rules and laws, telling her what she could and couldn't do. But nothing in her life and experience had prepared her for a man calling himself a rabbi to behave in such a way. There was something strange in his face, too, she realized, something that hadn't been there before, or that at least she hadn't noticed, that she had never experienced with a man of his age. An old man. No, not old, not exactly. An older man, she corrected herself mentally, a man the age of her father.

She looked away. Was this normal, for a psychologist to touch, to threaten like this? To get such a look in his face like this, a look she had sometimes seen in Duvie's in the moonlight, when he reached out to touch her? Or was she just imagining it? Perhaps he was only trying to do his job? Perhaps this *was* what all psychologists did when patients "didn't cooperate"?

She tried to calm herself down, to reason it out. Of course, counseling would be a waste of time if she didn't tell him the truth. But why did he need every detail? And how could she tell him what she had done with Duvie, lying there on his couch, with him watching her every move? With him *touching her*?

"So I see you haven't decided. So decide, Shaindele. And if you are not prepared to tell the truth, to answer everything I ask you, then don't bother coming back. Is that clear?"

He had already pulled his chair behind his desk again. He wasn't looking at her, but fiddling again impatiently with the pencils on his desk. "That's it. Time's up."

Slowly, she stood, backing away and turning the lock in the door that led to the waiting room.

"Not that door! Go out the way you came in." He seemed upset.

She stared at him, backing away, trying not to get near him. Only when she had closed the door behind her did she allow herself to breathe.

———

She was in no hurry to get home. The familiar streets seemed like a foreign country, the storefronts hazy and indistinct as if covered in smoke. The faster her heart beat, the more the streets seemed to whizz past her cartoonishly, her feet hardly touching the ground as she tried to put as much distance between herself and Yoel Grub as possible.

No one was home when she got there. Leah had no doubt gone to pick up the children. She was almost grateful not to be met with her stepmother's kind, searching eyes that would tempt her to allow all that she had experienced to pour out like pus from a wound. Better to wash it off with some tears and bind it up with silence and hope it would heal.

But again and again, the questions streamed through her, aching like the pain of a serious bruise. *What just happened? Who is this Yoel Grub? And, most of all, what am I going to do? What am I going to do?*

Obviously, she could never go back there. No, Yoel Grub was a fraud and a pervert. But who would believe her? Her parents, who were spending so much money to help her? After all, hadn't her father supposedly thoroughly checked him out? Her principal, who was his good friend and also Duvie's father? She had a brief moment of thinking about the expression "Apples don't fall far from the trees."

If she said anything, whose side would everyone take? The wayward girl's caught sneaking out with a boy she met in Moishy's Pizza, doing who knows what? Or the pious man entrusted with caring for such girls by Boro Park's distinguished Bobelger Rebbe for the last twenty-five years?

She closed her eyes and lay down on her bed. She was just a stupid teenager who had done so many foolish things in her life. Maybe she was just wrong? After all, what did she know? Maybe Yoel Grub had done nothing wrong. Maybe he was the tzaddik everyone claimed, and these were simply his methods, his professional methods, that he learned in a professional school that trained people to be psychologists and helpers? After all, hundreds of girls had gone to him over the years, and no one had ever complained, so what did she know? Maybe he really *could* help her. And she needed help, wanted it so badly. Wasn't it she who had asked to see a psychiatrist in the first place? She needed to get over the loss of her mother, to go forward in her life. She needed to understand why she didn't want to get married or have children. She needed to understand why she had let Duvie do those things to her.

Why had she?

Throbbing with fear and confusion, she turned her face to the wall. *What am I going to do now?*

Leah found her that way, fast asleep.

"Shh," she told Chasya, putting a finger to her lips and closing the door gently. "Your sister is sleeping."

"Why? It's not so late. It's not night. We didn't even eat our dinner or have a bath!" The child was indignant at this strange behavior.

"Yes, I know. But your sister is having a hard time. And sometimes, when we are older and having a hard time, HaShem helps us by letting us sleep and have good dreams. Then, when we wake up, we aren't so sad anymore."

"HaShem is so good!" exclaimed Chasya with such a sigh of saintly, heartfelt sincerity, Leah couldn't stop laughing and kissing her.

"*Good!*" Mordechai Shalom echoed, jumping up and down, a huge smile plumping out his already enormous cheeks, his long blond curls covering his big, blue eyes.

Such a gorgeousness, Leah thought, scooping him up, his chubby little body tender and sweet in her arms. How she loved them both, she thought, her attention drawn from the teenager to the little ones whose needs she felt so much more adequate to address. And for the moment, she tried not to worry.

"So how did it go?" Yaakov asked as soon as he walked through the door.

"Honestly, I don't know."

"You didn't talk to her?"

"She was sleeping."

"Sleeping? And where is she now?"

"Still in her room." Only now Leah realized how many hours had passed, and still Shaindele hadn't emerged.

Yaakov knocked on the door. "It's Tateh. Can I come in?"

"Come in, Tateh."

She was sitting up, her feet dangling off the bed to the floor, her pretty young face wrinkled from the indentations of the pillow. Her thick, dark hair had unraveled in messy wisps that covered her eyes. She pushed them back, gathering her hair in her hand and expertly rebraiding it. Her face was pale, pinched.

"What happened to you?"

"What happened?" she repeated stupidly, her mind still fogged from sleep.

"How did it go? With Rav Grub?"

She looked up into her kind father's eager, anxious eyes. She'd caused him enough problems, she thought. Besides, he couldn't help her. No one could.

"Fine, good," she answered like an actress learning a part. She had better learn it fast, she told herself, because it was the part she'd been given to play. No one else was auditioning. No one else wanted it. If she was going to get through this without breaking her father's heart, she was going to need to win an Oscar.

22

LOVE AMONG THE RUGELACH

Rav Alter heard the doorbell ring with surprise and—rare for the pious old man—uncharitable annoyance. Were even these few, sacrosanct hours of rest not to be vouchsafed him? Was there going to be no end to the intrusions on his life so that even his right to loneliness and mourning were not to be respected?

But when he looked through the peephole, he was shocked to see Fruma Esther Sonnenbaum. Quickly, he opened the door.

"I'm not bothering you, *k'vod harav*?" she said, thrusting out her foiled covered tray.

Rav Alter did his best to hide his considerable discomfort and even embarrassment. What was she doing here in the evening when his daughter wasn't there to chaperone? How could he invite her in, given the halachic problem of *yichud*? But on the other hand, she was no youngster, and she must no doubt be tired having walked all that way with . . . what *was* that she was holding? His mind, whirring with questions in the manner of a Talmudical exegesis, suddenly halted as he looked down. With perfect timing, Fruma Esther whipped off the cover. The indescribable smell of freshly baked rugelach still warm from the oven filled the space between them.

Rav Alter looked down at the little cakes. Every age has its desires, he thought. And after all was said and done, scholar or no scholar, rav or no rav, he was only human.

She saw his eyes light up with desire.

"Come in, come in, Rebbitzen." He opened the door widely but did not close it completely, hoping in this way to solve the *yichud* problem.

But Fruma Esther wasn't having any of it. "You should lock your door, Rav Alter. It's not safe these days."

He hardly hesitated. She was right.

More and more, strange things were happening in Boro Park. Men and even—*HaShem Yishmor, young women pushing baby carriages!*—had been mercilessly assaulted by gentiles for no reason, punched in the face, slammed to the ground, their head coverings and wigs torn off. And many others not physically harmed had become the recipients of hurled insults and defamations using the hateful, age-old idioms handed down from mindless anti-Semite to mindless anti-Semite; people with empty heads and empty lives to whom unfamiliar outfits and head coverings were trigger enough for mindless fury. Everyone was in shock. After so many years of telling themselves they were safe in their own country, Boro Park was now more and more a fearful ghetto in a hostile foreign land.

"This is true, *pekuach nefesh*," he agreed, locking the door. Anything that was a danger to life trumped any halachic requirement, permitting acts normally forbidden, like riding in a car on the Sabbath if you needed to go to the hospital or putting your arms around a strange woman if she was drowning in order to save her. But what to do about *yichud*? He suddenly went to the large living-room picture window, pulling up the shades and pulling aside the curtains, making it possible for everyone in the street to see into the well-lit room. Satisfied, he returned to his guest.

"I'm sorry to disturb you so late, Rav, but I wanted to bring them to you straight from the oven." She smiled. "I'll put them in the kitchen."

She bustled through the apartment with a familiarity and ease that stunned him. How did she know where everything was when most of it was still a mystery even to him? Then he remembered: the shiva.

"I'll bring you a cup of tea, Rav?" she called to him.

He followed her into the kitchen. "Only if you make two cups," he answered graciously. A woman in his kitchen. The smell of freshly baked cakes. Something in his heart leaped up.

Evenings were the worst. The big house so quiet with only his own breathing, the shuffle of his slippers from living room to study, the slight crackle of the well-worn pages of his beloved sacred texts. It had grown familiar to him like the deformed and ugly healing of a wound that you had no choice but to accept. And now, her voice, a woman's voice, comforting, bringing succor and sweetness into the sour loneliness to which he was never, ever going to become reconciled.

"I'm happy to have a cup, too." She opened the cupboards, somehow knowing exactly where everything was, which was fortunate because he would not have been able to tell her. Setting two cups and saucers on the counter, she switched on the kettle.

"The tea?"

"I'm not sure." He shrugged, feeling a bit foolish. But the kitchen was like a rented hotel room in a foreign country, an unexplored space.

"Maybe here?" She nodded, laughing, holding up a large ceramic jar with the word *tea* written in gothic letters in bright red. "Please, Rav, go sit in the dining room. I'll bring it to you."

"We could sit here in the kitchen; it'll be easier for you," he suggested, suddenly wanting to be a good host.

"If you want. But I always like to eat in the dining room. It makes the food taste better," she answered honestly, shutting off the screaming kettle and pouring out the hot liquid. She opened up a tea bag. It was the kind that made the water dark brown in seconds. "I'll use one bag for both?" she asked. "They are so strong."

"Yes, that is what my wife used to do," he murmured, remembering.

"And how much sugar? Or do you not take? Diabetes?"

"No, thank HaShem. Nothing like that. But the rugelach will be sweet enough."

They sat down across from each other at the long, elegant dining room table, the steam rising from the tea fogging their glasses. The cakes were piled up on a plate between them. But he made no move. She got up suddenly and brought two plates back to the table, placing one rugelach on each. Of course, she couldn't expect him to reach out for one! What if she reached out at the same time! Their fingers might touch!

She watched as he murmured the blessing over the cake and then over the tea, his lips moving silently before placing anything in his mouth. Always this restraint, always this remembrance of HaShem before enjoying any good thing; this *Blessed Be You King of the Universe Who Creates*— cakes, fruits, breads, and all other delicious things. How she'd missed that, sitting across the kitchen table serving a pious man, watching his lips move in prayer!

She watched him anxiously as he bit into the delicate crust. He closed his eyes, which almost watered in pleasure. Only then did she mouth her own blessing and take a bite herself. Oh yes. *Delicious,* she quietly rejoiced. A real pleasure. Among all the endless prohibitions and nitpicking don'ts of their lives as God-fearing Jews, how many pure joys were there unencumbered by guilt or shame?

"Just like my dear wife's."

"You must miss Malka Ruth so much. She was a wonderful woman. So kind, so charitable."

He looked up, his eyes alight. "You knew her?"

"Since we were girls in Bais Yaakov. She was always a special person. All the girls respected her, and the teachers only had good words for her."

"I didn't know that part of her life at all. It was over by the time we met. Did she like school?"

She hesitated. From what she vaguely remembered, Malka Ruth Diskin had been no scholar. But she had golden hands. "She used to knit sweaters. Beautiful mohair sweaters. All the girls were so jealous. She also liked to draw. Pictures of flowers."

He sat back, astonished. "I didn't know that."

"You know, a girl grows up, gets married. There is no time. You raise a family, work, help your husband, invite guests for big meals . . ."

He nodded, a bit sadly. "And now that things are slowing down, and now that there is a little more time . . ." He shook his head mournfully. "I knew your husband, Yitzchak Chaim. We learned together in the same *bais midrash*, and then in kollel. He was a great man. A true scholar. And as a teacher—so many students were blessed with his unique way of learning, his *middos*. He once told me he wanted to write a *sefer* about *middos*."

"He started it, but he never finished."

"But he published so many books!"

"Yes, on the weekly Torah portion, and also one on halacha. But the one he wanted so much to write, about how a person's character is the most important thing, more than any single observance, he was never able to complete before . . ." Her eyes grew blurry, and her mind wandered.

Rav Alter got up and brought her a box of tissues.

She took one gratefully. "Thank you."

"I know where these are at least. I use them. Often."

She looked across from him, her eyes softening. "You are still working, Rav Alter?"

He nodded. "Too much."

"But maybe . . . I hope it's not chutzpah for me to say . . . you should take some time now, do what you always wanted, planned, before . . ."

He lifted his cup and drained it. "*HaShem Yishmor,* who knows what will become of me now?"

"What will become of you? What's to become?" she scoffed. "Until a hundred and twenty! But maybe, like I used to tell my Yitzchak Chaim—and he was much younger than you—I used to say: *A mentsh tracht und Gott lacht.* Who can know what HaShem, May His Name Be Blessed, has in store for us, and when? My Yitzchak Chaim never got to finish that book, and it's a book we all need so much today. There is so much piety, but so few *middos.* What goes on in this world . . ." She shook her head, scandalized. "Even in Boro Park! I don't have to tell you."

He nodded in sorrowful agreement. "This is something that troubles my soul, too. People keep to the letter of the law but forget its spirit. So much *loshon hara.* So much unkindness. What does HaShem ask of us? To be like Him! To be just, and kind and loving. This is the hardest of all the mitzvoth! To love human beings."

"Gentiles, too?"

"Why not? They are God's children. He loves them. He created them."

"But, Rav, look what's happening on our own streets!"

"What's happening? A few lunatics. But the police, the doctors, they care for us, protect us, and they are mostly gentiles. And who's to say if we are not ourselves responsible? We need to be more involved in the world around us, to be kinder, and not just think about our own community's needs, our own poor. Selfishness brings hatred."

The great well of emptiness that was inside her ever since losing her

Yitzchak Chaim yawned open for a moment, swallowing his words. She remembered all those private conversations between husband and wife in which her husband's wise and compassionate words of Torah sank into her soul, making her want to be a better person. Now, there was only silence, or the poor substitute of rabbis up at their lecterns on Shabbos and holidays in crowded synagogues with screaming children and their gossiping mothers and grandmothers so you could hardly hear a blessed word! And even when your hearing aid was dialed up enough so that miraculously a few sentences came through whole, somehow it was never what you longed for, but some boastful, abstract erudition that threw around the names of ancient rabbis arguing over donkeys or kegs of wine, or goring oxen. So few rabbis talked about what was really important in life. But when you lived with a pious, learned man, the wisdom fell like manna all day long. All you had to do was collect it.

"Another rugelach?" she tempted him, seeing his plate was empty. "More tea?"

"I'm too full for more tea. But I can't say no to the rugelach."

Delighted, she placed another one before him.

Finally, both cups were drained, both plates empty. She got up to clear the table.

"Sit!" he commanded, taking away the plates and cups and silverware and taking them into the kitchen. "I'm not helpless."

"I can see that, Rav." Slowly, she pushed back her chair. "I'll just wrap up the cakes. Or should I put them directly into the freezer for Shabbos?"

He hesitated. It was only Monday. "You can put a few in the freezer, but leave the rest out, please."

"I'll leave it all out," she announced. "I can bring something else for Shabbos."

He looked at her hopefully. "Chremslach?"

"You eat them during the year, not just Pesach?"

"Malka made them for me all year round. With dates and coconut."

She looked back at him with barely hidden joy, her lips in a tight smile. "Actually, I was thinking a chocolate babka."

He could almost sense its scent rising like a phantom and filling the room.

23

❧

BREAKTHROUGH
WITH GRUB

Shaindele stood once again in front of the dingy door in the musty, dark hallway, feeling lost. He was there, inside, waiting for her. Grub. Just the idea of it sent a hot flash through her stomach and a cold shiver up her spine. She reached back to push in the bobby pins with which she had pinned up her braid into a mature matron's bun. She had also taken care to wear her ugliest, regulation Bais Yaakov footwear: orthopedic old lady shoes and 60 denier black tights. Her skirt was not mid-calf but ankle length, and her blouse buttoned up practically to her chin. Instinctively, she had done everything to make herself as unattractive as possible. She hoped she had done enough. Inhaling deeply, she knocked.

"Come in," he said, his authoritative, demanding voice reestablishing and confirming all the memories she had tried so hard to convince herself she had misunderstood. She trembled a little as she opened the door.

This time, he hardly looked up from his desk. She stood there, taking advantage of his momentary disinterest to look around the room. To her surprise, the beach scene was gone. Taking up its space was a truly toe-curlingly ugly oil painting of the Bobelger Rebbe, every gray hair and wrinkle garishly glorified and slapped into place by some color-blind hack who had no doubt learned his "art" through paint-by-numbers kits, she thought. But it was better than the women in bathing suits promoting an air of casual lust.

Finally, she noticed him stir. He put down his pen, smiling at her avuncularly. "How do you like the new artwork, Miss Lehman?"

She lowered her head, making no reply. And *Miss Lehman*? What was that all about? It sounded almost goyish.

"Please, make yourself comfortable," he said with studied correctness, waving her to a chair, which, to her surprise, was already waiting on the other side of his desk as if it were the most normal thing in the world; as if the last meeting with all its ugly innuendoes had never happened.

Confused and wary, but grateful for small mercies, she seated herself, crossing her legs demurely at the ankles and folding her hands together tightly in her lap.

He looked her over, then leaned back in his chair, tapping a pencil in front of him, first the point and then the eraser, over and over. She stared at it, hypnotized. "I think we might have gotten off to a bad start, Miss Lehman. So if I upset you, I apologize. Let's start all over again. Clean slate. Would that be all right?"

She exhaled, nodding. All of a sudden, he spoke perfect English, with not a trace of Yeshivish. That, too, was odd.

"So why don't you tell me what you would like me to help you with?"

Shaindele, who had spent the week preparing her defenses against the renewal of his merciless onslaught on her privacy and modesty, allowed herself to breathe. "I'd like to talk about my mameh."

"You lost her just recently, no?"

She nodded.

"That is very hard, especially for a young girl." He was silent for a few moments. "Were you close?"

Shaindele considered her next step. Was it better to cooperate or not? *Well, if I'm stuck here, might as well make some use out of it.* Besides, he was acting differently. Maybe he really *was* a psychologist, after all.

"She was everything to me."

"Please, explain," he said patiently.

"She was not just my mameh. She was my teacher. How to be a good Jewish woman, a wife and mother, from her I learned it."

"What kind of a person was she?"

She leaned forward eagerly. "She was so smart. She knew how to do everything. Such a good teacher she was! Her students, they love . . . loved her. She knew how to cook—such delicious food!—and take care of a house and children. Everything always smelled so clean and looked so shiny! I still don't know how she did it. And . . . and she would sew— the most beautiful Purim costumes, and not just princesses and brides. Once, she made me a costume to be a bag of flour! And Chasya she made to be a Hershey's bar." She smiled to herself, remembering. "And even though she had all that work for Shabbos, she was never too tired to play with us on Shabbos afternoon when she got up from her nap. All kinds of games and big jigsaw puzzles with thousands of pieces. All the pieces always looked the same to me, but she . . ." Her throat caught. "She could always figure it out. I don't know how she did it."

"You admired her."

"So much. She was perfect."

He steepled his fingers and rested his chin on it. "Well, not exactly. Can you allow yourself to remember your *not*-so-perfect mameh?"

She gripped the sides of her chair. "I don't know what you mean."

"I think you do," he said bluntly, sitting back and waiting.

She sat in silence for what seemed a long time. He made no attempt to fill it, seemingly content to simply wait for as long as it took.

"She . . . it always happened when she was pregnant or right after the baby was born," she said softly. "It was like she . . . went away somewhere and someone else came, a stranger, to take her place, someone who would yell at us and hit us and then weep and hide in her room. Everything fell apart. Clothes didn't get washed. Shopping didn't get done. Her job . . . the school had to hire substitutes . . ."

"And when this stranger came, who took care of you?"

Shaindele shrugged.

"And your brothers and sister?"

"I had to. It wasn't a choice."

"So this was also part of your 'perfect' mameh?"

She stared down at her fingers. "She couldn't help it. She was sick."

"Tell me about that, about her sickness."

Suddenly, it all came flooding back to her, all the ugliness: the smell of her mother's unwashed body, the stink of dirty dishes piled up in the sink, and the brown-crusted pots left over from Shabbos that stayed on the counters all week long. Then there were the stacks of unwashed laundry in overflowing bins that never seemed to get any lower; and the baby in clothes that he had long outgrown because there was simply nothing clean to dress him in. "I tried . . . to help. But I couldn't do it . . . take over. It was too much. I couldn't be *her*. And then . . . and then . . . she died."

"What do you remember about that?"

Every minute, every agonizing second. But she only said, "She died. From the sickness."

He looked at her penetratingly. "Try again," he encouraged her, not unkindly.

"I . . . I . . . was home with her, I was right there, on the other side of the bathroom door, the whole time. A whole bottle she swallowed! Aspirins. Why would she do such a thing? Why?" Tears fell softly down her young cheeks.

He handed her a box of tissues. She took one gratefully, blowing her nose and wiping her eyes.

"I didn't know *that* was what she was doing in there. I thought she was taking a shower. So I didn't do anything! Just waited . . . for her to come out. Waited and waited." Suddenly, she was back there again, alone. She forgot about Yoel Grub, the ugly little office in the nondescript building somewhere in the dusty streets of Brooklyn. She was once again at home, pounding on the door that could not be opened. "I should have known, I should have figured it out, when the water . . . it was turned off . . . and still she didn't come out. But I thought . . . maybe she's taking a long bath, or getting dressed, or putting on some makeup, or brushing out her wig? That was always a sign she was getting better. But it was taking too long, too long! It wasn't right. Something wasn't right. I knocked and I knocked. But she wouldn't . . . and then I tried to break down the door." She sighed, wiping her wet face with the back of her hand. "But it was wood. So strong. Nothing I could do . . . wouldn't budge. And when Hatzalah finally came—they took so long! Why did it have to take them so long?—it was too late."

"So *you* are responsible for what happened to your not-so-perfect mameh?"

His voice startled her. She'd almost forgotten he was there. She nodded tearfully.

"So it was you that made your mameh sick? You had a poison potion, and you poured it into your perfect mameh's coffee and made her crazy, is that it?"

"Of course not, but—"

"But what? According to you, it was all up to little Shaindele to keep her well, to save her. Right? According to you, children are completely responsible for the choices their parents make, no?"

She was struck dumb. Seen in that light, it was certainly ridiculous. "I didn't mean—"

He waved his hand, interrupting her. "No, wait. Let's think about this, be logical. If one person is completely responsible for another person being sick or well, then that person has to be more powerful, right? So that means that you—Miss Lehman, Shaindel, Shaindele—were more powerful than your mameh or your tateh, or your bubbee. You were the most powerful person in your whole family, in the whole world! Because, according to you, you had the power to heal, to save, a very sick woman who thought she wanted, needed, to die. Am I right?"

She leaned forward, trying to interrupt, to protest, but he didn't allow it.

"Or maybe, just maybe," he continued forcefully, "it's the other way around. Your mameh was more powerful, and she used her power to do a terrible thing to herself and to you."

"She didn't mean it! She was sick! Postnatal depression, the doctors said. She needed help, and I didn't help her!" Shaindele shouted.

"You didn't help her. Because on top of being the most powerful person in your family, you knew exactly what a very sick woman needed, and it was your responsibility to see that she got it, is that it? Not her husband's, not her mother's, not the community's? Just you! And you failed, right?"

She sank back, her passion spent. "I could have called the ambulance sooner," she said dully, barely above a whisper.

He nodded. "And maybe your mother *dafka* waited until only you were home so that she could do whatever she wanted and no one could stop her. Because you were a child and she was the adult, and it was her choice. She didn't expect you to save her. She didn't *want* you to save her."

Her eyes filled with tears. Her bubbee had told her the same thing, that day, at her mameh's grave. It was, she finally understood, the truth. "So how can *I* ever get married and have children? How can I know for sure this same sickness won't happen to me? That I won't do the same thing to my children?"

"What can anybody know about what life holds for us? All you can know is this: If you get married and have children and the same sickness happens to you, you won't behave like your mameh. You'll make better choices, smarter choices. You'll go to a doctor, get the help you need, medication."

"There are medicines for such a sickness?"

"Avadeh."

She let herself melt into her chair, all her limbs releasing their tight curl. She felt lighter, filled with sudden gratitude. From the corner of her eye, she studied him. He didn't even look like the same person as the one she remembered from just a week before—the scarily overbearing, aging man she was sure was a pervert. He looked younger, kinder. Handsomer, even, in a fatherly way. He looked like a respectable, God-fearing, intelligent professional.

How could she have so misjudged him?

"So what else?"

"What else?" She brought her attention back to the present.

"What else would you like to talk to me about, Miss Lehman?"

She considered. "I'd like to talk about what happened with Duvie Halpern."

"Duvie, the boy from the pizza parlor? Are you sure? Last week . . ."

She nodded, filled with new confidence. "I'm sure."

"So you've changed your mind?"

She nodded.

He smiled, folding his arms contentedly over his chest. "Go on."

"I liked Duvie. He was the first boy I ever looked at in that way."

"What way is that?"

"Like he could be my *chosan.* Like we could have a *chasanah,* and I wouldn't have to be afraid. It wouldn't be terrible."

"What wouldn't be terrible?"

"You know, having a *chosan,* getting into bed with him, having children . . ."

He nodded. "What did you like about him?"

"The way he looked. His hair, it was always falling in his eyes, but did he care? He just threw his head back a little to flip it out of the way. He could do that a hundred times. He didn't care. He was never changing his hair, cutting it. He didn't care what anybody thought."

"And you liked that, that he didn't care."

She shrugged. "I guess."

"What else?"

"I also liked his hands, his long fingers. Even though they always had tomato sauce and dough on them. But he acted like . . . like he was a prince in a castle wearing royal robes. Nobody could look down on him. He looked down on everybody, understand?"

He nodded, staring down at his desk, tapping his pencil.

"He was a joker, too. Made me, all of us girls, laugh. And when he smiled, he had white, beautiful teeth."

"You liked when he smiled at you."

She nodded shyly. "I liked that he liked me."

"And he knew you liked him?"

"Yes. I was there all the time. So he started to send me notes. When I ordered a pizza, there would be a piece of paper underneath the crust."

"Clever. What did they say, the notes?"

"Times and places where he wanted to meet."

"And this didn't upset you, frighten you? You weren't insulted, a good Bais Yaakov girl?"

"No. Why should it? To tell you the truth, I was happy. Excited."

"What did you think would happen at these meetings?"

She shrugged. "I didn't think about it. I was curious. I just wanted to be with him. To feel what it would be like to have him to myself."

"And for him to have you to himself," he murmured, not looking up. "Tell me about it, about the meetings. That is, if you want to."

She liked this new Yoel Grub, who put her completely at ease, making her feel no pressure at all, making her feel that whatever happened in this office, she was in control, and it was what she wanted. Maybe she had dreamed the last session? A nightmare?

And so, she began to tell him what had happened.

"At first, we just talked. He made a lot of jokes. I didn't even notice he had an arm behind me on the park bench, like he was just resting it there. And then somehow, his arm moved, and his hand . . . it was resting on my shoulder. That was it, for a while. But each time we met, he got closer to me."

"Physically, you mean?"

"Yes."

"He touched you?"

She nodded, ashamed.

"And you didn't tell him to stop?"

"I did sometimes, but then he would get angry and get up and threaten to leave."

"So you gave in?"

She nodded.

"And then what did he do?"

A small prick of discomfort began to inch its way up her stomach to her heart. This was a leap of faith, to open herself up to him. She hesitated.

"Would you like to stop now? Talk about something else?"

It was that sentence, that openness, that pushed her to overcome her fears and trust him.

"First, he used both his hands to pull me closer to him. He started kissing me. I'd never been kissed before. It felt strange, his lips on my lips."

"Strange bad, or strange good?"

That's odd, she thought. *At this point, he's supposed to get all high horse and moralistic. He's supposed to give me* mussar, *make me ashamed of myself.*

"Strange good, I guess. I liked it."

"How did it make you feel?"

Again, stranger and stranger. He was supposed to say, "What about *negiah*? What about *kedushah* and taharah?" On the one hand, she was relieved not to be scolded, but on the other, wary. He was, after all, a *religious* counselor, a rav, specially trained to help girls going OTD, Off the *Derech*. That was his job. But this rare opportunity to talk openly about her long-hidden struggle to make sense of her behavior—not just to someone else but to herself—was irresistible.

"It made me feel warm and cozy and beautiful. It made me feel loved."

He nodded. "Go on."

"But then, he started to do other things that made me feel not so comfortable. First, he unbuttoned the first button on my collar. The next time it was two buttons, until finally, a few weeks after we started going together, he took off my shirt altogether."

She looked up sharply. What was that noise coming from his throat? Like a gasp . . . of pleasure? "Weren't you afraid of someone seeing?"

"I was, but we were in the back of a car he'd borrowed. We went down to the beach in Far Rockaway, and sat there, talking, and then . . ."

"Go on!"

Now she stared. It hadn't been her imagination. There was a sudden urgency in his tone, an insistence. His face was red, bloated with excitement, his eyes burning, He was breathing heavily.

The old fear washed over her. Nothing had changed. He was the same. Everything else had just been an act to put her at ease. It was as if he had practiced this approach and perfected it. After all, he had done this to hundreds of girls. He was an expert. She shuddered.

"I think we should stop now. I . . . I'm a little tired," she said mildly. She didn't want to make him angry. All she wanted was to leave quietly, on good terms, and never, ever come back.

But it wasn't going to happen. He was furious. "I don't think that's a good idea."

"But isn't my hour up?"

He waved his hand dismissively. "I let special patients like you take all the time they need."

She squirmed. "But I'm not comfortable anymore."

"Why? I thought we were getting along so well!"

She could see he was making every effort to pull himself together, to find his "professional" face again and hide behind it. But he didn't succeed, his eyes still full of an unnatural urgency that frightened her. "Don't be a stupid child! Can't you see this is a very, very important conversation we are having? I absolutely refuse to stop now! I won't allow it! For your own good!" he demanded harshly. Then he took a deep breath, trying yet another tack. "Maybe, after all," he said, almost sweetly, "you would like to sit on my lap and have me caress you the way Duvie did when he made you feel so . . . what did you say? 'Cozy and warm and loved'?"

She shook her head violently, jumping to her feet.

He got up, moving toward her swiftly, blocking her way to the door. She stood there, paralyzed. He reached behind her head, pulling the pins from her hair, which fell down loosely around her shoulders, the braid unraveling. He seemed to gasp.

"You are a beautiful young girl. Why not dress like one? Modesty doesn't mean ugliness. HaShem gave you your youth and beauty. Honor it, child. It's nothing to be ashamed of. And don't feel guilty about what you've experienced, how your body felt when it was touched by a man. This is all normal, natural. HaShem is preparing you, your body, to become a woman, to welcome children." He moved closer, lowering his voice. "Don't you want to feel it? My whatyoucallit? All the girls do. Not at first, of course. But then they tell me they get addicted to it. They wait outside the office, begging me for it," he whispered, the words like a physical assault on her ears.

"Please," she begged, tears streaming down her cheeks. "It's wrong, shameful." She tried to turn around, but he held her by the shoulders.

"Only with the wrong person. Your problem was you chose the wrong person, Shaindele. Your pizza parlor boy was young and stupid like all young men. They don't have any patience. They grab what they want. They are coarse, insensitive. You need someone older, someone more experienced to help you." He paused, caressing her shoulders. "I've helped hundreds of girls, just like you."

The terrible thing was—the confusing, heartbreaking thing was—that he *had* helped her. And it was *that* which made this so much the worse. That he had the talent and ability to do so much good and instead was using it as a tool to gratify the basest, most despicable and selfish perversions of his nature, to carelessly bend the innocent to his will, to seduce and destroy them. A strange sensation of nausea and weakness enveloped her, making her knees wobble and her stomach lurch.

"Listen," she said with a strength that came to her suddenly out of nowhere, a strength born of living through tragedy and recovering from horrible choices; a strength grounded in the sure knowledge that you have a family that loves you and that there is a God that sees all and has set down clearly what is good and what is evil, "get your filthy hands off me, or I'll bash in your whatyoucallit and scream."

He dropped his hands, shocked. Swiftly, she got to the door, half expecting him to follow her and block her way. Instead, he moved back to the chair behind his desk, sitting down and leaning back, his hands folded serenely over his stomach. "All the young girls are like you at first," he called after her. "But you'll get used to it. You'll beg me to take you back. And if not, your parents will." He laughed, slapping the desk. "You know what? I think you need an extra session this week. Come back tomorrow at six o'clock. If not, I'll call your principal."

She glanced over her shoulder, shocked, then ran out the door.

In the hallway, she pressed her back against the wall, feeling her heart hammering its way out of her chest like a small, tortured creature desperate to escape. She fled down the staircase, snatching hurried glances over her shoulder in fear that he might be following right behind her. Only when the doors to the building delivered her safely to the street did she stop moving, staring up at the floor where his office would be. Even though she knew he had no windows, she could have sworn she saw him staring down at her.

24

❧

LEAH TAKES STOCK

Leah looked at the ton of papers scattered over her desk. And if that weren't enough, toys were lying underfoot, the laundry was piled up, and pots still waited to be scrubbed in the aftermath of the usual Shabbos turmoil. In the background was the incessant *ding, ding, ding* of email notifications from impatient customers, going off on her iPhone like little hammers to her skull.

The children had both been dropped off at school. Shaindele was at her psychologist appointment. And Yaakov had long ago left for work. She was all alone with no one looking over her shoulder for a change, she thought, pushing aside Mordechai Shalom's almost-shredded favorite blanket and his bedraggled teddy bear to make a space for herself on the sagging couch. This was the height of decadence, she scolded herself as she stretched out, closing her eyes. She was so tired, so tired! But more than that, she felt hopeless.

She hadn't expected it to be this way.

The initial euphoria of her marriage and the joy of being part of the religious community had not exactly worn off but had instead settled into a perhaps all too predictable familiarity. Now that the fear of being single without children to care for was no longer hanging over her like the pendulum in Poe's famous horror story, she found herself taking stock with a colder eye of all she had gained, and more surprisingly, lost.

It wasn't—God forbid!—that she no longer loved her husband, or her stepchildren or her Creator with the same fervent passion that had fueled her original giant leap into the unknown. She did, more than ever. Most of the time, she felt her heart brimming over with gratitude every time she felt her husband's warm embrace; every time the children dragged her off to see their latest play fort or work of art; every time she kissed them. And when she blessed her Creator for bringing back the sun each morning, or for the food she ate, or just the simple pleasures of being alive, her prayers were no less heartfelt and sincere. It was just that in becoming this new grateful, pious, loving person, she had lost touch with something equally precious and irreplaceable, the girl she had once been; a girl who soaked up knowledge in college classrooms and joyously climbed mountains, all her senses buzzing and alive, drunk with the joy of the earth's beauty. That girl hadn't been to visit her in some time.

She missed her. She missed jogging with her through open spaces, smelling mountain air so fresh you could almost taste it. She missed old trees, wide lawns, an uninterrupted blue expanse of sky. None of that existed in Boro Park.

Even more, she missed the simple courtesies: the politeness of strangers who were careful not to crowd you, who smiled and wished you a good day. Even if they didn't mean it, couldn't have cared less, it was helpful, even wonderful to have such encounters on a regular basis. This realization filled her with a newfound appreciation for good manners, which, unfortunately, the people of Boro Park did not share.

Indeed, the basic idea of "minding your own business" had never been heard of in this place, she often fumed, or if it had, been roundly rejected by popular demand. Every hour of every day, she lived among people where every stranger felt it not only their right but their duty to examine you head to toe and pass judgment on your adherence to community modesty standards. A place where people looked shamelessly into your shopping cart to check out your faithfulness to kashrut stringencies (according to their own very particular biases), as well as your extravagances or thriftiness. A place where neighbors thought nothing of looking into the windows of your home when they could or listening shamelessly through the walls to discover how often and how severely you disciplined—or failed to discipline—your children or argued with your husband, not to mention what kind of music you listened to and at what volume. There was absolutely no privacy.

She remembered that distant and none-too-friendly conversation with her mother at the beginning of her journey from secular to religious life. "It's not a cult, Mom," she had superciliously assured her. But now, she was not so sure.

She sat up, agitated, even frightened. All people who make radical changes to their lives must go through this, she told herself. It was normal to compare your new life to your old life and to feel certain things were missing. But it had never happened to *her* until now.

What was the trigger? That business with the music, the neighbors complaining? Or was it something deeper and more profound: Her failure to get pregnant, her inability to share some of her deepest thoughts with her husband? Was it her marriage itself?

She thought about her Yaakov, her kind, handsome husband. While he was as loving and considerate as ever, he, too, had changed. He was a different man since he'd started working full-time, leaving behind his beloved kollel and his study partner, Meir. Often, he seemed weighted down, joyless.

Like every other woman in the history of mankind married to an unhappy man, her first thought was: *What have I done wrong?* But aside from dancing around the living room, she really couldn't think of anything. On the contrary, she'd bent over backward to be supportive of everything he wanted to do, even at considerable inconvenience and heartache. For example, she'd accepted without protest the considerable amount of time he was spending in evening and weekend Talmud study groups at the expense of their time together. But that wasn't to say she didn't resent it.

As much as she tried, she couldn't help not only missing his company but also feeling unfairly burdened with household chores and childcare. After all, she also worked, and her salary was often even greater than his! Was this not his house as well? Were these not also his children? So far, she had chosen not to bring it up, aware that just a hint from her would get him to drop some or even most of these activities. But what would she gain? She couldn't risk having a man on her hands that was even more depressed and unhappy than he already was.

While he hadn't exactly opened up about his feelings, she knew him enough to understand that he, too, was in mourning for his old life. Together, these shadows from both their pasts had cast a pall over their life together. While she very much wanted to help him, more and more, the unfair distribution of their chores and responsibilities was making her feel like a martyr. And that, she realized, wasn't sustainable. It was a stop-gap, not a lifestyle. At least not for her.

How did other women do it? Fruma Esther? Basha? Her neighbors? Their entire lives were dedicated to helping their men study, taking every burden off their shoulders to do that. And yet they went about cheerfully, with kind and ready smiles, earning salaries, cooking enormous meals, cleaning, and taking care of a horde of children, not just the two little ones and a teenager that she had to deal with. These women had seven, ten, even twelve children! And more grandchildren than you could count were always turning up on their doorsteps for advice, meals, money, and love. She envied them their serenity, stamina, and dedication; their endless faith and wisdom.

Was it her secular American upbringing that made her view the equal distribution of household chores and childcare as a right? Not to mention her own particular belief that every person also had an inalienable right to leisure. What was there in her character that was so hopelessly flawed that even her blessings sometimes became unbearable burdens?

Her mother's words echoed in her mind, refusing to be silenced, no less harsh and far more relevant than she had ever dreamed possible: *Why would you want to be some man's kitchen slave and babymaker?*

If only, she thought, hugging her stomach. Rather than fulfilling her need for motherhood, her love for her stepchildren had only strengthened it. Her longing for a child of her own had grown exponentially with time, becoming more and more like a sailor's passion to finally see dry land. She couldn't help it. If she could love another woman's children the way she did, what would it be like to have one that was totally her own, with no memory of other soft hands and warm eyes that had caressed them in the not-quite-forgotten twilight that was early childhood?

The ticking of her biological clock added another layer of resentment toward the forced separations from her husband. Quite apart from her sexual longing, for a woman desperate for a pregnancy, it was cruelly maddening! It was breaking her apart; even bringing her, she worried, to the edge of her sanity.

She thought of her mother sneaking out of her bedroom window in Flatbush to a waiting van filled with grungy rock musicians headed for San Francisco. For the first time in her life—to her horror and shame—she felt a bit of envy. To be free of rules! To be true, only to yourself, and your own desires and needs with no one judging you, proscribing your life in ways that could neither be endured nor challenged!

Impulsively, she took out her phone and dialed her mom. Since the wedding, they'd spoken sporadically a few times a month. She, too, was going through hard times. Her live-in boyfriend of seven years had recently absconded back to Punjab, where his Sikh parents, unbeknownst to her, had arranged a marriage with a young Sikh bride. As she'd explained it to Leah, his half-assed, long-distance apology had been: "It's not too late for me to have children," no doubt quoting his doting parents.

Never mind that he already had a child, Balvindra, whom he never bothered to visit. When she pointed that out to him, his inadequate response had been: "I screwed up that relationship. She calls her stepfather 'Dad.' I want other children, kids who will know me."

Cheryl, Leah's mom, couldn't pretend she didn't understand. Still, it was another huge disappointment in a life filled with them. And if she was honest about it, the most galling part was financial. His salary combined with the profits from her hairdressing salon had allowed her, for the first and only time in her life, not to worry about money. But talking to her daughter, Cheryl Howard was careful to shrug that part off.

"It's not the money. I've always supported myself. And there are plenty more where he came from," she'd asserted bravely. "Besides, he was getting religious again, growing his hair. He even wore his turban to your wedding, remember? Honestly, this was bound to happen sooner or later. Me and a religious fanatic? Can you just see it?"

But Leah wasn't buying the cheerful insouciance. While her own feelings about Ravi had always been mixed, she knew her mother had loved him deeply. As for money, while she knew her mother had always been careful financially from long habit, she also knew that as proprietor and main employee of her own small business, she didn't have much of a cushion if something went wrong. Leah couldn't help worrying.

Despite being polar opposites, it had always been just the two of them, and a mother is a mother. Always. As Judge Judy never tired of pointing out, "See that guy standing next to you? Take a good look. You won't remember his face in ten years. Now look at your mother. She's going to be your mother forever."

"Mom, how are you?"

"Lola! I mean Leah. Great, and you?"

"Okay, I guess."

"Guess?"

"I'm just tired, Mom. Monday blues."

"Everything okay with you and Jacob?"

"Of course. Why wouldn't it be?"

"Newlyweds . . . men . . . religion . . . little kids . . . take your pick."

Leah had to laugh. "All of the above, but leave out the kids. I love the kids. I just wish . . ."

"You had one of your own, right?"

"I suppose."

"Patience."

"I go nuts with jealousy when I see these pregnant Boro Park teenagers pushing double baby carriages with a stomach out to there. I even get teary when I see a pregnant cat! I think I'm going insane."

"When you decided to move to Boro Park and become one of them, you went insane. Now you're just like the rest of them."

"But I'm not like the rest of them, Mom. That's the problem. And don't you dare say 'I told you so.'"

"Even though I did."

"But you weren't right . . . about . . . everything."

"Just some things."

"I guess I am a feminist, after all."

There was a short silence, during which Leah imagined her mom air-punching and saying a silent *yes!*

"I'm really sorry to hear that, honey." She sounded absolutely sincere.

"Don't get me wrong. I haven't changed my mind about that whole crowd. I don't have to remind you I grew up in Flatbush, so I knew what you were getting into long before you did, but I like Jacob. He's a good guy. And I know how much you love the kids and they love you. I really want you to be happy. And life is a compromise. Nothing's perfect. Remember that. It's hard to have a life that fits all your needs, no matter where you are or what you believe in. And when you finally get there, there is nothing to stop it all disappearing in a second."

"Have you heard from him?"

"Ravi? You're kidding me? He's on his honeymoon with his twenty-something and back in his turban, until it starts giving him headaches—which it certainly will, trust me—and he takes it off again. Then she and the in-laws and his parents are going to come down on him like a ton of bricks! But hey, it's a free world, and it was his stupid choice. So not my problem anymore." Her voice trailed off unconvincingly. "But don't worry about me. I've got someone new. His name is Jerry. He's also originally from Brooklyn, like most of Florida. He runs the coffee shop down the block. Lost his wife last year. Cancer. I've known him for years. And yes, he's Jewish. You see, I'm not prejudiced."

Leah smiled. "Well, I've got a pile of work to do, Mom. I just wanted—"

"Listen, honey, why don't you come down to Florida one of these days? Take a little vacation. Bring the kids, why don't you? I've got a pool. I'll buy a new barbecue and kosher food for you, and paper plates and stuff. You could use a few days off. Go jogging on the beach."

"That sounds wonderful."

"Think about it. Talk it over with your husband. How is he, your hunky Hasid?"

"He's not a Hasid. And he's trying to get used to working downtown instead of studying all day. It's hard for him."

"Well, I give him credit. I was wrong about him. I guess they are not all the same, living off their wives while they bitty-bitty-bum."

"Let's not get into this, Mom. Really, we've had such a nice talk."

"Okay, okay, I never know when to shut my big mouth. And next time, let's FaceTime. I want to show you my new hair color."

"What, the spiky short blond with the black roots is gone?"

"With the wind! I was cloning too many of my clients. I let it grow, and now it's your color, strawberry blond, but more strawberry. Jerry loves it."

Good for Jerry! And for Tom, Dick, and Harry who would surely come along if Jerry didn't pan out. Which was fine, Leah supposed, with grudging admiration for her mother's resiliency. Strangely, Leah sort of missed Ravi, although theirs had not been the most wonderful of relationships; he had practically thrown her out when she'd wound up at her mother's doorstep after losing her job and being betrayed by her cheating boyfriend. In fact, it was his "What are your plans?" that had propelled her to get involved with a Chabad summer program, her first step in abandoning a secular lifestyle for a religious one. Ironically, it was in Ravi the lapsed Sikh that she'd found an unlikely ally. He understood about religious obligations and guilt and family, something her mother had always refused to do. She wished him well in Punjab with his dark-eyed bride.

"I've got to go, Mom. Just wanted to hear your voice."

"I'm so glad you called! I'm sending you a big kiss and a hug, honey. And think about that vacation. I'd love to see the little rug rats. They'll have a blast in the pool."

"I'll think about it." Probably way too much since it was impossible, Leah thought, sighing. "Take care of yourself. And send me a selfie. Dying to see the hair!"

Long after she'd hung up the phone, she lingered prone on the couch, unnerved by the strange, incomprehensible irony that her mother, Ms. I-Don't-Believe-in-Anything, was now comforting *her* in her religious doubts and encouraging patience!

"Please, God, don't punish me. I know I'm a wretched ingrate. But just between the two of us, why would You let me meet the love of my life, experience the love of children, and then not allow this marriage to give me children of my own? Please, please give us a child, our own child!" She found tears rolling down her cheeks. "And please help me to understand my husband better, to make him happier. I know he also works so hard."

She got up looking for a tissue. She blew her nose and wiped the moisture from her face before straightening her aching back and heading determinedly into the kitchen, where the grimy pots awaited.

But before she could even turn on the hot water, she heard the front door bang open and saw Shaindele walk in and head directly for her room. Even for Shaindele, who was not the president of her fan club, Leah thought, this was a bit extreme. She wavered between resentment, curiosity, and real concern. "Okay, okay, HaShem. I hear you," she whispered, going to the teenager's door and knocking. If you ask for *chesed* for yourself, you must first bestow it on others.

"Are you okay, honey?"

The reply was muffled. Were those sobs? She quickly opened the door. The girl was as white as a sheet, tears contorting her sweet, young face.

Leah sat down next to her, putting a tentative arm around her. To her surprise, Shaindele clutched her, shaking.

Leah had never seen her like this. "Hey, hey, what's wrong? What's happened, sweetie? Was it a difficult session with the psychologist? Sometimes that happens. It's not a bad thing."

Shaindele shook her head, gulping down the phlegm that was now choking her, wiping away her blinding tears. How to explain the complicated situation with this man to her stepmother? She wasn't even wholly convinced she understood it herself. And yet one thing was clear: Yoel Grub was dangerous, and she was no match for him.

"I can't go back, Leah. I just can't!"

"Hey, no one is going to force you, I promise you. But can you just explain to me why?" She tried to be gentle, sympathetic, but her heart dropped, imagining the repercussions at Shaindele's school, not to mention with her father! Another thing on his plate for him to deal with! No, for *them* to deal with; something that would take up more of their precious time together, putting new pressures on their relationship, new obstacles in the way of their intimacy.

Shaindele shook her head. "I don't know if I can."

What was that supposed to mean? Despite her sincerest efforts to be understanding and sympathetic, Leah found herself filled with irritation. "Try."

Something in her stepmother's tone sobered her up. She drew back sharply, stilling her sobs. "It's not safe for me there."

"Not safe? In what way? What are you afraid of, Shaindele?"

How to explain how his face looked when he said things, the unspeakable implications? She tried to remember something he'd said that was outrageous, which she could now repeat to win her stepmother over to her side, but she couldn't. It wasn't the words, it was the *way* he said it, and even more, the way he *didn't* say things, things she'd expected . . . wanted . . . him to say, the correct, religious things a rav should say to a young woman he was supposed to be counseling. Most of all, it was a feeling deep in her stomach, an ache, a fear, a desire for flight that was instinctive and uncontrollable.

"He's not helping you?"

She couldn't even say that! For most of this past session at least, he had been perfectly professional and very helpful.

"I can't help you if you won't talk to me, sweetie. Please!"

It all went through her head, an avalanche of words, impressions, and feelings: the way she felt splayed out on his couch. The way he'd brought his chair close to hers. How she'd blushed when he told her he "wanted to be her friend." How he touched her skirt when he'd said, "I want to know every detail of what you did with him." The threat: "Get comfortable!" The things she'd told him about Duvie and how he'd said, "You need someone more experienced." The way he'd pulled the pins from her hair . . .

And then the word came to her, the perfect word that explained what was wrong with Yoel Grub, what was unacceptable and unspeakable. "When I'm there with him, it's not *tzniusdik.*"

Leah looked at her blankly, trying to remember exactly what that word meant to *haredim.* You used it to describe clothing, which was either *tzniusdik* and acceptable, or not *tzniusdik* and wanton. You used it to describe a person's behavior among other people, to describe a loud-mouth, an exhibitionist, as opposed to a modest, shy person. And then it dawned on her, *tznius, tzniusdik: that* also described physical relations, situations, between the sexes. Stunned, she looked into her stepdaughter's young, frightened eyes.

"Are you telling me that this psychologist, this Rabbi Yoel Grub, hasn't behaved in a *tzniusdik* way with you?"

The girl nodded, relieved.

Leah's head was spinning. "Are you sure it's not just a misunderstanding? Can you give me some details?"

"The first time I went to him, he had a picture of women at the beach in bathing suits on his wall. He asked me why I kept looking at it, and I said I didn't think rabbis had pictures like that on their walls. And when I came back the next time, it was gone."

"So you told him you didn't like the picture and he took it down. That was nice of him, right?" Leah said, bewildered.

"And whenever I told him about what I did with Duvie, he never said what any rav would say, that it was wrong, that I shouldn't do such things. Instead, he seemed to like it! Something's wrong with him!"

"Maybe he was just being understanding, trying to help you."

"No, no! I can't explain it. With the picture, it was like I caught him and he was trying to cover up. And with Duvie . . . he was demanding details. He got all excited, Leah."

"But that could just have been your imagination, honey."

"He keeps touching me!"

Leah's mouth opened in astonishment.

"He touched me over my skirt, and then he reached over and took my hairpins out, told me to dress younger. He gives me the creeps, Leah."

Honestly, Leah was getting the picture. But she was still doubtful. Had this been happening anywhere else, she would have been instantly wary and would have taken Shaindele's side immediately. But because it was Boro Park, and because Yoel Grub was apparently so highly regarded by the *frum*est rabbis who sent all their teenage girls to him, how was it possible that something could be so wrong?

Leah put her hands in her lap, squeezing her fingers until the knuckles were white. She took a deep breath. "Shaindele, you're sure, about the touching? You couldn't have imagined, misunderstood . . . You're absolutely certain?"

Shaindele nodded, tears streaming silently down her cheeks. "He asked me to sit in his lap, Leah. He asked me if I wanted him to caress me the way Duvie did. He said he was older and could do it better."

Leah felt her heart begin to pound. This was no misunderstanding. There was not a single doubt left in her mind that Grub was grooming her. Thank goodness Shaindele had had enough sense to figure it out in time and ask for help.

"Oh my good Lord! Come here, sweetie." She gathered the girl in her arms. "You did the right thing, telling me. And you are never, ever going back to that sicko again, you hear me? We will find you someone else from outside Boro Park. A professional."

"But what about my school, the principal? And what will Tateh say?"

"Never you mind about that. I'll deal with all that."

The girl wrapped her arms around her stepmother's shoulders and leaned into her. "Thank you, Leah. Thank you so much!"

"Try to relax, honey. Be glad you were smart enough to figure this guy out sooner rather than later. I'm sure a lot of the other young girls the rabbis sent to him weren't. I'm very proud of you, Shaindele."

These were the words that in the future the girl would hold on to and carry with her. For what was to come, she'd have no choice.

25

A RAY OF HOPE

Yaakov was sitting at his desk trying to concentrate on his work. Outside, the sun was shining, and the sky was blue. He had felt the spring coming the moment he stepped out of the house that morning. In only a few weeks, it would be Passover, the official inauguration of springtime.

How he looked forward to all the preparations that turned the house upside down! Everything would be thoroughly cleansed. All the most beautiful dishes and cutlery, used only one week a year, would be unwrapped from their cartons and readied. Special groceries would be purchased, unique dishes prepared.

This is what I need, he told himself. Renewal. Spring. Beauty. To get in touch with the ancient story of the Hebrews released from brutal slavery to freedom and life as sovereigns in their own land.

He leaned back, stretching his cramped arms. Often he found his fingers heavy and dead as they roamed over the keyboard, the pins and needles painful as he rubbed his circulation back into life. He closed his eyes, thinking of the time not so long ago when all a man had to do was fill in some simple numbers in worn ledgers to know everything they needed to know about their enterprises: how much spent, how much earned or lost, the profit. While the bottom line wasn't that much different today, the ways one got there were labyrinthine, cut up into arcane specializations that were being sliced ever finer: amortization, standard engagement revenue, transaction tax. He himself was involved in the audit division and focused on liabilities.

It was actually a bit depressing focusing on loans, unpaid utility bills, bank overdrafts, mortgages, expense accounts—each one a negative. He often thought he'd be happier in assets, or even equity. If his lifeblood and the hours of his day were to be sacrificed on the altar of such work, he wanted to feel himself at least part of a successful enterprise.

But this way, he knew so very little about each client. He hardly ever got to meet one of them in the flesh, these niceties being handled by gentiles in impeccable Brooks Brothers suits and handpicked silk ties. Often, he missed the humanity that would have turned the numbers in the ledger into a comprehensible human drama. Were all these hotel bills, for example, strictly necessary, or a cover-up for something nefarious? And the loans that had been taken out, were they a wise choice, harbingers of progress and expansion, or frivolous measures boding ruination? He would probably never know.

As low man on the totem pole, he was tasked with the unfolding of crumpled receipts that needed to be put in order. Measuring his worth as he did according to other criteria altogether, he didn't actually mind that. This was, after all, simply a job for which he was being paid. But the boredom! The lack of intellectual stimulation and challenge! It was doing to his once fine mind what the keyboard was doing to his fingers. Often, to his embarrassment and chagrin, he found himself dozing off. He had taken to playing games with himself to keep alert, making up stories to explain the receipts and expenditures, some of them quite risqué. More often, he went on automatic, allowing himself to use the time to think about his family, his problems, his hopes and dreams, and especially his fears.

He often thought about Leah. He was more in love with her than ever, he realized, longing to see her when they were separated, suffering through the obligations that prevented him from spending more time with her. It seemed as if they were always being pulled apart. From the moment he got up in the morning, all his religious obligations hit him like a fierce undertow, tearing him out of her arms and dragging him far away: shower, get dressed, *daven,* eat, and then once again board the dirty, crowded, dilapidated tin box that took him far from her to an alien place he more or less despised. And then, when he was at last released, his children awaited him with their little anxious eyes and grasping hands, clamoring for his time and affection. The precious little time left unclaimed he had piously invested in Talmud study classes to assuage his guilt at leaving kollel and to combat the rot he feared was spreading in his soul. Aside from his children and Leah, they were the only part of his life that brought him joy.

And where was his wife, his Leah, in all of this? While she never, ever complained, he missed her so much, especially when their beds were pushed apart and they could not legally resume their intimate life together. He found it maddening.

All this came to him as a strange surprise. After all, the rhythm of married life for a devout Jewish couple never varied, and he had experienced all this before with his first wife. *I somehow forgot that part.* He shook his head. *Or is it so much different this time around?*

Leah was not the bride of his youth, when everything was new and thus unquestioned. She was the wife of his maturity, when everything in him had ripened and bloomed and deepened, his desires as well as his problems. The difficulties of his new secular job in an alien culture among strangers had hollowed out an emptiness in him that had not existed when he was a young husband among his own kind in kollel. He needed comfort and connection more now than he had then, more than any other time in his life.

And in the middle of this wrenching struggle to keep his balance and walk the tightrope between this difficult new job, his family responsibilities, and his spiritual life, had crashed this enormous, unexpected asteroid from outer space: Shaindele's secret treachery!

It was unthinkable what had been going on behind his back. Unthinkable! Unheard of! That a daughter of his . . . He had never heard of *anyone* in his family or among his friends being faced with such a challenge. He was torn between the instinctive fury, disappointment, and disgust that welled up in him, and an equally instinctive fatherly love. It was his little, orphaned girl, after all, and she had suffered so much.

But why should suffering lead to wantonness? It had not, after all, affected his sons that way, those serious young Talmud scholars learning in one of the Jewish world's most respected yeshivas. Why, the reports he regularly received about their piety, their diligence, and their intelligence were glowing!

He gnawed his lip. Yes, the decision to send them off to Baltimore to board in yeshiva and spend Shabbos and most holidays with his brother's family had been wise, if wrenching. He missed them so much. But by shielding his sons from all the harsh realities of their mother's death, he had allowed them to fall all the more heavily and with crushing consequences on his teenage daughter. While the boys' lives had scarcely changed, for Shaindele, it had been a life-shattering upheaval, the burdens of housekeeping and childcare falling on her like an avalanche.

He felt sympathy for her, he did. But he refused to accept that as an excuse for her outrageous behavior. Through the millennia, Jewish girls had always faced harsh realities: the pogroms in the shtetlach of Europe, the upheavals of immigration, and finally the Holocaust itself. Religious girls, far from losing their faith and their piety, had been the stalwarts, the ones who made it possible for the Jewish people to continue despite all odds.

As a member of a religious family and community, he had always been taught that women were naturally stronger and more pious with a boundless *emunah*. Even in the times of Egyptian slavery, it had been Jewish women who had risen to the challenge, saving the nation from annihilation by enticing their despairing husbands to continue marital relations even as Jewish babies were being thrown into the Nile. From their unwavering faith had finally emerged Moses, a redeemer.

So no, he couldn't fathom what had happened to his daughter. It simply broke his heart, filling him with guilt and depression. Only now, with this new, school-sanctioned arrangement with the psychologist, had a small ray of hope begun to shine into the dark recesses of his soul. He pinned all of his hopes on Rabbi Yoel Grub, who everyone said specialized in young girls who had lost their way. Only Grub could give him back the little girl he loved so much, bright and whole, healed from all the ugliness that had deformed her life. Please God that it would happen! He had it in him to forgive. He knew he did.

Tonight, Leah would be going to the mikvah. The longing in his heart to be with her once more, a husband and lover, banished all his misery. He would take the whole night to himself, he thought. He had already put in a call to Meir telling him he would not be able to come to their weekly study session together. He would buy her flowers and candy, just as he did when they were going out. He would wipe his mind and heart clean of all the aggravations, doubts, and unhappiness that infected it. He would be with her, only her, in completeness and devotion, the way he had not been for so long, he told himself.

Then he sighed, taking up the little pieces of paper and smoothing them out, trying not to think about the people who generated them.

26

LEAH, YAAKOV, SHAINDELE

The bright flowers were damp against his hands. His heart leaped up with anticipation as he viewed the fragrant pink roses, magnificent dotted purple stargazer lilies, the peachy pink alstroemeria. He was glad then that he'd spent the extra time and money to let the florist work her art instead of grabbing a ready bunch of predictable red roses from one of the buckets. He rejoiced, too, that he'd splurged on the chocolates: kosher Swiss pralines boxed in festive gold with a large red ribbon that had been curled with the joyous and delicate devotion given a favorite little girl's precious hair. His whole body felt light as he clutched his gifts heading home along the dusty streets of Boro Park, barely conscious of his feet touching the cold ground.

"Here, these are for you, my lovely wife," he would say to her when she answered the door. And her face—her lovely, kind face—would dimple, her beautiful eyes deepening with joy, as she flashed him a smile of pure, white light. She would take his gifts and lead him past the children to the intimacy of their bedroom. "I have been to the mikvah," she would whisper into his tingling ear, as she . . .

"Shalom aleichem, Reb Yid," a voice boomed into his consciousness.

He looked up, his face blushing red as if his thoughts were flashing across a neon sign emblazoned on his forehead. It was a person he vaguely recognized who sat near him in the synagogue.

"On your way home? I'll walk with you. Flowers, candy? It's a simcha?"

Yaakov's heart sank. He knew the man meant well and was just being friendly, but he fiercely did not want his company or his intrusive questions to replace the silent joy of his anticipatory dreams. To make things worse, the man was elderly, and his pace was slow. But Yaakov could think of no way to extricate himself that would not be unkind.

It could not have taken more than ten minutes before the unwelcome companion turned off, bidding goodbye. But to Yaakov, it had felt like hours. He tried to make up for it by increasing his pace, almost running. Once home, he didn't bother waiting for the elevator, taking the stairs two at a time. Instead of ringing the buzzer, he used his key, turning it as quietly as possible so as not to alert the children.

But their small, perfect ears were not fooled.

"Tateh!" Chasya and Mordechai Shalom screamed, attempting to jump into his arms.

"What's this, what's this, Tateh?" Chasya cried out, trying to wrest the candy from his hands, crushing the bow.

"Stop!" he shouted at her in exasperation.

The children froze, their smiles transformed into frowns. Mordechai Shalom broke out into huge wails of indignation.

Leah came rushing into the room. She looked at him with shocked disapproval.

"I'm sorry, I just . . ." He held out his offerings to her.

Her frown vanished, confusion taking its place. "Yaakov . . . thank you. But what happened with the children?"

He watched as she hurriedly set aside his carefully chosen gifts on the dining room table, turning her full attention back to the children, crouching down and cradling them in her arms.

"I didn't want them to . . . They were ruining . . . ," he faltered, coming close to her and lifting Mordechai Shalom out of her arms into his own. The child was still sobbing softly.

"Tateh frightened you?" he asked remorsefully. "I'm so sorry, Icy,

Cheeky. They were presents for Mommy. I wanted to keep them pretty for her. Will you forgive your tateh?"

Mordechai Shalom nodded, his thumb in his mouth, his little body shaking from big, trembling intakes of air.

Yaakov reached out to Chasya, too. But she pulled away, burying her face in Leah's skirt. "Tateh didn't mean to scare you," Leah whispered, nuzzling the child's ear.

Something about this focus on his crimes suddenly filled him with unreasonable anger. "Can't Tateh come home and have two minutes' peace?" he fumed, putting Mordechai Shalom down and stamping his foot, which set the child off again, joined now by his sister. But this time, Yaakov didn't care.

"These children have to learn a little discipline. I never jumped up and down on my father. I would never have dared," he said with more vehemence than he'd intended, his spoiled hopes turning bitter as he watched the ignored bouquet already beginning to wilt, the festive ribbon of the pralines flattened against the table from the weight of its bright cardboard box.

Leah, shocked, said nothing. This was so unlike him. Then she sighed. "Come, children. Say good night to your tateh and come to bed."

Yaakov went into the bathroom. He stared at himself in the mirror, shaking his head slowly, astonished. How had it all gone so wrong? He washed his face with cold water, patting it dry. She was waiting for him alone in the living room. The flowers, he saw, had already been carefully placed in a large glass vase of fresh water.

"They're gorgeous, Yaakov. Thank you! What's the occasion?" she said, reaching for the chocolates and smiling as if the whole wretched scene with the children had never happened.

He exhaled gratefully, smiling back. "Remember the days of our courtship when I tried so many times to bring you flowers and candy?"

"'Goyish romantic presents,' you used to call them." She chuckled. "I always found some way to pretend they weren't actually meant for me."

"You'd leave the flowers for us for Shabbos and let the *kinderlach* eat the chocolates."

"Not all of them," she protested with a wry smile. "Well, I admit I only allowed myself one or two."

"Should we open it now, while it's quiet?" he suggested hopefully.

She hesitated. "Don't you want to kiss the children good night first?"

The children. Of course. Always the children.

"Just this once, can't we just . . . ? I'll talk to them in the morning."

She shrugged unhappily. "Okay, if that's what you want, but there is something else that just can't wait," she pushed on, even though it was perfectly clear to her that now was not the time. She couldn't help it. She simply needed to know, without delay, what Yaakov intended to do about Yoel Grub. It was something that just couldn't be put off, however wise.

This burning urgency was more for her own sake than her stepdaughter's, she admitted to herself. What she needed, without delay, was an iron-clad reassurance that he wasn't "one of them," those Boro Park sheep who did whatever their community machers told them; that he was going to think for himself, especially where his own daughter was concerned. Most of all, she needed uncontestable proof that she and he really *were* part of a free, sincere, devout religious fellowship of individuals trying to live a good and pure life and not mindless members of some cult. Only his immediate and unwavering indignation over Yoel Grub would silence the voices of fear and negativity in her mind, dispelling once and for all her budding doubts over her decision to become part of this community.

"What's so important it can't wait a minute?" he asked with sullen impatience, feeling ill-used.

She sat down beside him, also frustrated. How she had longed for this—undivided attention, intimacy! He'd even, unbidden, canceled his evening *shiur* with Meir! This was the time she'd been preparing for, finally convinced she could trust him enough to be completely honest with him, even if it upset him. And now, instead, she was about to sacrifice this precious moment, to ruin it without any benefit to herself at all. But it couldn't be helped.

"It's Shaindele."

She already sensed him inching away, his face and body stiffening.

"Must we? Now?"

"It's not what you think!"

"But isn't she being taken care of? Aren't we paying a fortune for professional help? Not like when her mother was sick when we didn't . . . Aren't we doing whatever we can? Why do we need to talk about it? It's upsetting."

"What I'm going to tell you now is a thousand times more upsetting. I'm very sorry to have to do it now. I know you were hoping . . . looking forward to . . ."

He leaned back, making a curt, dismissive gesture with his hand, then clasping them together tensely in his lap as if to say, *What does it matter what I was hoping for, what I want?*

The gesture wasn't lost on her. It took Leah aback. She had no idea he was so angry, that he was feeling the lack of intimacy between them as much or even more than she herself. But it didn't change what she needed to do now, good timing or no.

"It's Yoel Grub."

"The psychologist? Nu? What?"

"He has been behaving inappropriately with her."

"*Vus is dus?* 'Inappropriately'?"

"His behavior is not *tzniusdik*. He's ignoring *yichud*. He's touching her. He's talking to her about forbidden things. I think he's a big fake. A pervert in rav's clothing. We need to find her someone else. And while we're at it, to inform all the people who recommended him that it's dangerous to send young girls to him for counseling."

Yaakov stood up. He took a step toward Shaindele's room, but then he reeled, falling heavily backward onto the couch, almost knocking into Leah. She reached for him, concerned.

"Are you all right, Yaakov? I know it's a shock—"

"A shock?" he repeated dully, his eyes wild. "A shock!" He was breathing heavily.

She was frightened he was having some kind of medical issue. "Please tell me you're all right!" she pleaded.

"Tell you I'm all right? You tell me such a thing, that a pious man—recommended by Rav Alter, after he discussed it *with the Bobelger Rebbe himself,* who sends all the troubled girls in his community to Grub—is making sinful advances to my seventeen-year-old daughter? And that you heard this from a girl who has been sneaking behind her parents' backs for months to meet and do who knows what with some yeshiva bum she met in a pizza parlor? And on the basis of that, you want to ruin a man's reputation? Take away his livelihood?"

A searing disappointment, like a hot knife, ripped through Leah's stomach. "Yaakov, I understand this is a shock. But I spoke to Shaindele. I asked her many questions and insisted on hearing all the details, and I'm telling you she is not making this up. He has been grooming her."

"I don't know what that means! *Grooming, inappropriate.* I'm not as smart as you, Leah. I never went to college. I'm just an ignorant, haredi yeshiva boy who has lived in this neighborhood—which is apparently Sodom and Gomorrah—his whole life," he spit out in fury.

She was at a loss. She had never seen him like this. She didn't know who this person was sitting next to her, filled with ignorant, unreasonable resentment and anger. She shifted her body, moving away from him.

The gesture incensed him even further. "This is not the first time that girl has come between us. Remember? Right after we got engaged, how she ran away to my brother's? I wanted to let her stay there."

"You wanted to let her get married! She was sixteen!"

"I never!" he began indignantly, then thought back on it. "It's true I was angry. I said some things, but of course I wouldn't have."

"No? Are you sure?"

He was cut to the heart by this, and by her closed and furious face and molten eyes that couldn't even bear to look at him.

He jumped up. "Where is she now? I'll get the truth out of her!"

"She's at Fruma Esther's. I wanted to have a chance to talk to you about this without her. She's terrified you won't believe her and that you'll force her to go back."

"Of course she has to go back! If she doesn't go back, Halpern will throw her out of school. She won't graduate. You heard him!"

"That's another thing. What is the principal of a girls' school doing directing teenage girls to that pervert?"

"*Vus is dus,* 'pervert'?"

Did he really not know English? Had he not been born and raised in America? "It's a *soteh.*"

"This . . . that is *loshon hara*! *Rechilus*! You've completely taken her side without looking into it! Just because a silly girl makes accusations to cover her own sins!"

"She's your daughter! And please keep your voice down; you'll wake the children. Or don't you care about them, either?"

He was wounded, staring at her in disbelief.

"Aren't you even going to ask me what she said? Aren't you even curious?" she whispered with a sudden dispassionate calm he found more frightening than her anger.

"Oh, that's allowed? You let? I can question?" he retorted sarcastically, digging into his position, pushed by shame, regret, and disappointment to an extreme stance that was not natural to him.

"*Allowed?* When is a person not *allowed* to hear the truth? Maybe because I'm an ignorant *baalas teshuva*, practically a shiksa, who didn't learn in kollel for twenty years, but I never heard of that halacha."

His eyes smarted. "Maybe we shouldn't talk about this now," he backtracked, feeling overwhelmed with sudden regret.

"When, then, Yaakov? She has another appointment with Grub tomorrow."

"What, she goes every day?"

"No, but Grub insisted because she ran out of there in tears. If she doesn't go back, I'm sure he'll cover himself by calling Halpern with his version first."

"I need to talk to her myself. To hear it firsthand."

"Please don't put her through another inquisition! You're her father, but you are also a man. Don't embarrass her by making her repeat it to you."

"She can pull the wool over your eyes, but not mine! I'll get the truth out of her!"

"Instead of interrogating *her,* why don't you go speak to Yoel Grub?"

"And ask him what? If he . . ." He couldn't even think of how to phrase it! "If he behaved in a way unbecoming a rav with my teenage daughter?"

"He locked the doors! He touched her, pulled the bobby pins from her hair! Told her to sit in his lap, that she needed someone 'more experienced' than Duvie Halpern! He threatened her that if she didn't do exactly what he wanted, he'd get her expelled!"

He listened with only half an ear, horrified and disbelieving. It wasn't possible! A man even older than himself, married with nine children. A grandfather of four. A man well known and respected in the community, recommended by Rav Alter himself! He simply refused to consider any of it could possibly be true. And if it wasn't true, then it was another monstrous lie cooked up by his wayward daughter for reasons only she understood.

He suddenly felt weary. "What is it you want from me, Leah?"

"I want you to fight for your daughter! To believe her. I want you to prove to me that this whole holy world I've given up so much to be part of is real and not some make-believe stage set, like Disneyland."

"I can't understand you! Don't you remember all the lies she made up about you, trying to break us up? Why would you do this for her?"

She was astounded. "Because . . . ," she began, trying to clarify her thoughts. "Because you are a righteous man, Yaakov, and this is—or is supposed to be—a righteous, God-fearing community that protects its children! Because this is an evil situation that must be stopped once and for all. That's why, Yaakov."

They were at an impasse.

"All right. I'll look into it," he said dully.

"Thank you," she answered formally, rising stiffly to her feet and going into the kitchen. She brought back a plate of food for him, placing it on a mat on the dining room table. "Your dinner," she said.

"Aren't you going to join me, Leah?"

"I'm going to the mikvah. I don't want to get there too late."

Silently, she put on her coat and, covering her hair with a warm hat which she would need on the way back when she emerged into the cold streets with hair still wet from her ablutions, headed for the door.

He sat alone in the living room, listening to the sounds invading the silence: impatient car horns, an ambulance screeching in terror, the motor of the refrigerator coming to life, the ticking of a clock.

So this is what it has come to after all his efforts in forming connections, marrying, having children. *This loneliness, this silence,* he thought bitterly with a growing self-pity. He moved from the couch to the dining room table, looking down at the plate of carefully prepared food. It was still warm and looked appetizing, and yet he felt no hunger, no desire to nourish himself. Out of habit, he picked up a fork and pushed the food around, reluctantly bringing some to his mouth, barely tasting the fragrant vegetables and the chicken. He soon put the fork down. It was no use. He leaned back, pushing himself away from the table.

What was my crime? he thought, getting up and pacing. And then, unexpectedly, another thought: *What was* her *crime?*

He remembered the other women he had met on those pitiful, not-so-long-ago shidduch dates, women carefully selected by aging matchmakers who had long ago forgotten the meaning of love. None of the women had shown any interest at all in his children, viewing them as a burdensome and inconvenient part of a bargain to which they had no choice but to agree to attain what they wanted for themselves and their own children. The worst were those who had made it perfectly clear that under their regime, his children would be whipped into shape by rules that would downgrade their needs to those of the furniture's.

And then there'd been Leah, who had no rules. Leah, who'd simply loved them.

She had become their mother, he realized, startled. Their mother, not their babysitter or stepmother, and she would fight for them like a lioness. For her, they would always come first. This was a blessing, he thought, his sense of its rightness and goodness dissolving his anger. *I should thank God for that, not resent it. It was one of the reasons I fell in love with her.*

He went to his children's bedroom, quietly opening the door. Mordechai Shalom was fast asleep, his breathing even and deep. Tears still stained his beautiful round cheeks, Yaakov saw, stabbed with remorse.

"Tateh?" a little voice called out to him in the darkness.

He sat down beside his little girl, tenderly gathering her in his arms. Because she was so smart and so funny, it was so easy to forget how really young she still was. Her bones were like a little kitten's, her body still rimmed with baby fat. A little girl, a sweet, small girl. How he loved her! He kissed her cheek and laid her down again. "You said your *shma*?"

"Yes, Tateh. I didn't forget. I was crying, but I think HaShem understood anyway."

He smoothed her hair off her delicate forehead.

"Tateh?"

"Hmm?"

"Did you and Mommy eat all the chocolates?"

"We didn't eat not even one," he admitted, and was rewarded with a sleepy smile.

"You could have one. One each," she added generously, yawning and turning over.

"That's very kind of you, Icy," he whispered, tucking her in. "Now go to sleep."

He closed the door carefully behind him, then leaned against it, breathing deeply.

Next, he opened the door to Shaindele's bedroom. He put on the light, looking around the room. There was her desk, piled high with her schoolbooks; the Code of Jewish Law, the second volume of the Five Books of Moses, with commentaries, the prophet Isaiah, a book of English grammar, and a workbook for algebra. Her notebooks lay open, sharpened pencils in holders stood up straight and ready. A Shabbos dress that had been carefully ironed was hanging on the closet door. A cork bulletin board held a printout of her weekly class schedule and some photos of herself and her friends and cousins at various weddings. And there was a framed wedding photo of himself and Leah smiling into the camera. After everything, all the turmoil, she kept a picture of Leah in her room!

Then his eye was caught by something else, something he didn't remember seeing before. There, over her bed, hung a huge, framed photo of herself dressed as a bride with a crown of flowers on her head. She couldn't have been more than Chasya's age, he realized. She was sitting on Zissele's lap, her mother's arms draped around her small shoulders. It had been taken in kindergarten one Friday morning when she had been chosen as Ima Shabbos, a great honor for the little girls, who got to dress up and light candles and make the blessing. Both she and Zissele were smiling into the camera, but already he could see the traces of grimness and despair darkening his young wife's eyes as they looked into the future. Someone had carefully and painstakingly braided and pasted small bunches of dried flowers lovingly onto the picture frame. It must have taken hours.

He stared at the photo. She, too, was his little girl. Then suddenly the idea burst in his brain like a bomb. What . . . what if. . . . what if . . . it were . . . true? What if this man, this Grub, was not to be trusted? *After all, I don't know him personally. I'm not a Hasid, part of Grub's community.* And neither was Rav Alter, who had never actually said he'd spoken personally to the Bobelger Rebbe and who didn't know this Grub either. Rav Alter had simply passed on the assurances of others, people in a completely different community who followed very different rules and had a lifestyle unique to themselves alone.

He began to think about the terrible scene Leah had painted that he had been too upset to even consider. Pulled the hairpins from her hair? Locked the doors? Touched her? Words could be misinterpreted. But actions? These concrete, physical manifestations of the man's will, his power? Even if only one of these things had occurred between Yoel Grub and his daughter, the man should be stoned! There was no room for discussion here. He had either done these things or he hadn't. Why would Shaindele make this up? She had nothing to gain and everything to lose.

He walked to his bedroom, quietly opening the door. It was dark and silent. The beds, he saw, had already been pushed together, a sign that she, too, had been joyously anticipating the end of their difficult two weeks of separation. Hopefulness began to beat once more inside him.

Undressing quickly in the dark, he climbed in, waiting for her to come home.

He'd almost dozed off by the time he heard the bedroom door open. He watched her move through the shadows, hanging up her street clothes, then disappearing into the bathroom. She emerged in her nightgown, then silently climbed into bed, turning her back to him.

Tentatively, he touched her shoulder.

She turned over. Her face was wet with tears.

"My love, don't," he whispered, taking her into his arms. "I'm sorry. I'm so sorry."

"Thank you," she answered, snuggling against him. "Yaakov, I'm so frightened."

"Of what?"

"That all this isn't real. That Boro Park isn't real. It's like the theater, where people present some reality to an audience, trying to make people believe it's true, when the storefronts are made of cardboard and the clothes are all costumes they put on and take off, along with the expressions on their faces."

"I don't understand."

"You grew up here, Yaakov, but this is all new to me. I wanted . . . want . . . so much to believe that people here are different. That they practice what they preach. Otherwise, what am I doing here?"

He moved closer, holding her to him. "I understand, my Leah-le," he murmured. "I really do."

She held his face in her hands and kissed him. "I know this is hard for you, but you have to promise me you won't send her back to him . . . not until you look into it."

"*Bli neder,* you have my word."

He felt her face next to his, the warm flesh of her arms in his hands. Her skin was like silk, he thought wonderingly, and her hair smelled of roses. *Flesh of my flesh, bone of my bone,* he thought with passion. With her help, he slowly lifted her nightgown delicately over her head.

But even carried away, he needed to be careful, he told himself, to remember how different she was from him, where she had come from, her fragility. And before he was completely caught up in the joyous rhythm of their coming together, ending the isolation and maddening loneliness, while his mind was still capable of reason, he was overcome by a terrible thought. *If what Shaindele says happened to her is true, I will have to ask myself the same question: What am I doing here?*

27

WILL THEY BELIEVE HER?

"I don't understand, *maideleh.* What is going on with you?" Fruma Esther asked her granddaughter Shaindele the next morning. "Explain to me again why Leah wanted you to spend the night with me?"

"I told you last night, Bubbee. I need a little time for myself. Away from the *tummel.*"

"What *tummel?* You mean the *kinderlach?* Your brother and sister? That you call a *tummel?* Like you're not used to it?" She shook her head shrewdly. "Last night, I saw you were suffering, so I left you alone. But now I want to hear the truth."

"Please, Bubbee. I don't want to talk about it."

"*Ich farshtey.* But want, don't want, you'll talk."

How was she going to get out of this? She wouldn't have minded telling Bubbee all about Yoel Grub, but if she did, she'd have to explain what she was doing there in the first place; she'd have to explain about Duvie Halpern, and the trips to the city and out to Far Rockaway . . .

"You're cold?"

Shaindele shook her head, crossing her arms defensively over her shivering shoulders.

"You had a fight with Leah?"

Shaindele looked up, startled. So that's what she thought! She hesitated, wondering if she should simply latch onto that for the sake of convenience. But the unfairness of it was too much for her. She shook her head. "Leah has been wonderful to me, Bubbee."

The old woman raised her eyebrows. This was a new story. Now Fruma Esther was really worried, whereas before she had just been mildly concerned, convinced that some minor rift between Shaindele and her stepmother was at the bottom of this unexpected visit. That would have been understandable, even expected. The girl had been so against the match, and no one could say she was completely in the wrong. After all, her father was a respected *talmid chocham,* and Leah had been a girl from the street, a *baalas teshuva* from a single mother who dressed like a . . . Oy. Better not to even think such thoughts. As much as Fruma Esther had come to respect, even like, Leah, certain things still rankled.

"So what, then, *shefelah?*"

"I'm going to a psychologist. The school sent me."

"A psychologist," she repeated. After everything that had happened to Zissele, just the word made all her nerves tingle and her stomach ache. "For *vus?*"

"I'm having . . . had . . . some . . . problems," Shaindele said slowly, selecting every word as if it were a live grenade.

"What kind of problems?"

"Bubbee, you know!"

"Still from your mameh? From all that business? But didn't we talk about it?"

"We talked. But it doesn't go away so fast."

"So this psychologist, what do you do with him? Also talk, no? And he's helping you?"

"Yes, but . . ." What was she going to say now?

"Nu?"

"He was helping me a little, but I don't like him. I'm not going back."

"So it's decided? From what, then, are you shaking so much from what's decided already?"

"I decided. But the school . . ."

"What does it have to do with the school?"

"They made me go. Otherwise, Rabbi Halpern will expel me."

"And you told the school you're not going back? They know? They agree?"

"Not yet. But I told everything to Leah. And she agrees with me!"

That, sniffed Fruma Esther Sonnenbaum, was neither here nor there. "So tell me also what you told Leah."

"Please, Bubbee, it's hard for me!"

"Truth surfaces like oil on water. Out with it!"

"I don't like the psychologist. He isn't . . . *tzniusdik.*"

"*Vus?*"

"He locks all the doors. There's *yichud*. And he has dirty pictures on his wall. And he touches me and says things to me, talks to me in a not *tzniusdik* way."

"He's a goy?"

"No, Bubbee. He's a *frum Yid*. A Bobelger Hasid. Rabbi Halpern sent me to him."

"He has a name, this *frum Yid,* this Hasid?"

She hesitated. "Yoel Grub."

"Grub?" she exclaimed. "That's a name?"

Shaindele shrugged.

"When is your next appointment with this *grubber yung*?"

"Today. Six o'clock."

"You're going?"

"I'm never going back to him," she stated vehemently.

Fruma Esther nodded. "*Far zikher.*"

"So you're not mad?"

"Mad? On who should I be mad? If this is the way he behaves, it's a *shandah*. Of course you don't go to a person like that. You're telling me the truth, *maideleh,* for sure?"

"For absolutely sure, Bubbee."

"So where is the problem? Why did you have to leave the house, come here?"

"Leah had to tell Tateh. She was afraid he would be mad on me."

Now a little red light lit up in the old woman's shrewd head. "And why would that be?"

"I don't know. She just did."

There was something more going on here, something she didn't quite understand, and anything shrouded in darkness and mystery she didn't like. In her long experience with life, she'd found sunlight was the best disinfectant for hidden evil. Bring it out in the open, and the "mystery" disappeared, replaced by perfectly clear, foul truth.

She weighed her options. Of course, she could pressure her grand-daughter now, and she would talk. But there was something fragile about the girl this morning, she thought. Maybe it would be better to get the information from her parents.

"So go get ready for school, *maideleh*. You ate something?"

She nodded. "Rugelach."

"That's a breakfast? Come, I'll make you eggs, toast . . ."

Shaindele shook her head, her face pale. "No, Bubbee. I'm not hungry."

"So I'll make you a sandwich for later, *maideleh*," Fruma Esther said, concerned but not yet alarmed. That would come later that morning as sure as the sun rose, she told herself, all her warning bells going off like firecrackers on Lag B'omer.

———

He was going to have to take a few hours off work, he told his boss. It was a personal matter.

"Nothing serious, I hope?" the older man inquired politely.

"Nothing I can't handle in a few hours," Yaakov assured him with a certainty he did not feel.

"And you're caught up with your work? We have the tax deadlines in a few weeks, remember."

"I'm caught up. It's not a problem."

In gratitude, he applied himself with renewed diligence to his work, barely lifting his eyes from the screen and the columns of numbers he was calculating. At lunchtime, he opened his brown lunch bag, eating at his desk.

His phone rang several times before he begrudgingly took time to answer it.

It was Fruma Esther. "I know you are at work, so let's not waste time."

"And hello to you, too, Rebbitzen," he told her, barely breathing as he considered what can of worms was now about to open.

"I spoke to Shaindele. She told me about this psychologist, this *grub-ber yung.*"

He smiled to himself. Leave it to Fruma Esther to cut to the chase. "I'm looking into it."

"She has an appointment today. I told her not to go."

"I also told her. Actually, Leah told her."

"And you agreed?"

"I honestly don't know yet. I'm still looking into it."

"What's to look into? You heard what the child said?"

"I heard. But Shaindele doesn't always tell the whole truth."

She caught her breath. "Since when?"

"Bubbee, you don't remember?"

"That was last year, with all the *tummel* with getting a new stepmother. But since then?"

"She didn't tell you?"

"Only about Grub she talked. That he wasn't *tzniusdik.*"

"Did she tell you why the school sent her to him?"

She shrugged. "Problems. Zissele . . . what happened . . ."

"Not exactly." He hesitated. But he had promised himself long ago that he would not hold back information because of shame. If it could be done, it could be talked about. The truth needed to be dealt with. "Shaindele has been seeing a boy behind our backs. Duvie Halpern."

"Her principal's son?"

"Yes."

"So?"

"What?"

"So he's Rabbi Halpern's boy. He's not a *shaigetz,* not even a *baal teshuva,*" she said pointedly. "What's the harm?"

"It wasn't a shidduch. She was sneaking around with him at night, going to the city with him and who knows what else. We only found out by accident."

"She admitted to this?"

"To everything. And then Rav Halpern called us into his office. He was thinking of expelling her."

"No!"

"Yes."

"But it was his son!"

"So because of that, he agreed to keep it quiet if she'd go see a psychologist."

"And he is the one who picked this Grub?"

"Yes. But I also checked him out with Rav Alter, who spoke to the Bobelger Rebbe himself. Grub is very respected among his Hasidim. All the girls with problems are sent to him for counseling."

"So you think Shaindele is lying about him?"

He hesitated. "I don't know. I'm looking into it. But in the meantime, she is not to go back."

Now she had it, the whole panorama. But like a jigsaw of a thousand pieces, some significant parts were still missing, making it impossible to fully comprehend the entire picture. That being the case, she honestly didn't know what to say.

"She'll get in trouble with the school if she doesn't go back to him?"

"Probably. That's why I need to look into it more closely, right away."

There was a beat as Fruma Esther considered the entirety of the situation. "Whatever you find," she said slowly, "don't send her back. A young, innocent girl doesn't make up such things out of her head."

The exact same idea had occurred to him. But what he kept to himself was the agonizing question of whether or not his daughter was still such an innocent.

————

He left work early, arriving in Boro Park at five thirty. It was a short walk to Yoel Grub's office. It being early, he decided to check out the office itself. There were two entrances, he realized. First, he used the service elevator, carefully turning the doorknob to Grub's office. It was definitely locked. Then he went down and took the main elevator up, walking casually through the waiting room to test the door from Grub's office on the other side. It, too, was locked. From where the office was placed inside the building, he could tell there were no windows, no way to observe what was happening inside.

Of course, you would expect privacy, the front door to a counselor's office would be locked against unwanted intrusions. But for exactly that reason, the back door to the office of a religious counselor should have been wide open. There was no getting around it; Grub was in clear violation of religious law. Yoel Grub might be a rabbi, but he was no tzaddik.

It was a quarter to six. Yaakov sat down in the waiting room, but a certain strange impulse made him rise to his feet and once again go down and take the service elevator up to the back entrance of the office. He stood there, waiting. At five to six, the door to Grub's office flung open. A young girl rushed out, frantic. She was younger than Shaindele. She had long blond hair and a sweet, young face that was crumpled in distress and fear. Grub walked out and reached out, gripping her shoulders roughly when he suddenly looked up and noticed Yaakov standing there. Without a word, he returned to his office, slamming the door.

Yaakov, shocked, approached the girl, who was now sobbing.

"Are you all right?" he asked gently.

She wiped her eyes, nodding, refusing to look at him.

He walked her to the elevator. "My daughter was also sent to him," he told her quietly. "She also complained."

She turned to him, blinking and astonished, a small glimmer of hope in her face.

"She's seventeen. How old are you?"

"Almost thirteen," she told him. "What did your daughter . . . How did she . . . ?"

"She told us he is not *tzniusdik*. She says she won't go back."

"And you believe her?" she asked, her voice so pitiful and fearful, it broke his heart.

"Why wouldn't I? And you must tell your parents, too. And your teachers and your rebbe."

"The Rebbe was the one who sent me to him. They won't believe me. No one will help me."

"I believe you, and I will help you. Here," he said, handing her a piece of paper and a pen, "write down your name and address and phone number."

She hesitated, searching his face as if for answers that would help her make a decision. "They would be angry if they knew I spoke to a strange man. They'll say it's my fault. That's what he tells them all the time. That I'm not cooperating."

"What does he want you to do?"

She stared at him in terror, clamming up. Then she suddenly filled out the paper, handing it back to him wordlessly, then running quickly down the staircase.

He folded it carefully, placing it into his wallet. Then he took the elevator down and rode up once again to the main entrance to Grub's office.

He sat on a chair in the waiting room until the door opened and Grub came out, scanning the room. When their eyes met, Yaakov got up and walked toward him.

Grub looked at him, puzzled.

"You are expecting my daughter, my Shaindel. I'm her father. Can I come in and speak to you?"

Grub backed away, blocking the entrance to his office, but Yaakov pushed past him.

There it was, the picture with the women in bikinis at the beach.

Grub followed him in, carefully closing the door behind them.

Yaakov took in the couch-bed. He sat down, trying it out. It was not a lounge chair but a bed that took up almost the entire office.

"So where is she?"

"Shaindele?"

Grub nodded arrogantly. "You'll have to pay for this session. She never canceled."

"We need to talk, Rav Grub."

"About what?"

"About what goes on in an office between a religious married man, a grandfather, and teenage girls when the door is locked from both sides and there is a big bed between you."

"I'm a professional, licensed . . . ," he blustered.

Yaakov scanned the diplomas on the wall. There was no license and nothing from a recognized institution. It was mostly letters of gratitude from various Hasidic charities and a certificate that he had passed a ye-shiva program in religious counseling.

"Your license?" He pointed to the wall.

"Licenses are for goyim. I have twenty-five years' experience."

"I'm sure you do. But what kind of experiences—that's the question, isn't it? My daughter says you've been touching her, saying things to her that I won't repeat. Threatening her. Just like that poor little girl I just saw with my own eyes!"

Grub shot up. "I don't have to talk to you. What right do you have to stand outside my door and spy on me and my patients? That girl you saw is very troubled. She has a right to privacy! From this minute, you can tell Rabbi Halpern I refuse to accept your daughter. She's too far gone even for my help. A wayward, stubborn girl who has no business being in the company of other religious girls. She'll infect them with her disgraceful behavior. You wouldn't believe the kind of things your daughter told me she's done with this boy! Even I, who thought I'd heard everything, was shocked. I'll be writing all this to her principal. So it's good you came by, saves me a phone call."

Yaakov leaned back, fighting down the almost irresistible urge to smash his arrogant, sneering face to a pulp.

"Is that so, Mr. Grub? I want *you* to know, I had a chance to talk to your last patient. She's younger than Shaindele. Barely thirteen. That's a criminal offense. Child molestation. Remember Nechemya Weberman? How many years behind bars did he get for what he did to that poor girl? One hundred and three? But I'm sure he'll appeal. And with mazal and time off for good behavior, he'll be out in no time, only fifty or sixty years!"

Grub sat down at his desk, playing with a pencil.

"You see, Yoel, can I call you that, since you are on such intimate terms with my daughter? You see, it's not like it used to be, when the whole community elected the Brooklyn DA and then all the judges and all the machers here had to do was complain to get charges dropped and sentences thrown out. Today, it's not like that. Ask Nechemya Weberman during visiting hours in the penitentiary."

"I suggest you don't start fires you won't know how to put out, because your own house could burn down, Yaakov Lehman. After all, it's her word against mine. And who do you think they'll believe? The re-spected friend of the Bobelger Rebbe himself, or some wayward Bais Yaa-kov girl, with a mother who committed suicide and a father who married a *baalas teshuva* who dances around in her underwear in front of open windows? You see, I do my homework."

Yaakov jumped to his feet, his fists clenched and murder in his eyes.

Grub stood up, swiftly opening the door to the waiting room and backing out as quickly as possible into a room full of mostly Orthodox Jews waiting placidly to talk to someone about their aching backs or their sore feet.

28

THE RECKONING

Yaakov opened the door, quietly putting his briefcase down as he awaited the standard rush of greeting from the little ones. To his surprise, it didn't come.

"Yaakov! How did it go?" Leah asked him, putting her arms around him and pulling him close.

His face was pale, his eyes listless. "Where are Icy and Cheeky?" he asked her, concerned.

"In their room. I told them not to jump all over you when you came through the door. To let you catch your breath."

Only now, in the quiet of the house that had all but ignored his return, did he realize how precious that moment was and how he couldn't live without it. He walked down the hall and opened the door to their bedroom. They were sitting on the floor playing. They looked up at him with big, sad eyes.

"Who is going to guess what I have in my pockets?"

They jumped up and ran to him, hugging him and digging their small hands into his pockets, pulling out little handfuls of candies in cellophane and foil-wrapped chocolates.

"Tateh, Tateh, Tateh!" they screamed in joy, practically knocking him over.

He sat down on the floor, letting them climb all over him.

Leah hung back at the door, watching them, happy. "But you can't eat all that stuff now before your dinner," she cautioned, smiling. "Give it to me, and I'll put it away for you in a magic box, and once a day, you can pick one to eat, all right?"

Quickly, Chasya opened a few chocolates, stuffing them into her mouth. Mordechai Shalom tried to follow suit, but he wasn't fast enough. Yaakov compassionately helped him open one before Leah collected the booty.

"Come, wash for dinner," she told them as Yaakov got up and dusted himself off. They ran off into the kitchen.

"I have to talk to Shaindele," Yaakov whispered. "Is she home?"

"Yes, in her room. She's afraid to come out and face you."

He shook his head. "My poor little girl."

"You've changed your mind? What happened?"

"I'll tell you everything after we put the *kinderlach* to bed."

He knocked softly on Shaindele's door. "It's Tateh. Can I come in?"

He heard a barely audible *yes*.

She was sitting at her desk, books and notebooks opened, a pen in her hand. Could she really concentrate on homework amid all this turmoil, or was it a pose?

"How are you, *maideleh*?"

She was struck by the compassion in his voice, which she had not heard for a long, long time. She put down her pen, closed her book, and swiveled to face him. "I don't know, Tateh. I really don't."

"I went to see Grub today."

She was shocked, steeling herself, just about imagining the show that pervert had put on. "And?"

"And now I know that everything you told Leah is true."

Shaindele stood up and walked to him, throwing her arms around him.

He hugged her, smoothing down her hair. "My lovely girl, my Shaindele," he murmured, kissing the top of her head.

She wiped the tears from her eyes. "What's going to happen now, Tateh? Are they going to throw me out of school?"

"Of course not! Why would they? It's Grub who has to be worried, not you. What was your *aveira*? That you told the *emes*? That you stood up to that *chazzar,* that *bulvan*? I'm very proud of you. Not all young girls would," he murmured.

"I was so afraid you wouldn't believe me! I wouldn't blame you."

"I never want you to be afraid to talk to me again. You can tell me anything. Anything. Please promise."

"*Bli neder.*"

Leah stood outside the door watching. She, too, was close to tears. All the memories and longings of her journey toward a deeper life, a richer happiness, built on the firm foundations of love for a husband and children in a place where good was sought, and evil and corruption exposed and destroyed came flooding back to her. At this moment, in this humble little apartment in Boro Park, she saw it, a place where God's light flooded in unimpeded, warming her soul.

"Leah!" Shaindele called out to her. "Thank you!" Slowly, they came together, hugging long and hard, finally bridging all the emotional and cultural gaps that had so long plagued their relationship.

"Come, let's eat. I'm starving," Yaakov said, smiling as he looked at them, treasuring the moment even as he struggled against the fear that still lingered in his heart, a fear that this was not yet over. But he was not too worried. Despite Grub's ugly threats, as a man nourished by decades of learning the laws of goodness in the Torah, he simply assumed that he lived in a place that had internalized those laws as he had and that he would surely be believed.

As soon as he explained the situation to the school, he told himself, they would apologize and thank him, making sure they never sent Grub another young girl. Not only that, but they would help him to inform the parents of Grub's other young patients of the dangers and the need to switch their daughters to another counselor, as he intended to do immediately with Shaindele.

As for the girl whose name he held in his pocket, he would discuss the matter with Rav Alter. If her family was part of the Bobelger community, it would be best if Rav Alter informed the Bobelger Rebbe, giving him the opportunity to deal with Grub and all the other terrible things going on in his community right under his nose. Loss of the rebbe's support would be the most devastating blow they could inflict on Grub. He and his family would be shunned, banished from their place in the community. While he felt sorry for the man's wife and children, it was a punishment Grub himself richly deserved.

As all this flashed with lightning speed through his consciousness the way thoughts do, he found himself almost buoyant with a newfound peace. *You can never know if something is a good thing or a bad thing,* he thought, smiling at his lovely young wife, who smiled back. Instead of destroying them, all these difficulties were just bringing them closer, exposing their hidden wounds to the healing sunlight of truth. *God of the Universe, thank you! You are so good to us in so many hidden ways,* he prayed with exultation.

Later that evening, they all sat around the dining room table enjoying tea and some of the rugelach Fruma Esther had sent.

"But what did he say, Tateh?" Shaindele probed.

"What you would expect a *rosha* to say!" he answered, frowning. "Shameless." He shook his head in disgust.

"You mean he denied everything?" Leah asked.

"Nu? You think he beat his breast and said, 'Guilty'?"

"So, then, Tateh, why are you so sure? Why do you believe me and not him?"

"Because I saw it with my own eyes! I went to the back door near the service elevator and waited. A young girl, no more than thirteen, was running out, but he grabbed her. Only when he noticed me, he let go. Later, I spoke to her. I can't believe he's gotten away with this behavior for so long and that prominent rabbis—the Bobelger Rebbe himself!—back him up, send him other young girls. He is a very good liar! But now it's over for him."

"But what about my school?" Shaindele asked. "Rabbi Halpern?"

"I'll call him tomorrow from work and go in to see him when I get a chance. I can't take off any more time."

"But I missed today's appointment. What if Grub called the school? They won't let me in tomorrow!"

"I'll go with you and talk to Halpern," Leah offered.

Yaakov thought it over. "Yes, thank you. And maybe you should take Fruma Esther with you."

"That's a good idea. But you'll have to call her and explain first so she knows what's going on."

"Do we have to, Tateh?" Shaindele gnawed on her lips apprehensively. She was terrified of her grandmother finding out about Duvie.

"She already knows most of it."

"Really? About me and Duvie, about the trips to the city?" She couldn't believe it. And Bubbee hadn't said a word! She'd been so nice to her! Quick tears sprouted in her eyes, and her throat grew a lump. "You are all so good to me, and I don't deserve it. All I do is make trouble for everyone all the time."

"No one ever lived a life without mistakes, even the biggest tzaddikim," Yaakov assured her. "Look at Moses. He forgot to give his son a bris and was almost punished with death! And then Aaron, the High Priest of all Israel, made the Golden Calf! And the great Rabbi Akiva believed Bar Kochba was the Messiah, and because of that, thousands of his students died in the revolt against the Romans and our Holy Temple was burned to the ground, and we Jews were exiled from our land for three thousand years!" He had begun with the intention of comforting her, but was comforted himself by this realization. The entire book of Leviticus was filled with instructions on how to atone for sin, assuming mistakes would be made by everyone, no matter how wise and exalted.

"So I guess going to a jazz club with Duvie wasn't so terrible, after all." She smiled through her tears. Yaakov shook a finger at her in mock anger. Leah reached out, squeezing her shoulder encouragingly.

"You are a good girl, Shaindele," Leah told her, "but you have suffered, and suffering brings out different qualities in people, sometimes their weaknesses and sometimes their strengths. The important thing is to understand where your behavior is coming from. Once you understand yourself better, you'll be able to cherish all HaShem's gifts to you and to figure out how to use them to have a good and happy life, full of *chesed* to others."

"It's going to be fine, you'll see," Yaakov added in all innocence, looking at his wife and daughter—two people he loved with all his heart and would do anything to protect—honestly believing what he was saying was true.

It wasn't. Not by a long shot.

———

"Maybe you don't have to come, Leah," Shaindele protested as they drove to drop off her siblings and then on to her school. "Maybe nothing will happen."

"I promised your father, and it's better than sitting at home worrying."

Shaindele exhaled slowly, immensely relieved. "Thank you, Leah. And, Leah?"

Leah glanced over at her briefly. Shaindele seemed curled up, tiny, and very young. "Yes?"

"I'm so sorry, for . . . everything. I really . . . love you."

Leah's heart expanded. "My dear Shaindele, I love you, too. Like Tateh said, none of this is your fault. You can't imagine how proud I am of you for sticking up for yourself!"

And your mameh would be, too, was at the tip of Leah's tongue, but she held back. Was that true? Would she be? Really? Or would Zissele, the perfect product of her haredi upbringing on the streets of Boro Park, be absolutely appalled that her daughter had gotten herself into a situation like this in the first place? Would she be one of those people urging her to hold her tongue at all costs? Considering Zissele's own behavior, it wasn't a stretch.

Or maybe, Leah tried to convince herself, if Shaindele's poor mother had survived postnatal depression by getting the help she needed in time, instead of being pushed to suicide by the paralyzing "shame" of needing psychiatric help, she would have been a different person, one capable of truly cheering her daughter on right now.

"And I think your mameh would be, too," Leah added solemnly.

The girl sobbed twice, heavily, then inhaled, controlling herself. Leah pulled a tissue from the glove compartment and passed it to the girl. "Now wipe your eyes and pinch your cheeks to put in some color. Hold your head up high. You are a hero, remember that. You not only saved yourself but who knows how many other innocent girls from being sent to that monster's office."

They walked in together. "You go to class. I'll deal with this. Where is the principal's office?"

Shaindele showed her, then waved a small, hesitant goodbye as she went off.

Leah knocked on the door. When she heard nothing, she opened it. A bewigged matron sat behind a cluttered desk, looking up briefly with a glance that computed Leah's worth with lightning speed, the algorithm no doubt a certain combination of the length of her sleeves and skirt, the thickness of her stockings, and the modesty of her head covering. A frown was the final sum, Leah realized, wondering which element had pushed down her score.

"Yes?"

"I'm Leah Lehman, Shaindele's mother . . . stepmother . . . and I'm here to see Rabbi Halpern."

One brow shot up. "Shaindele Lehman," she repeated slowly with a slight shake of her head. "He knows you're coming?"

"I'm sure he's expecting one of Shaindele's parents this morning."

"Oh yes? And why is that?"

"I'd rather talk to him about it personally."

"Well, he's not in yet."

"When do you expect . . . ?"

The woman shrugged.

"I'll wait, then." Leah looked around for an empty chair and sat down in it.

The secretary ignored her.

It was more than a half hour before he turned up, lumbering into the office with slow, heavy steps, not bothering to look around or even greet his secretary. He disappeared inside, slamming the door.

Leah heard the intercom buzz and saw the secretary answer, cradling the phone between her chin and shoulder, all the while throwing surreptitious glances in her direction as she listened. "Hmm, well, okay."

"Good that you're here. You can take her home with you."

"What?" Leah jumped up.

"Rav Halpern just told me to have Shaindele sent home immediately."

"Don't you dare!" Leah shouted at her, striding past the startled woman and slamming open the door to the principal's office. "I'm here to talk to you, Rabbi Halpern. Don't look so surprised! Did you think throwing my daughter to the wolves was going to be easy? How dare you! Who do you think you are?"

He hardly moved, looking her up and down contemptuously. "Tell Hyman the mashgiach to get here immediately," he called through the open door.

The secretary poked her agitated head in, pulling her wig down over her forehead as if it was about to slide off. "Should I call Shomrim, too?"

At the mention of this private haredi police force that patrolled the neighborhood, ostensibly to protect its citizens from unwarranted anti-Semitic and criminal attacks, Leah momentarily froze.

"Just Hyman. For now," he added ominously.

"Why are you doing this? Did Yoel Grub call you? Well, you should know that he is a sex pervert and abused Shaindele in his office. And she's not the only one. We have proof—names and addresses," she bluffed. "And unlike you, the police won't be impressed by Grub's Boro Park credentials. But you can bet they'll be extremely interested in him—and in you—for sending young girls to him. How many exactly have you sent?"

With surprising agility and speed, he suddenly went to the door, poking his head out. "Wait with the girl," he told his secretary.

"So you *don't* want I should send a note to the teacher?"

"*Wait!*" he shouted, slamming the door behind him. He sat down heavily behind his desk, facing her. "Sit down," he ordered.

Leah sat down.

"First of all, it wasn't Grub that called me. It was the Bobelger Rebbe's nephew. He called to tell me that the Bobelger Rebbe himself told him Shaindel Lehman is a danger to the other girls."

"Based on what? They've never even met her! Just because Grub told him? Did you, or the Rebbe, or the Rebbe's nephew ever visit Grub's office? The 'counseling' comes with a big bed in a tiny room with no windows and two locked doors decorated by pictures of practically naked women."

His mouth fell open slightly. Then he gathered himself together, pressing his lips closed. "I understand you're a *baalas teshuva*? From California? And how long have you lived here with us?"

"Close to three years. But what does that—?"

"Rav Yoel Grub has lived here all his life, as did his father. He has been a respected counselor in Boro Park for twenty-five years and a close friend of the Bobelger Rebbe. But you wouldn't know that, being who you are."

"Twenty-five years!" The implications were staggering. "And how many other girls has he done this to?"

"Done what?"

"Sexually groomed, touched, used for his own sexual gratification?"

"We've never had a single complaint from a parent or a child about Grub."

"You've never had a complaint because everyone is afraid to open their mouths, afraid they'll be treated the way you're treating me and my daughter, pressuring us to keep quiet!"

"Pressuring you? What pressure? How dare you make accusations against innocent, respectable people. You have no proof. Nothing. '*You shall not a talebearer be among your people,*'" he said piously in Hebrew.

"Oh, so we're playing that game? Okay, fine. And what about '*Justice, and only justice, shall you follow,*' or '*Let justice be done though the heavens fall*'?"

"I see you took many *shiurim,*" he said sarcastically.

"And I remember them all, everything I was taught about how good and holy a person becomes when he follows God's just laws."

The door opened. A burly man in his fifties with a large black skullcap burst in. "You called me? There's a problem?"

Rabbi Halpern exhaled, making a dismissive hand gesture. "It's all right, Hyman. She's just leaving."

"If I do, I'm going straight to the police. So you might want to think about this a few minutes longer. And it won't just be about Grub either but about your son Duvie, too."

"Get out!" Halpern shouted.

She shot up.

"No, not you. You sit."

The man disappeared, closing the door.

"What about my son?"

She thought fast. "My daughter was a minor, and your Duvie wasn't. Sexual abuse—including statutory rape—is a felony in New York. And Grub is going down the same rabbit hole as Nechemya Weberman. And you, and your precious Bobelger Rebbe, are both his accomplices, so you are going down with him! Because you are right. *Being who I am*, you're dealing with a woman who didn't grow up on your sacred streets and doesn't understand the unwritten codes here and won't be intimidated. Got that? You throw my daughter out of school or hurt her in any way, and this conversation is over, and I won't be coming back without the NYPD."

He sat there, stunned and speechless. The minutes passed. The secretary poked her head in, concerned at the sudden silence. He waved her away, furious.

Finally, he composed himself. "*Eppes,*" he began mildly, in sharp contrast to his previous outbursts, "*zeit ois az ich hob zich zu geheilt.* Oh, you don't know Yiddish? Maybe I was too hasty," he quickly translated.

"Maybe we both were," she said with equal restraint.

"Why don't you ask your husband to come and see me, Mrs. Lehman?"

"And until then?"

"Maybe it would be best not to involve the girl."

"So she stays in her class, without harassment, and without *loshon hara*?"

He raised two palms upward in surrender. "For now."

"Thank you so much, Rabbi Halpern. As it is written in the *Ethics of the Fathers*: 'Three things sustain the world: justice, truth and peace.'"

She got up with dignity, turned her back, and walked swiftly out of the office, then out of the school. Only when she got behind the wheel of her car did she realize that her hand was shaking too much to put the key into the ignition. She sat there, her brave front collapsing, filled with a sudden terrible fear and regret over her outburst. Halpern would soon realize the emptiness of her threat; seventeen was actually the age of consent in New York, so his precious Duvie was safe. And despite what she had said, she had lived in Boro Park long enough to know the codes and to realize she had finally broken every one of them. *There will be hell to pay,* she thought, tears rolling down her cheeks as she wondered what her husband was going to say when she told him.

29

SHOWDOWN

"Yaakov, can you talk now?"

He put down his sandwich, holding the phone closer. "Yes, I'm on my lunch break. What happened? Your voice is hoarse. Have you been crying?"

"Yaakov," she whispered, "I had a fight with Halpern. He was going to throw Shaindele out today. I said some things . . ."

"Going to throw her out! What . . . that's . . . disgusting!" He paused. "What things?"

"I lost my temper. I'm so sorry; please forgive me." Her voice cracked. "He wants to see you."

"Maybe that would be best. I'll call the school. Did you take Fruma Esther with you?"

"No, I forgot all about it! I was dropping off the kids and just decided to go in to see him for a few minutes, but it was a mistake. I wound up telling him I was going to turn him into the police."

"Turn in Halpern?"

"And Grub, and the Bobelger Rebbe who backs him and sends girls to him."

There was a sharp intake of breath on the other side of the line, then silence.

"We'll talk about it tonight, Leah. Try not to worry."

"Oh, Yaakov, I'm such an idiot! I've ruined everything!"

With a keen understanding of the bottomless abyss she had unwittingly opened up by threatening the Hasidic leader himself, a man basically worshipped as infallible by his fanatic, cultish, and often violent followers, Yaakov nevertheless made a superhuman effort to comfort her. With a calmness and patience that took more self-control than he had ever imagined he possessed, he said, "You are my darling wife, and I love you. You were only trying to make things better."

"Thank you, my love. Thank you." She blew her nose. "Okay. Enough. I'll see you later. Bye."

She hung up and sat on the couch, twisting her hands together, unable to gather her thoughts. There was a sudden knock on the door. "Who is it?"

No one answered. She looked through the keyhole, but there was no one there. She opened the door a crack, and there on the floor was an envelope. She widened the opening, stepping through and looking down the staircase. But it, too, was empty. Picking up the envelope, she hurried back inside, locking and bolting the door behind her.

The envelope was not addressed. She tore it open. It was a short note, primitively handwritten in all block letters as if by a first grader practicing the alphabet.

> Shaindele Lehman is a Prutza. and her
> Stepmother is an American Whore. do Anyting to
> Harm the Santly Rav Grub, or Insult the Holy
> Bobelger Rebbe, and Police Can't Help you. You
> have been Warned!

Her hand trembled. But before she had time to fully absorb what was happening, the phone rang. She listened, terrified to pick it up. But what if it was Yaakov? Or Shaindele? Or one of her clients? She couldn't allow herself to be paralyzed by fear. She wasn't going to give them that!

"Shalom?"

"Shalom to you!" To Leah's enormous relief, it was a woman's voice, and she sounded positively cheerful.

"Leah? Is that you? Leah Howard? Sorry." She laughed. "I mean Leah Lehman! Sometimes I forget."

"I'm so sorry, who is this?"

"Oh, it's Gittel. Rav Weintraub's secretary. You have a minute? The rav would like to speak with you. Can I put him through?"

Rav Weintraub, her mentor, the person who had allowed her to enter this community, who had vouched for her, invited her to attend *shiurim*, employed her, found her a place to live, got her customers for her new internet advertising business. The kindest, most devout man in the world. Oh no!

"Yes, of course," she murmured barely audibly, her throat closing.

"My dear Leah, it's been a long time!"

"Yes," she answered, barely breathing. *Please, God, not Rav Weintraub, too!*

"So you're probably wondering why I'm calling," he said.

"Does it have anything to do with Rabbi Grub, or Rabbi Halpern, or the Bobelger? Because I want to explain."

"Grub? Halpern? The Bobelger?" He seemed surprised. "Sounds very interesting, but no. Listen, I have a girl here, a *baalas teshuva*, who is also a computer whiz. I told her how successful you've been. I think she's also from California. Maybe you could invite her for Shabbos, talk to her about your own journey?"

Leah felt the lump form in her throat as relief flooded through her wildly. She coughed, making it possible to speak. "Of course, I'd be happy to, Rav. Just send me her name and telephone number."

"I'll ask my secretary. Thank you, Leah-le! How are you, the new bride?"

"Not so new anymore, Rav." She smiled, already feeling a little better, as if she were still anchored to those safe shores to which Rav Weintraub had rowed her.

"And how is it to be a mother?"

She breathed deeply. "Rav Weintraub, I never thought I could love so much, so deeply. I never thought I could be this happy."

"Not every mother is so enthusiastic all the time," he joked. "I'm sure it isn't easy."

"That's true, but it's worth everything to take care of your children no matter what. Isn't that true, Rav?"

His voice was bright, rejoicing. "Baruch HaShem! No sacrifice is too great for our children. Whatever we do for them comes back to us in blessings a thousandfold. May HaShem soon bless you with your own child."

"Thank you so much, Rav Weintraub. You have no idea how much your phone call means to me right now!"

There was a beat. "Something is going on I don't know about?"

"I can't talk about it right now. But if you hear any *loshon hara* about me, know it isn't true."

"We don't listen to *loshon hara*. So not to worry, Leah-le," he joked. Then his tone turned serious. "If you need my help, you know you can always come by."

"Thank you so much, Rav."

"My secretary is sending you the girl's number. Thank you, Leah-le."

She put down the phone, the letter still clutched in her shaking fist.

She called Fruma Esther and asked her to come by in the evening, if it wasn't too much trouble.

"Something happened?"

"Yes, I'm afraid. We need your advice."

Later that afternoon, when she picked up the little ones from school and took them back to the car, she found the windshield had been smeared with broken eggs. *Harlot* appeared on the glass in red Magic Marker.

Chasya looked at it, startled. "Why did somebody paint on our nice car, Mommy?"

"Maybe they didn't have paper," she answered, tight-lipped and furious. She strapped the children inside, took out some rags from the trunk, and sprayed the windshield with glass cleaner, rubbing away the writing as quickly as she could, aware of strangers slowing down as they passed to take in the scene, their faces surprised and a bit excited. How many had managed to decipher the writing before she got it all? She worried, scrubbing away only until the word disappeared and she had just enough clarity to safely drive home. She didn't want to linger an extra second with the children in the car in case the vandals were still nearby.

When Shaindele came home from school, she went straight to her room, closing the door. Leah followed her, concerned. "Are you okay?"

she asked, poking her head through the barest opening, not wanting to infringe on her privacy.

Shaindele nodded, coming to the door and opening it, then returning to sit on her bed. She pulled several stuffed animals—relics of her childhood—into her lap, wrapping her arms around her favorite, a brown teddy bear bedraggled of fur. Her face was streaked with dried tears and reddish splotches, Leah noticed. She looked like a frightened child.

Leah sat down next to her, putting an arm around her. "Tell me."

"On the way home, a Hasid crossed the street and yelled at me. The names he called me, Leah! In the middle of the street! And then he opened a bottle and threw some liquid at me." She lifted her feet. "My shoes and socks are soaked."

"Take them off immediately! And take off the rest of your clothes. I'll wash everything! Do it now! Then take a bath and scrub yourself."

Leah lifted the wet shoes and stockings gingerly. They had a strong, acrid stench.

"It was urine. But it could have been acid," she told Yaakov later, hiding in his arms, exhausted. The children had been put to bed early. Shaindele was still in her room, and Fruma Esther had not yet arrived.

They sat side by side on the fraying brown couch in the living room whose walls badly needed a fresh coat of paint; a place that had sheltered them since their wedding day and had been home to Yaakov and his first wife and five children. It was a home like many in their community, modest in size and poor of furnishings but rich in love and devotion and piety. Always in the past, they had convinced themselves that the physical discomforts of such a place were more than compensated for by the joy of living securely among their own kind, sharing in the bounty of their rich, spiritual life. But now doubt chipped away at that certainty as they clung to each other, Leah describing her visit to Halpern, the incident with the car, and what had happened to Shaindele. When she finally handed him the letter, she did so wordlessly.

Yaakov sat up, opening it, then shooting to his feet as he read. He paced the room. He was furious, appalled, frightened, and completely helpless. "May the God of Abraham protect us!" he cried out as the range and depth of the attacks on his family merged in his mind into one unbearable assault.

In Yaakov Lehman's sheltered life among God-fearing Torah scholars and their families, he had never come into contact with people who used this kind of language, let alone who were responsible for these kinds of deeds. He didn't know what to do. Even if he had wanted to, he had no idea how to resort to brute force, threats, lies, or ugliness. He knew nothing about underhanded stratagems. In his straightforward, simple life, his whole experience had been in perfecting his character so as to live ever more honestly and kindly, treating those he came into contact with as he himself would have wanted to be treated. He had no weapons of self-defense. None. But these people, he thought, they were also part of his community. They were his brothers. But they were also his enemies, evil people incapable of repentance who wished him and his family harm. They were Esau to his Jacob.

He crushed the letter in his fist.

Leah caught his hand. "No, don't. We might need it."

"For what?"

"Evidence."

He nodded, feeling distraught at the very thought of breaking the community's strong taboo against bringing in outside, secular authorities. Yet simultaneously, something inside him shouted wildly, *They all belong in jail!* Those who would harm his wife, his young daughter, should be strung up, beaten to a pulp! But even if they went to the police, until they did anything . . . Police were reluctant to get involved in Boro Park disputes, trying to stay out of the neighborhood. For the first time in his life, Yaakov Lehman wished he had the unrestrained physical power of a simple, primitive man with no conscience.

"We need to find out ourselves who's behind this."

"Who do you think?" She was bitter.

That alone was the worst thing they could have done to his family, he realized: taken the light from his happy, loving, kind, devout wife, filling her soul with darkness. Never would he forgive them for this, not if they asked for *mechilah* a thousand times! They needed to be found! To be punished! Surely, the good people whom he had known all his life would help him: Meir, Rav Alter, the men he had studied with for over twenty years, the rav of his shul, the friends of his father, of his father-in-law . . . surely? But then he thought of those men, those good, kind men, and how they, too, disliked to get involved in anything unpleasant, anything that smacked of scandal. How they actively avoided openly taking sides in public quarrels. They were men of peace, of dignity. Men who watched their tongues out of piety but also men who lived in these narrow, congested streets who could ill afford to make enemies of the Hasidim who ran the businesses, owned the apartment houses, and established free loan funds.

Slowly, the confidence inside him collapsed. He felt shattered. "Maybe we should take her out of the school, before the girls start a campaign against her," he suggested. "I could send her to my brother in Baltimore."

"But it's only a few months until the end of the school year. She'll be graduating!"

He paced, more and more agitated. "Yes. She deserves to graduate, after all she's been through. It will hurt her so much to leave now. It's not right!" he fumed, changing his mind again and again.

"And also, she's in the middle of therapy. She has to continue. We can't just stop."

He hadn't thought of that. "Yes, we need to find her someone new, someone she—and we—can trust."

"I'll call my friend Dr. Glaser. She'll know. But you're right. Maybe we should keep her home, at least for a few days?"

"We shouldn't have to give in to this kind of *rishus*. We shouldn't bow to it, obey it. It's like bowing to idols. There is a God, and He will protect us."

"But, Yaakov, be practical."

"All right. What if we pick her up from school and keep her from going out on her own for a little while until we figure this out?"

"Yes, all right. I can do that, pick her up with the car." *Unless they slash my tires,* she thought, wondering with a cold chill what would be next.

The doorbell rang, and the sound sent a frisson of fear through them both. They were under siege, she realized, and the benevolent place she had so lovingly embraced and wanted to call home had become a jungle of dark forces, wild, uncontrolled, and unpredictable.

Fruma Esther bustled in, her hands full of heavy plastic boxes holding various delicacies. "I made so much for Shabbos, I thought you could use—" She stopped, caught by their stricken faces. She put the food down on the dining room table instead of immediately unpacking it in the kitchen. "So tell me, I'm listening," she said, hanging up her coat and settling into a chair.

Yaakov and Leah exchanged glances. Neither one of them wanted to hurt the old woman by telling her any of this, which reflected so badly on the world of which she was so proud to be such a prominent member. And truthfully, neither did they relish the idea of being subject to a long list of recriminations. After all, they were hardly blameless in all of this. Perhaps involving her wasn't such a good idea, after all?

"Nu? I'm waiting!"

Yaakov moved a chair opposite hers. "We have a problem."

"With Shaindele and this Grub. I know all about it. So what else is new?"

"They want to throw her out of school."

"Who? That Halpern? But his own son started it! A yeshiva bum from the pizza parlor, *nuch*!"

"That's what we told him, so he said if she gets therapy, the school won't bother her. They forced us to send her to Grub, who's a Bobelger Hasid."

"Shaindele told me all about him."

"The Bobelger send all their girls to him. I even asked Rav Alter before I sent her, and he said the Bobelger Rebbe himself vouched for him."

"The Bobelger Rebbe himself, you say?" She shook her head in dismay. "He's an old man. Maybe he doesn't know what's going on. But Shaindele is sure about what happened?"

"She's sure. But even if I didn't believe her, should I not believe my own eyes?"

"*Vus is dus?*"

He described his experience with the young girl.

"*Rosha*," she said softly, shaking her head. "And the Bobelger close their eyes! A *shandah*! And their daughters the most sheltered of all the girls, except for Satmar. They're so careful about every little thing, buttoning the last button on the shirt collar, wearing closed shoes not to show the cleavage between their toes, dark stockings, no makeup. They marry them off at seventeen after one date, that's it."

"We also can't understand it. But it's the truth."

She shook her head. "No one will believe it, Yaakov."

"Then we have to make them believe it, Bubbee!" Leah said passionately. "Our Shaindele got out of it before he hurt her too deeply, but what about the other girls? Hundreds of girls over the years. When is it going to stop? Who is going to stop it, if not us?"

"You're putting a healthy head in a sickbed."

"What does it mean, then, when God says to us, *Tzedek tzedek tirdof*? Justice, justice pursue it."

Fruma Esther looked at her. "You're a *baalas teshuva*. You take everything word for word. But that's not how it works here."

"So explain it to me, Bubbee. How does it *work* here? What is it exactly I don't understand? Didn't God say in the Torah, 'All Israel are responsible one for the other'? And 'Chastise your brother'? What part of this am I confused about? And aren't people who live in this neighborhood called *haredim*, meaning 'people who shake with the fear of God'? Don't they keep the tiniest letter of the law and make up lots of extras just to put a fence around what God is asking of us, so we don't ever even get close to sinning? And these things are written clearly for all to read. It's HaShem's will."

Fruma Esther leaned back, breathing heavily. It was all true, all true, she thought. But no one in their community spoke that way, thought that way. It was foreign and strange, this way of thinking, of looking at things. The community had a way of doing things, laws that were outside what was written in the Torah. And overarching all was the respect for the old rabbis, the leaders, whose words were not to be questioned, whose great wealth of knowledge of the holy books granted them almost prophetic wisdom far beyond the ordinary Jew's. You didn't always understand their decisions, which often made no sense, which even seemed, in fact, contradictory to the laws of the Torah. For example, the way you held your tongue when a man beat his wife or cheated the government out of money with false benefit claims. You couldn't understand it, just as a person could not understand why a just and compassionate God would create a lion who had to kill in order to eat instead of living on grass; or why an innocent child should be visited with illness that brought horrible pain and suffering. So, too, you could not always understand how the great rabbinic leaders, the Gedolai Hador, ruled.

"I'm just a simple Jew," she answered. "And so I cannot answer you the way a learned scholar would. But I will tell you this, Leah: if you and Yaakov come out publicly against Grub and the Bobelger Rebbe, no one will be able to help you, not your friends, other rebbes, or the police even."

"So what exactly are we supposed to do, Bubbee? Let them destroy us?"

"What, you mean already they started in on you?"

With a heavy heart, Yaakov handed her the note.

She put on her glasses and read it, her mouth falling open. Then they told her the rest—the car, the urine . . .

"This is how they behaved in the shtetlach in Europe." She nodded sorrowfully. "My father, he should rest in peace, told me they used to put nails on the floor of the mikvah to get back at rival groups. And before the Holocaust, when the *shluchim* came from Eretz Hakodesh to talk to the people about moving to Palestine, they would throw stones at them until they ran away. Even when the Nazis took over, some of these *rabbonim* were still telling the people to stay put, while they themselves ran away! They saved themselves, but did their Hasidim—the ones lucky enough to survive the camps, or the ones in America, remember any of this? No. They flocked back to their leaders here in America, stumbling after them in blindness, throwing piles of money at them, enough to build new yeshivas and *batei medrash,* not to mention luxurious houses for them to live in like kings. Even after what happened in Europe, their Hasidim still hang on their every word, letting them decide who their children will marry, which surgeons will do their operations, even how they should invest their money, as if they were still the wisest of holy prophets." She grimaced. "Yes, so wise they were," she murmured, tilting her head, her eyes narrowing.

"I didn't know you felt this way," Yaakov whispered.

"I don't like to talk about it. We are not Hasidim. Neither was your family. We, too, had *rabbonim.* We followed them when they told us what *hechsher* to use, but on other things, we made up our own minds. I'm only telling you this so you'll understand: don't get into a fight with them! You can't win. The best thing to do is nothing. Find another counselor for Shaindele and send her back to school."

"And Halpern?"

"You leave him to me. As for the Hasidim, tell them if they don't bother you, you won't bother them. That you'll keep your mouth shut about Grub."

"I'm sorry, Bubbee. I know you are right, but I just can't do that," Leah said softly, looking at Yaakov, who looked back at her helplessly.

Fruma Esther studied the two of them. *Two lovely young people,* she thought, *so good and upright and pious.* They were exactly the kind of people this community always pretended they were trying to raise with all their Torah institutions and all their *shiurim* and all their charities. But if Yaakov and Leah tried to change the world, make it a better place, they and their family would be utterly crushed, maybe even physically harmed. She was so afraid for them.

"I see I cannot talk any sense into either of you," she said sadly, getting up.

"I'm so sorry we involved you in our problems, Bubbee. Thank you so much for coming, for giving us your advice, which I'm sure is good. Please, don't worry about us. We will take care of it," Yaakov said, smiling bravely, helping her up and bringing her coat.

"Put this one in the freezer; it's for Shabbos. Chicken legs. And this one is a babka. Chocolate. The kind the *kinderlach* liked from last time," she said, pointing to the plastic containers on the table.

"I'll drive you back," Leah offered, but Fruma Esther just shook her head. "My doctor tells me enough with the sitting around all day! The more I walk, the better it is for me. But thank you." She touched Leah's smooth cheek, looking into her worried eyes. *And I once thought this girl wasn't frum enough to marry into our family, to live in our community!* She and Yaakov were truly the bravest and most pious people she knew, God should only bless them. What was going to happen now? Perhaps Yaakov would be able to defend himself. But Leah? The gossipmongers and backtalkers would rip her to shreds if she dared to take them on. What had happened so far was nothing.

30

THE *CHORBYN*

The next day, Yaakov called Halpern from the office. "I can't take off time from work, Rav Halpern. I want to thank you for your patience. My wife, Leah, she's very protective of my children. Maybe she got a little *verklempt*. No, of course we aren't going to the police! And we have only the deepest respect for the Bobelger Rebbe." He paused, listening helplessly to the furious diatribe of the man on the other side of the line. "So what happened, happened," he mollified. "I understand Rav Grub isn't going to take her back even if she wants to go . . . What? What do you mean if we beg him? We are not beggars, and besides, he isn't the right psychologist for her. And we all want what's best for her, right? I'm glad you agree. You don't? Listen, Rav Halpern, I don't think threats are good, not from me and not from you. So let's settle this like *frum Yidden*, with *rachmones*, all right? The child has only a few months left until she graduates."

He was silent, his lips stretched thin, his fists turning his knuckles white as he heard the reply. "I'm sorry you feel that way, Rav Halpern. But in that case, let me remind you of what happened to the Eshet Chayil school in Brooklyn, and the principal, Rav Yankel Hochman, and his assistant, Mrs. Surah Schneider. They threw out a girl and the parents sued '*for negligence, defamation, intentional infliction of emotional distress, engaging in behavior with malice and intent to harm and breach of contract,*'" he read from the internet article he had printed out. "And the parents could have won if they hadn't decided to settle with the school. How many thousands of dollars in damages? You can just guess." He waited. "No, I'm not saying we *want* to be *moissar* you to the secular courts, but you know the *rabbonim* permit this under certain circumstances. So if you don't act toward my daughter and my family like a *frum Yid,* what choice do you leave me?" He listened, his lips loosening, his fists uncurling. "I appreciate that. I'm sure in a few days, this will all be taken care of. Yes, thank you. So we're agreed to do nothing in the meantime? Okay, thank you. Shalom."

His relief was brief, because even as he put down the phone, his boss was standing at the door looking at him with an expression that no employee ever wants to see.

"Can you come into my office for a minute, Jacob?" his boss said curtly.

Trembling, Yaakov followed him.

"Please, sit down."

Yaakov sat.

"You've been with us how long now, Jacob?"

"Eight months," he said, wiping his suddenly parched lips with a nervous tongue.

"And would you say you are happy here?"

"Yes, very happy. And I hope you have found no reason not to be satisfied with my work."

"Well, we have actually had no complaints until now."

A sudden ache went through his stomach, and his heart began to pound. "I'm sorry to hear that. Can you tell me which client complained?"

"The Weiss Shoe Company."

Yaakov exhaled. "But I don't work on their business. They aren't with me."

"No, but they have been with this company for many years and are a treasured client that brings in a great deal of business for us. And they're not alone. Glick's Diamond Factory. Shaindlin Fabrics . . ."

"None of them are my clients. I have never been assigned any work for any of them," he protested.

His boss seemed confused, shuffling some papers on his desk. "Really?"

Yaakov nodded, and then it dawned on him. "Can you tell me, please, if these companies happen to be run by Hasidim?"

"Actually, I think they are."

"Bobelger Hasidim?"

"Well, I'm not the one to ask. They all look the same to me . . . Sorry, didn't mean to offend."

Yaakov waved his hand. "I'm not offended. But let me explain the background." He explained, watching his boss's face change colors and his body grow more and more uncomfortable as he shifted in his seat.

"Well, I understand, and that is, of course, most unfortunate. But I'm sure you can appreciate that as a business, we have to keep our clients happy."

There it was, the *chorbyn*. After all the sacrifices he'd made! All the hard work he'd invested! And now they were going to fire him, take away his livelihood, plunge his family back into an unbearable poverty. *She's going to leave me*, he thought. And who could blame her? Who would want to be married to such an *umglick*?

"What if . . . ," Yaakov began in desperation, clutching at straws. "What if I tell you that in a few days all these complaints will disappear and the problem will be solved?" He made a herculean effort to sound confident, even as he recognized he had no idea how to make that happen.

"So you're telling me, on your word, that I can call these clients back and assure them that the problem will be solved right away?"

Yaakov nodded, terrified of the commitment he was making. But what could happen that would be worse than getting fired? It was a risk worth taking. *After all, miracles happen*, he told himself.

"Well, I'm glad we had this little talk, then, Jacob. It's been most fruitful. I'd hate to lose you. In fact, your own clients have had nothing but good things to say."

"I'm happy to hear that. And I'll take care of this. I appreciate your confidence in me and your patience."

The man nodded with a stiff, dismissive smile.

Yaakov returned to his desk in a daze, the office and all its people, furniture, papers, lighting merging into a confused sound-and-light show that played out in front of him the way he imagined narcotic-fueled dreams displayed themselves in the minds of the drugged. But he had ingested nothing but a large dose of misery, enough to weigh him down and drown him in sorrow forever.

———

"What can I tell you, Basha? Everything is falling apart. The world is falling apart," Fruma Esther said almost breathlessly as she leaned back on the easy chair, the most comfortable chair in the living room of her dear friend, the chair Basha's husband, Rav Aryeh, used when he wasn't out learning or teaching or being part of some neighborhood committee that decided the most difficult halachic issues. So most of the time, it was empty.

"Oy, I hate to see you like this, Fruma Esther! It's not good for your heart!"

"Or my head, or my liver, or my varicose veins," she muttered. "But what am I going to do? My Shaindele says he touched her. That the man touched her, took the pins out of her hair and talked to her in a way that is not *tzniusdik*! Think of it, Basha. A fifty-year-old, with grandchildren!"

Basha tilted her head, giving her friend a long, sideways look.

"All right. I know my granddaughter doesn't always tell the exact truth, but my Yaakov looked into it. The man counsels young girls in an office with no windows, locked at both ends! With his own eyes, Yaakov saw another young girl coming out of there crying. Besides, why should Shaindele make it up?"

Basha considered this for a few moments, then shook her head. "You're right, Fruma Esther. She's a bit *tsumisht,* but she is a good girl. I'm proud on her that she told her parents and didn't go back."

"But it's a serious problem, Basha. This counselor, this Grub—"

"Such a name!"

"Right? Who has a name like that and doesn't change it? Anyway, Grub is very good friends with the Bobelger Rebbe."

"*Oy vey!* You can't start with him. His Hasidim are animals. They're dangerous."

"Not all," Fruma Esther remonstrated mildly, with a distinct absence of the passion she reserved for good causes that she actually believed in. Both women, longtime residents of Boro Park, had watched with growing alarm and resentment as over the years Hasidim of various sects had displaced the longtime Litvish misnagdim from their homes and institutions, buying up everything in sight, causing a stampede of the older residents from Boro Park to places like Lakewood and Monsey.

"But Halpern, her principal, isn't a Hasid and Bais Yaakov isn't a Hasidishe school. Why would he send girls to a Bobelger Hasid for counseling? And why would he side with him?"

"I think that there are very few *frum* psychologists for girls in Boro Park, and he's sent so many girls to Grub that if it comes out something is wrong, it will be a *shandah* for him personally. So he's threatening to throw Shaindele out if she doesn't go back."

"Remind me what you told me about why she was sent there in the first place? I'm so forgetful."

"I never told you."

"So tell me now."

She hesitated.

"I'm listening."

"Shaindele was going out with Duvie, Halpern's son."

"The one that's OTD? The one from the pizza parlor? I didn't know she already started with a shadchan."

Fruma Esther sighed. "She isn't. She did it *on her own*. Behind her parents' backs."

The other woman gasped. "I can't believe it! Our little, sweet Shaindele who was always so *frum*?" She shook her head sorrowfully. "If her mameh were still alive, it never would have happened." She sighed. "But you know, Fruma Esther, if it wasn't your Shaindele, you'd be the first one to say it's not fair to the other girls to have such a girl in their class, that she might be a bad influence on them."

"*Emes.* Believe me, I know. But what can I do, Basha? She's my little Shaindele. I lost my dear daughter Zissele. What, am I going to lose *her* now, too? She'll have to leave the community. She'll be pushed out to who knows where? To what *Gehinnom*? Maybe even off the *derech*!"

"*HaShem Yishmor!*"

Fruma Esther nodded. "Blood is thicker than water. Anyway, like you said, she's *tsumisht*, not evil. Basha, the child has only four months until she graduates. Then she'll go to the matchmakers, do everything respectably. But if she gets expelled . . ."

"No matchmaker will go near her, and the boys, her brothers, will also be in trouble."

"Even worse, she'll never be able to become a teacher like her mother! No religious school would accept her. And she would make a wonderful teacher."

"So what you're telling me is this has to be hushed up, and fast."

Both women nodded. "I told Yaakov and Leah this. But there's a problem."

"*Vus?*"

"Leah. She doesn't know from such things. She's mad on the world! She goes to Halpern and threatens him *she'll go to the police.*"

"She didn't!"

"I'm telling you, when I heard this, *it's getting black in my eyes!* She'll turn him in, she tells him, and Grub, and also—listen to this—*the Bobelger Rebbe himself* for recommending Grub!"

"I'm *plotzing*, Fruma Esther, *plotzing*!"

"What are we going to do? Such *a broch*. To threaten their rebbe. His hoodlums are already worked up." Fruma Esther shared the long list of attacks the family had already suffered.

"I can't believe it! To Shaindele, in the middle of the street, in front of everyone! Such chutzpah. *Behemeis*. So the word is already out."

"Was it Halpern or Grub, you think?"

"Probably Grub called Halpern, to complain on Shaindele and get her expelled. But before he could do it, Leah started in with him about the police. Halpern for sure called Grub to tell him what she said."

"Such a *chorbyn*!"

"It was an easy way out for Halpern. But don't worry on him; he's a *nishtikeit*! He should only meet a fire! He hasn't been principal very long. And that son of his, that Duvie, we've all heard the stories. So Halpern's been on shaky ground awhile. You know, my Aryeh sits on the board of Bais Yaakov."

"I didn't know that!"

Rebbitzen Basha Blaustein shrugged. "Like he doesn't have enough to do! So I can ask him to give a call to Halpern, that he shouldn't dare throw Shaindele out."

"That would be a big mitzvah. But what are we going to do about the Bobelger? Leah threatened their rebbe! Once the attack dogs are sent out, only the rebbe can call them back."

"If you want to beat a dog, you find a stick!"

"*Emes,* Basha. But how?"

"What we need to figure out is why the Bobelger want to protect this Grub. I can't believe no one else has ever complained. So why do they keep sending their young girls to him? They are so *frum,* so careful. Five minutes their girls talk to a boy, they're already dragging them under the chuppah."

"Did you ever think, Basha, that the Rebbe himself just doesn't know?"

"What?"

"Think about it. The Bobelger Rebbe is almost ninety years old. No one sees him, talks to him, except his nephew and a few of the big machers with the money who support him and Bobelger institutions. Even when the Rebbe sends out new rulings, people never see him, only the nephew and the machers. Maybe one of them has some connection with Grub."

"I think I once heard one of the machers' sons is married to one of Grub's daughters. Or maybe it's the nephew's daughter, or his sister? Anyway, he's a relative."

"Oy, you could be right, Basha!"

"So who knows what's really going on there, who's really in charge? And even if people could get through to the old rebbe, get around the nephew and the machers, who's going to tell the Bobelger Rebbe the truth? They'd be terrified to be called yentas, talebearers, liars, accused of *loshon hara* and *rechilus.* They'd have to risk being thrown out of the Hasidus."

"What we need is a very *choshuva* rav that everyone respects, that even the nephew and the machers wouldn't dare to turn away. Only such a person could go to the Bobelger Rebbe himself and tell him the truth about Grub.

That would be the end of this. A word from the Rebbe, and Grub would be out, and my family's good name would be saved."

"But who is important enough and well-respected enough to walk in to see the Bobelger Rebbe from today to tomorrow?" Basha scoffed. "And who would want to get in the middle of such a tzimmes?"

"Who?" Fruma Esther's mind was blank. But then, like a gift from heaven, a brilliant flash of clarity lit up her brain, sending her the obvious solution and the answer to her prayers.

31

❧

MORE THAN A FRIEND

The first call came in as soon as she'd arrived home after dropping off the kids.

It was a veteran client—one of her first, in fact—a very demanding butcher who always wanted everything done yesterday and never paid his bills until she threatened him with a *din Torah*.

"For me, you're not working anymore," he said without any prefacing niceties, something she was used to from him. "I'll find someone better, cheaper," he told her nastily.

"That's fine, Mr. Schecter. Just pay me for the part of the job I already sent you."

"What part?"

"The updated mailing list of your clients?"

"I'm not using it."

"Well, that's up to you. But I did the work, and I want to be paid."

"You should get off your high horse, lady."

"I don't know how to ride. Pay me, or I'll sue you."

She hung up, annoyed. *I should be happy to get rid of him,* she told herself, but still, it rankled. How many times had he begged and wheedled her to do one more job and then one more after that even though he hadn't paid his bills? And how many times against her better judgment had she given in? Well, this was it, then, and good riddance.

Not fifteen minutes later, the phone rang again. This time, though, it was a new customer for whom she'd completed a small but really excellent little online sales campaign. The pitch had been clever, the graphics stunning. She'd been quite proud of it. He'd thanked her profusely, paid her promptly, and enthusiastically asked for a quote for a great deal more. She smiled to herself. That was quick! She'd only sent the proposal out yesterday. It was very competitively priced, but still a great deal of money she could really use right now. But her smile soon faded. No, he said apologetically but firmly, he had decided, after all, to go with someone else. They exchanged the usual polite regrets. She hung up, surprised and disappointed. Two clients leaving her in the space of a half hour? What were the chances?

She decided to do some laundry and clean up before opening the computer and beginning her morning's work. The noisy, energetic dance of the loaded washing machine masked the long series of constant dings heralding incoming messages. By the time she'd finished, made herself a morning cup of coffee, and checked her messages, she was shocked to find dozens of her clients had contacted her—almost all of them cutting ties.

This can't be happening, she thought, dumbfounded. She called her favorite, a kosher coffee shop for whom she had set up internet advertising, a website, a customer list. It was run by a young, religious couple from Israel who were both chefs. They had invested everything in their homey little business and had become quite successful—creating a popular local hangout where mothers came to meet over croissants after dropping off the children at school and where portly religious businessmen trying to lose weight often ordered a healthy salad for lunch.

"Hi, Tirza, it's Leah. I just got your message. I'm so surprised. Can you just tell me what I've done wrong? I thought you were happy with my work."

"Leah!" The voice on the other side of the phone was low and embarrassed. "You haven't done anything wrong. You've done a great job for us."

Leah couldn't believe her ears. "So then . . . why? Why are you firing me?"

There was a long silence. "Some men came by yesterday afternoon. They said they were Bobelger Hasidim and that you had insulted their rebbe. They warned us to cut our ties with your business, or else they would see that our kosher certification was canceled."

"They can do that?"

"The Bobelger run Boro Park. They are on every religious council; they have ties with the mayor and the district attorney. And no one in our district gets elected judge or councilman without their backing. Of course they can do that!"

She couldn't believe it. It was like scratching beautiful wallpaper to find the wall beneath was crawling with termites. Such injustice, corruption, and ugliness underlying all that she had believed was so holy and righteous and just! She felt as if she had dived into a pristine pool of crystal-clear water in the mountains, only to find it was fed by sewers. Something bright and lovely died inside her.

"Listen, Leah. I don't know what you did to upset them, but you have to undo it and fast. They've gone to every business in Boro Park. I'm so sorry, but we have everything invested in our coffee shop. We just can't afford to go against them. And neither can you."

Leah's heart sank. She said she understood. No, of course there were no hard feelings. She thanked them for their business, wished them well, hung up, then cried her eyes out. By late afternoon, almost every single one of her customers had either called to fire her or had done it online.

Everything she had built up, all her work, gone, just like that.

She stared at the closed computer and silent phone, feeling as if she were making a shiva call where someone very young and dear had unexpectedly and shockingly passed away. Those were the worst; there was nothing you could say, no comfort you could offer.

She got up and paced through the dingy little apartment where she had fallen in love with the children, and then their young father, starting a life with so much promise, so much richness. She touched the laminated jigsaw puzzles hanging on the discolored walls put together over long Shabbos afternoons by the children and their mother, pictures of pretty forests and rivers, children playing by the shore. She paused at the shelf of family photos: Shaindele's sweet round face, her hair tied in bows; baby Mordechai Shalom with his long, golden curls in his mother's young arms; Chasya in her Queen Esther Purim costume. And there, too, was the wedding photo of herself in the lustrous white dress she'd borrowed from a *gmach* that fit her so well, her red curls elegantly gathered and dressed with pearls, standing next to her tall, handsome husband, both of them beaming with happiness. Only recently had it even been framed!

And now, she realized, their lives as they knew them were over. So soon!

She tried to think of how she had unwittingly destroyed all that was so precious to her. What had been her sin? Where had she taken a wrong turn? She tried to remember every act she had committed, every conversation she had had, combing through them the way a mother combs a child's hair looking for lice and the little white eggs that cling to the cleanly shampooed hair waiting to hatch and multiply, to infect and destroy. That was it! She had obviously missed one or two—little sins. Perhaps she had held resentment in her heart for something she overheard a neighbor saying about her and, instead of confronting them, had held it inside? Perhaps she had been unkind to her husband without realizing it, or forgotten to give charity? Little eggs, clinging, that had now hatched and were multiplying, crawling over her life. Or perhaps it was much worse: not small sins but inexcusable transgressions like the sin of ingratitude, of always wanting, pleading, for more, more, more instead of counting all God's many blessings?

She sat down at the dining room table and took out Maimonides's *Sefer HaMitzvos,* which she had been in the process of learning before her wedding. According to Jewish law, there were 613 commandments that a Jew was obligated to observe. Some were positive like love your neighbor, love God; and some were negative like don't steal, don't gossip, don't commit adultery. One by one, she sifted through them, judging herself as harshly as she could.

And then suddenly, out of nowhere, she felt a sudden revelation. She closed the book and kissed it. No, it wasn't a just God punishing her for her transgressions but a corrupt community of hypocrites trying to destroy her for *all she was doing right!* It was because she had taken this community at their word, loved God, and kept His commandments; because she had refused to betray all the ideals that *they* had instilled in her and that she loved. For that, they would never forgive her.

I am *doing the right thing,* she understood. *No matter what happens, I must hold on to that. All that I've learned here, all that I've been taught from the holy books of the Torah has led me to this moment, to these decisions that will now destroy my life here, making me an outcast.*

The words of the psalm came back to her:

My enemies abounded with life and they that hate me wrongfully were multiplied.
They that repay evil for good oppose me because I pursue that which is good.

She would not, *could not,* do differently. Something in her had changed permanently, she realized. She was not that morally compromised girl who had been able to keep working for a corrupt company producing bogus products that destroyed lives to keep her paycheck. She had truly done *teshuva.* She was a different person now, she thought. A better one.

She closed her eyes and felt God streaming inside her, illuminating the darkness, lightening her heavy heart. She laughed out loud. Against all reason, she suddenly felt happy. *He* was real! And *He* was still there. *He* had not left her. The same God that lit the streetlamps, sent a jogger and his son to rescue her eight-year-old self from the monster who had threatened to taint her young life with the lifelong horror of violation and pain, transforming the experience instead into a touchstone of faith and gratitude, would always be there for her. And what she was doing now, she told herself, would please Him and make Him proud. It was as simple as that.

She stretched, walking to the window. Spring had come to Boro Park. The sparse trees that lined the gray sidewalks were becoming lush and green again, and the dull, cold light of winter had been replaced by a warming golden glow that slid through the narrow gaps between the crowded brick houses like honey.

She took out the old vacuum cleaner, dustcloths, and glass cleaner, going into a frenzy of tidying up, trying to keep her body and mind too busy to think about the moment Yaakov would come in through the front door. Should she call him now and tell him what had happened? Or let him have a few more hours of peace? How would she be able to break this news to him at all? Would he be angry—at her, at Shaindele? Or simply, and more likely knowing him, just heartbroken at the awful behavior of the people he lived among?

Exhausted, she finally turned off the vacuum cleaner, staggering to the couch and almost falling into its soft cushions. *What,* she thought with rising panic, clasping her hands together tightly, *are we going to do? How are we going to pay our bills?*

Well, there was always Yaakov's salary. They could manage on that while she built up a new client list, gentile businesses outside the neighborhood who couldn't care less about Hasidim. But that would take time. And then, of course, there was always the possibility of finding a job in Manhattan, far away from this insular little community. After all, how far did the influence of these shitty little Hasidic thugs go? But it would mean such inconvenient hours and hiring babysitters for the children . . .

Her head spun.

Before she knew it, it was time to pick up the kids. She hurried down to the car. This time, it was not eggs on the windshield. This time, just as she'd feared, it was the tires, all four of them, slashed. She gave out a little cry, holding her hand to her mouth. But there was no time! She would have to walk to pick them up.

She hurried, trying not to allow hatred to fill her heart as she looked at the strangers passing her by, the people who either ignored her or looked her brazenly up and down finding fault, or so at that moment did it seem to her. She felt besieged and friendless among hostile strangers. *Why,* she thought, *did I ever come here? And how could I ever have thought it was better than what I'd left behind?* Secular life might have been empty and careless, but it hadn't been deliberately cruel. She counted her friends: Fruma Esther, the Blausteins, who had mentored her, Rabbi Weintraub, Dr. Shoshana Glaser, who she'd met in a hotel ladies' room, both of them escaping from horrible shidduch dates, Shoshana's Rollerblading group. How had she ever imagined she could make a life here? That these people would ever see into the heart of a stranger among them and accept her as an equal?

Chasya was already standing with her teacher inside the gate waiting. She smiled and waved. Chasya's little face lit up, and she waved back.

And then it hit her. She felt her body propelled violently forward, her arms instinctively outstretched, bruising along with her knees as she slammed against the hard pavement, her forehead and nose bumping and scraping against the rubble and slivers of glass. For a moment, she didn't even try to move, afraid of becoming aware of some tragic, irreversible damage. She simply closed her eyes, assessing her pain. But then she heard the voices. She looked up. Dozens of strangers surrounded her, peering at her, shocked and concerned. A young mother, horrified, moved toward her wanting to help. But a chorus of voices stopped her.

"Don't move her, don't move her!"

"I'm calling Hatzalah!" a man with a cell phone declared.

"He rode right into her!" the young woman insisted, clutching her baby closer. "It was no accident. It was clear like the day. He did it *dafka*. Slammed right into her!"

Leah's head throbbed, trying to make sense of all this information, to put it together, but it was impossible. She was too tired. All she wanted was to sleep.

Then she heard Chasya's terrified voice. "*Mommy!*"

She opened her eyes, trying to lift herself up off the ground, to turn over, but it was impossible. Everything hurt. Kind hands patted her down, urging her to lie still, informing her that medical help was on the way. Someone else handed her back her purse, and still another offered her baby wipes to clean her hands and face.

She lifted her head slightly, looking toward Chasya. The child was terrified, crying. Leah motioned toward her teacher to bring her, and her teacher picked her up, carrying her to Leah and setting her down.

Chasya looked down, hysterical. Leah reached up to touch her face. "Don't cry. You know sometimes when you are playing and you fall down you get a few boo-boos? That's what happened to Mommy. That's all. I'm going to be fine."

"But the bad man on the bicycle . . . He's a *rosha*."

"I'm sure it was an accident. Maybe he forgot how to ride? Next time, he's going to break his own head."

She saw the child suddenly stop crying. "Maybe his head will crack open like a big egg," Chasya said with a cautious smile.

Leah reached for her hand, kissing it. "Your teacher is going to call Bubbee to pick you and Mordechai Shalom up," she told the child, nodding at her teacher, who nodded back.

"Please don't worry, Rebbitzen Lehman. We'll take care of it. Can I do something else for you?"

But an ambulance was already pulling up to the curb, the EMTs jumping out and hurrying toward her.

"You go with your teacher now, Chasya. Mommy will be fine. The doctors will put a Band-Aid on my boo-boos."

The child wept, but she didn't struggle, taking her teacher's hand and walking back into the building, all the while throwing kisses over her shoulder.

A young bearded man—a Hasid? she wondered—wearing a bright orange EMT vest crouched down beside her. Instinctively, she recoiled.

"Listen, we're from Hatzalah, the local Boro Park volunteer ambulance group. Someone called us. Can you tell me your name and what happened?"

"My name is Mrs. Leah Lehman, but I'm not sure what happened."

"It was an accident," a man offered.

"No, it was *dafka*. Some Hasid, a *meshuganah bulvan* on a bicycle, was riding on the sidewalk and rammed right into her! Didn't even stop!" an older woman informed him, adjusting her head covering. "What's going on in this neighborhood? A *shandah*!"

The EMT nodded, surprised. "A Hasid? Are you sure?"

"I don't know a Hasid from a *misnagid*?" the woman scoffed. "*Payis* down to his *pupik*."

"A *frum* person to do something like this. Disgusting," the young mother agreed, incensed.

"Teenagers," someone else suggested.

"Teenagers don't have long beards," the irate older woman continued. "Here, sweetheart, I'm writing down my name, my number. I'll put it in your pocketbook. I'll be a witness for you. *Zay gezunt! Be well.*"

"Someone called the police?" the EMT asked.

No one spoke.

"Okay, we'll report this. But first, let's take care of you," he said, his wide, dark eyes filled with concern and sincere sympathy. "Tell me how you feel."

"Like I got into a fight with an angry three-hundred-pound gorilla."

He smiled. "Do I have your permission to examine you?" he asked.

"Are you a doctor?"

"No, but we are all trained professionals, and we will only do first aid. In ten minutes, you'll be in the emergency room of Maimonides Medical Center. We've already called ahead."

"Okay, thanks." Gently, and very delicately, they lifted her onto a stretcher and carried her to the ambulance. Behind a curtain pulled closed for modesty, one of them very professionally examined her wounds, cleaning them and applying disinfectant. "The good news is that mostly you've just got some superficial scrapes and bruises. We can't tell for sure, but you don't seem to have a concussion. The bad news is that it looks like one of the fingers on your left hand might be broken. Can you try moving it?"

She shook her head. The pain was excruciating.

———

By the time Yaakov arrived at the hospital, her head had already been x-rayed, concussion and bleeding ruled out, the finger set, and all her wounds—all of them ugly but superficial—bandaged.

She touched the bandage on her forehead. "I must look like an extra in a disaster movie."

He sat down next to her, a flash of fury and anguish in his eyes as he looked at her wounds. He reached out for her unbandaged hand, kissing her fingers. "You look beautiful. Leah, Leah, why were you walking? Why didn't you take the car? We spoke about this!"

"Yaakov, the tires were slashed."

His shoulders slumped, and his face stiffened furiously.

"And, Yaakov, I've lost all my customers. The Bobelger threatened them."

He turned away from her, looking at the ground. "My boss called me in, too. Told me he'd had complaints about my work from clients, people I don't even work for, Hasidim. I tried to explain, but he doesn't want to hear. They can't afford to lose customers, he says. He wants me to deal with this or he might fire me."

"Deal with this? What, send her back to Grub? Apologize to him? Pretend we were mistaken?" She searched his face, holding her breath.

"Never!" he said emphatically, and her heart filled with love for him, for this brave, upright, kind man.

"Oh, what are we going to do? This is what it must be like to live with the Mafia in places like Sicily or Naples."

"And this is how criminals spread their evil and torture the innocent. Whatever happens, we can't give in!"

Then she thought of something. "Did Shaindele get home all right?"

"Fruma Esther took a taxi. Picked up all the children and took them home. She's waiting for us."

"What would we do without her, Yaakov?"

He nodded. "She's a blessing."

"When are they releasing me?"

"I think they want we should wait another hour, just to make sure you aren't dizzy or throwing up."

And then, there was nothing left to say. She closed her eyes, giving him her hand. He sat by her bedside holding it like a precious jewel.

Help me, he prayed. *Dear Lord. Help me.*

32

❧

GOD'S MESSENGER

When they got home later that night, Chasya was still up, sitting in the living room with her sister and Bubbee.

"Mommy!" Chasya screamed, running toward her. Yaakov smiled at her but held up a hand, cautioning her not to get too close. After he helped Leah walk toward the couch and sit down, he lifted the child in his arms.

"You were worried about Mommy," he said gently, and the child nodded.

"The *rosha* knocked her down—his head should only crack open like an egg! And someone should steal his bicycle!" she added for good measure.

"Come here."

Yaakov sat the child on the couch next to Leah, who wrapped her uninjured hand around the little girl's shoulder, pulling her close. She brushed away her silky dark hair from her forehead and kissed her.

"Why did he do it, Mommy?" the child asked, putting her thumb in her mouth and leaning her head against Leah's shoulder.

Leah looked over her head at Yaakov, who looked back at her, his jaw flinching.

"We can't know why people do things. HaShem allows everyone to decide what they're going to do all by themselves."

Chasya took her thumb out of her mouth. "Except for Pharaoh," she whispered sleepily.

Despite their pain, Leah and Yaakov pressed their lips closed to hide proud smiles, winking at each other.

"What do you mean, Icy?"

"HaShem made his heart hard like a stone so he couldn't change his mind and do *teshuva*, so HaShem could give him the worst punishment for what he did to the *Yidden*," the child told them. "The man on the bicycle, he's worse than Pharaoh! HaShem should give him eleven plagues!"

"My Icy." Leah kissed her again, squeezing her gently. "I'm so proud of you. You've been so good. But you've had such a long day! So many things happened. Are you ready for your tateh to carry you to bed and tuck you in?"

She nodded sleepily, lifting her arms up to her father, who hovered over her.

"Did you say thank you to Bubbee for taking you home?" Yaakov whispered to the child, who lifted her tired head from his shoulder. "*A dank,* Bubbee."

Fruma Esther got up and walked to the child, kissing her. "Your mommy is right. You were a very good girl, Chasya. Not even a minute's trouble did you give your bubbee."

The child nodded happily, acknowledging the compliment, settling her head back into her father's chest as he took her to bed.

"Where's Shaindele?" Leah asked, suddenly realizing she hadn't seen the girl.

"She's in her room. She's ashamed from you. She thinks it's her fault."

"Please, tell her to come, would you, Fruma Esther?"

Shaindele came into the living room and just stood there, staring at Leah, then burst into tears.

"*HaShem Yishmor, HaShem Yishmor,* this is all my fault!"

"Come here and sit down with me, Shaindele."

The girl obeyed, her movements slow and reluctant. "Now listen to me. Who are the guilty ones? All the criminals in jail or the people they attacked, robbed, and murdered?"

"I don't know, I don't know." Shaindele wept, covering her face with her hands. "If I hadn't sneaked around with Duvie and hadn't been sent to Grub, none of this would have ever happened."

You can't argue with that, Leah thought, moved by the girl's sincere contrition and sorrow. She put her arm around her heaving shoulders, just as she had her little sister's. "And if you hadn't gone to Grub, he'd still be abusing little girls from our neighborhood and no one would ever know. It was *beshert* you should go through this, to expose him, to help others. I'm so proud of you!"

But Shaindele refused to be comforted. "Please forgive me, Leah. I'm so, so sorry. I'll never do anything like that again. I—" She was crying so hard, her voice became incoherent.

Yaakov moved into the room and stood in front of her. "I'm going to say this, and I'm saying it to all of you, not just Shaindele. '*Fret not because of evildoers, nor envy workers of violence, for like grass they will soon be cut down . . . trust in the Lord and do good,*'" he said in Hebrew, quoting the words of Psalm 37. His voice shook, and his body trembled.

Leah reached out a steadying hand, caressing him.

"This is what I've decided. Leah, you are going to visit your mother in Florida, and you'll take the little ones with you. Shaindele, you are going to your uncle in Baltimore to be with your brothers."

"But what about school, graduation?"

"Your uncle has arranged for you to finish school in Bais Yaakov in Baltimore. He knows the principal, and they are happy to have you."

"But I won't know anyone," she began, then suddenly stopped, swallowing hard. "Yes, Tateh. Thank you, Tateh."

"It's a very good idea," Leah said. "But what will you do here all alone, Yaakov?"

"I won't be alone. After all, I've lived here all my life. I have friends, neighbors."

He sounds very brave, and very foolish, Leah thought, loving him more than she ever thought possible.

"You are also going to Florida, Yaakov," Fruma Esther interjected suddenly. All this time, she had been sitting quietly in the big easy chair, her face white and drawn, her eyes shocked as she took in Leah's injuries, the bandage on her forehead, the splint on her finger, the hint of leg bandages slightly visible beneath her long, modest skirt. She couldn't believe it had happened in Boro Park, on these kind, familiar streets where she had spent her entire life! That a Jew would do this to another Jew . . . It was unthinkable!

Then, suddenly, she remembered the vague stories over the years of what went on among the Hasidim—here and in Kiryas Yoel, Meah Shearim, and B'nai Brak—scandalous tales about how different warring sects vandalized each other's synagogues and study houses, beat up rabbis, broke into homes and businesses, and all in the name of God. She remembered what Basha had said about the Bobelger. She hadn't wanted to believe it, but like medicine with a horrible taste, she forced herself to swallow. And if this *was* the truth, then it was better for Yaakov and Leah to take the little ones somewhere else until she could try to put an end to it.

"How else is she going to get to Florida? You'll drive her down, Yaakov. She's not fit to take care of the children and drive yet."

"We can't drive down," he said.

"Why not?"

"Well, the thing is, the tires on the car—" Leah began.

"Don't tell me!"

"That's why I was walking to pick the kids up."

"We'll call the tow company now. It's Heschel Altshuler's nephew. He'll pick up the car, change the tires, and bring it back by noon tomorrow."

Leah shook her head. "It's going to cost a lot of money, and right now . . ."

Fruma Esther looked from Leah to Yaakov. "Something else happened?"

"I lost all my customers. The Bobelger threatened them."

"They threatened my boss, too," Yaakov told her suddenly. He hadn't planned on it, wanting to spare her, but there it was. It was a relief to him. He was so tired of secrets, of making up lies to save face, to cover crimes, to make their world seem a better and more benevolent and upright place, imbuing the people around him with all kinds of superior qualities that in reality they didn't possess. They were no different from anyone else, he thought bitterly. No better and no worse. Simply the same as all godless people who stepped over others to get ahead.

OTD, short for people who had left the good and righteous path of Orthodoxy to live lives that adhered to no law or ritual. How we pride ourselves on how superior we are to them! How deep is the sorrow we profess for their parents and relatives who must suffer the disgrace of their relationship to such miserable creatures! But if the truth be told, who was really, firmly, on the path of righteousness, and who far afield? It was not what the people of Boro Park wanted to admit to themselves.

"I'll take care of it," Fruma Esther said firmly, waving away all their objections. "Listen, children," Fruma Esther began sadly, "I understand what you are going through, and it breaks my heart. But there are still good people in this place. We are not Sodom and Gomorrah. Let me see what I can do."

"What can you, or anybody, do? We can't apologize to Grub. We can't send Shaindele back to him. And that's what they're demanding in order to leave us alone."

"Are you sure that's why all this is happening? Because Grub is so important to the Bobelger?"

"Not directly, but because it is known that he is supported by the Bobelger Rebbe himself. And so, if we say anything against him, it's like we are insulting their rebbe."

"That's what this Grub wants you to think, him and his followers. That's why he's gotten away with this for so long! I'm sure the *menuvel* on the bicycle who did this to Leah is a close relative of his, another *grosse tzaddik*. He probably cut the tires, too. Believe me, it's only a few bad apples. And they are only angry and helping Grub because they don't know the *emes*. Yaakov, you said you had a name, a girl who you saw with your own eyes coming out of his office, crying?"

"Yes, but she won't testify against him. She wouldn't even agree to talk to me."

"Never mind. Give me the name."

"What are you planning to do? Please, Bubbee! Don't start with these people. You could also be in danger."

"I should be afraid of these *nishtgutniks*?" She scoffed. "Let them threaten the bedbugs! I'm too old for that. Besides, I have a plan."

"Please, I beg you, don't get mixed up in this, Fruma Esther, please!" Leah begged her, truly afraid.

"Yaakov, give me the name of the girl, and give me the car keys. Leah, you call your mother and pack up for the trip. I'll try to make sure the car is ready for you around noon. Don't leave it out front, Yaakov. Drive away as soon as you get it back. Are you listening to me?"

"But what are you planning to do?" Yaakov asked her helplessly, unable to think of any alternative.

"Never mind. Sometimes old people have an advantage that young ones don't. I ask you to trust me."

Defeated, Yaakov gave her the car keys and the note with the name of the girl. He was out of ideas and out of hope. He had to trust that the God he loved and believed in really could work miracles that were beyond his comprehension, and that Fruma Esther was His messenger.

33

⚜

A DANGEROUS MISSION

"I'm not bothering you, *k'vod harav?*" Fruma Esther asked humbly, her arms filled with plastic containers and tinfoil-covered pans.

He stood by the door, smiling at her. "I'm disappointed. Last time, you promised to call me Shimon Levi," he admonished her with mock severity. "Here, let me help you."

"It's all right, all right. I can manage," she insisted, but he wouldn't budge, taking the heaviest parcels from her, scrupulously careful not to touch her in any way. She followed him into the kitchen, automatically leaving the door open behind her because of *yichud*.

He looked at her quizzically. "What, it suddenly became safe in Boro Park?"

"Oy, the door!" She went back, locked and bolted it, then pulled up the shades.

"It's all right?"

"It's fine," he assured her. "If everyone in the neighborhood can see what we're doing, it's not *yichud*. So what have you brought me this week?" Rav Alter smiled.

"Schmaltz herring with apples. Chicken soup with knaidlach. Stuffed cabbage and a tzimmes kugel. And for dessert, pareve chocolate ice cream."

"What, no rugelach?" he said jocularly, wide-eyed with mock indignation.

"Actually"—she blushed—"this time, it's a babka."

He raised an eyebrow. "With chocolate, or cinnamon and nuts?"

"Both!" she told him triumphantly. "One you'll put in the freezer for Shabbos. Go sit. I'll warm everything up and bring you."

"You're not going to make me eat alone?"

She pursed her lips, happy as always to keep up the pretense that she was simply bringing him food as a *chesed,* and they were not actually spending the evening together. "Oy, I'm so full, but I'll keep you company. Maybe just a spoonful."

It had been going on for the past three months, a private celebration of friendship to which Rav Alter looked forward all week. It wasn't just the food—although he was thrilled with that as well—but mostly the happiness of having familiar, homey smells permeate his sterile house. No one cooked here anymore. On Shabbos, he went to his married daughter's or his daughter-in-law's. And during the week, he ate at the yeshiva.

Yes, the food was a pleasure. But most of all, he enjoyed the company. Spending time with a kind, pious woman so much like his dear wife who, for a few hours at least, chased away the bottomless loneliness and bereavement of his life, helping him to remember what it was like to be a couple.

What a joy it was to have a normal conversation where he wasn't forced to rack his brains for brilliant insights or agonize over the correctness of halachic judgments! With her, he could take off his black suit jacket and smack his lips over his favorite foods, eating more than was good for him without risking the admonishments he got from his well-meaning daughter and daughter-in-law who watched over him as if he were an irresponsible child. The older you got, the fewer things life had to offer that still gave you pleasure. Food was the last, joyous bastion that made it worthwhile to get out of bed in the morning, he sometimes thought.

She arranged the rolls on the table. From the scent, he could tell they were still warm from her oven. "Go wash; I'll bring the herring and the soup," she said.

He filled the special two-handled cup with water, performing the ritual of sanctifying his hands with water before reciting the sacred blessing over bread—the beginning to any meal in a religious home, reminder of the priestly temple ritual. Only then did he tear off a piece of bread, dip it in salt, and eat, closing his eyes as he savored the moment.

She watched him proudly. "Now come try the herring, and then I'll bring the soup with the knaidlach." She bustled from the kitchen to the dining room, carrying the plates carefully.

"Why do you have to work so hard, Fruma Esther? You know I'm happy to eat in the kitchen." He said this every week, knowing it was hopeless.

"Such food deserves the dining room," she replied.

He sighed, resigned. How could you argue with that? The last thing he wanted to do was insult such food! Only after she'd served him did she put down a plate for herself. They ate silently, enjoying the food and the company as if they had been together forever.

It had been like this with her Yitzchak Chaim, may his soul rest in peace. Quiet, friendly meals where neither felt obliged to do more than just sit beside one another in a shared activity. Talk wasn't necessary when you were married to a man for forty years. You already knew what he was going to say. More than that, you knew when he was about to sneeze and needed a tissue. You knew from the wrinkle of his nose if he liked or disliked something. And you knew when you told him a story, exactly what it was going to remind him of and how he would react. Because in many ways, you'd become one person with two bodies, your experiences, beliefs, frailties, and needs so familiar to one another that you could almost feel the others aches and worries, their pride and enjoyment, which could not but strengthen your own.

A long marriage with a compatible partner enhanced and heightened everything. Losing that person, being just one instead of two, was not like being single again; it was like being torn in half, leaving a vast emptiness that nothing else could fill. Unless, of course, you found someone who—like a long-lost puzzle piece—was so miraculously similar in shape and color they filled the void completely.

The stuffed cabbage and *tzimmeskugel* were next.

"Just like my Malka used to make. *Geshmacked*," he complimented her. "But the *tzimmeskugel*, this I never tasted. Delicious!"

"It's my mother's recipe. And she got it from her mother."

"They were from Poland?"

"No, Lithuania. Vilna. Descendants of the Vilna Gaon," she said proudly.

He pushed himself back from the table. "I didn't know. Such an important family."

"They were. All heads of yeshivas, community rabbis. The Holocaust destroyed them. Did you ever hear of the Ponary forest?"

"I heard, I heard." He shook his head sadly.

"Once, twenty years ago, Yitzchak Chaim and I took a trip to Vilna with other religious Jews. The tour bus drove out to Ponary. We drove down the road that the trucks took to bring the Jews of Vilna from the ghetto. They let us off by the little museum. We looked down the road and there were stone slabs as far as you could see, so many of them, and every one marked a mass grave. As far as you could see," she repeated, her eyes unseeing as she remembered. She felt her body shiver. "It just went on and on and on."

He shook his head slowly. "My own family were from Czechoslovakia, the Carpathian Mountains. During the war, the town changed hands and became Hungarian, and then the Nazis took over, and afterward the Russians. Now it's in the Ukraine. My grandfather was the chief rabbi, as was his father before him. My father was a brilliant young Talmud scholar who was being groomed to take his father's place. In 1938, he was the father of two small girls and was drafted into the Hungarian slave labor force. It was a miracle that in 1939 they allowed him to come home for Passover. I was born nine months later. My father, blessed be his memory, never lived to see me. The people of the town—my father's congregation and students—were able to arrange for my bubbee and zaidie, my mother, my sisters, and myself to be smuggled out of the ghetto to a gentile farmer's house, where we spent the war in hiding. I don't remember much. But my grandparents didn't survive the hardships. After the war, we came here, to America, to Boro Park. I was raised as the last remnant of my family's rabbinic line."

"A great honor."

He shrugged. "A great obligation and an even greater burden. To be the only one left . . ."

They sat there silently, the ghosts of their families twirling around the room, filling the space between them.

"It's hard for people to understand. Even for the *kinderlach*. Impossible to explain the heaviness we carry around with us."

"So many souls depending on us, making demands on us," he agreed.

"It is the will of the *Aibishter*." She sighed. "We do what we can do, no?"

He nodded. "Which means we should try not to be sad if we can help it. You can drown in sadness, like the ocean."

"Which is why, no matter what, I always have dessert," she said brightly, smiling.

He laughed, patting his stomach. "I don't know if I have room, Fruma Esther."

"Of course you have the room! And I also will make the room," she promised.

"To something like that, a man cannot say no."

"Even a very wise man," she teased him.

The babka—a delicate crust smothered in mouthwatering chocolate filling—was scrumptious enough to send even the ghosts out the window. They washed it down with cups of deliciously brewed green jasmine tea, something Fruma Esther had discovered unexpectedly only recently.

"The tea is good, no?" she asked him.

"Wonderful! I never tasted such tea!"

"It was a present from a woman I know."

"A *frum* woman knows about such things?"

"Not *frum, frei*. Someone I met from the hospital who drove me in her own car all the way from Manhattan to Brooklyn when I had my eye operation. Didn't ask for even a penny! A volunteer. Such a schlep. We got to talking. I told her about my Zissele, and she told me she also lost a child, beautiful son, from that terrible sickness, that AIDS. I was surprised she even talked about it."

"May HaShem watch over us! Such a tragedy." He shook his head.

She nodded sadly. "A very kind woman, full of *chesed*. We still talk once in a while."

"We *frum Yidden* have no monopoly on goodness."

"It took me a while to understand that, Shimon Levi. But when

Yaakov married a *baalas teshuva,* I began to see things differently. I saw things in the community—among our own kind, Shimon Levi!—that made me ashamed, may God forgive me! And I wasn't any better. I also didn't want. I was trying so hard to find him a *kallah* from a *choshuva* family, a *frum*-from-birth Bais Yaakov girl. But once I got to know Leah, his wife, I understood what a pure heart she has, just like him. It was *bashert.*"

"You know, in the Talmud, two sages, Rav Chisda and Rav Abbahu, discuss who is holier, the tzaddik or the *baal teshuva.* You would think for sure the tzaddik, who has lived a sinless life. But Rav Abbahu disagrees. He said, 'Where the penitent stands, even the tzaddik cannot.'"

"Why is that?"

"The Rambam says it's because the *baal teshuva* has tasted sin and yet separated himself from it, defeating his evil inclination. Their efforts are heroic and unceasing. While the tzaddik doesn't have to work so hard. And the first Lubavitcher Rebbe said that the enthusiasm and passion of the *baal teshuva* makes his worship of God special."

"I never thought of it that way," Fruma Esther murmured, moved almost to tears of pride in Leah, and of shame for herself and all the others she knew who looked down on the newcomers to their community.

"So they're happy, then, the young couple?"

She hesitated. "They were."

He straightened up in his chair, alert. "What happened?"

She opened her purse and handed him a letter. "Yaakov asked me to give you this."

He sat there reading, shaking his head, his silence punctuated by an occasional heartfelt *oy vey.* When he had finished, he folded it up and gave it back to her.

"No, I think he meant for you to keep it."

"It's a terrible story."

She nodded. "If Yaakov hadn't seen these things with his own eyes . . ."

"So tell me, what's happening now?"

She brought him up to date: the threat of expulsion, the urine, the car tires, and worst of all, the bicycle that had sent Leah to the hospital.

He slammed a fist on the table. "Tell me, who is responsible for this? A *shandah* and a *cherpeh!*"

"We don't know, but we have our suspicions."

"You know, Yaakov asked me about this Grub. I'd never heard of him, but since he is a Bobelger Hasid, I called the Bobelger Rebbe."

"What did he say?"

He hesitated. "Well, in the end, I didn't actually speak to the Rebbe. His nephew controls all the phone calls, the visits. The Bobelger Rebbe is very old, you know. But not so long ago, we would sit together on all the important community boards. A very wise and learned man," he said wistfully. "He's not well, they say. *Nebbech.* But the nephew told me they send all their girls to Grub. That he is one hundred percent reliable."

"The nephew! He's a youngster." She lowered her voice. "And from what I understand, he surrounds himself with criminals."

Rav Alter held up a restraining hand.

"I'm sorry. I know it's *loshon hara.* But look, all I'm saying is that if the Rebbe himself would get involved, look into what Grub has been doing all these years, he could save the *neshamas* of so many innocent young girls. And then . . . and then . . . when the truth came out, they would have to leave Yaakov and Leah and the children alone. We don't know what else to do. You're our last hope."

"Let me ask you, Fruma Esther, because this is a very serious accusation that can ruin a man's life and reputation—aside from Shaindele's word, you have proof about Grub?"

"Only what Yaakov said he saw."

"Yes, I read. But this is not really proof. After all, Shaindele is his daughter. He was looking for proof; he wanted to believe his own daughter. His judgment could have been affected. We must have objective proof."

"There was another young girl. Yaakov saw her coming out of Grub's office, very upset. He found out her name. Maybe you could talk to her, to her parents?"

There was a moment of silence.

"But maybe it's better you shouldn't get involved." She sighed, gathering the dirty plates and carrying them slowly into the kitchen. She put them into the sink and turned on the hot water.

He should stay out of it, for his own sake. That was clear to her now. Even though the position he held in the community equaled that of the

Bobelger Rebbe and therefore no one would dare to molest him, still, what did he need it for? There would be accusations against his rulings, accusations against his piety. There was no shortage of things these criminals could think up if you went against them. She would never want to put him in harm's way. Even with so much at stake, she found that she cared for him as deeply as she did about her own family.

"Fruma Esther."

She turned around. He was standing by the counter holding the rest of the dishes. "Give me the girl's name. I'll look into it."

She shook her head. "Forget I asked you. It's a bad idea. It's dangerous, *k'vod harav.*"

"Shimon Levi," he corrected her, his sad eyes suddenly twinkling once more.

34

◈

A DIFFERENT WORLD

"Lola? Is that you?" Cheryl Howard asked sleepily, confused. She had just spent the last hour by the swimming pool in the brutal Florida heat, and her brains felt like sautéing mushrooms, soft and shrunk to a fraction of their size.

"Leah, Mom. Did you hear what I said?"

"What?"

"We are on our way to your house."

"We?"

"Yes. Me, Yaakov, Chasya, and Mordechai Shalom."

"The whole family?"

"Well, the older kids are in Baltimore."

"Where are you now?" she asked, just to make sure she wasn't dreaming. Lola was coming, bringing the rabbi and his little kids? To Florida? To her nonkosher, secular house? Just like that? After she'd politely rejected every single invitation for over two years? Had it not been for the worry that something must be terribly wrong to have unglued her daughter from that backward neighborhood of religious fanatics she'd been clinging to with all her might, Cheryl Howard would have been over the moon.

Despite her fatigue, Cheryl did a quick review of their last conversation, mining for clues. Well, Lola had remarked that she was, after all, still a feminist (who would have thought?). Then there was that admission about the "ups and downs" of newlyweds. Did that mean something? But if Jacob and the kids were coming with her, she couldn't be hightailing out of fanatics-ville à la *Thelma and Louise*. But maybe—could it be?—that she was planning on dumping yeshiva boy once she got there, then kidnapping the kids? Go know.

"Where we are is someplace on I-95." Leah's voice interrupted her thoughts, answering the question she'd already forgotten she'd asked. "We'll spend overnight somewhere along the way to break up the drive. It's okay, Mom, isn't it? I mean, you did invite us."

"Of course it's okay! I'm just surprised is all. How are the little rug rats?"

Leah turned her head to look at the children in the back seat. Cheeky had a rubber steering wheel toy connected to his car seat and was happily steering, pressing all the colored buttons and pretend-tooting his long-disabled green horn. Icy was more subdued, tracing invisible pictures on the window as she stared at the scenery. She seemed sad, Leah thought, troubled. "They're fine, I hope."

"You *hope*? Why, what's the matter?"

"Well, you're going to find out anyway soon enough. We've gotten into a bit of neighborhood controversy. My stepdaughter Shaindele—"

"The chubby, vindictive one with the personality of a politician who's just lost an election? That one?"

"Really, Mom, she's just a kid, a kid who recently lost her mother. Be charitable."

"No, that's your department. I'm your mother, and I'm allowed to not adore the little troublemaker for everything she's done to my daughter."

"But we get along fine now, really."

"So why isn't she coming with you?"

"It's a long story, but she's graduating in a few months. She has to study."

"Okay, fair enough. So what is it I'm going to find out?"

"That there is this vendetta against us and we've been attacked." As she spoke, Leah anxiously scanned the children's reaction in the rearview mirror. Oh no! Chasya's eyes—alarmed—were taking over her little face. She pressed the phone closer to her mouth and tried to whisper. "I can't talk now. But it's not safe for us there right now. We've made some very powerful people angry."

"So what did they do? Show up with machetes?"

"It's Boro Park, Mom, not Sinaloa."

"But they did *something,* right?"

"Yes, but I can't talk about that now because Chasya's . . . Hi, Chasya"—she waved and smiled at the child's serious face—"wants to play I Spy with me. Right, sweetie?" She nodded at the child, smiling.

"But you're all okay, right?" There was an edge of alarm in Cheryl's tone. She was waking up fast.

Leah looked at her bandaged knees and splinted finger. "We'll live. Not to worry. But I can't talk right now."

"Okay, okay, I hear you. I'll get you some food and meat at Super Glatt in Boca, and a brand-new barbecue."

"Don't forget the paper plates and plastic utensils and cups—"

"I know the drill, believe me. My parents were from Flatbush, remember?"

"I remember. Mom?"

"Hmm?"

"Thank you so much for always being there. I don't know what I'd do without you."

Cheryl felt her eyes well up from such totally unexpected (and long overdue and totally deserved, in her opinion) praise. "Well, you're most welcome. Have a safe trip. See you in two days."

"Bye." Leah turned around in her seat. "I spy with my little eye . . . something green . . . ," Leah began, and was rewarded by Chasya's immediate attention, her little face alive with interest. She felt Yaakov's hand reach out to hers, giving it a gentle squeeze.

The road whizzed by, rocking the children to sleep.

"What did your mother say?" Yaakov whispered.

"She put on a good show. But I think she's flabbergasted. And worried. This is so sudden. She can't figure out what's going on."

Yaakov nodded. "We should have come to see her months ago. It wasn't right."

Leah looked at him meaningfully. "Even though she's not religious? I always thought you didn't want the children exposed to the way she lives."

He seemed genuinely shocked. "No, no! That was never the reason. I just couldn't get away from work." His expression was grim.

"It hasn't been easy for you, has it?" she murmured, suddenly realizing just how unhappy he'd been all these months.

"I don't mind the work, the actual accounting. It's even interesting in a way. But being part of the 'team'—my boss, the other people, the clients—having to go to bars with them, to pretend I'm one of them just to get ahead . . ." He shook his head. "I hate it so much, I can't even tell you. And that was before my boss threatened to fire me over something that has nothing at all to do with my work!"

She was genuinely shocked. So that was it, what had been eating away at him all these months, turning him into another person? She felt an enormous relief, bordering on joy. "I thought it was me you were un-happy with, me you wanted to get away from."

He clutched the steering wheel, giving her a quick, astonished glance. "*HaShem Yishmor!* Oy, Leah. I'm so sorry."

"I'm also sorry. I never really asked you what was wrong. I guess I was afraid of the answer."

"So then maybe it's not so terrible we had to run away together." He chuckled, and she joined him.

"Maybe it's a *chesed*."

They were both deep in thought as they passed the turnoff to Balti-more.

"Didn't you want to stop and see your family?"

He shook his head. "I want to give Shaindele a chance to settle in first."

"You called your brother after she got there?"

He nodded.

"So how is she?"

"He says she seems tired after the long train ride but relieved to be out of Boro Park."

"Are they arranging for her therapy?"

"They are checking out counselors, women counselors, who have real academic degrees and have been working with teenagers in the community. They have a number of recommendations."

"HaShem should bless us that they find the right one."

"Amen."

"So where do you want to spend the night?"

He shrugged.

She took out her phone. "We'll probably be near Virginia or South Carolina when it gets dark. I'll try to find someplace in that area that has a kosher restaurant."

"There would be such a place? Down South?"

She smiled. "Yaakov, there are religious Jews all over America. Little communities with synagogues and *kollelim* and kosher food stores and religious schools."

"I never knew that! I mean, Kiryas Yoel—"

She laughed. "I know. You thought they pulled up the drawbridge in Lakewood and the *Vaad Harabbonim* sent policemen to stop religious Jews from going any further."

He smiled self-deprecatingly. He *had,* actually. "Yes, I'd like to see a place like that," he said, his eyes shining with excitement. "A religious community far away from Boro Park, Flatbush, Crown Heights, and Williamsburg; far away from Bobelger Hasidim."

"A place full of kind, nonjudgmental religious Jews who truly love the Torah, and each other," Leah whispered, her voice cracking as the pain from her wounds suddenly throbbed.

Noticing the flash of agony that momentarily clouded her features, he clutched the steering wheel with a sudden ferocity. "If I could just get my hands on the person who did this to you . . . You know, sometimes I actually fantasize about being a six-foot-three, two-hundred-and-fifty-pound goy who grew up in the South Bronx and knows how to pound his enemies into a pulp!"

She laughed, but he cut her short.

"No, it's not funny! I'm not joking. All those years I spent, invested, in learning how to be holy and good! How is that going to help me—us—now? An eye for an eye. I know the Oral law explains that means paying damages, but sometimes I think HaShem meant it exactly the way it's written and that He understands evil much better than we do. That person on the bicycle? I want to break both his arms and legs, to see him trussed up like an Egyptian mummy in some hospital bed! It's the only thing that's going to make me feel better . . . feel like a man." He heaved a sigh of despair. "My beloved," he said softly, taking her hand. "Please forgive me for not taking better care of you."

"Yaakov, the best thing you can do for me is to stay the man I fell in love with. A good man. A kind man. A loving man whose whole life has been dedicated to making the world a better place. The world is full of two-hundred-and-fifty-pound gorillas pounding people into pulps; it doesn't need another one. There *has* to be some good people in the world. Otherwise, why would HaShem keep it spinning? Why would He bother to put the sun in the sky every morning? It's a way of being grateful, isn't it? Showing Him that what He's created He did for people who deserve it? Don't ever change, Yaakov, please. Let HaShem deal with the bicycle man."

But her words didn't reach him. "Sometimes I think I've wasted my time," he said bitterly. "I can't do anything. Earn a living, even protect my wife and children!"

"Please, don't tell yourself that! What happened to us just proves the opposite, that people are desperate for truly wise men and educators, teachers who can take our Torah out of the hands of the hypocrites who distort and twist its message, presenting themselves as the most devout, the most knowledgeable, when they don't know anything at all."

"They are arrogant, ignorant," he fumed, the violence rising inside him again.

"'*Who is a hero? The person who conquers his Evil Inclination*,'" she admonished softly, quoting the well-worn adage from *Ethics of the Fathers*. She reached out to him, touching his arm, which was as hard and tense as the gleaming cold metal of a weapon.

Her touch traveled through him, breaking down the barriers inside him, wrapping itself around his inner wounds like a healing salve. He sobbed, pounding the dashboard.

"Don't," she implored, frightened. She had never seen him like this, this gentle man, this scholar; the man she looked up to and wanted to emulate. He, too, was wounded, she realized. He was losing his faith. Not in God but in his friends and neighbors, the world he had grown up in and cherished, and which had cherished him back even as it had despised her and tried to keep them apart; the world whose foolish mores had condemned his young wife to death and pushed his innocent, troubled teenage daughter off the rails, turning her into an outcast. It was a world she had for some time ceased to believe in and trust. Ironically, they were now more than ever on the same wavelength. And that was a blessing, an answer to her prayers, no matter how it had come about.

———

They took a few rest stops to use the bathrooms. And when they got hungry, they stopped and laid out a picnic on a roadside table, buying the children rabbinically approved brands of ice cream in the nearby convenience store.

The light was fading fast as they reached the exit ramps for Folkestone, Virginia.

By the time they pulled into the parking lot of a motel, everyone was exhausted. It was inexpensive, but clean, and they were given the keys to a large suite with a kitchen and two bedrooms, one of which had a crib.

"Let's just feed the kids and bathe them and put them to bed. I'm falling off my feet," Leah admitted.

"But I thought you picked this place because it had a kosher restaurant?" He was disappointed.

"It does, but I'm more tired than hungry, and we still have some sandwiches in the cooler. We'll try it tomorrow for breakfast?"

"All right. If you want," he answered, realizing he, too, was exhausted.

By the time everyone had eaten and bathed, they sank into the clean, cool sheets and comfortable mattresses, sleep coming as soon as their heads touched their pillows.

The next time Leah opened her eyes, the sun was streaming through the edges of the blackout curtains. She turned over luxuriantly, closing her eyes and listening to the riot of birds singing outside their windows.

"Yaakov," she whispered, reaching out for him, but he was already gone, probably to find a synagogue where he could say his morning prayers with a minyan. She sat up, moving slowly out of bed, careful to protect her bandages. First she checked on the children, who were still sleeping soundly. *We're in no big rush,* she thought grimly, not looking forward to having those conversations with her mother or baking under the relentless Florida sun.

She went into the bathroom, performing her morning ablutions. She longed for a shower but couldn't risk wetting her bandages. Instead, she used a washcloth to do the best she could. When she was done, she tucked her voluminous hair inside a headscarf and put on her clothes. Then she picked up her prayer book. She looked around for a place to say her morning prayers. There was a small terrace, so she stepped outside. *Oh, how lovely,* she thought, leaning over the balcony as she breathed in the clean, sweet smell of cut grass and the heady perfume of a flower she could not name. They were in a residential neighborhood of neat houses on wide lawns. Everywhere she looked, the lush tops of old trees danced in the gentle spring breezes. To the right, she glimpsed a harbor with small sailing craft and the sun glinting off the sea. She said her morning prayers with a calm she had not experienced in some time.

Afterward, she leaned back in the lounge chair, putting up her feet and closing her eyes. She felt happy and peaceful, united with God and her fellow man. She luxuriated in the feeling, refusing to think about the past or the future. This now, this moment, it was a gift. She would not throw it away.

The door slid open and the children came bounding out, exploring this new place, going from zero to 150 miles an hour in a second. She bent down to Mordechai Shalom and kissed him. In response, he gently nuzzled against her. How she loved him! "Come," she urged him, carefully holding out her arms. "A new diaper, then potty?"

He shook his head. He hated potty training and was resisting it with all the cunning and stubborn will of his terrible twos. She laughed. "You are going to have to learn someday, young man, or no pretty girl will agree to a shidduch date with you!" She tousled his bright, golden curls, then tickled his little round stomach as he giggled uncontrollably. It was so infectious she found herself laughing, too, until tears ran down her cheeks.

Chasya, who had also been laughing, stopped. "Why are you crying, Mommy?"

"I'm not. I'm laughing." But then, suddenly, it wasn't true. She wiped her eyes with her uninjured hand. "Come sit down on the potty for a little while, and then I'll put you in a clean diaper," she cajoled.

But he wasn't having any of it. He shook his head vigorously. "No potty. Diaper!" he demanded firmly like some dictatorial potentate.

Chasya went over to him and whispered something in his ear. Without a word, he slipped out of his diaper and held his arms up docilely for Leah to help him onto the toilet. To her shock, for the first time, he waited patiently until something actually happened. It was a first. Even those times he'd reluctantly agreed to sit, he'd absconded long before anything could be accomplished.

"Such a good boy! He went potty!" She praised him to the skies, with the enthusiasm reserved for heroic war acts and sports victories. "What did you say to him, Chasya?" she asked as she wiped him clean.

"That Mommy has a lot of boo-boos and he shouldn't make her cry."

She felt her eyes tear up again as she hugged the little girl. "You are a sweetie, and I love you to the moon and back."

"I'm a *tzadakis,*" the child intoned solemnly.

Leah nodded at her, making a tremendous effort to keep a straight face. "Absolutely, without a doubt!"

Then she took the baby in her arms, laying him flat and putting him on a fresh diaper.

"Kiss boo-boos and make all better!" Mordechai Shalom said enthusiastically, hugging her dangerously close to her bandages and trying with all his might to kiss her hand. "Gently!" she told him, allowing him to place his soft little lips on her wrist.

"Wow, that's amazing. All better now!" she told him. "What a great little kisser!"

He was absolutely thrilled, filled with pride in the potency of his boo-boo-healing powers.

"Are you hungry?" They both nodded.

She opened the refrigerator to rummage through the leftovers from their picnic bag. But just as she was about to kick herself for not preparing more food, the door opened.

"Breakfast!" Yaakov declared, placing two paper bags on the counter.

She unpacked. "This milk is *cholov Yisroel*! Where did you get it? And the little yogurts, they are the same ones we buy in Boro Park."

"And there are also fresh rolls and cheese, cereal and cookies! I asked people in the synagogue, and they showed me where the kosher stores are, and the Jewish bakery and diner. All of them with the best hechsher!" he exulted like an oil prospector whose land has finally produced a gusher.

"I want to hear all about it!"

"You were so right, Leah! There is a large Orthodox Jewish community here! I couldn't believe it. I walked to the shul, and on the way, I saw so many homes with mezuzahs! I couldn't believe how full the weekday minyan was. And many of the men dress like I do," he said with enthusiasm. "And there are two kosher restaurants, one milchig and one fleishig, both with an excellent hechsher."

"Two? Wow."

"After I went to the kosher supermarket and bakery and was walking back here, I saw two boys riding bikes ahead of me on the sidewalks. As I got closer, I saw they were both wearing yarmulkes, and one even had *payos*! I started talking to them. They both go to a local yeshiva. The older one, who's in eighth grade, told me he's learning *Meseches Succah* in *Bava Metziah; Davarim; Shmuel Bais* . . . And then the other boy told me they also learn math, English *composition*—that was the word he used, imagine, a little boy knows that word already!—and history, and a few other things I don't remember." He shook his head in amazement.

"Sounds like an excellent school."

But Yaakov just continued to shake his head, murmuring again and again, "Imagine, in Virginia!"

"I was thinking we could take the day off instead of driving straight through. Do some sightseeing in the area, then head to Florida tomorrow?"

"And I could go to shul for the evening minyan, and then we could eat out lunch and dinner?"

She nodded. "And maybe we could check out the school, meet some of the parents . . ."

Their eyes met in perfect understanding.

35

THE PROPOSAL

Although Rav Alter tried everything to arrange for a personal meeting with the Bobelger Rebbe himself, explaining to the nephew that they were old friends, once again his request was politely and respectfully denied.

"I hear he has Alzheimer's," Rav Alter's gabbai, Zevulun, whispered. "The nephew doesn't want anyone to know. So he makes up pronouncements and halachic rulings himself, then tells everyone it's from the rebbe."

Rav Alter shook his head. "If what you are telling me isn't true, Zevulun, it's *rechilus*. And if it is true, it's a *chilul HaShem* and a *shandah*," Rav Alter answered, discouraged. He had hoped that, face-to-face with his old friend, they could put an end to the violence. But with the nephew in charge, there was no chance of coming to an understanding. He would have no choice but to act independently.

"Call the girl and her parents. Arrange for them to meet me in my office."

"They'll want to know why. What should I say?"

"Tell them the truth. It's about Grub."

"Is that wise?"

Rav Alter looked into the familiar face of his very efficient and practical gabbai. "Why not?"

"If the child is seeing a counselor, they'll want to keep it quiet."

Rav Alter smacked his palm against his forehead. "Of course they will! So maybe tell them I'll come to see them, in their home, in the evening. Discreetly."

"I'm sure they'll be honored, *k'vod harav.*"

They were not Hasidim but actually members of the Ashkenazic, Lithuanian community, the gabbai informed him. They were surprised but honored to invite the head of their community into their home.

"They are simple people—he has a shoe store, and she is a housewife. They have three children. Their eldest daughter, Menucha Sarah, is four years younger than Shaindele."

"That makes her how old?"

"Thirteen, *k'vod harav.*"

"A baby!" He sniffed. "What do you hear is the reason for the counselor?"

"Her father has a heart condition. Times have been very hard for them financially. Her mother went to work to supplement their income. The children are a little lost."

"What did you tell them about why we are meeting?"

"I didn't."

He sighed. That evening, he walked to a large apartment house in the poorer section of Boro Park and rang the bell.

A thin, pale, sickly man with a large black velvet yarmulke opened the door. He seemed overawed. "Such an honor for us, *k'vod harav!*" he gushed, ushering him into the modest apartment.

The place, poorly furnished, had clearly been scrubbed until it shone, the windows sparkling, the old bookcase polished to a dull shine. Light refreshments in the best Sabbath dishes were laid out upon the dining room table.

Rav Alter sat down in the easy chair they offered him, facing the parents, who took a seat opposite on the worn sofa.

"I understand you are going through a difficult time. You know there are funds available, free loans. I'd be happy to arrange that. Also grants," he added delicately.

The parents exchanged embarrassed looks.

"Many thanks, *k'vod harav*. But praise be to God, we are managing."

"I am happy to hear that, but that is not the reason I came to see you," he hastened to add.

They nodded, relieved, their eyes questioning.

Rav Alter took a deep breath. This was not going to be easy. "As you know, many young people in our community are having difficulties. This is a confusing time in the world, with so much *pritzus,* so many temptations. The internet . . . We need to protect our children."

They nodded approvingly. If anything, they looked even more perplexed, Rav Alter noted, floundering, then having no choice, pushing ahead as best he could. "So as one of the heads of this community, I am talking to the parents of teenagers who are seeing rabbinically approved counselors, to see if it is helping them, and if we should send other children. I understand your daughter is going to see Rav Yoel Grub?"

"Who is spreading such things about us?" the father asked, absolutely furious.

It was not only the therapist, Rav Alter realized, but the idea that they might need charity. *Oy vey!* I need to learn to be a more accomplished liar! "Please, please. This is completely private; you can rely on me never to tell anyone."

"But, *k'vod harav,* how did *you* find out?" the mother persisted.

"Just by chance, someone whose own child was also going to Grub saw your daughter coming out of his office. She was crying. He heard Grub call out her name. This person was so concerned that he shared this with me in the strictest confidence and wanted to find out if your daughter is all right."

They were shocked, he saw, and yet clearly relieved as well. Someone in the same boat wasn't likely to spread rumors that could come back to bite them. That their daughter had been in distress was clearly secondary.

"Has she said anything to you?" Rav Alter asked.

"No, not a word."

"And has Rav Grub helped her?"

He could see the parents exchanging confused looks. "She is a quiet girl who doesn't share much. Maybe it would be better for *k'vod harav* to ask her himself?" The father signaled to the mother, who got up and went into the bedroom. When she returned, a girl no more than a child was with her. She seemed like a small, skittish night creature longing to scurry beneath the nearest bush. She looked very young and very scared.

"Say shalom to *K'vod Harav* Alter, Menucha Sarah," the father demanded.

"Shalom," the girl whispered, not looking up.

"He wants to ask you some things about Rav Grub."

For the first time, she raised her head. She looked terrified, Rav Alter registered.

"Please, Menucha Sarah, don't be afraid! You haven't—*chas v'shalom*—done anything wrong. This won't take long, and it would be a big help to me."

Reluctantly, she sat down.

"Can you tell me if Rav Grub's office has windows?"

She seemed relieved. "No," she exhaled, shaking her head.

"And how many doors are there into his office?"

"Two," she said softly.

"And when you are in the office, does he leave one of them open?"

She shook her head, suddenly fidgeting with her fingers.

"Tell me, does he lock both doors?"

"Yes," she answered, gaining a bit of confidence.

"And what about his walls? What does he have hanging on the walls of his office?"

"Pictures."

"Please, describe them to me."

"He doesn't always have the same ones. Sometimes it's a picture of the Bobelger Rebbe, but other times . . ." She hesitated.

"Go on, it's all right."

"Women in bathing suits at the beach."

The parents' eyebrows shot up.

"And what do you do at these sessions in Rav Grub's office?"

She looked beseechingly at her father and mother, then stared at the floor.

"He asks me questions."

"What kind of questions?"

"All kinds. I don't remember," she whispered, not meeting his eyes.

"It can't be that you don't remember anything," her father declared, annoyed. "Try harder! You've been going there for months!"

"Please, I can't!" she begged.

Rav Alter cleared his throat. "Can you tell me, Menucha Sarah, do Rav Grub's questions sometimes make you uncomfortable?"

She looked at him steadily, nodding slowly.

"And can you tell me, child, has Rav Grub ever touched you?"

She nodded, tears suddenly streaming down her cheeks.

Her parents half rose out of their seats. They looked astounded.

She ran into her mother's arms, hiding her face.

"Can you tell me, Menucha Sarah, do you like going to talk to Rav Grub?"

She shook her head vigorously, her whole body trembling.

"How would you feel, Menucha Sarah, about going to talk to someone else? A woman counselor?"

"Please, *k'vod harav*," she implored.

He nodded, smiling, rising to his feet. "Thank you so much, Menucha Sarah. You have been very helpful. HaShem should bless you and your dear family."

Her parents walked him to the door.

"What does this mean? What are you saying . . . ?" the girl's father began.

"It means she shouldn't go back to Grub; he isn't the right counselor for her. She should go to a woman. I'll have my gabbai call you with the name of someone else."

The father, who looked devastated, seemed to be about to ask more, but then thought better of it, pressing his lips together. Finally, he whispered, "Thank you so much, *k'vod harav*!"

He took the man's trembling hand in both his own, patting it warmly, then nodded to the wife. "Don't worry. It will be fine. One day, we will all dance at her wedding."

"*Mirtzashem!* Amen."

Rav Alter walked slowly down the quiet streets, his body trembling with quiet anguish and controlled fury. So many years! So many young girls! And if not for the courage of little Shaindele Lehman, no one would have ever known! It was monstrous.

As soon as he got home, he called Fruma Esther.

"Nu?"

"Shaindele is telling the truth. Leah is right. It's a *shandah*. But"—and here he caught his breath, leaning against the wall—"I can't publicly condemn Grub."

Her heart sank. "Why not?"

"The girl and her parents will never admit anything publicly. Even to get her to describe the pictures on Grub's wall was like splitting the Red Sea. And even if I could get her and her family to talk to the police, which is as likely as the Messiah appearing on my doorstep in the next ten minutes, they would suffer what Yaakov and Leah are suffering. But I can and will do something else."

"Something is better than nothing," she sighed, heartbroken, but resigned.

"I can make sure no girl from our community ever goes to him again."

"That, too, will be a blessing. But he'll just go on with the Bobelger girls."

"I think what I plan to do will help those girls, too."

"And what about Yaakov and Leah?"

He felt helpless. "Fruma Esther, you know how it is here in Boro Park. There is not much I can do. But I will try."

"Yes," she said. "I know. Thank you, Shimon Levi, really. And forgive me for making your life even harder."

"No. Thank *you* for helping me to see my responsibility to right a great wrong." And more gently: "And thank you, Fruma Esther, for making this unbearable year of mourning a little easier for me."

She blushed in a way she had not for decades. "I'm glad. And please don't be too hard on yourself. I know you are doing the best you can, Shimon Levi. May the *Aibishter* bless you."

He hung up with a heavy heart. The best he could. But today, to his great shame, he recognized how little power he really had. If only his word were law, as were the words of his father and grandfather before him in the little eastern European villages where they held positions of chief rabbi; when their fearless voices thundering from their pulpits were enough to silence all dissent and settle all conflicts. Now his voice was just one of many trying to make itself heard above the cacophony of those competing for the community's hearts, minds, respect, and money.

The next morning, he called in his gabbai.

"We need to find a psychologist, a *frum* woman, who lives in Brooklyn and specializes in children. Can you call Rav Kunditz at Yeshiva University? They have a training program for psychologists there, I understand. Many of them are *frum* women. Ask him for his recommendation for the top person who got the best grades and who has the most experience. And when you get it, please contact the parents of Menucha Sarah and give it to them. And now you need to help me draft a proclamation."

The gabbai was startled. This hadn't happened for years.

"I want it to say the following: 'In the name of the *Vaad Harabbonim*, and for reasons of modesty and holiness, from now on, all girls in our holy communities needing psychological counseling should be sent only to women psychologists approved by the *Vaad*.' I will sign it, and you will ask the other *rabbonim* on the *Vaad* to sign it. I'll write up a note for you to give them."

"And then what will we do?"

"We will run off hundreds of posters with this proclamation, to be plastered all over Boro Park, Flatbush, Williamsburg, and Crown Heights, endorsed with the signatures of the entire *Vaad Harabbonim*. Or as many as we can get."

"The Bobelger will never sign."

"Don't be so sure."

Sure enough, the Bobelger Rebbe was the only one who refused to sign. Rav Alter called the nephew.

"This is Rav Alter. I'm calling on behalf of the *Vaad Harabbonim*. Can you please explain the Bobelger Rebbe's objection to joining our *psak*? After all, doesn't your Hasidus pride itself on being the strictest when it comes to *tznius*? And is it not more *tzniusdik* for a young girl to talk of intimate things with another woman rather than a man? Look what happened with Weberman! I'm sure if you explain this to your uncle, he will be only too happy to join us."

"Don't think I don't know what this is all about!" he replied nastily, all pretense gone. "You are very close friends with Yaakov Lehman even though his wife, the *baalas teshuva,* is an immodest woman who has been seen—"

"Please no *loshon hara*!"

"—dancing around with no head covering and worse? That she is a *moissar* and a *motzi shem rah* who threatened the Bobelger Rebbe himself! And now she is spreading *loshon hara* and *rechilus* about a good man, a family man, with a wife and many children to support—and who just happens to be my brother-in-law. She is even threatening to go to the police, to ruin his reputation and destroy his *parnosa*!"

Rav Yoel Grub was the nephew's brother-in-law. This explained everything.

Rav Alter took a deep, calming breath. "You know, it takes time for *baale teshuva* to understand how we do things here in Boro Park. I'm sure if I spoke to Leah Lehman, explained to her that the matter is now closed and that she and her family will no longer be harassed and all the harm done to them already"—and here Rav Alter raised his voice—"*will be corrected and compensated*"—he paused briefly, allowing his voice to return to its natural mildness—"then maybe I can agree to convince her and her stepdaughter to show a similar *chesed* and forget about filing complaints with the police. But just so you know, Shaindele Lehman is not the only one of your brother-in-law's young women patients to make these kinds of complaints against him."

Tellingly, Rav Alter thought, the nephew didn't immediately demand "What kind of complaints?" Instead, all he asked was, "Who?" His voice was as cold as ice.

"I have given her and her parents my sacred word never to discuss it. But I have the name written down."

"They came to you?"

Was there a sudden touch of fear in the nephew's tone? A slight lessening of the arrogance? "No, I actually went to them."

"For what reason?"

"Because someone saw the girl leaving your brother-in-law's office in a terrible state and came to me for help. And because she is only thirteen years old."

There was complete silence. Rav Alter took advantage of it. "Listen, it's a *mazal* you're family. You can help him. Please advise your relative that it might be better for him to take only male patients from now on. As it is written: *For lack of wood a fire goes out.* And did you hear—Nechemya

Weberman, *nebbech,* had his sentence reduced by half, and he'll *still* be sitting there another fifty years! As for the *psak* of the *Vaad Harabbonim,* it is final and will be printed and put up all over Brooklyn in another two hours. Do the Bobelger *really* want to be the only group left out of a *psak* protecting the *tznius* of our women and girls?"

An hour later, the Bobelger Rebbe's signature on the proclamation arrived at Rav Alter's desk. Along with it, was another envelope addressed to Yaakov Lehman. He opened it. It was filled with cash.

After the posters had gone up all over the religious communities of Brooklyn and Manhattan, Rav Alter took the envelope out of his desk drawer and put it in his pocket. Brushing off the luxurious felt of his best Shabbos hat and donning the long black coat he wore to the synagogue on festive occasions, he walked through the streets of Boro Park. His progress was slow, as every two minutes (or so it seemed to him in his eagerness to reach his destination), another member of his large congregation stopped to bless him and shake his hand. One even waylaid him with great excitement to discuss the new *psak* going up around town, whose ink had barely dried, filled with curiosity and hoping to uncover the treasure of a juicy nugget of exclusive information from a famous rabbi to be shared as proof of one's exalted status.

Rav Alter was polite, but distant, looking down at the ground while these people whispered eagerly into his ear. In reply, he said absolutely nothing, until finally even the densest got the picture and backed off, raining down pious clichés like a brief summer shower that leaves everything annoyingly damp rather than nourishingly watered.

He rang the buzzer. Fruma Esther took a while to answer. "Yes?"

"It's me. Shimon Levi. Can I come up?"

She buzzed him in immediately and stood by an open door as he made his way from the elevator. "You're here!"

Only now did he realize how strange that was. He hardly ever went anywhere except to the synagogue, kollel, or his children's homes. Everyone usually came to him. And although he had been meeting with Fruma Esther for months, he had never been to her home.

"I can come in?" he asked, suddenly shy.

"*Avadeh.*" Smiling demurely, she opened the door wide.

It was a neat but modest home, he thought, much smaller than his own one-family house, but furnished similarly: the floor-to-ceiling book-cases, the large dining room table that could open to host fourteen people on a Shabbos, the family photographs and oil paintings of the *kotel*.

"A drink I can get you?"

He nodded gratefully.

"I'll go get you tea. Sit, sit. Why are you standing? You look tired, Shimon Levi."

He nodded, taking off his large black hat and setting it neatly on the coffee table, then taking off his black overcoat and draping it neatly over an armchair. Cooler, he slipped gratefully into a dining room chair, suddenly exhausted.

She bustled about, hardly knowing what she was doing, bumping into closets, nearly smashing her good teacups, which seemed to have a life of their own. He was here, in her home! Shimon Levi!

She brought him tea and a tray of her latest baking.

The eyes in his tired face lit up. "Mandelbrot! Taiglach!"

"Still warm from the oven," she boasted, pleased, taking a seat across from him.

"I came to tell you that I think I was able to influence whoever was behind the attacks on your family to stop."

"You think, but you're not sure?"

He took the envelope out of his pocket and put it down on the table. "I didn't count, but it should be enough to cover the car tires, the medical expenses . . ."

She looked inside, overwhelmed. "You're not going to tell me where you got this, right?"

He shrugged.

"And the rest?"

"Time will tell. But in exchange, no more talk about calling the police."

"*Avadeh.* I'll explain this to Leah. She doesn't understand. And what about Shaindele?"

"Was she thrown out of Bais Yaakov?"

She shook her head. "After what happened to Leah, we took her straight out and sent her to her uncle's in Baltimore. The head of Bais Yaakov there is a relative of her aunt's family. They will let her graduate."

"I can arrange for her to come back, to finish with her class, if she wants."

"No, this is *besser*. A little distance, less wagging of tongues. It's good like this. And what about Grub?"

"I put up posters all over Brooklyn with a *psak* from the *Vaad Harabbonim* that says girls needing counseling should only go to women counselors."

She sat back, staring at him in admiration. "Shimon Levi, it's brilliant!"

He shrugged, pleased, taking a slice of mandelbrot.

"It's good?" she asked, not that she had any doubts. But she wanted to hear him say it.

He simply closed his eyes in pleasure, nodding.

"I'm so sorry I made so much work for you, Shimon Levi."

"What are you worrying? Believe me, if it wasn't this, it would have been something else," he said wearily. "I'll tell you the truth, I'm not sure how much longer I can go on like this."

"You know, I was thinking the same thing. The *kinderlach*, they should only live and be well, I love them. But so much *tummel*, such *mishugas*! And it never stops. Ever since my Zissele, God should watch over her soul, passed, I've been like a chicken without a head. I need a vacation. In fact, after this is all over, I'm thinking I'll visit my daughter in B'nai Brak."

"Go to Israel? Aah. Yes. This is where my soul has longed to be for such a long time. I have a little apartment in Jerusalem, in Geulah. I bought it many years ago. Malka Ruth, may her soul rest in peace, and I dreamed of retiring there. I have a child and many grandchildren in Bayit V'Gan."

Now, he thought, pausing for a moment before launching into the speech he had long planned to the last word, which contained many learned Talmudical references, flowery quotes from the psalms and *Ethics of the Fathers*, a speech he had not yet had the opportunity or courage to deliver. But as he opened his mouth, the entire perfectly and laboriously composed discourse went straight out of his head. Instead, he found himself saying simply, "Fruma Esther, maybe we'll get married and go together?"

36

THE CORRECTIONS

They spent the day at the zoo, then took the children to the local botanical garden, which was so thrillingly beautiful, it made Leah feel like crying. *Just this,* she thought. *Just this.*

The next morning, they loaded up the car, strapped the children in with their toys, and got in themselves. Her eyes were wistful as they drove by the pretty little homes with their large backyards and jungle gyms. The children, drowsy from their full breakfast, immediately fell asleep.

"It's good we spent the extra day. I feel much better now," Leah said.

"Yes," he agreed. "I'm glad I went back to the minyan again. I didn't rush out this time, and people were so friendly, almost all of them said hello to me and asked me about myself. I also loved the prayers."

Leah studied him carefully. "What was so special about them?"

"Well, the people are a mixed group—some are black hats like me, and some are knitted skull caps, but there was no talking at all. They all seemed really devout. People asked me all kinds of questions about my studies in kollel and accounting. And then one of them said to me, 'We are looking for educators, men like yourself who have been in kollel so many years.'"

Leah's heart did a somersault. "Really? Do you know who the person was?"

"It was the rabbi, someone told me later. Such a young, kind man. He said, 'If you want, we could also help you set up your own accounting firm here. Everyone in the Jewish community would go to you, and all of us have jobs in businesses downtown.'"

Inside her, a small flicker of hope ignited with a sudden flare. "Wow!"

"And after davening, some of the men took me to see the local religious day school and kindergarten. They even have a small kollel! It was *gevaldig*. Imagine, in a place like this, so far away."

"From Brooklyn, the center of the universe," she murmured, smiling.

"All right, laugh at me. But I never knew."

Just then, her phone began a series of dings. They came fast and furious.

"What?" he asked, but before she could answer, his own phone rang. He put it on speakerphone.

"Hello?" *It's my boss,* he mouthed to Leah silently. "Yes, I took another vacation day."

"When do you think you'll be back?" the male voice asked—anxiously, she thought.

"The day after tomorrow. I'll fly in."

"Excellent, Jacob. And listen, about that talk we had . . . not to worry. It's all been settled."

"What happened?" he asked instinctively and then thought better of it. He had, after all, promised to take care of it. But he had done nothing.

"Well, damnedest thing. I have just heard back from all the clients who were complaining. Not only do they want me to drop the subject but they suggested switching their accounts to you! And they wanted me to be sure to let you know."

He was speechless.

"Jacob, are you still there?"

"Yes, well, that's great. Thank you for letting me know. We'll talk about it when I get back."

"Of course, of course. Have a safe trip back and regards to the wife. Leah, is it?"

"Yes, thank you. Well, goodbye."

"Goodbye."

The dings kept coming to her phone, but she ignored them, her eyes wide. "What was that all about?"

Yaakov slammed a flat hand on the dashboard, his laugh exultant. "I have absolutely no idea! But I have my job back, even though I haven't done anything!"

"That's fantastic, Yaakov!" she said, finally looking down to check all her incoming messages. "You're not going to believe this! All those dings? They are messages from my former clients, all asking to come back."

"Baruch HaShem!"

"Yes, God be blessed, but for many other reasons," she murmured dully.

He turned to look at her, astonished. "What's wrong?"

"Yaakov, I don't want these clients! And . . ." She finally had to say it, what had been secretly going through her mind for months now. There was no choice. "I can't go back there . . . to Boro Park. I just can't."

What she had loved about becoming an Orthodox Jew was the valiant optimism of the attempt to cast out all that was base and ugly in human nature and behavior. Only the true God who created mankind would have the audacity and optimism not only to believe it possible but to provide a pathway. And it was not just the big things—murder, kidnapping, adultery, theft—it was the exquisite exactitude of the little things: You must not go into a shop and ask the price of something if you had no intention of buying; it was considered fraud, because it wasted the time of the poor shopgirl or store owner; you must have scrupulously accurate weights if you sold things by weight; you mustn't look at a beautiful home with envy in your heart, even if you didn't know who it belonged to, because envy might lead to coercion, and then to theft, and finally to murder. And even if the envy never led anywhere, but simply settled in your heart, that, too, was forbidden; you mustn't take revenge, even if it was only in the form of refusing your neighbor a cup of sugar because they had denied you a cup of milk; you mustn't gossip, tell tales, humiliate someone even in private. And if you did it publicly, causing the blood to rush into a person's face, it was akin to murder; you mustn't put a stumbling block in front of the blind or curse a deaf man; you must give back lost items, and guard lost property until the owner could be found, expecting nothing in return; you must love your neighbor as yourself. You must do nothing to him that was hateful to yourself . . .

The laws went on and on, laws created for Jews, by Jews, over thousands of years that in their strict observance would make a human being little less than an angel and would create a nation of the most kindly, honest, decent human beings who had ever walked the face of the good earth. She had wanted to live among such people in the hope that it would help her to become one as well.

She thought of Boro Park. In her short time there, she had met such people. There were, perhaps, even many of them. But they were like that not because of that place but in spite of it.

It was a shadow world, a place of shame and secrecy where saving face ruled lives and ruined them; a place of fear and forced conformity to rules that were the opposite of the godly ones she had learned to cherish. It was a place where human needs, compassion, and justice were sacrificed daily on the altar of pretense, appearances, and status; a hard-hearted place that rejected the stranger and convert with the utmost snobbery. A place that cowered before evil and discarded justice; a place where cowardly appeasement and conformity and dishonesty reigned; a place that made it impossible to follow the spirit and letter of the Torah to which all paid lip service, but in reality had replaced with the twisted interpretations of an arrogant, self-serving leadership.

For all its rabbinical courts and synagogues and vast study houses where thousands of students sat learning the laws of God; and despite its fanatic delineation of what people were permitted to eat and wear, somehow true piety and goodness had eluded it. It was no different from any other neighborhood in any other twenty-first-century city, she thought, rife with selfishness, lust, materialism, superficiality, and greed—everything she had thought she was leaving behind her when she had joined them.

How had this happened? How had they veered so far from their goals? How had they, possessors of God-given rules and traditions thousands of years old, ancient blueprints for purity and goodness so powerful they had inspired all three monotheistic religions and still served as their bedrock, been blown so far off course?

How had it all gone so wrong?

Because, she thought, human beings were flawed. Even the most devout were sometimes too weak to fight their demons. But instead of admitting defeat, they had institutionalized and rationalized all their failures, twisting God's laws into something unrecognizable and intimidating all those who protested.

She didn't belong there. She wanted no part of it.

But it wasn't too late. It was never too late. A new community with young families, refugees from the falseness and corruption, from those continuing to go through dead motions, pantomiming with silent mockery all that had once been so holy, so revolutionary and exciting. Like the young tribes born in the desert who had heard the very voice of God Himself, seen miracles with their own eyes, listened to the prophet with their own ears, they, too, could cross the Jordan, smash the old idols, expose and uproot to the core the secret dishonesty and debauchery and child sacrifices, creating a new land to nurture those willing to accept without compromise the pure, living tradition that could never be destroyed, that was there waiting for them to rub off its tarnish until it shone with beauty once more.

"You mean never?" Yaakov asked her breathlessly, shocked.

She nodded. "Never. I just can't. And not only for myself . . ."

He pulled the car over, parking, then shut off the engine.

"Then for who else?"

Her fingers touched her belly. "When I was in the hospital, they gave me a blood test. Yaakov, I'm pregnant! That maniac who ran me down? He could have killed our baby!"

He undid his seat belt, looking at her in horror and wonder. "Is the baby all right? Did the doctor check?"

She nodded, smiling. "The baby is fine. I am fine."

He looked into the back seat to make sure the children were fast asleep. Then he moved toward her, enfolding her gently in his arms. "Then God has answered all my prayers."

She, too, looked over at the children. Satisfied, she lowered her voice to a whisper. "And there is something else. Something I've been afraid to tell you."

"You never have to be afraid of me. Ever."

"Yaakov, I can't stand not touching you two weeks every month! Not sitting next to you. Not handing you anything. It makes me feel shunned, dirty, ugly. I know this is the halacha, but I just can't."

"The halacha is that I can't make love to you while you are menstruating and for seven days later, until you've been to the mikvah. All the rest are fences around the law." He reached out to her, holding her hand. "We will find a way to climb over the fences together without falling off the cliff."

They smiled at each other, tears of joy streaming down their cheeks as they felt the warmth and familiarity of the precious, permanent bond they had formed that would last until the day they died, a bond which had truly made them one.

"It won't be easy. We'll be starting from scratch," he whispered.

"Not easy. But not impossible. Going back is impossible."

He nodded, a joyous, completely unexpected sense of freedom making him suddenly laugh. *Yes*, Yaakov thought, putting his seat belt back on and starting the car, moving his little family on to the open road. Despite all the difficulties and hardships that awaited them, he felt nothing but happiness, realizing he, too, couldn't go back. He also didn't want those clients, those coworkers, that boss. Instead, the two of them would begin again, in a better place, taking their children, their love, and the God of their fathers with them. For the first time in many years, he felt confident that the future held blessings.

EPILOGUE

THREE YEARS LATER

"Did the plane land on time? When do you expect to be home? How are they? Tired? Well, at their age . . ." Leah smiled as she spoke, pressing the phone against her shoulder with her cheek as she held her newborn son.

"Mommy, Tikva Sarah won't get off the swing, and Mordechai Shalom wants his turn."

She turned to Chasya. How tall the little girl was getting, and how pretty! Her pale cheeks had bloomed in the three years they'd been in Virginia, practically living outdoors, the weather so much milder than New York's. And the big backyard of the lovely home they'd purchased with the help of a community fund and their own burgeoning success in both their careers was more luxurious than she'd dreamed they'd ever be able to afford. The roses she'd planted last spring were rioting in all colors, she rejoiced; and the big, old apple tree was heavy with fruit, giving abundant shade over the tables set up for the celebration of her new son's circumcision ceremony later that day.

"I put all the drinks in the spare refrigerator," Cheryl said, coming up behind her, her arms juggling little flower-filled vases. She placed them carefully at the center of each table. "There, done," she said, pushing back her hair, now below her shoulders and a sophisticated shade of ash blond that suited her. She wore slim jeans and a white top with a not-too-low neckline and elbow-length sleeves, as modest an outfit as she was ever likely to wear in this lifetime, she thought. She knew the jeans—well, any pants at all, actually—were taboo, but the top was a clear effort at accommodation, a far cry from the usual low-cut, sleeveless style that was her wardrobe staple. It had taken years, but she and Leah had finally internalized that neither of them was likely to change and that their relationship would entail an ongoing series of compromises. She was doing her best, and so was Leah. Their connection had actually blossomed. She was single again, but wouldn't be for long. She had her eye on a few eligible candidates. But she was in no rush. She liked her house, her business, her dog, herself. And most of all, she adored her grandchildren, step or otherwise. "What else? Oh, let me steal that baby, what an angel!"

"He's all yours, Mom," Leah said, adjusting her head-covering, which had come loose, letting some of her wild red curls cascade over her shoulders. But she wasn't worried. Unlike Boro Park, in their new community, no one would care if she took it off altogether. Or if she played her music and danced around her living room in joy—something she did regularly. It was live and let live. It was her choice to keep covering her hair. It was a gift to God, she thought. A way of saying thank you and demarcating boundaries.

She walked swiftly over to the jungle gym, pausing for a moment to watch the back of her daughter's head with its wild curls—the golden shade of her father's—lifting in the breeze each time she propelled herself forward into the air. She was a little over two years old and already completely fearless.

"Tikva Sarah, you have to give your brother a turn. He's been waiting patiently. Do a *chesed*," she told the child gently.

The tiny girl looked over her shoulder at her mother, frowning, but she immediately stopped and got off. Mordechai Shalom gave her a hug and kiss, climbing on in her stead.

Leah lifted her up, kissing the child's soft cheek, smelling her hair. "What a lovely, kind little girl you are to be so nice to your brother! I'm very proud of you, Tikva Sarah. Are you tired now? Do you want your nap?"

Of course she shook her head. "Want cookie," she demanded, then stopped, marveling at the beautifully set tables, the colorful flowers, that had transformed the familiar backyard into another kingdom. She squirmed to be let down.

Leah laughed. "Oh, I know where you're headed, young lady! No way. Come into the kitchen, and I'll give you a cookie."

"And juice," she negotiated.

"And juice," Leah agreed.

"And ice pop," she pushed her advantage.

Why not? Leah chuckled. "My future CEO," she told the child.

Someone was ringing the doorbell. It was a little too early for the caterers.

There she stood, Shaindele, and beside her a tall, handsome yeshiva boy dressed in a black suit and wearing a large Borsalino. She was a woman now, completely, Leah thought, embracing her. The once chubby, red cheeks had given way to high cheekbones a delicate pale rose, and the long, dark braid was now an elaborate updo held back by two fashionable, glittering barrettes that were the latest style, as was the expensive pale pink suit of shantung silk that made her look like a gracious princess on a walkabout.

"What a surprise!" Leah laughed, pulling her stepdaughter close and hugging her. "I didn't expect you until this evening!" She turned to the young man. "Akiva! How are you?"

"Baruch HaShem," answered the young man affably.

It was Yaakov who had made the shidduch. Akiva's parents were prominent members of the Folkestone community whose son had found religion during his studies at MIT. He had been a rising star in the local kollel, where Yaakov found great joy in teaching part-time in addition to his accounting business. Yaakov had been so impressed with the serious young man. Despite his prestigious degree in computer engineering and a completely nontraditional upbringing, he had developed a burning passion for learning that reminded Yaakov of himself. He had soon outgrown the local kollel, and Yaakov had arranged for him to continue his studies in the prestigious yeshiva in Baltimore where his own sons—both of them married now and fathers—were still learning in kollel. *If I'm lucky,* he thought when suggesting the shidduch to Shaindele . . .

He was. They all were. Everyone loved Akiva. Especially Shaindele.

The plan was for him to learn full-time for a number of years before joining the working world. Shaindele, like her mother before her, would support them by teaching, which she loved.

"Can I also give you a hug?" Leah asked Akiva.

"Of course!" He laughed, moving in closer for a maternal embrace.

"They would never have allowed that in Boro Park!" She beamed at them. "Come in, come in, sit down. I'll get you something to drink."

"Juice," Tikva Sarah piped up. "Pops!" she insisted.

"Oh, you're adorable," Shaindele said, lifting her out of Leah's arms.

"She-she." The child grinned widely at her big sister.

"I'm so happy to see you both! It wasn't too hard for you to get away, with your wedding coming up and so much to do?" Leah said.

"Are you kidding? We wouldn't miss this! Are Bubbee and Rav Alter here already?"

"Any minute. Your tateh is on his way from the airport with them. They were coming in, anyway, for your wedding, now they'll also make the bris. Such a good baby! He came right on time!"

"We can't wait to see him! Another little baby in the family." Shaindele smiled, looking meaningfully at Akiva, who returned her look with love. Years of therapy had taken away her fear of having her own family. Unlike her mother, she would know what to do if things went wrong. Her experience with Grub had left a surprisingly positive residue: she knew now that there was no shame in speaking out to get the help you needed, and that her family could be trusted and relied upon to put her needs above every other consideration.

"How was the drive from Baltimore?"

"Not bad. It took us about four hours."

Once again, Leah appreciated how fortune had smiled upon her. The community was not far from Baltimore and not too far from Florida. They had made the drive numerous times.

"How are your parents, Akiva?"

"Baruch HaShem. My father had a business meeting in Hong Kong, but Mom will be here."

"We are looking forward to seeing your whole family next month."

She heard the tires of the car crunching up the gravel path. "Wait, I think they're here!"

The family ran out the front door and down the porch steps of the lovely wraparound veranda.

Fruma Esther got out first, carrying a large picnic basket. She had a new, gaily coiffed wig and a stylish dress. Even her orthopedic shoes looked more fashionable than the kind she'd worn for decades.

"I baked in Jerusalem for the bris," she told them. "Oy, it's heavy."

"I'll get it, Bubbee, not to worry," Yaakov said.

He stepped out of the car and walked around, holding the door open for his former teacher and mentor, picking up the bags, then helping Fruma Esther up the steps.

Rav Alter had aged, but not deteriorated, Leah saw with relief. Even after the brutal flight from Tel Aviv, there was still a spring in his step as he looked over the children.

Hearing the commotion, Cheryl had joined them with the baby, and Chasya and Mordechai Shalom went running to greet their grandparents.

"Oy, the *kinderlach,* so beautiful!" Fruma Esther exulted, her hand over her heart, whispering a silent prayer to the *Aibishter,* who was always nearby in her heart and her mind. "Look at that baby! What, red? Really, red curls? A *broocha* on his *kepelah!*"

"Like King David," Yaakov said, laughing, as he caught his wife around her waist and kissed her, something else they would never have done in Boro Park.

He, too, had grown older, his short *payos,* neatly tucked behind his ears, a light but definite gray. But the lines around his mouth that had once turned down had now deepened into laugh lines, and the look of shock and despair that had once settled in his calm blue eyes had disappeared, replaced by a merry sparkle of happiness.

"And my Shaindele, my *kallah-moide,* come here to your bubbee," Fruma Esther urged, taking in the young woman from her shining eyes to her lovely, slim figure. "Just like your beautiful mameh, may her memory be a blessing! She would have been so proud, so proud," Fruma Esther whispered to the girl, hugging her. Then both of them wiped away a tear as they all headed inside the house to prepare for yet another family simcha.

ACKNOWLEDGMENTS

I have never before had any desire to compose a sequel, leaving my characters behind in various situations to muck through to the future by themselves in each reader's imagination. But with *An Unorthodox Match,* the future of Yaakov and Leah came to me in a rush. By then, however, I had already written over four hundred pages, and so decided their future deserved a book of its own. This is that book.

I am imparting all this to make it clear that this book, too, is indebted to all those I acknowledged in my last book: those *baalos teshuva* who shared their life stories with me, my friends in Boro Park who took me in and guided me, and the teachers of the Hebrew Institute of Long Island, an Orthodox Jewish day school in Far Rockaway, who guided me to the life-altering decision to take my faith seriously. All the things Leah has experienced in turning from a secular to an Orthodox lifestyle, I, too, have experienced (with perhaps the exception of being run over by an incensed Hasid on a bicycle, although I, too, have often felt the wrath of the religious community in pointing out the lead feet of many a cherished community idol).

I am grateful to author Varda Polak-Sahm, whose book *The House of Secrets: The Hidden World of the Mikveh,* published by Beacon Press, helped me discover fascinating details about the intimate rituals of Orthodox married couples. I found similar information online at heb .KabaLove.org in the published pages of the pamphlet "The Perfect Behavior of the Groom on His Wedding Night."

I thank and acknowledge as well all the many authors who have written and published online, in magazines, and in books about the growing transition of yeshiva and kollel students leaving full-time studies to join the workforce, helping me to understand the complex emotional, religious, and psychological aspects arising from this situation.

Thanks go to my excellent editor, Anna deVries at St. Martin's Press, for her meticulous reading and excellent suggestions, as well as to my agent, Mel Berger at William Morris Endeavor, for always being there to help, encourage, and guide.

As always, my partnership with my husband, Alex, grows stronger and more profound with every year and every book. Thank you, my love. Our fiftieth anniversary has come and gone. Looking forward to celebrating our sixtieth! Thanks also go to the four lovely children we have raised, and their wonderful spouses; and the *nachas*-creating machines that are my precious grandchildren (all thirteen of them—so far!), thank you for the love, laughs, pride, joy. You are, and will remain, my strongest sources of inspiration.

GLOSSARY

a broch. A curse, a plague.

a dank. Thank you.

a mentsh tracht und Gott lacht. A person plans and God laughs.

Aibishter. "The One on High," meaning God.

assur. Forbidden.

avadeh. For sure, certainly.

aveira. A sin, transgression, offense.

ayniklach. Grandchildren.

baal teshuva. Literally, "possessor of repentance." Refers to one who leaves a secular lifestyle to become religiously observant. **baalas teshuva** (feminine). **baalos teshuva** (feminine plural) **baale teshuva** (plural). Refers to penitents of both sexes. **teshuva.** Penitence. To repent is to **"do teshuva."**

Bais Hamigdash. Temple in Jerusalem.

balabus. Literally, "house owner," but often used in a derogatory way to indicate status: bourgeois, prosperous merchant or working class as opposed to scholar.

balabusta. Laudatory term for efficient, hardworking housewife.

bashert. One's perfect match as ordained by God.

beheimeis. Derogatory, "Beasts!"

bekesha. Black frock coat worn by Hasidic men.

besser. Better.

bli neder. A formula that accompanies a vow used to prevent a person from swearing in vain.

broocha, **also** *bracha.* A blessing.

bulvan. A boorish, rude, coarse person.

chas v'chalilah. God forbid. Also **chas v'shalom**.

chasanah. A wedding.

chazzar. Pig.

cherpeh. A disgrace.

chilul HaShem. A desecration of God's name.

chizuk. Strengthen. To give *chizuk* is to help strengthen someone.

cholov Yisroel. Kashrut stringency that demands a cow be milked by Jews to ensure nonkosher milk is not added.

chorbyn. Complete disaster and destruction.

choshuva. Important, highly respected.

dafka. Specifically and emphatically.

din Torah. A trial and judgment given by a rabbinical court.

emes. Truth.

eppis. Somewhat.

Eretz Hakodesh. Literally "the Holy Land," i.e., the land of Israel.

far zikher. For sure.

farshtey, farshteist. Understand.

farshtunkene. Stinking.

frum. Devout or pious, committed to the observance of Jewish religious law, often exceeding the bare requirements of **halacha**, the collective body of Jewish religious laws.

gadol hador. The greatest and most revered Torah scholar of the generation.

Gehinnom. Purgatory.

Geshmacked. Delicious, yummy.

gevaldig. Tremendous, huge.

gmach. Free loan fund that distributes a wide variety of goods and services as a good deed. **gmachim.** (plural).

gornisht. Nothing, zilch, zero.

gribbenes. Crisp chicken or goose skin with onions fried in schmaltz.

grosse tzaddik. Derogatory, "a great saint."

grubber yung. Coarse, uncouth, crude youth.

HaShem. Literally "the name," a periphrastic way of referring to God in contexts other than prayer or scriptural reading because the name itself is considered too holy for such use. **HaShem Yaazor.** God should help. **HaShem Yisborach.** God be blessed, interchangeable with **Baruch Hashem** and **Yisborach HaShem.** **HaShem Yishmor.** God watch over us.

hechsher. Rabbinical stamp of approval, mostly referring to kosher status of food.

hishtadlus. Personal effort toward a goal.

ich farshtey. I understand.

k'vod harav. Honorific. "Most respected teacher."

kepelah. Literally "little head," a term of affection.

kinderlach. Diminutive, affectionate term for children.

Litvish. Of or pertaining to Jews from Lithuania.

loshon hara. Gossip.

mamash. Really, truly, actually.

mechilah. Formal forgiveness for sin.

mechitza. Divider separating men's from women's sections in synagogue.

menuvel. A person who is always causing grief, can get nothing right, and is always in the way.

middos. Character traits.

mirtzashem. God willing.

mishagas. Craziness. **meshuganah, meshuga**. A crazy person.

misnagdim. Rabbinical opponents to the rise of the Hasidic movement, centered in Lithuania.

moissar. Squealer who turns over fellow Jew to secular authorities.

musaf. Afternoon prayers.

mussar. Ethical behavior in the spirit of the Torah.

nebbech. Sad, unfortunate.

negiah. Literally "touch," the concept in Jewish law that forbids or restricts physical contact with a member of the opposite sex (except close family).

neshama. Soul.

nesoyon. Spiritual test, usually something difficult or tragic. **nesyonos**. (plural).

nishtikeit. A nobody.

nishtgutnik. No-good person.

OTD. Abbreviation for "Off the *Derech*," meaning those leaving the true path of Orthodoxy.

pirchei. Literally "blossoms," name given to choirs of young haredi boys singing religiously themed songs.

plotzing. To burst with strong emotion, frustration, or annoyance.

potur. Exempt.

prutza. An immoral woman, a whore. Also **pritzus.** Immorality.

rachmones. Piteous.

rosha. Hebrew word for villain. Also **rishus.** Evil.

shaine. Beautiful.

shalom bayis. Domestic harmony.

shandah. Shame or disgrace.

sheva brachos. Seven blessings, parties held seven nights postwedding to honor the bride and groom.

shluchim. Emissaries (plural). Usually sent to promote a religious or ideological cause, or to collect funding. Also **shaliach** (singular).

shma. A fundamental prayer affirming one's faith, recited morning and evening.

shpilkes. Pins and needles. **on shpilkes**. On pins and needles.

taharas hamishpacha. Family purity, a code word for abstention from sex during menstruation, counting seven clean days, and immersion into a ritual bath before resuming marital relations.

taka. Really, actually.

tisch. Literally "table," but refers to joyous Hasidic gathering of wine and song around rebbe.

treife. Foods forbidden by Jewish law, especially meat from nonkosher animals, or animals not slaughtered according to Jewish law.

tummel. Confusion, uproar, noise.

tzaddik. A saintly man. **tzaddikim** (plural). **tzadakis**. A saintly woman.

tznius, tzniusdik. Referring to modest behavior in dress, deportment, and relations between the sexes.

umglick. A born loser, unlucky.

"Vus is dus?" "What is the meaning of this?"

yenne-velt. Literally, "other world," used to indicate the afterlife or the world to come. Also used in the context of a place that is really far away or in the "middle of nowhere."

yichus. Good pedigree, important lineage.

yungerman. A married male learning in kollel, as opposed to working for a living. A term of respect.